I0606553

GENERATION DEMENTIA

MICHAEL HARTNETT

© 2015 by Michael Hartnett

All rights reserved. No part of this book may be reproduced, stored in a retrieval system or transmitted in any form or by any means without the prior written permission of the publishers, except by a reviewer who may quote brief passages in a review to be printed in a newspaper, magazine or journal.

The final approval for this literary material is granted by the author.

First printing

This is a work of fiction. Names, characters, businesses, places, events and incidents are either the products of the author's imagination or used in a fictitious manner. Any resemblance to actual persons, living or dead, or actual events is purely coincidental.

ISBN: 978-1-61296-592-5

PUBLISHED BY BLACK ROSE WRITING

www.blackrosewriting.com

Printed in the United States of America

Suggested retail price $18.95

Generation Dementia is printed in Book Antiqua

To my parents, Jerry and Bridget, my wife Amy, and my
children Brittany, Patrick, and John.

To my parents, Jerry and Bridget, my wife Amy, and my children Brittany, Patrick, and John.

GENERATION

DEMENTIA

1

THE ANSWER

The family left Levon Gallagher's past on the curb. He had a box of five-and-a-quarter-inch floppy disks with labels scribbled in magic marker: true relics from the 1980s. The top one was named "The Answer." And if that was the first, what would be below it? The meaning of life? Anyway, I probably possessed the only machine in town – a Commodore 64 the Joan left me – that could read these disks. That was the first time I kept some of his trash for myself rather than drop it into the back of the truck.

My garbage truck had witnessed the death of Levon Gallagher. The Monday pickup arrived just after the early morning ambulance to his house, and on Thursday I saw the hearse pass by, the leaves of his big maple tree yellowing across the October sky. The following Monday Levon's relatives were clearing his possessions. Boxes of moldy clothes and Christmas decorations were shoved onto the street, next to a stained mattress and ugly sea-foam crockery.

I had been tempted before to take something left out as

garbage. Some of my buddies had an eye for copper wiring; others took busted shoes with missing soles. I resisted until I saw Levon's legacy left out there like the better part of a man's life. While the floppy disks were the most artificial of everything discarded, even more than the stack of Tupperware and the single whiffle ball bat, I snatched them instead of vacation albums marked the Poconos, Florida, and Civil War Battlefields.

Six years ago when I was just a boy, Levon Gallagher told me a story I've never forgotten. I had a feeling the moment I opened these disks, the story would make sense to me.

In many ways, taking Levon Gallagher's disks kicked off the last year of my boyhood. From that day forward, I would always grab something left for garbage. Soon the neighbors were expecting it. This rescued junk would become my personal contribution to Generation Dementia.

But that was before I learned of the twenty years of lost garbage, before Operation Pick-up Kids had gone viral, before the TV cameras came and more TV cameras came, before I heard Lee Lee's violin pierce through the damp morning air, before Eva had three frying pans sizzling on my stove and the scent of garlic seeped into the kitchen cabinets, before Frick Village stepped into the brave future and became Garbage Free, and before I opened any of the files of Levon Gallagher.

Now in the soft autumn light, I hung from the garbage truck with one paw on the orange handle like an orangutan. The trash and I were out there together at the curb, awaiting the grand collection. Let's see what's on the menu today. We've got boxes and boxes of pencils tossed away. They were broken or scribbled down to nubs. They had never been sharpened. They were tossed out of time, like old tape cassettes. We've got two heavy safes, but locked up tight. I imagined sparkling jewels inside. We've got paint cans stuffed with kitty litter, since we won't take the cans if they're sloshing about. We've got a huge bag of rotten potatoes which smelled even worse than diapers from the Alfords. We've got a tuxedo, hanging from the branch of a tree. Looks like the type an accordion player might wear or perhaps a trash man with big dreams. I looked at Louie, my tough bowling ball of a trash mate, and lined the suit up to his chest. "You want it?" I asked him. "Looks like it'll fit you." Louie answered by throwing it into the compactor.

Louie tended to frown at me, telling me I was eighteen going on eighty. When I selected the one item that I would keep from all that day's rubbish, he said, "What do you want that crap for? You're like an old bum." I wouldn't bother to explain to Louie that when I picked up the object, I would own its history and carry its scars. On each trash run, I picked up many objects, not knowing if I would encounter anything better. In the darkness of 4:57, I tossed a cracked plate on my hidden stash shelf next to the compactor lever, but I flipped it into the loader at 5:04 in favor of a small digital camera that I spotted bulging at the bottom of a tall kitchen bag. I thought it would be nice to search for lost images inside a camera that had probably lost its focus. Yet that too found its way into the back of the truck.

As the run was nearing its end, I was tempted by the 8:22 discovery of a narrow farmer's spade with a splintered handle, for what could have greater possibilities but an instrument for digging? Well, I'll tell you what's better: Levon Gallagher's floppy disk that started with "The Answer."

* * *

Louie Sacco was once considered the perfect trash man. He threw away everything. The pails would return scrap free and whatever debris was left on the curb would be taken away without a speck remaining. The neighbors would put out bizarre and awkward items – massive stereo consoles that had once filled up entire living rooms in 1964, family outhouses passed down for generations, even a handsome electric chair expropriated 30 years ago by a devoted corrections officer – just to test Louie.

The ancient Peggy Murphy dedicated a month to constructing a dummy corpse. In the wee hours of pick-up day, she spent more time than expected arranging the body stuffed under the lid, a casual hand peeking out. Peggy wanted to make sure that Louie would have no doubts about what was in the can. When the truck rolled up to the Murphy curb, Louie merely grunted, expecting a heavier load – the dead tend to weigh more than the usual take-out containers and hair-care bottles – and tossed it casually into the back of the truck, cranking on the compactor to smash the body face up against a video game console. Louie even banged the side of the can onto the truck's thick metal edges to flake off whatever dried blood he could (it was actually a corn syrup Peggy had dyed red). Louie must've figured out that the corpse was a fake . . . at least, I hope he did. As she dragged the pail back to her garage, Peggy thought perhaps she might try cannibalism for Louie's next test. She envisioned a collection of half-chewed limbs, piled up in a lidless pail, like they were just an innocent stack of old shoes. She would jamb them in so forcefully that Louie would have to shove his gloved hands in there to pry them out.

Peggy and the rest of the neighbors had no idea that Louie would be taking his trash collection in another direction.

The day came in late September when Louie started to throw away everything.

I mean everything.

Louie no longer waited for his customers to bring the trash

to him. He made decisions single-handedly on what was indeed waste. His opening attacks were scooping up some horrible resin lawn animals, disturbingly cute chipmunks and rabbits that Louie ripped from a petunia patch. The neighbors generally applauded his bold, yet highly tasteful decision. For a while it was just what was near the curb: a stray garden gnome or a carelessly tossed rake. Gradually, he moved onto balls and bikes within arm's length.

But then he ripped out Alice Harvey's wishing well.

The following week, when he took a sledgehammer to Nonna D'Antonio's cement lions that guarded her driveway, Louie had clearly crossed the line. About that time Big Bill Hannah put me on the truck with him.

* * *

Operation Pick-up Kids has been a model program for Ben Wright High School and the entire community from the moment Mr. Pulaski joined forces with his old war buddy Bill, who happened to run the village sanitation department. Troubled students would clean up the neighborhood. With the village bankrupt and having let go most of its staff, the residents were willing to allow slightly disturbed teenagers to clear trash from their curbs. The last thing Big Bill wanted to do was to fire Louie, which would be a black eye for the program and shake the confidence of the community.

Which is where I came in.

I had only been on the job four days when I grabbed the Gallagher disks. Big Bill watched me hoard scraps of trash in the ensuing weeks. He thought my tendency to preserve rather than to destroy might serve as a calming influence on Louie. "My good lad, you are a true scrounger of mongo," Big Bill told me after the garbage run. He spoke with a charm and courtesy of someone whose childhood was populated by knights and maidens and drilled with lessons in manners. Big Bill gave the impression that he spent many hours at colleges but perhaps had not been very dedicated to completing degrees. Peering through the windshield with his big wrinkled forehead, he drove the truck but rarely said a word during the entire journey. He only focused on following his path that snaked through Frick Village and on spotting our dropped pails, so he knew when to lurch forward. In the morning Big Bill would regularly greet me on the way to the truck with, "So, how's my good man Hash today, you ole' mongomaniac?"

Louie would spit out the word "mongo" like it was a curse, especially every time I carefully picked through the trash. He fed the compactor like it was a starving child. When tough, awkward items hit the curb, like the tar squeegee poles and driveway sealant buckets at the Stevens' house, Louie jerked the lever back and forth to snaps the sticks and crush the barrels deep into the hold, all the time the gears grinding and the motor growling under incredible pressure. Even if he had to flip the lever twenty times and shove his boot into the compactor to give that last nudge inward, Louie would make sure the truck always had room to take in more trash.

My presence alongside Louie gave the neighborhood a new wrinkle of entertainment as our pail pick-ups were often interrupted by Louie's looking to compact a pot of impatiens or a wind-catcher while I grabbed him by the sweatshirt and wagged my finger. He wouldn't let go and we'd wrestle about. Louie was powerful for his 5'1" frame, but still small enough for me to hold him back. One October Monday I had to get him in a head lock before he relinquished his grip on a particularly lovely set of Tibetan chimes. He always bounced up laughing, his eyes scanning down the street for something else to toss.

To keep things interesting, I made it a morning tradition to slide a package out from one of my many pockets. "What's that?" Louie asked.

"Free range tofu."

Louie shook his head. "You mean that tofu got to prance around in the fields before it was slaughtered."

I'm not sure Louie grasped the spirit of the product. "This way it's healthier for everyone involved."

Louie jerked his head toward the packet. "How much did that set you back?" When I didn't answer, Louie eyed me like I was a lawn ornament he considered dumping in the compactor.

After the rubbish run, I would sit down with Louie for breakfast at the diner, and we would talk over the morning's business, which generally featured his trying to destroy the neighborhood and my trying to destroy Louie. Even at breakfast, Louie was disposing everything, this time in his mouth, consuming enough for three larger men. The pancakes were followed by eggs, then by Belgian waffles, with bacon along with each course, all chased by sausage patties and then sausage links as dessert (Louie believed the links were sweeter).

"If I could just get rid of all the crap," Louie told me. He shoveled in a scoopful holding a couple of eggs and a three slices of bacon. "Everything would be a hell of a lot clearer."

"Can't argue with that." I saw all this rubble and debris not only in my nightmares, but my daydreams.

Louie ate happily and spoke sadly. "I can't keep up. People never seem to stop making crap. I used to love the Styrofoam in the big delivery boxes. It's light, like I'm throwing a bag of balloons into the truck. But it takes up a lot of room back there and it doesn't compact as much as it should."

If somebody else were telling me about Styrofoam, I might think he had an environmental agenda. Not Louie. He just wanted to clear more space, so he could throw more of Frick

Village away. Unfortunately for Louie, a garbage truck doesn't exactly sneak up on unsuspecting neighbors. Even at 5:47 in the morning, you are awakened by the rumble two blocks away. So when Louie went after Derek Standish's lawn jockey, Derek swung an aluminum bat and tried to knock him into right field.

Hannah was also uneasy about having me on the truck. As he put it, "there is something terribly odd, my good man, about a garbage man being a hoarder." Fortunately, since he was driving, he never caught me eying some of the garbage already crushed in the truck. He wouldn't have understood how tempting a compacted metal shopping cart could be now that it was transformed into a marvelous crab trap.

As opposed to their noisy protests when Louie stepped off the truck, the neighbors kept a hushed vigil for my appearance. At first I think they saw my scavenging as an invasion of privacy, an effort to peer into their souls through the discarded skins they shed. They soon understood I had interest neither in their perversities – often involving obsessive shoe consumption and small plastic objects – nor in their porn, which incorporated strangely similar materials. No, I wanted what they once thought valuable, and soon they saw my inspections as a validation of their own worth.

As I passed by the Carters, I could almost hear the old man say to himself, "Will the boy take the microscope or the telescope? Will he look inward or outward?" It was my turn to wonder if the pick-up would measure their values or my own.

The story passed through the neighborhood quickly about how on one leaf-drifting morning I plucked a discarded wooden dragon puppet with a broken wing that I spied under an ice cream carton. When Mrs. Stevens came running out the front door with a panicked expression, I walked toward her with the puppeteer cross in my hand, the dragon dangling below, one wing soaring while the other folded in and out weakly, like a maimed hawk caged at a bird sanctuary. "May I have that back?" she pleaded.

"Of course," I bellowed in a voice I borrowed from St. Nick. "I'm so happy you decided to keep it. It would have been a shame to lose it."

While I'm pretty sure I had done nothing wrong, Big Bill had gotten word that I had tried to steal toys from little kids. "That's the kind of rumor, my good man," he said, "that could destroy the program."

"I would never," I said, acting a little defensively. "Don't worry. I'll be a good boy."

Bill smiled. "That's what I like to hear."

I wasn't sure how to handle the complaint. I had a feeling Mayor Heine was behind my problems. The other day Heine came out as he saw me grab his pail.

"Hey Hash, you looking for something?"

"Yeah," I said, not happy that he knew my name.

"Well don't." He nodded to me in a way that he could claim was friendly, but I knew was threatening. Heine regularly sent out troubling Tweets, such as, "The Frick residents should watch what they put near their curb. I've heard a few things have gone missing." The last thing I wanted was to get tossed off the truck, but the residents were sending me mixed messages. I noticed whole families would be up in the wee hours staring out the window to see what I would take out from their trash. At first, I took little, but seeing their disappointed faces, I stopped holding back and started grabbing away. I understood how humiliating it was for my neighbors to have garbage worth absolutely nothing. We all must possess such an embarrassment of riches that some will inevitably spill over into the trash pail, don't we now?

2

PASSED WORDS

At the beginning of my senior year, I had no plans to climb onto a garbage truck. The Joan had died in August, which left Aunt Vicky asking me a lot of stupid questions about back-to-school clothes. After learning that I had no interest in her mothering me, Aunt Vicky consumed most of her hours like she had before she moved into the Joan's house: online dating. I will not waste your time with disturbing tales of creepy guys who "chatted" with her. I started to warn her once, but thought I sounded an awful lot like her when she had talked to me about drug use ("I don't know what your mother was thinking when she named you Hash"), so I let her fall apart in her way while I was given the distance to travel my own road to ruin.

The troubles started when the school made me change my password to log onto its website. The next day I couldn't remember that password. Then I forgot my gym number. Then my locker combination. Then my cell phone access code. Then my phone number. Then Louie's phone number. Then the password for my sports fantasy teams. Then my social security number. Then my birthday. Every time I thought I had summoned up familiar numbers from my memory, they scattered like pigeons in a thunderstorm. I met often with Pulaski, my guidance counselor. I held my chin a lot when he was watching me and raked my hand through my hair when he wasn't. I knew some of the passwords I typed in once belonged to me, but they turned their backs on me now, apparently having an easier time moving on with their lives than I've had. I'd written some of the codes and numbers on my forearms, but I'd done so with such nervous haste that they were very hard to read. When the machines rejected me, they never told me how many letters or numbers I had right, or whether the problem was a mere case issue, where I typed in lower, yet dreamed in upper. Mr. Pulaski said all the numbers and codes might come back to me if I just tossed away tons of trash. For Pulaski, hauling trash was the cure for all miseries.

"It'll clear your head," he said, sounding more like a physician than a counselor, scribbling words on a pad as if he was handing out prescriptions (I'd rather he was handing out passwords). When I grew tired of every electronic device that wired me to humanity rejecting my attempts at a meaningful relationship, I found myself spending hours at my school locker, spinning the dials both left and right trying to discover the actual combination. I moved my hands softly and slowly, hoping to feel the click signaling that everything was locked on, but never hearing it. I passed hours that way, missing class after class.

The bell would ring and the students would filter into classes through Ben Wright High, but I remained at my locker, trying to get a door open beyond my mental capacity. On the wall stood a plaque with a message from none other than our hometown genius Ben Wright: "Don't expect anything to be what you expect." There were whispers throughout Frick that the great inventor Wright had killed himself, so he might've known what he was talking about.

Ms. Spiegel, the school psychologist, told me that I'd forgotten all of my passwords because I missed my family. It took all my self-control not to say to her, "What are you trying to tell me? No family, no passwords?" I hoped that the next number I'd forget would be the one on her office door.

Students would watch me spin the dials. Some seniors would rotate in and out, and a couple even cut class to watch me. I couldn't figure out if they were hoping I would succeed or fail. Perhaps they just enjoyed seeing the dial go around and around, or relished the moment when I turned in the other direction. Mr. Pulaski would shuffle along on his scraped-up shoes toward me, making the daily journey to my locker to gently nudge me away. The counselor wore soft, checkered button-down sweaters of a brand long out of business. He was kind, smart, and patient, but my behavior challenged these qualities. The students seemed to savor that little show the most, especially since Mr. Pulaski said, "stop spinning," and after a pause said, "stop spinning," and after a pause said, "stop spinning," and after a pause said, "stop spinning," until he sounded as compulsive in trying to make me stop spinning as I had been in actually spinning.

Pulaski dipped his head below his chin and peered up at me like a friendly bulldog, so I couldn't avoid making eye contact with him. "You get on the garbage truck and you won't have to worry about any of this."

"Yeah?" I patted his head like he was my pet (I couldn't help it). "What's the password to get on the truck?"

"I'm the password." Pulaski walked away. I muttered to myself, "He's the password," hoping I'd remember.

Unfortunately, my difficulty with passwords and codes

seemed to spill over into my everyday conversations. When Jen said, "Hello," I replied, "I'm fine," and when Max said "Good morning," I said, "bacon and eggs." When Mr. Long said, "Take out your copies of *Hamlet*," I responded, "he isn't home right now." Then April asked if I wanted to go out on Saturday night, which I definitely did (if you saw April, you'd understand). I answered, "Broken1234," which I'm pretty sure was my College Board password. April said, "whatever," and walked away looking a little annoyed.

I was beginning to sound like Levon Gallagher near the end. He would stop by to see the Joan, even though he'd kept promising her that he'd never return. No matter how weak she was, the Joan would always smile happily and ask, "What are you doing here?"

"What do you mean?" he'd say. "I'm not here."

Not wanting become a ghost like Levon, I decided to try my luck online. The only password I seemed to be able to type was "Love2". I must've typed "Love2" fifty-nine times in the next few days – the computer would kick me off after a few attempts and then I'd have to wait three minutes to try again. No matter how many times I said "Love2," the only answer I received was "Invalid."

* * *

Ms. Ackerman looked over my shoulder during art class. "Mmm, that's interesting." She played with her dangerously straight hair, hair that I'm sure had once been dyed Goth black. "Why do you only paint reality TV stars?"

"What else is there to paint?" I asked her. She said something about the sea and the stars and family. I frowned and thought of survivors, idols, bachelors, bachelorettes, big brothers, hillbillies, housewives, hoarders, top chefs and bottom feeders. My image of Kim Kardashian was just about complete. I needed to soften the smoky eyes a bit, so that my dazzling, air-brushed Photoshop vision would be true to the way she appeared on magazine covers. I grunted approvingly at my beautiful image.

Then I took out my lighter and led the flame to each of the four corners of the canvas.

The painting's edges curled and the flames rose. Ms. Ackerman screamed and pounced on the blazing painting with surprising speed, extinguishing the flames with her thick smock. My classmates dropped their brushes, laughed, and used the word "freaky" a lot.

"What are you doing, Hash?" asked Ms. Ackerman. "You could've set off the fire alarm."

"I didn't want to look at it anymore," I said.

She stared at the painting, smudges and soot all over the Kardashian brand. I thought she was going to cry. Instead, she sent me down to Pulaski's office to have a "chat." She wouldn't let me take the painting with me.

I waited in Pulaski's office (he'd "stepped out"). Then the hallucinations began, which always seemed to happen whenever I had a free moment and kept my phone in my pocket.

The visions tended to open in a church, which was odd, since I hadn't attended a mass since the Joan died. I'd peer down at the pew in front of me where I spied a kneeled woman whose shoe soles were exposed: her left sole had a yellow circle with a big "9" at its center and the right sole had a sales sticker (marked down to $29.99). The priest was at the altar and he had pulled out his I-Phone and scrolled down until he found his prayer. After he read the text with great solemnity, he tucked the phone inside his white robe and suddenly the light from an app illuminated his whole person and left him aglow. The I-Phone Priest floated in my visions, sometimes blocking my view of the mirror behind me or the sandwich in front of me.

To ground myself, I pulled out my phone and called up Louie. "Yeah."

I asked, "Did you know Levon Gallagher?"

"The dead guy? A little. He nearly had a stroke when I tossed his typewriter. I told him if he didn't want to get rid of it, then he shouldn't have dropped it on the front grass. He said it was lawn art. The crazy bastard."

"Poor guy," I said, wishing I could've grabbed the typewriter before Louie.

"He said he wanted it back. I pointed to the compactor 'Do you really think that's a good idea?' I asked him." Louie had funny ideas about anything that made it into the truck, like it could never leave, like it was dead.

"That wasn't right Louie." I shook my head. "You should've just gotten it for him."

"I would've, but I wanted to see him at least move toward the truck, just to make sure it really meant something to him. Instead, he didn't budge and mumbled something about making me pay. I don't think that's going to happen now."

I said goodbye to Louie. My vision returned of the I-Phone Priest who now laid his hands onto the typewriter and turned it into a Commodore 64. One time Grandpa Artie asked where was the antenna on the computer. I laughed, which was a really bad idea. That old bastard was another one I couldn't get out of my brain. Almost daily, Grandpa Artie rattled around my subconscious, his cane in hand forever probing. A little, old man, Artie was wiry and muscular, even though by the time I was in 4th grade he was already fading. Artie had just finished smacking me: an open paw swinging across my head and clipping me on the right ear, followed by another just to make sure the sting stayed with me. Moments earlier, I had asked him about my father again. He muttered something about, "I told you not to talk about that bastard." Still, I continued to ask Artie because I could tell by his spastic anger (the swats aimed right at my ear almost missed me) that he was clearly conflicted. "I forgot which story your mother wanted me to tell you about him. Anyway, he's gone and he's not coming back, so forget him, O.K.?"

As I held my ear, Artie took a breath of remorse. "I hit ya because I don't want you to be a pussy. Now pick up that rifle." Artie had always taught me manly things, trying to counterbalance the Joan's coddling. "Put it tight against your shoulder," he growled. I tried, but when I tugged the trigger, the kick sent me onto my back.

Artie laughed, lifted me up, kissed me on the forehead, said I was a good boy, and pressed the butt of the rifle tight against my shoulder.

The next thing I knew Pulaski was shaking me on that shoulder and leading me into his office. "So you're burning your artwork now?"

"Don't get all worked up. It was just Kim Kardashian."

"Oh." He studied me. "But Ms. Ackerman said you spent two weeks painting her."

"I couldn't get rid of her until I made her."

Pulaski smiled grimly, indicating that the world no longer worked that way. He blew his big honker and stuffed his handkerchief into a pocket of his faded checkered sweater. "You do know that setting something on fire is usually an automatic suspension."

I gave him a good, steady stare. "I want to get on the truck."

Pulaski acted like he was surprised, even though he had recruited me. When in the previous weeks I had spun the dials at my locker, he jabbed a promotional flier into my free hand. His Operation Pick-up Kids was designed for the non-academic types, so I guess his pretending to be stunned was his way of keeping my dignity.

I tried to explain. "I need to touch something heavy, something I can hold onto, and then I need to make something of it."

Pulaski had known about my artistic ambitions. He had been there when I received all those writing awards in ninth grade, and now that I'd turned to drawing and painting, he'd always taken the time to congratulate me every time I won a contest or a gallery spot. "So this journey into trash land is about your work."

I took a deep breath. Pulaski's office had hundreds of books stacked on his shelves. All of them looked dog-eared and beaten up, like he'd read every one of them. He knew too much to jump at every teenage drama. Hell, I had to talk to somebody, and I liked how quietly he cared. So I told him. "I know I need to see things a little differently. I need for my eyes to stop hurting and for these hallucinations to go away." At least I didn't tell him about the Joan's voice.

Pulaski raised his eyebrows and shut the door. "Son, what are you taking?" he asked in such a way that told me we were talking confidentially and that he wouldn't go running to Principal Collins or to the police the minute I returned to class.

"That's just it. If I was taking something, I'd understand. The fact that I'm not and still hallucinate is what's bothering me."

Pulaski had a pad and pencil out now. "What kind of hallucinations?"

I told him, taking a good five minutes.

"Damn," he said. "I guess we oughta find a spot for you on the truck." He told me I'd have to go out over to Mayor Heine's office to fill out paperwork. "Wait till you see what you have to sign."

"What, like insurance forms?"

Pulaski smiled. "That and . . ."

"What? A blood oath?"

"Pretty close, and a liability release form that might send you running for the door."

"Yeah, I'm not planning on getting my arm crushed in the compactor."

"Good man."

I shook Pulaski's hand. As I closed the door behind me, I could've sworn he muttered to himself, "Friggin' Generation Dementia."

Over the past few months, I had heard Pulaski muttering through the hall the mantra "Generation Dementia" as a way to soothe the aching heartburn that accompanied every daily meltdown by one student or another who lost his grip on what seemed like a few minutes ago a reasonable approach to passing through senior year. He was convinced we were all on the verge of breakdowns.

A couple of marking periods ago, nobody thought Andy Pulaski had any good ideas. He should've retired a dozen years back, and yet when he created Operation Pick-up Kids, he sold the hell out it, like he was trying to make a name for himself at the school. He'd show up in our classrooms explaining that he gave seniors a chance to learn what real hard work was like and to clean up the village at the same time. And then he'd tell us the story of the conversation he had with his partner, his big, equally geriatric friend Bill Hannah, who would come into our classroom sporting a hard hat, those heavy workboots, and a smell that no soap could scrub away. Pulaski told the audience with a smiling Hannah looking over, "Bill would say to me, 'Andy, I don't think they're tough enough. They haul trash a few days with me, and I guarantee you they'll suddenly start planning out a real career'." I have no idea why this chunk of cheesy child psychology worked, but from the day the first openings for Operation Pick-up Kids were posted, the line stretched all the way to the cafeteria.

"Damn," said Max Goodman, "there are more people here who want to pick up garbage than want to get into Harvard."

Pulaski offered a sly grin. "Harvard's application pool is less competitive."

In the halls, everyone called the program Operation Pick-up Kids by the phrase Pulaski so obsessively muttered, "Generation Dementia." Now Generation Dementia was a program we could get behind.

Operation Pick-up Kids would've been unthinkable if Frick Village hadn't fallen into bankruptcy after heavy investments in the failed mapping program, lost.com. lost.com promised to take people places they couldn't get to before. With a faulty algorithm that sent drivers into the Atlantic Ocean, lost.com took Frick Village to the cleaners. Herman Heine, our mayor for thirty years, threatened to cut the entire sanitation department to prevent the village from being taken over by the state. The neighbors whispered that Heine had long desired to reorganize the department, so he could kick out the Mexicans who left Frick's streets spotless and Heine's reputation soiled. You see, Heine tried to keep immigrants out of his village, and had beaten up Hannah in the press for hiring them. When I was a cub reporter this past summer for the local rag, *The Frickin'*, I watched Heine and Hannah go at it, with the mayor calling Hannah a criminal while the big man hollered back "You, my honorable mayor, are a racist." Some of Hannah's buddies at the village had even whispered that Heine had fiendishly driven the trustees to invest in lost.com – with map apps that led to nowhere (the locals joked that the website was aptly named, since to logon was to leave even the most directed individual dazed and confused). Only with the village flat broke could Heine gut Hannah's department.

Finally, Frick Village was living up to its many nicknames, everything from Hick Village to Sick Village to Mick Village to Spic Village to Dick Village to Prick Village: Frick's a name that essentially cried out to be replaced by a more offensive relative. Meanwhile, the trash piled up at the curb. Big Bill tried to pick up all the village trash on his own, driving the truck and then getting out to empty the pails. It was an act of failed heroism, so when Andy Pulaski reminded Hannah of his standing offer, Operation Pick-up Kids emerged.

I should've seen it coming during a raucous village meeting on a sultry, early September night. With the editor out sick, I had been assigned as number one cub reporter to cover the meeting for *The Frickin'*. Before then, Hannah was just a local character to me and much of the neighborhood. He was the huge guy who spoke to everyone like he was their personal servant; he managed to do so in a way that was kindly, respectful and amused . . . he was never a kiss ass. "Yes, my good sir," I'd hear him bellow phrases that belonged more in a King Arthur tale than in a supermarket deli line. The three times I spoke to him he called me Master Hash, which made me sound either like a rapper or an expensive brand of canned meat.

What I witnessed was a slew of brutal attacks on Mayor Heine as Bill Hannah stood in the front row and listened to the community raise him to the status of a Marvel superhero.

Hannah was just one aging man alone on a huge garbage truck, trying to clean up the neighborhood – a job until recently reserved for a half dozen strapping, incredibly industrious young Mexicans. After Heine laid off the Mexicans, Hannah got them jobs with an old buddy (Hannah had a lot of old buddies) at a construction firm, where they earned more than they ever had on the trash truck. That left Big Bill as the lone member of the sanitation department. When I pulled Hannah to the side and asked him why he tried to take on a job he clearly could not do, he answered with the calm of a yoga instructor. "My good man, was I going to stand by and watch the great Frick Village just go to hell?"

The community appreciated the nobility in such a commitment, one that they found clearly lacking in Mayor Heine. Glancing from Big Bill to Mayor Herman, Peggy Murphy pointed an accusatory finger at Heine, "You are trying to kill that man, you bastard!" The mayor looked like he didn't understand the language she was speaking. A notorious multi-tasker, Heine further incited the crowd by scrolling down through his I-Phone screen, riffling through long legal documents, eating a meatball hero, and yanking out ear hairs, all while he banged the gavel and ran the meeting. Many residents brought up how another mayor would have made across-the-board cuts when hit with this budget crisis, but such was Heine's vendetta against Hannah and the Mexicans who worked for him that only the sanitation department had suffered. In between bites of his sandwich and taps on his phone screen, Heine answered that he had no problem with the sanitation department and had only the greatest respect for its supervisor and the workers. In response to the mayor's defense, many voices were yelling at the front of the room for a long time, long enough for Heine to toss aside planning board documents and move onto his examination of the zoning board briefs.

Levon Gallagher, who had come out of hiding to attend the village meeting, walked right up to the board table and asked, "Are you even listening to us?" Despite the fact that Levon seemed so weak and frail, he summoned a gaze of hatred for Heine that even the mayor could not have missed.

After checking two Twitter accounts on the phone, signing two zoning approvals, spearing a meatball, and plucking a particularly long follicle from his lobe, Heine looked up at the hostile crowd and at the still angrier Levon and answered, "Yes."

"That's just what I thought," said Levon as he staggered out of the hall and was never heard from again.

That night I caught whispers that some of the residents on rubbish runs greeted Big Bill's truck by personally dumping their own trash in the back. The next morning I woke up an hour before the sun and met Big Bill on his truck, notebook and I-Phone in tow. In the jerky stops and starts of that run I discovered a humanity surprising in its generosity of warmth on a hot, humid day. Yes, there was self interest in Derek Standish lifting his own pails, but how do I explain his heading down the block and dumping the trash for the three elderly couples at the far end or how indeed do I explain Derek's gathering up the debris from the other houses whose residents were already working. Derek said to me, "I don't need to watch Big Bill have a heart attack, do I?"

Better yet, Peggy Murphy was too old to haul trash, but she had just the right combination of sinewy arms and martyr commitment to make for a wonderful picture. The entire

Gulotta family came out, with the son Anthony even jumping on the truck for a few blocks. I got photos of every moment; that was until I started lifting a few pails myself.

Indeed, my friends, on that September day I lurched toward becoming a garbage man.

3

THE FLOPPIES

I kept a special eye on Levon Gallagher's house. The family members would come and go irregularly, leaving additional bits and pieces of his carcass on the curb. Usually, the grievers would get all the material out quickly and stick out a For Sale sign with an accompanying price that would let it turn over within a few months. But these family members lingered as if they had some unfinished business at the house, as if they were looking for something.

I had become increasingly curious about Levon – you can get that way when you pass the dead's house every day. I gave his trash special inspection and kept more of it than all the other residences combined. When I inspected my Gallagher collection, I tried to figure out why hadn't I put the floppy disks into the Commodore 64? I was generally practical about my mongo. Everything I collected from the other residents I put to use, transforming these materials. Gallagher's junk, however, lay untouched. I should indeed find out what The Answer was on that top floppy disk. He'd been connected to my family for many years, particularly his long friendship with my grandfather Artie. I had met Levon a couple of times when I was in sixth grade. He was clearly in love with the Joan then and stopped over occasionally, handing me bubble gum and asking me to punch his stomach, then showing me how to snap a jab. One night, drunk, he told me some story, I tell you. I always wondered whether it was true. From then on, every once and a while he'd stumble back into our lives, especially when the Joan got sick. I tried to figure out whether I cared he'd died.

I guess I had cared enough to chase down Gallagher's obituary on the Internet. He was a curious man, a man worthy of my scavenging. As the obit writer noted, his life was founded in a new age. "He was a baby born on August 6, 1945, the very day the Enola Gray dropped its Little Boy nuclear bomb on Hiroshima."

The Joan used to gush about Gallagher being a famous Pulitzer-prize-winning reporter, yet I had avoided him when I started to string for local newspapers last year. I didn't want any favors. Gallagher's obit was of a size worthy of a governor. Newspaper people love to write about their own. The rest of the obit made me wonder whether his life would be a good blueprint for my own. It read –

For years, Gallagher was known as the man who had the best job in the world. His *Off to Work* column featured his taking employment at almost every possible position available in the second half of the 20th Century. "What made his job so good is that he had every job and no job," said Shelley Kornfeld, his longtime editor at *The Herald*. Those jobs ranged from performing mating dances with whooping cranes under the guidance of ornithologist George Archibald to storing spent nuclear rods in underground pools to applying makeup for one of Liz Taylor's many red carpet appearances. His most famous employment was the week in 1984 he worked with then-President Ronald Reagan, during which Gallagher was given full security access.

A man of many scars and limps, Gallagher was legendary for throwing himself deeply into every encounter, often at a cost of great personal injury. One such adventure that left him deeply wounded was his sperm collection of a genetically engineered bull, an incident from which he suffered several cracked vertebrae.

"The problem was always that I lacked the skills and the familiarity to really do any job safely," Gallagher said in an interview last year. "I would regularly lament leaving a job once I was getting the hang of it, but then I'd get to the next job and be even happier. Look if that leaves you a little bruised up, then so be it."

Those bruises accumulated to such an extent that they probably expedited his demise as his doctors claim he suffered from several degenerative conditions, including brain injuries that led to early dementia.

Gallagher was famed for the many fights he had with celebrities, fellow journalists, and assorted private citizens, most of which landed him in a short stint in either a hospital bed or a jail cell. Yet, despite his difficult reputation, the employers who took him on for his *Off to Work* column rarely complained about him. "He was willing to do anything," Kornfield explained, "and he'd never whine and never questioned his bosses. I'd gotten many calls from his employers who, when I asked if Levon was giving them a problem, would say, 'Are you kidding me? I wish I had a hundred Levon Gallaghers'." He was also known for his decades-long friendship with wunderkind inventor Ben Wright, with whom Gallagher caught up regularly during roll-outs of dazzling new technological gadgets and gizmos until Wright's untimely death in 1997.

Despite the fact he traveled the world in his job, Gallagher lived his entire life in Frick Village. "The village nobody leaves" lived up to its reputation when it came to Gallagher. There he became involved in all local matters, particularly in his fights over immigrants with Frick's longtime mayor, Herman Heine. Heine could not be reached for comment on Gallagher's passing.

Even as he grew gravely ill, Gallagher seemed to harbor no ill feelings. Last month, while in the hospital, apparently aware that the end was near, Gallagher told *The Herald*, "I always thought the big bomb would get me. Christ, I was born with the bomb. That would be poetic justice, you know, the bomb getting me, getting us all. But it didn't. I'm a lot happier going this way, I tell you."

That night I fired up the Commodore 64, took a deep breath, and shoved in the first of Levon Gallagher's five-and-a-quarter-inch floppy disks.

The Diary of Levon Gallagher: Pushing Buttons

The Answer:

They made me duck under the desk during the air raid drill. I've been wondering all day where I will be when the bomb drops. My first answer was definitely not under the desk. Fight like the bomb's coming tonight.

November 22, 1963

That morning I was a boy of 18 at Cornell, and by evening I had become a man. At the Royal Palm Tavern I got into it with Artie Cornwall. I probably should've been more gracious. He'd driven up four hours to see me, but by the time he arrived I was already at the bar in a bad mood. Artie had been a mentor to me during my high school years, introducing me to wonderful contacts when I worked as a cub reporter at *The Frickin*. He had set up an interview for me with Ben Wright, who, because of his friendship with Artie, gave me access to the inventions he was working on. Ben probably should've shut his mouth, but Artie told him "to give the kid a break." Ben's work on new audio devices got me a byline in *The Herald*. Artie gave me connections. Artie explained why Ben's inventions were a big deal. And, most importantly, Artie gave me quotes for my articles.

But tonight Artie was wrong. In fact, everyone at the Royal Palm was wrong, especially Keith Stevens. I had flashed Keith a wonderful little cartridge given to me by Ben that would actually play music. I told Keith that I knew the inventor, the inventor of a device that would change the way we live. Keith just growled at me. To see the future, I clearly had to peer past a forest of apes.

I had been pouring packets of Tang into Seagrams and soda to cheer myself up, since I had decided that Tang makes everything taste better. Most of the dopes at the bar didn't agree. I tried to get Artie to swig some, but he just crinkled up his face like I offered him a cup of piss. And when I told him about Keith's reaction to the cassette tape, Artie didn't seem too interested. All he wanted to talk about was the latest Ben Wright innovation, the push-button phone. "It just came out a couple of days ago."

He pulled out a phone from his briefcase. Where the rotary dial was supposed to be square, numbered buttons were lined up in a grid. God, it looked awful. The elegant ring holding the ten inner circles that would spring back with the twist of a finger was gone, replaced by something clunky and boxy like those big dull rectangular skyscrapers rising all over our cities. I'd been hearing from Artie that Ben was off in Pittsburgh (Pittsburgh for Christ's sake!), working at Bell Laboratories on a device that would change the world. I heard that all summer long before Cornell, and again in Artie's letters. I sure hoped to hell this new piece-of-crap wasn't it.

I tried to be diplomatic. "It's not very impressive looking, is it?"

Artie scowled. "Have you gone off to college and turned into a moron? Look at it." Artie's mouth twisted north like he'd caught me eating dog food.

"The rotary's gone," I said, not backing down. "That was the most attractive and intriguing thing about a phone, and Ben's taken it away."

Artie gave me a look like he'd just sipped my Seagrams and Tang by mistake. He got the bartender to drop the tavern's phone on the bar, handing him a five dollar bill before he transferred the jack wire from the rotary to the push-button phone. "Give me the phone number to the pizza place next door?"

Artie, who rarely missed anything, knew I loved pizza and knew I'd have the number to the local place. "It's 427-8294. Why? You hungry?"

"No, you idiot," Artie was never really the sweetest talker, but he was especially foul tonight. "We're going to do an experiment, so you can understand what Ben has achieved." Man, Artie propped Ben up on such a high pedestal he made the Statue of Liberty look like a Chatty Cathy doll. Artie reached in his pocket. "Here's a dime. Go over to that payphone and let me know when you get a dial tone. We'll start calling at the same time."

I put the dime in the phone, heard the buzz, signaled Artie, and started turning the dials. When I was done, I got a busy signal. I returned to Artie.

"I ordered us a pepperoni with extra cheese." The bastard even remembered how I liked my pie. He smiled. I wanted to punch his smug yap. "I did that in the time it took just for you to dial a number."

"Yeah," I said, "So what. You saved a couple of seconds. Big deal. That's supposed to impress me."

"How could it not?" Artie was flabbergasted. I sipped my Seagrams and Tang and decided I'd show him what a real innovation looked like. Ever since I'd met Ben, I'd been scratching around to find new inventors and to share their contraptions with the world. I'd become known as a journalist on the cutting edge. For the past few months, I'd been corresponding regularly with Bette Graham. She created this wonderful new substance she called Mistake Out. Bette was a secretary in Dallas. She understood what a waste it was to retype entire papers all because of an error or two. She formulated a paint to cover up the errors. The substance dried quickly and could be typed over. Absolutely brilliant. Now that was a real time saver. I thought Bette's only miscalculation was changing the name from Mistake Out to Liquid Paper.

I made Artie write down on a cocktail napkin, "The Push-Button Phone is the greatest time-saving invention of our era." Then, I took some Liquid Paper out of my pocket and showed it to Artie. I started to paint over the words "Push-Button Phone" and blew on the napkin. "The push-button phone saves what? A few seconds here and there? But this wonderful little bottle," I shook the Liquid Paper, "saves hours and hours." I then wrote Liquid Paper over the whited-out area of the napkin.

Artie lifted up the napkin delicately and respectfully like it had been transformed into the Declaration of Independence. He acted so reverentially and with such an aura of sincerity that you really had to know Artie well to realize he was giving me the business. "So what you are saying is painting over a few typos is a greater feat than taking the most important instrument of our time and making it work ten times faster than it used to. I guess you're right. The tremendous increases in productivity that could occur when businesses can call so many more clients and customers per day is nothing compared to the ability to white-out the words 'promising young scholar' so you can correct them to 'infantile, self-righteous prick'."

In case I missed his meaning, Artie lifted the now hallowed napkin to his nose and discharged a load of snot into it.

I'd had about enough of Artie Cornwall. "You

wouldn't blow your nose in it if your boyfriend Ben Wright invented it!" Artie did not like what I was implying and hit me with a quick right that dropped me and left my nose bloody. By the time I got back up, Artie was thrown out and my pizza arrived.

It took two handfuls of napkins (boy, we were chewing through the napkins tonight at the tavern) to stanch the bleeding. I returned to my barstool, grabbed a slice of pizza, and slurped on my Seagrams and Tang.

Artie had been a good friend to me, almost like a big brother really, but he would pay for his mistake. I would wipe that error away like I was using Liquid Paper. I was not in any rush though. This would be rotary-dial revenge. No push-button nonsense. The following week I made my first trip to the other side of Ithaca.

* * *

Boy, I'd seen Grandpa Artie enough to know that he was a hothead. Levon never showed that side to me, although the rumors I'd heard in Frick about the prize-winning journalist were in line with the story. Both men seemed to be capable of arguing and fighting about anything. It was a miracle they were friends. They must've made up since I know from Artie that the Royal Palm Tavern was not the last bar they frequented together. So why did Levon bother writing that story and saving it to a floppy disk? I did notice something familiar about the date, so I looked that up, only to discover that it was the day President Kennedy was shot. On that very evening, Levon chose to record this story? I went to bed that night anxious to return to the truck.

The next morning, hanging off the orange compactor handle,

all I could think about was Levon's mention of revenge and his journey to the other side of Ithaca. Maybe it was the assassination of Kennedy in my head, but the whole thing sounded pretty ominous and sinister. Artie walked with a limp in his right leg, an injury he refused to explain to me (my questions would be answered by a smack in the head). I wondered whether Levon gave him that limp. Then there was that old story Levon told me about Artie, Ben and my grandmother, a story sufficiently disturbing to understand that with Levon, anything could be possible. All I knew for sure was that I would be on the lookout in my trash runs for old phones – rotary and otherwise. When I brought them back, I knew that the house would feel a bit more like my own.

4

MY INHERITANCE

Aunt Vicky left the house in late August. She told me it was a once-in-a-lifetime chance at love, and she had to go down to Florida to find out if they really had something special. She met the former *Banana Republic* model and retired hedge fund manager on the internet. I wasn't worried about Aunt Vicky. I figured if this romance didn't work out, she'd have another once-in-a-lifetime opportunity next month. Those prospects tend to present themselves with surprising regularity. Anyway, that meant I had the house to myself until she returned, which didn't seem like anytime soon. We spoke every couple of days, exchanging lies. She'd tell me how great everything was going with Evan. I'd make clear to her that I wasn't going through any sort of existential crisis, and that I had a very clear direction for my future as a hedge fund manager.

Her absence gave me free reign to fill the Joan's basement, shed, backyard, and, when desperate, den with all the castoffs I collected on my daily runs. I dragged the mongo into the house, trying to correct the impression that I lived a life no reality television producer would bother filming. Like some dusty, balding homeowner, I gloomily paid the utilities with the five years of stamps, return address labels and checks the Joan left me. To further demolish my social life, I never responded to a couple of party invites, guaranteeing no more would follow. I had been tempted to join the partygoers, but I couldn't figure out how to be there and not talk to anyone. Could mongo, if I melded it together in weird and angry ways, break the routine? I owned the house now and was steadily filling it up with the castoffs of other people's lives. Maybe I could star in a reality TV show called Waste of Time.

Last year, my mother suggested we could have our own reality series called *Dying with the Joan.* "It'd be a great way to attract girls," she told me. "Who can resist a grieving son?"

During those months when I visited the Joan in the hospital, she would remind me every day that "the insurance money is enough to keep you in the house and pay for college." She said this right after her simple acknowledgement that she was dying. As if, on the bright side, I'll be pretty well off.

We would laugh grimly. She made sure before she died that I sent in all my college applications; they were months early, but she didn't trust that I would do them otherwise. She knew me too well. Now that I'd been accepted to 13 different schools ("Apply to them all, Hash, just to be safe"), I didn't feel like going to any of them.

I liked being home more every day. Each trash run meant I brought something else to the house that I could mate with the other castoffs. Some nights I printed out sections of my mother's blog that she wrote online in her final year with brain cancer. I had not looked at a word of it back then. Hours before she started, she had just become the twenty-third follower to *my* blog. Then she asked me how to write her own. After a couple of weeks, Levon Gallagher stumbled onto it, followed her around for a couple of days, wrote about it in *The Herald*, and within a month, her blog moved from seven followers to one hundred and fifty thousand.

Before she became too sick, Levon dropped in regularly, helping her write her blog. One day, he dressed in a cheap checkered suit and matching suitcase. Calling the Joan to the couch, he opened up the suitcase, took out a volume of the *Encyclopedia Britannica* and broke into a sales pitch, delivering in rapid speech lines like "big, fat books make big, fat children" and "know so much that nobody will ever want to talk to you." Even though her feeble, cough-rattled frame could hardly take it, the Joan was laughing the entire time.

At the end of the pitch, Levon dragged a mahogany bookcase from his car, aligned it in a prime corner of the living room, and started shelving the thirty-two massive volumes. "Hey Mister Encyclopedia-man," the Joan said playfully, "I never said I wanted to buy these."

"You don't have to pay a cent," Levon said. "I'm giving this 32-volume set, the final one ever to be issued by Encyclopedia Britannica, to you for free, my dear."

The Joan laughed again. "Some salesman you are."

"Well, I enjoy selling much better when I don't want the customer to buy anything."

When Levon left, the Joan grew all weepy. "Do you know how much he must've paid for that? I'm sure it was more than a grand."

I looked at my mother with hope. "You think you'll get through all the volumes?"

She wiped away a tear. "Oh Hash honey, he didn't get the set for me."

Maybe not, but most of the time Levon came by to let the Joan talk and write, as much of both as she could get out of her system. She blamed her cancer on microwave ovens and cell phones, which only increased the attention on her blog. I had to wait until after the funeral to get my I-Phone, and I still didn't have an operating microwave in the house.

In the hospital, she indirectly blamed her cancer on oatmeal. "Everyone said how good oatmeal was for you. You know a heart-healthy diet and all. So every morning for a month I put a bowl with water and oatmeal into the microwave and turned it on for two minutes. And it was never done. So I'd put it on again for another minute and just before the time was up, the oatmeal would bubble over and explode. I'd run to the microwave and stop it. As I opened the door, I felt the waves pulse through my skull. Every day, I picked another number between two and three minutes for the microwave and every day my oatmeal would either be underdone or explode. In the end, making oatmeal would always lead to an explosion I couldn't stop no matter how fast I popped open the microwave door."

"I don't remember this," I'd tell her. "I don't remember you ever eating breakfast."

"I never did," she said, shaking her head simultaneously in a Yes-and-No motion. "Not in front of you." As you're probably figuring out, I didn't understand everything the Joan told me.

She would apologize for having Aunt Vicky take over as my guardian. "I don't have anybody else." When she would say that (and yes, she tended to repeat things, particularly in her hospital bed), I wanted to shrink into my socks. I tended to stay the night in the green vinyl chair next to her bed whenever she spoke of Aunt Vicky and my future. We both knew Aunt Vicky hated the cold and that summer would be the Joan's last season and that there was a reason Aunt Vicky never had children or even a pet and that Aunt Vicky's complete lack of interest in me may have been my best chance of getting to decide my own path in life.

God, the weeks after the Joan died, too many people at Frick High tried to support and advise me, the counselors, the principal, the psychologist, the social worker, assorted teachers, even the cafeteria monitor. The only one who left it at, "Sorry about your Mom" was Pulaski, and he hasn't brought it up since.

When she wasn't talking about all the ways she contracted brain cancer, the Joan would sit in her hospital bed and tell me about her grandfather. "You know he put your Grandpa Artie through college hauling trash."

"Yes the Joan, I know," I tried to say agreeably. Her stories became simultaneously more repetitive and more detailed. A week before she died, and the last time she was truly conscious, she told me about when her grandfather was just 14 and was starting in the garbage business, that pigs were herded to eat much of the rubbish. I admit that at the time, I believed she was just making up stories, hoping to keep my attention, which made me miserable since I had been *trying* to pay attention . . . although death has a way of distracting me. Here was the Joan, looking for that last bit of company and comfort, and she had to make up stories about pigs eating trash and her grandpa picking up what even the pigs wouldn't consume. I didn't feel like Son of the Year, I tell you.

Now I found that each day I wanted to believe that story more. My hours on the truck gave me something to look forward to, even if it was just to mess around with Louie. This morning, he looked at the packet I drew from a pocket. "What is it this time?'

"Farm-raised seaweed."

"You mean that stuff is grown on a farm, not the sea?

"I think so."

"Then why isn't it just weed?"

"Because it's seaweed, you dope. Sometimes I don't think you're smart enough to haul trash."

"Someday," said Louie, managing to look down at me even though I stood a foot taller, "I might just meet the rigid qualifications."

We were both in great moods today because it was a recycling run, the cleanest and noisiest of all runs. The glass clattered and clanked, sometimes crashing so furiously that I thought a dozen chandeliers had fallen. The plastic bottles were the most satisfying to collect, since when all the air was crushed out of them, only small disks remained. Just to make sure we weren't too happy, Mayor Heine regularly threatened our continued employment on the truck, sending out Tweets to turn the community against us. Today's was: "If Frick residents have any problems with their garbage pick-up, they should contact me immediately." And when I picked up his pail, Mayor Heine said to me, "All the valuables are under the dog crap, Hash." I didn't see any dog crap. Heine didn't even have a dog. We knew that Heine would fire us the first chance he'd get.

That night, I turned on the television and didn't see the MTV shows about America's wild, troubled kids, but instead I saw a herd of pigs, forever munching, and her young grandpa tiptoeing through the dung, snatching up rims of bike tires and broken vinyl records. I knew one day I would weld a statue of my great-grandpa from those rims and records, but I hadn't figured out how to make the two work together yet. Some of the hours after school were just a lot of thrashing around the house alone, flashing on memories the Joan explained to me, memories I never actually experienced. I just needed to pass the hours until I could get back to hauling trash.

Tonight, after being greeted by my mother's insignificant question in the hall, I walked through her words to the refrigerator. Ever since I started working on the trash truck, I heard the Joan's question echo through my head: "Did you take out the garbage?" At first, I laughed. But each time I heard it again, the comment became a little less funny. Walking past that bookcase stuffed with encyclopedias, I ate pork chops and put on the television only to discover I had seen all the shows before.

My trip to the bathroom didn't improve my mood. I kept envisioning a screen that captured me doing my business, uploaded for all to see. Oh man, to get the angles for that video, the cameras must've been above and below, reflecting off of water and mirrors. Yet I didn't spot a camera anywhere. Although I suspected I was once again hallucinating, I saw everything on a screen before my eyes so clearly, down to a tagline naming the reality show *True Evacuations*, that I googled it. There was no such show, and surprisingly nothing like it on television or even YouTube. Yet I still couldn't shake the spooling video of relieving myself. My trips to the bathroom became quite uneasy. I read the Joan's blog until late into night and then I knew by the way I was hugging my pillow that I wasn't going to sleep, so I stayed up reading the rest of the Joan's days until I climbed out of bed, threw on my overalls, and hopped onto the truck.

5

THE ANTIBIOTIC VIDEO

Max burst into Pulaski's office to announce, "I want a gig on your stinkin' trash truck." Then he bowed his head, fell to his knees, and pulled down his right fist to complete the dramatic effect. "I'm giving up."

Max had been convinced since seventh grade that he'd be famous before he left high school. "What do I need? One lousy video to go viral? Hell, I should have enough by the time I reach puberty that I'm a household name." Yet word never spread of Max's brilliance. Not that Max hadn't tried. One day after we viewed Max's latest, Louie had argued that Max tried too hard and then he attempted to right-click the YouTube video of his good childhood friend into the desktop trash, not realizing he did not have such authorization ("Sure, it's easy to point and drag, but if the crap never goes in the virtual can, then I think I'll stick with the heavy, stinky pails, thank you"). Some of the videos were pretty entertaining. I think his best one was of customers walking into a consumer electronics store to buy televisions only to find the actors on all the TV screens were looking out at the prospective buyers. Some appeared like orphans, pleading cow eyes welling glumly up to potential adoptive parents; others gave sales pitches, and yet others featured super models who switched between blank stares and suspicious glances. The viewer had the strange experience of watching a video of customers being watched by televisions. Max explained to me that the work played with our understanding of the nature of attention – something Max was a particular student of.

Unfortunately, once you threw enough videos on YouYube without robust reactions, the audience began to view you as not worth even the trouble of clicking an icon. Like the rest of us, Max was used to having too much attention, but no stroking from his parents, his teachers, and his friends could soothe the devastating outrage of discovering that the rest of the world really had no interest in him. The interest didn't have to be sincere; at least, they could've had the common courtesy to see the video without actually watching it. Unfortunately, Max's true gift wasn't in videos, but in computer hacking. Administrators, teachers, and students all believed that Max had information on them, which meant they stayed away from criticizing him or his videos, and stayed away from him in general.

So when Max broke down in Pulaski's office, he'd get a little more attention than the everyday student. I was becoming particularly used to such outbursts in that office. Operation Pick-up Kids had quickly become the sanctuary where the anxious and desperate rushed in, hoping to run away from whatever today's crisis happened to be: college application, college acceptance, college rejection, no parking spot, bad cafeteria food, etc. It seemed that half the school suddenly wanted to toss around trash. Operation Pick-up Kids had become glamorous, which of course was exactly the opposite of the plan, since hauling pails was supposed to provide the kind of anonymity that the disturbed and demented seniors craved. Instead, now residents gawked at the carters like they were avatars in some video game. Sometimes, when I lifted up a pail, I caught the piercing eyes, eyes hoping I would do a couple of flips, maybe smash the truck with a sledgehammer, and then send game coins showering onto the street.

Max was given a crack because Louie had gotten so many complaints that Pulaski needed to keep him off the truck for a shift or two to show the Frick residents that he and Bill were listening. Plus, Pulaski never knew what Max had lifted off his own hard drive.

I handed Max a uniform and he smoothed wrinkles from it like it was his wedding suit. From the driver's seat, Big Bill gave Max a proper greeting. "Welcome, my young junior flip. Are you ready to empty the piss pots?"

"Piss pots?" Max looked alarmed.

"Don't worry," I assured Max. "He just means we're going house to house."

"Oh."

While he had to empty no actual piss pots on the run, Max was surprised about how much liquid sloshed around the bottom of the truck. The compactor squeezed out the oozing juices from all the decaying produce and dairy in the pails, which had already been liquefying. As the roiling gray soup slopped about the truck bed, the churning of the compactor transformed the waters into a toxic tidal pool.

After he twisted his mouth a couple of times at the sight of this diseased sea, Max adjusted. However, he presented a whole new slew of challenges on the truck. At every stop, Max saw murders – murders of a distant past, murders of the moment and murders of next Thursday.

As we dumped the remnants of a big TV antenna from the Gulottas, Max wrinkled his eyebrows, which he did constantly whenever he thought and talked simultaneously. "I betcha they skewered a couple of bodies before they left the weapon for us to dispose of."

I shook my head. "You just don't go around killing people and leaving the evidence with the trash man."

The eyebrows danced. "Of course you do, that's how nobody gets suspicious. If you act like it's just junk instead of something you stabbed a man through with, then nobody will bother with you."

I pointed to the rod. "Why don't you hold onto it then?"

Now the eyebrows seemed to grow even bigger. "And get myself implicated in a homicide, no thanks." He dumped the rod into the compactor. I had a feeling I knew whose hard drive Max would be hacking tonight.

"You know," I said, "you could've made a few bucks in scrap metal from that."

More shadows from the furrowed brow. "Not worth the risk."

As Big Bill drove us along the route on that late October morning, the oaks deciding to start dropping their leaves, Max saw suffocation in the Standish's discarded plastic bag, poison in Peggy Murphy's recycling bin, a cut jugular from the jagged lid of Nonna D'Antoni's tomato can, a bashed-in skull from a cast iron leg of Keith Stevens's outdoor table, and oh yeah, the collection of bodies that the Mavella clan clearly stashed since they were guilty of leaving no trash and therefore no weapons at the curb.

"Max, my friend." I patted him on the shoulder. "You are looking for stories that aren't here. You've got the classic first day trashman syndrome. You think that there are big secrets in this trash. There aren't. There are only little, rotten, awful secrets."

"Well," Max smiled, his eyebrows shrinking, "that's better than nothing."

"Believe me, Max, the videos you play in your mind are much better than anything you'll find out here."

I figured I had talked some sense into Max because once we landed at Mayor Heine's house, Max stopped shooting out theories of blood and mayhem and rushed toward the single pail on the curb. Finally, I'd get some work from another part of his body besides his gums. But Max wouldn't lift up the pail. His hands were rifling through the contents like he was sifting for gold. He rose up with paws full of shredded documents that he waved through the cool autumn air.

"What are you looking for?"

"Anything private."

"You want to dump the pail now?"

"Oh yeah." Max stuffed the shredded papers into his pockets. He looked like he'd just celebrated New Year's.

I pointed at him. "Why?"

"My other videos will be nothing compared to the one I'm making on Mayor Heine."

I rolled my eyes. "I'm sure that'll be thrilling." I tried not the show my discomfort; of course, Max was antagonizing the one bastard I could not afford to piss off, the one bastard who could get rid of me, and, I figured, would get rid of me, any day now.

Max was pulling out of his kinky hair strips of paper, each possessing long slivers of single letters. "The Mayor's got some crazy secrets."

"You mean the stuff about the garbage scandal."

"Oh, that's nothing. There's the Ben Wright disaster and that's only the beginning."

Most of us in Frick always carried around strange feelings about the afterlife of our local hero, especially about allowing Mayor Heine to exploit his legacy. Ben Wright became the star of the most original reality TV show even though he was dead at the time. *The Invention of Life* dragged up footage from Ben's last year in Frick before his mysterious death. Ben had spent the previous thirty years bounding across the nation from Tech Alley to Silicon Valley laying his divine hands on great inventions and inevitably improving them. During that final year in Frick, much of his life had been secretly recorded on videotape. That footage, plus hours of stock promotional tape from the various tech firms he joined and many commentaries from Mayor Heine, became the basis for *The Invention of Life*. Ironically, the show made the previously little known Ben Wright famous as an innovative genius. Only after the reality show aired was our high school named after him.

The Joan had been saddened by Ben's unwitting participation in the TV show. "It's not like he had a choice," she had said to me more than once. "He left his estate to the village and we say thank you by showing America how this genius fell apart. Oh God, the way he scratched away his own skin. When he took his shirt off, Ben looked like he'd been rolled across barbed wire. No wonder the poor man wore gloves. Every day he ripped himself up. And we showed that to everybody. I'm pretty sure most of the time he had no idea he was being filmed."

When the Joan brought up *The Invention of Life* to him, Levon Gallagher shook, frothed, and kicked the encyclopedia case before he pulled out the W volume and showed her Ben's entry. However badly the Joan, Levon or anybody else felt about what happened to the inventor's legacy, there was general agreement Mayor Heine bore most of the responsibility for laying out Ben

Wright's brilliant, broken life to the world and forever associating Frick Village with reality television.

Now Max was telling me Mayor Heine had even more skeletons in his closet. "Data mining is where he made all his money."

The truck started moving again and, staring at Max's pockets, I yelled to him over the grinding gears and engine. "And you think that confetti will give you some answers?"

He shook his head, frowned, and hollered. "You've got a lot to learn about making a viral video."

I muttered under my breath, "So do you."

Max didn't notice because he was too busy arranging his papers in an effort to make them look less assembled. Then he shouted out, "These are Heine's actual shredded papers here. I put these all over the screen, it will definitely show that he's hiding something. Add that to the other stuff I've dug from his trash and I have a beautiful story here about the Mayor's crazy, intrusive data mining."

"You've gone through his garbage before?"

"Every Tuesday and Friday morning at 4:30 a.m."

"You doing my job for me?"

"Just looking for dirt on a few of my neighbors, that's all."

"Some life you have."

"You should talk."

I tried not to be offended. "Don't you think you'd find a lot more out hacking than rummaging through people's garbage?"

"Of course I do. But I need the visuals."

Max had to realize that suspicion goes both ways. It's one thing to hack into the neighbors' computer screens and they're none the wiser for it, but it's another to spread your mistrust with every pail you dump. I thought it was important to talk a little sense into Max before he dropped right over the curb. I pointed to a blue house at the end of the block. "You know what they're thinking in that house right now as they look out and see you out here, the new trash kid?"

"No, what?"

"What'd that boy do to get this job? He must've killed Louie. Did you do it with a pail to his thick Ginny head or just stuff the little Italian meatball into the compactor?"

Max nodded, his eyebrows now barely visible.

I patted him on the back and said reassuringly, "Understand now?"

"Yeah, I get it. I'm glad I did the trash run. Tell Louie to be ready for the next one. I'll talk to Pulaski when we get back."

"Good man," I said. "You're not made to be on the truck. You're better off making a video of us."

"Nah, that's O.K. You're no Mayor Heine. If it's not interesting enough with me on the truck, it certainly won't be interesting without me there."

I felt relieved, yet I also felt sorry for Mayor Heine. When I signed my insurance releases at Village Hall last month, Mayor Heine said to me in a tone meant to be affectionate, "Son, you wouldn't believe how much you learn from what people throw away." At the time, Heine's comment creeped me out. The words kept gnawing at me. Maybe Max and Mayor deserved each other.

I rummaged around my pockets, searching for the "present" I wanted to get rid of before Max finished the run. A few weeks ago, I had come to realize I needed to throw away some of my past cluttering the house, especially with all the mongo I hauled in. I struggled to toss any of it out. Last Monday on the trash run, I stuffed an old kitchen mitt in my pocket, figuring if I casually tossed it into the compactor I wouldn't feel like I had just strangled a puppy.

Then I saw Peggy Murphy dragging back her empties.

I drew the big glove from my pocket with what I hoped was a stylish flourish. "This is for you." I handed Peggy Murphy the ragged, orange mitt, scorched and blackened over the years.

She picked it up without smiling. "There are holes in it. Did you ever get burned when taking something out of the oven with it?"

"Yes."

"Oh."

"It was a good glove."

I made sure I left before she threw it away.

Now I gave Max the Joan's cancer wig, the one she refused to wear. I figured he could use it in one of his videos. From his smirk, I knew that Max didn't realize it came from her. He must've thought I snatched out of the bin of some drama queen like Peggy.

"That's a good move, getting rid of that thing," he said, stuffing it in his pocket with the speed of someone who'd just been handed a bag of heroin.

"Why?"

"Because the mayor's after you and the program."

"What does he care about trash?"

"The only hands he wants in Frick's garbage are those he can control."

As usual, Max sounded a little paranoid, so I pushed back. "Do you think Heine has security cameras at his house?"

"Of course he does."

"So what do you think he's going to do when he catches you rummaging through his pail?"

"Oh, he'll go nuts, but," and here he gave me a sharp stare, "I won't be back on the truck. Trash is not my life."

Easy for video boy to say. What the hell would my mornings

be like without the truck? I had a hard enough time getting up on weekends.

As he stepped off the truck for good, Max gave me some parting advice. "If you don't figure out how to deal with Heine, you'll lose it all." He spread his arms out like he was giving a tour of paradise, walking away with a sly little chuckle.

* * *

After the fall mornings of garbage pick-up, the hours at school just sort of floated by. When I wasn't hanging around Pulaski's office, I did just enough in my classes to not raise any alarms. I had been out so often late last year that my friends were not on top of me, and I didn't make any effort to start conversations. My only remnant of my past role at Ben Wright High as an involved and sharp kid on the fast track to a top college was my continued presence on the Class Spirit Committee. Since I'd already been accepted to too many colleges, I had no desire to continue any of the extracurricular activities that filled out my applications. I even resigned as editor of the school literary magazine, *The Bleeding Soul*. But among the stupid promises I had made to the Joan in that hospital bed of awful fluids was that I wouldn't give up all my clubs when she was no longer around to nag me. Since the other activities only met before school, the Class Spirit Committee was the one place I could keep my word. Of course, I couldn't possibly hate any committee more than this one. Most of the members gathered in the mornings, but the chair, the very enthusiastic Megan Stevens, held extra afternoon meetings just for those with scheduling conflicts. The only ones to gather afterschool were Megan, me and Max, who must've consumed his mornings picking through Mayor Heine's trash and filming god-knows-what.

Today, we were discussing what the float would be for the Homecoming Parade, and Megan tried very hard to act like the decision hadn't already been made by the morning crew. Megan was particularly good at smiling and laughing as she muttered words that left me annoyed at the moment and bruised for days to follow. Everyone was certain that she'd win the Senior Superlative for Class Cutie, but she never put me in the proper mood to notice. She wore very tight stretch pants from a designer so hot that I'd never heard of him. In the classes I had shared with Megan, I listened to her give many correct answers, but never a smart one. Now she was in charge. Great.

The senior class theme was Our Time. I made what I thought was a pretty good suggestion – to create a three-dimensional Facebook Page for the float.

"Oh that's a great idea," said Megan. She was snickering and tried hard to let me know she was suppressing a laugh. "Has anyone ever told you that you have an old soul?" Why, yes, Megan, everyone tells me I'm like an old man, particularly since you spend an awful lot of time telling people that I'm not very clued in and act like one of your dad's friends. She smiled at me some more. "It's just that Facebook hasn't been popular for years."

"Isn't it still big?"

"Maybe with my Grandma." Now, Max's eyes zoomed in on me like they were camera lenses. I tucked my hands into my jean pockets, wondering if he had a device on somewhere.

"Well then how about Twitter?"

"Twitter?" she laughed again. "That's such a cute idea."

Instead of clutching my hands around her neck, I offered, "Tumblr?"

Megan doubled over in laughing spasms, but she remained

completely silent in her convulsions. It was as if my cluelessness was so monumental that she couldn't register the stupidity of what I was saying and simultaneously figure out how to get air in her lungs to wheeze out noisy chuckles.

I tried one more time with my good idea. "Instagram?"

After Megan recovered, she asked if I wanted to go to the mall when the meeting ended. I made an excuse about a load of homework. I wasn't up to watching her sprawl of the floor when I thumbed through last year's fashions. Funny, for years I thought I had kept up on everything. In the early hours of the morning, I would read dozens of Wikipedia entries. I would walk into school with crazy terms and trivia that drew friends toward me, talking and joking in the happiest of ways. But starting about two years ago (before the Joan got sick, so I can't even pin it on that), those bleary-eyed studies made me sound a bit off. I had been writing a lot too and most of what came out of my mouth were sentences that belonged in research papers rather than in casual conversations ("A chance for the alumni to reexamine their past through the eyes of present-day seniors, the Homecoming Float should be both a sign of our times and an emblem of nostalgia.") About that same time I had fooled around with Megan at a party. I remember throwing up underneath a street light on my walk home, and then throwing up again at home. The next day Megan acted cool. I didn't, behaving like something important had happened. I made the mistake of posting on Facebook a picture of me drunkenly and lovingly staring at her. Immediately word spread that I was a stalker. How that impression transformed into casting me as an old man, I can't tell you. I immediately took down the picture from Facebook and trashed all copies. Unfortunately, the image had been shared more times than I'd like to remember and my status as an old man only grew. In the weeks that followed, my new identity was being shaped by a whispering Megan and a circle of giggling friends who could barely restrain their screeches.

It has been harder to reinvent myself as Hash the Rugged Trash Man than I had figured. My mornings on the garbage truck have started to break up those phrases of an old man. Yelling over a grinding engine tends to simplify the way you talk. Now I only preserve that vestige of my overread, overaged self for you.

Megan didn't seem too interested in allowing me to remake myself as a young senior. She explained that the committee would go with the recommendation of the morning group: a float featuring comic book superheroes. I kept my mouth shut while she and Max decided on the color of the background where all the seniors in spandex would stand. I'm pretty sure after a few minutes they arrived at blue. Meanwhile, I read another inspirational statement up on the wall from good old Ben Wright: "You often only discover the truth when you are searching for lies."From my cargo pants of many pockets, I pulled out a Gameboy that must now be six years old. I had spent two years digging, excavating and erecting an empire in CraftMeister. My world was filled with trickling fountains, sycamore-lined boulevards, and old women who washed the sidewalks with bleach. One day as I was constructing the final vents on a bakery, my world froze up and wouldn't respond to any button I pushed. When I restarted CraftMeister, all I could access was a screensaver image of Main Street, a tiny glimpse into the world I'd so intensely envisioned and erected. Since then, what appeared whenever I turned on the Gameboy was merely that single image. As I tried to enter the world I spent two years constructing, the program froze. I explained to Megan, "All it shows of what's trapped in the machine is that one image." She actually accepted the Gameboy from me. I guessed she'd take a picture of it and shoot a message off to her friends of just how pathetic I was.

I don't know why I wanted her to possess such a record of me, but I strangely felt it was important, even if remnants of me were humiliated.

* * *

When I got home that night, I was greeted by the Joan's voice, asking me whether I'd taken out the garbage, her voice so clear I turned the corner, hoping to see her face. I whispered the words my mother said. They were not cruel or profound or happy or sad or powerful words. They were so achingly common and meaningless. They were everywhere, even as I muttered them opening the refrigerator or shampooing my hair in the shower.

And I had enough problems in the bathroom, what with the camera angles everywhere upon me. I was starring in another episode of *True Evacuations*. It mattered little that the reality TV series had yet to air. I couldn't help but notice the product placement surrounding my embarrassed body – Right Guard Deodorant, Ivory Soap, Barbasol Shaving Cream, and Suave Shampoo. The hallucination clung to me like a scared baby.

To distract myself, I spent the first hour following my routine of reading and deleting Emails. That didn't help my mood because I started counting the trash violations sent to me. The six I received were petty citations, like leaving the pail more than six inches from the curb. Their nature convinced me that Mayor Heine indeed had it out for me. I scanned the rest of the Emails. I opened every one in five – the subject line better be a winner or the subject better be a girl I like. I had three Email accounts, and each one warned me that the mailbox was full and that I'd better start hacking away at the messages. I would guess I wasted a good twenty minutes each day deleting SPAM, a fine use of my time. Then I deleted the regular bloggers who courteously sent me "personal" Emails to promote their brands. At those moments when I hit the final, point-of-no-return trash icon, I suffered from twinges of regret. For that reason, two bloggers always got a second look. The first was Reverend Alexander Burr, who was awfully kind to my mother near the end and was a lot less preachy in person than on his blog. He knew what was going on around Frick, since he was a man people tended to confess to. The other blogger, Selena Omaha, told even more. Frick was small enough for me to know that nobody named Selena lived in the village, and I couldn't figure out who she was. She sounded like one of my classmates. All I knew was that she was even more interested in trash than I was. Both the Reverend and Selena got a once over before I deleted them, and even then I got this funny feeling that I missed something terribly important. In fact, I was sure I did.

From the October 31 Trash Folder

Are you sure you want to permanently delete all the items and subfolders in the Deleted Items Folder?

The Daily Bread from Reverend Alexander Burr

The average person peers down unto his phone 150 times a day. That is far too many occasions to bring forth bitter and poisonous fruit. This child of Satan Max has brought a video camera into my sacred sanctum and delivered a cell phone into my hands. He thinks this phone will make me walk in slippery places, that I will succumb to the immoderate and boundless furnace of fire and brimstone. I explained to the loathsome, lens-burdened worm that I will not gaze upon the cell phone.

That devil Max smiles and stands ready to capture my fall even as he breathes lies. He says that he just wants to record my rejections, that I will lord over YouTube, sending a message the world hungers for.

Staring out beyond his lens to a congregation only I can see, I cry out, "My children, stop looking down at the accursed, damnable phone." The fallen seek solace in the phone, but I sayeth, keep your hand on the plow and stare straight ahead. I sayeth again and again, unhand me, handheld devices, for you are dragging me unto the path of desolation. I say, vanity, vanity, all your channel capacity. Before you seized the phone, I could forgive you for you know not what you do. Now your fraudulence, your phoniness, is a yoke. That devil child Max, I am certain, hoped to record my fall. Instead he is witness to my prophecy.

The Epic Life of Selena Omaha

So are you ready for the inside scoop about what's popping in Frick Village?

You better be because I've been out all night turning up your trash before the garbage men come. And the stuff I know is real fresh. Don't be shaking though. You can be chilling because I'm not throwing shade at you. I'm starting with the dead, and you won't believe what Levon Gallagher's fam left out on his curb.

A gun.

I mean not a real killa, but it still could make Levon a playa. When I brought it home, I thought it was a toy gun, but my Pops told me it was a BB gun. He bought me some BBs. I went into my backyard, cranked the handle, and fired. I must've shot a hundred BBs at mason jars, hub caps, lawn mower blades, and ceramic lawn ornaments. Plus, I found out you could kill a squirrel with a BB gun. After I saw all the BBs I left in the fences and trees, I decided to return to Levon's backyard to see if he mad liked his gun as much as I did.

So one morning as the sun rose before Hash and Louie and Big Bill showed up at Levon Gallagher's curb, you could've found your bae, Selena Omaha, picking BB pellets with her pocketknife from a herd of wet, smelly stuffed animals. Yes, on the stumps and patio furniture Levon propped up stuffed animals to use as target practice. Pretty crazy, right?

But Levon's just the start. I'll definitely be giving you the swag money smack, straight up. And don't think about digging up my trash to chirp on me. I don't leave even a crumb out on the curb. Sorry 'bout it. As for the rest of you, get ready to listen up.

After I hit delete, I shut my eyes only to see mounds of rubble shot through with whispers too muffled to recognize.

6

THE GARBAGE THAT NEVER QUITE MADE IT

I sat in the inner room, filling out my log for Operation Pick-up Kids. Mrs. Woods, Jen's mother, had entered into Pulaski's office, delicately blowing her nose, letting out the faintest of toots. She was one of those incredibly skinny, more incredibly nervous women of that age, who if not for the two "incrediblys" in front of her descriptions might be an incredibly attractive woman of that moment and situation; instead she was incredibly annoying. She had come in crying about her daughter.

"I don't know what to do with Jen. I think she needs to go on the garbage truck." Poor bastard Pulaski. Ever since he created the Operation Pick-up Kids program, every parent who had any issue with a son or daughter thought it could be solved by handling a healthy wad of trash.

Pulaski certainly knew how to be sympathetic, asking "What's wrong?" A two-second question that generated a twenty-minute explanation so detailed ("you know the day she wore the red Gucci pumps and the Coldwater Creek sheer blouse that claimed to be salmon even though I swear to this day it's mauve") and bizarre ("she collected her toenails in her change purse, some are even wedged against her applicator") that I couldn't fill out a line of my log. The upshot finally arrived in the twenty-seventh minute of the twenty-minute complaint: "Mr. Pulaski, she won't look up at anybody anymore. She just gazes down at her phone. She won't talk to anyone except on the phone. She won't even talk to me unless I call her or text her. Her friends tell me that Jen does the same thing to them. She even brings the phone into the bathroom when she showers. I don't know where she puts it in there." I heard a soft swallow and another genteel toot. "Once I called her in the shower and she answered."

"What'd you call her for?" asked Pulaski.

"I wanted to know if she needed more shampoo. I could hear the shower water splashing down as I remembered she told me the other day that she was almost out. Mr. Pulaski, this is serious, I'm afraid Jen might be electrocuted."

I heard a familiar grunt from Mr. Pulaski, which I'm certain Ms. Woods did not clearly interpret. "I don't advise calling her in the shower," he said, trying his best to drain the last drops of irony from his tongue.

"What if someone else calls then?" Mrs. Woods countered.

"I see your problem," Pulaski said sympathetically with those four words I have heard him say frequently in my hours filling out the log. There was a long pause and then Pulaski asked. "Why haven't you taken her phone away?"

Mrs. Woods started crying. "I tried, but Jen won't give it up."

"Can't you just cut off the service?"

Mrs. Woods sobbed for a good two minutes, a few placid

toots along the way to assure Mr. Pulaski that her suffering was borne with dignity. She initiated a half-hearted attempt to speak, interrupted by Pulaski passing tissues and the desolate mother sniffling delicately, with again only the faintest squeaks spraying from her nostrils, before she confessed, "I can't do that to Jen. What if without her phone she shuts down completely and doesn't communicate with anyone."

"I see," said Pulaski, and I believe he did indeed see the source of the problems and what would not be done about them.

"She's afraid someone will Tweet or post something bad about her. If she doesn't catch it, she said her life will be over."

Ah, teenage girls. But the problem was larger than that. Jen wasn't the only one peering at her phone instead of looking over her shoulder to see if the past or the present would catch up with her. Aunt Vicky cradled her phone like it was a newborn.

"Unfortunately," Pulaski said gently, "she is not a candidate for Operation Pick-up Kids, since given Jen's condition," – I imagine Mrs. Woods smiled at this moment, happy the counselor called the problem a condition – "Trash pick-up would be a danger to her. Her eyes can't be staring down at her phone when she's hanging off the back of a moving vehicle."

While she could not be on the truck, Jen clearly belonged to Generation Dementia, and I decided to get in touch with her. That cold night, the first of November, I stopped by the Woods' house with one of my pieces I'd been working on. The subject matter was a bit risky given Jen's "condition," but I think sometimes a gift just needs to be given whether someone wants it or not. I had snatched from the Hosbachs an old black rotary telephone with all the wiring still attached; I connected one end to an extremely large cell phone from the 1990's dropped in the

Forrest's recycling bin, and the other to a Styrofoam cup which had been tossed onto the Alford's front lawn (I snatched it before Louie could crush it), a rescue effort I had just mounted that morning. With black magic marker, I wrote on the Styrofoam cup the work's title: "The Calling."

I tried to hand the contraption to Jen, who naturally would only look down at her phone. So I clicked a picture of it and sent it to her. A moment later – God she was a lightning-fast texter – she sent her reply. "Thank you. It's lovely."

I took out a string, attached it to yet another Styrofoam cup from the Stevens' collection and connected it to its sister cup on "The Calling." Into my cup I bellowed, "You're welcome," hoping she might pick up the other end. Hell, if nothing else, "The Calling" had to be considered a phone. I spoke again into the cup. "Would you like to try it?" and paused, listening for the reverberation. She did not answer, so I texted her the same message.

"Sure," she wrote back.

I waited a good hour to see if she would lift her head from her cell phone to use my fine contraption. She never looked up. I continued to call her from my cup until the Styrofoam ruptured. I left my broken end at her house with the rest of "The Calling."

The next morning when I made my rounds, I found that Jen (or could it have been Mrs. Woods) had left "The Calling" out on the curb. I took it back with me. Jen could deem it garbage, but from my first day, I made the commitment that nothing was really garbage until I said so. I wasn't hurt by her rejection. I might as well have been a bachelor on a reality TV show who didn't get handed a rose.

Louie shook his head, smiling. "So now you're trying to pick up girls from the curb too?"

I scratched my thickening razor stubble. "Whatever I can get my hands on." I wasn't kidding either. Whatever I could get to take home, I would grab.

I pulled a fruit bar from my pocket. Louie gave me a look almost of approval. "Nice to see you're eating something somewhat normal for a change instead of those overpriced, annoying organic turds you're usually chewing on."

I pointed to the label on a fruit bar. "This bar is 77 percent organic." After I took a bite, Louie snatched the rest, lightning fast, and tossed it in the compactor. "Why the hell did you do that?" I asked.

"You just ate the 23 percent that was any good."

* * *

Louie found that we needed a good half hour to decompress after we got through with the garbage run. We'd hang out and talk to Pulaski. I'm pretty sure if we didn't have that time, I'd end up hurling a trash can across the physics classroom (try studying *that* trajectory), and Louie would be ripping half-filled water bottles from the dainty hands of dehydrated sophomores and tossing them into the recycling buckets. As we filled in our log sheets, Pulaski told us tales about the sordid and lurid history of sanitation in Frick Village. "At least you guys know that your trash ends up in the resource recovery plant. You can see what comes out the smokestacks. You weren't around for the bad old days. There's about twenty years when we have no record of garbage. It's like we didn't make any of it at all."

"How's that possible?" I asked.

"Oh, anything could happen in the days of the landfill. You had to pay by the tonnage, and, if you know Mayor Heine, he doesn't like to pay for anything, let alone garbage. The carting industry, ahem, wasn't exactly well regulated back then. It was the Wild West of refuse. Some say we were burning trash in small metal containers in spots all over the village and that in those days the haze filled the sky so thickly that it would make these wonderful fat rainbows after a storm. Others say a herd of hungry hogs fed off our trash until after too many years of munching on poison, they died in the landfills that fed them. Most say that story's not likely since we've never found a single hog carcass, not a skeleton, not even a hoof. Some say the old garbage carters shipped it off to a town out west that was looking to fill some breaks and gaps in its huge valley so the engineers could level a new turnpike. Some say the trash is all buried somewhere around here still today, seeping down into our land and into our water."

"What does our cheap mayor say?" I asked. "Hasn't he been mayor forever?"

"Mayor Heine doesn't say."

"Well, I guess we won't know then unless one day a neighbor's planting geraniums and he unearths a shoe."

"A shoe might not be garbage," Louie pointed out. "That might just be attached to a dead body." The thought got Louie going. "Maybe we should continue the tradition."

"How so?" I played along.

"Maybe . . ." Louie gave Pulaski a serious glance. "Maybe, we should hide our garbage too."

"There's no way," said Pulaski, dismissively. "Everybody would know about it in a day."

"Hey Pulaski," said Louie, "you've got a big house and big yard, don'tya?" Pulaski merely scratched his big nose. "You always call us Generation Dementia. How about we live up to our name? Maybe if you got a little trash in your yard, you'd start appreciating me more, instead of putting me on probation anytime I pick up a stray coffee cup from a yard."

"When Peggy Murphy's still drinking from the cup? I just don't think you can call that a stray cup."

"She looked like she was done." Louie pointed to the contraption I named "The Calling," which I had placed atop the log desk. "Look at this guy with the Styrofoam cups and all the phones here. You telling me I'm worse than him. I see an empty coffee cup, I throw it away. Hash sees an empty cup, he clings onto it like he's some weird, hoarding elf and then starts attaching other worthless crap to it."

"I see your point," said Pulaski.

"Damn right you see my point. Hell, I wouldn't worry about me hauling trash from your lawn. I'd worry about Hash giving you that Frankenstein monster of phones and foams and wires as a present."

"By the way," I tossed in, "Mr. Pulaski, when's your birthday?"

For once, Pulaski didn't laugh. "Seriously boys, you've got to cut off the nonsense on the truck. I've heard Heine is setting up a hearing with the sanitation board, and if the board doesn't like what the residents tell them, they'll shut us down right away."

Louie whistled. "I thought that was just talk."

"Not anymore," said Pulaski. "Big Bill told me Heine's pushing to get the hearing on the agenda of the next meeting."

Louie and I glanced at each other. That very morning, as I popped the lid on Heine's trash can, I saw our Frick Village sanitation department job applications resting neatly above an overstuffed tall kitchen bag, the applications we had submitted months earlier. Clearly, they were photocopies, and we had indeed gotten those jobs, but Heine wasn't exactly mysterious when he wanted to deliver a message, eh? Plus, the mayor's

Tweets about us were becoming increasingly strange and aggressive: "If Frick residents observe any sanitation worker improperly dressed, let me know immediately." We wore orange jumpsuit uniforms, and we always wore them on the job. We couldn't figure out what Heine could get us on our outfits, unless it was their cleanliness. Would we have to make sure no speck of trash lands on us in our hauling? Louie and I knew we'd better think of something.

Pulaski ended the conversation the same way each day, "Don't you baboons have classes to attend?"

When I was finally done for the day learning how the forces of math, English, science and history protected the world from the great plague of ignorance, I returned home and subsequently fiddled with "The Calling," ringing out messages to any who would listen. If my life were a reality TV show, a pretty girl would answer, and we would flirt meaninglessly until I hung up from embarrassment. Too much time passed in my head watching reality shows I could have no chance of joining. I ignored the loneliness of the house and spun my finger through the old dials.

If someone did answer, I was ready with a surprisingly relevant question: Do you have any idea what happened to all those tons of trash Frick Village lost all those years ago?

7

THE DIARY OF LEVON GALLAGHER: ACT 22

April 3, 1968

We were at the Gray Pony. I told the guys how I had drunk Carnation Instant Breakfast forty-two days in a row: "What could be better than to start every morning with a chocolate shake?" Sometimes I even had it for my lunch. Derek Standish suggested I had gained a few pounds. I decided I didn't want to listen to his yapping. I'd been having a great day. I had just put the finishing touches on a story that I'd been working on for months. It filled one of those black marble composition notebooks, and I'd been reading it over between sips of whiskey. Old Ben Wright got his paws on another invention, working with those boys at Texas Instruments on a handheld calculator. I type in 43,567 and multiply it by 757,412 and see the answer 32,998,168,604 before I can blink.

An amazing story.

No, I wouldn't let Derek bother me. I saw in

the glaze of his eyes that Standish was only capable of adding up very small numbers, and he needed a very big pencil just to accomplish that. To keep the mood light, I tossed out my favorite barroom topic: "Who is the better actor, John Wayne or Sydney Poitier?"

"That's a stupid question. John Wayne, obviously. Why? Who do you think?"

"Sydney Poitier of course. He has shades."

"Poitier has shades alright, huh, huh, which is part of the problem." I knew just by bringing up Poitier I was asking for trouble. You mention a black actor, a black singer, hell a black anything at the Gray Pony, and a bigoted slur will slip out faster than a belch.

"I see. You won't admit John Wayne's limitations."

"John Wayne is an American treasure. A myth, a legend."

Here we go. I could see where this would be heading. "That might be true. But he's not a very good actor. Sydney Poitier can tell you a story just by closing a car door."

"He can't shine John Wayne's shoes." Derek gave one of those deep, discriminating laughs, a chortle filled with dirty, white gas. Now I would have to carry the argument to the tense, miserable spaces these conversations inevitably inhabit.

"I thought it'd get back to that. Poitier builds more tension shining shoes than John Wayne can winning the entire West."

"John Wayne is the representation of all that's good in America. He's one man by himself with a gun standing tall, dealing with the bad guys, crushing through his strength of character those who would oppose our way of life."

I drew my face right up to Derek's brutal chin and answered, "Yeah, Sydney Poitier does all of that and without a gun."

Derek growled something about my calling John Wayne a coward and the conversation grew ugly quickly. I poked him in the chest with my black marble composition notebook to drive home a point. Then I might've made a comment about Derek's knuckle-dragging stupidity. That's when he grabbed me by the collar and tossed me out door. Then he took my notebook, ripped it in two, and threw it at me. His big paws must've been like vice grips to do that.

I dropped the tattered remnants that were my notebook and me into the car and headed, as usual, to Sarah's and Artie's. Sarah had given birth just six months ago but looked damn good, I must say. I entertained them with this night's skirmish. Sarah asked why I would get into it with someone twice as big as me about something as stupid as who was a better actor. I told her somebody had to set Derek straight. Sarah sipped Ruinite on ice. Sarah pointed out that I may not have succeeded in my goal.

Artie handed me a whiskey, lifted his own, and said as a way of a toast, "Here's to leaving the Tang for the astronauts." It had been such an old joke between us that no liquor could touch our lips without Artie delivering that blessing. I lifted my glass and the baby gave one of those weak, snuffling cries. Sarah swaddled her on the couch.

As usual, we sat there swapping stories. Sarah and Artie had richer lives and better stories than I did. Sarah would present dramatic renditions of her encounters at the gallery, about how Andy Warhol told her to stop selling paintings. "Darling, you should be an actress," she said in a dead-on droll impersonation of Warhol, "then you'd be as deeply superficial as I am." Artie would offer the inside scoop on the shenanigans going on at City Hall. "Grady walked out of the maintenance department with a chainsaw stuffed inside his suit jacket, like nobody would notice. He shops at that warehouse like it's Sears."

Tonight, I finally could tell a story worthy of them, and it wasn't even about Ben Wright. "A new homeowner leaves a big sealed steel drum he found in the crawl space out at the curb. The garbage man refuses to take it unless the drum is opened and emptied. The drum weighs more than a sack of crap. The homeowner opens it to discover a dead woman soaked in formaldehyde. Of course the guy calls the cops. The cops chase down the previous homeowner who claims the drum was there when he bought the house and that he never bothered to move it. The autopsy corroborates his line. The body had been dead for twenty years. It was a black woman, and get this, she was pregnant."

Artie let out a low whistle; Sarah clung to the baby a bit more tightly. "The cops found the owner from 1948, a Hank Miller, down in Florida. He told them he knew nothing about the barrel or the woman. The next day Miller blew his brains out. Miller's grief-stricken widow explained to the cops that the dead woman, Lucinda Meadows, had been their maid. She told the cops that one day Lucinda just disappeared. 'We guessed she was homesick and needed to go back to North Carolina,' she told them blankly."

I knew better than to give Sarah and Artie details about the relationship between Hank and Lucinda. Instead, I kept nice and quiet, the way Artie does when he negotiates deals down at City Hall.

"Did that really happen?" Sarah asked.

I smiled grimly at her. "You can read about it in tomorrow's *Herald*."

I got ready to leave. As she held the baby in one hand and passed me my coat with the other, Sarah told me, "You're right, you know."

"About what?"

"Sydney Poitier is the better actor."

I felt pretty good there for a couple of moments, though my return to my car and my torn notebook blackened my mood. Everything I needed to tell Ben Wright's tale of the calculator was in that notebook, but now I couldn't figure out how to reassemble the ripped pages. The story stopped making sense to me. I wasted many days thinking about my lost story and my argument with Derek. Then I met with a friend of a friend and purchased John Wayne's best friend. I may straighten out Derek yet.

* * *

Another frustrating diary entry. My first question was who the hell is Sydney Poitier? I had heard of John Wayne, but like most names I had heard, I didn't know who he was either. I looked up John Wayne on *Wikipedia*. "An Academy Award-winner, Wayne was among the top box office draws for three decades, and was named the all-time top money making star. An enduring American icon, he epitomized rugged masculinity and is famous for his demeanor, including his distinctive calm voice, walk, and height."

Then I looked up Sydney Poitier. "In 1963, Poitier became the first black person to win an Academy Award for Best

Actor for his role in *Lilies of the Field*. The significance of this achievement was later bolstered in 1967 when he starred in three successful films: *To Sir, with Love*; *In the Heat of the Night*; and *Guess Who's Coming to Dinner*, making him the top box-office star of that year. In all three films, issues revolve around the race of the characters Poitier portrays. In 1999, the American Film Institute named Poitier among the Greatest Male Stars of All Time, ranking 22nd on the list of 25."

While maybe I should have focused on his being the first big black star in Hollywood, I couldn't get my mind off his being ranked number 22 of all time. I wondered whether I'd like to be on any list that I was 22. I think I'd rather be left off as some oversight. Plus, the list was just male stars; add the actresses and another 15 years of acting updates on that list and who the hell knows where he would've ended up. I did look up the date and discovered that Martin Luther King was assassinated that day. Maybe I could make some connection there. Yet I couldn't get over Poitier's rank of 22nd, so I looked up the list of Greatest Male Stars of All Time and John Wayne was listed 13th.

No wonder Levon got his ass tossed.

Levon's hints about buying guns and getting revenge started to gnaw at me: the bitterness was reminiscent of the story he told me long ago. Bringing Ben Wright into the entry only complicated matters. Yet Levon didn't talk about him directly, even though Ben's achievements were clearly in his head. Sure, Artie was back in his story, but what really struck was the appearance of my grandmother, someone I'd never known. Plus, the newborn had to be none other than the Joan. What did any of these fragments add up to? I couldn't piece it together. When they had arrived at the Gallagher house, I figured the family members were looking for memorabilia. I wondered whether they found a bunch of dead bodies in the basement.

I felt a little better knowing that Derek Standish was just outside yesterday with a baseball bat in hand, making sure Louie kept his paws off of his huge Vietnamese planter that held a very small arborvitae. I noticed for the first time that Derek walked with a pronounced limp, a limp similar to Artie's, a limp which I now decided came from an old wound. I spent the rest of the night wondering how, where, and when that wound occurred.

Then there was Levon's story about the dead body in the steel drum. Even more incredible than the story itself was that the garbage man refused to take the drum. Louie would've had it in the compactor before I had a chance grab it. And if I had been strong and quick enough to wrestle it away from Louie, the barrel would have made its way into my living room as a cool, industrial-style end table.

That is until I opened it.

Despite the disturbing nature of the story, I knew I would be in search of a steel drum. For months, I had been out on the curb searching for piece of my identity. The drum would be my own little conversation piece. I might be the only family member in the house, but that didn't mean I lacked full rooms of other people's memories to share. The only problem was that nobody in Frick left steel drums out on the curb. Either they were scarce or still down in somebody's crawl space.

8

THE FALLEN PRODIGY

Lee Lee thought she had an appointment with Mr. Pulaski, but since last month, Lee Lee regularly appeared at meetings she didn't really have. I had been in all the advanced classes with Lee Lee, only Lee Lee had taken more of them. She supplemented her seven AP courses with evening science research and winter break science research and summer science research camp, which featured 18-hour days in the lab. That schedule barely left enough time for Lee Lee to run the Student Council, edit the literary arts magazine (taking over *The Bleeding Soul* when I resigned), and organize the numerous charity walks, runs, and dances (those last series of exercises served as a remedy for bake sales that she ran to fatten the student body). And then there was the violin that Lee Lee must've played in her sleep, since she managed to perform at every town, county, state and regional venue atop any platform that could be deemed a stage. Little wonder that those students who witnessed Lee Lee's feats firsthand tended to run howling into Pulaski's office, confessing their worthlessness and begging to be set up on the trash truck first thing tomorrow morning.

When Lee Lee came into the office, she was having her own little crisis of order. Even before she visited Pulaski, she showed up in Macroeconomics when she was supposed to be in AP Calc., appeared in Calc. when she should've been in AP Physics, and missed her Intel Science Project deadline because she had mistakenly appeared in a 10th grade health class – a class Lee Lee had naturally completed in 7th grade. The crisis intervention team – replete with a cadre of psychologists and social workers – had met repeatedly trying to figure out what was happening to Lee Lee, who was supposed to be named valedictorian of Ben Wright High that very week. Unfortunately, Lee Lee missed most of these meetings, since she was lost somewhere else. Last Tuesday, the crisis intervention team waited an hour for her, only to discover her in Phys. Ed with her gym socks pulled up high, trying to play volleyball in a class she'd never taken with a teacher she had never known.

When Mr. Pulaski found her in the gym, he asked gently, "Lee Lee, what are you doing?"

She stared at him mildly and said, "Oh."

Pulaski slid his hand across his big nose. "I'm not sure what you mean by that."

She was on the sidelines, pointing to the ball going over the net. "I'm just waiting for my rotation. I love to rotate."

Pulaski leaned over to her and whispered, "You know you're not in this class, right?"

Lee Lee smiled warmly. "Now I am."

Today, in Pulaski's office, she brought her violin with her. Without any other form of greeting, she announced to him and to me, "You know, I'm not strong enough to lift a garbage can." Pulaski shot me a look as if to say, do you want to handle this one.

Lee stood about 4-foot, 10 inches and could not have hit 89

pounds on the scales without carrying a two-pound bag of baloney under her arm. "I imagine trash disposal would be quite a challenge for you," I said.

"That's what I thought too," said Lee Lee, her eyes bright and her whole aspect indicating that she was in a chatty mood.

Pulaski threw in. "Well, considering how much you have on your plate, getting involved in the Youth Waste Management program might be extraordinarily difficult for you anyway."

"Nonsense," Lee Lee said. "I have plenty of time. I can always make time." Pulaski and I exchanged looks. We were momentarily envious of how Lee Lee had managed to figure out how to make time – show up to wherever you wanted whenever you wanted; the key was just to make sure you showed up somewhere.

"Well, then what would you like to do? You just said the pails are too heavy for you." Pulaski made this inquiry with what I could tell was a bit of mischievous curiosity. He knew the principal would lose a testicle if his prized student ended up on the trash heap next to me, who was also once a small twinkly moon, compared to the soaring ringed Saturn that was Lee Lee. If Pulaski kept heading in this direction, he may well steer last year's entire state championship Mathletes team into waste management.

She lifted her violin. "I would like to play music on the truck."

Pulaski, who was well trained to never laugh at a student comment no matter how absurd, let out an involuntary chuckle. "Play music?" was all he could get out.

"Sure." She paused. Since neither Pulaski nor I could think of anything to say, she continued, "Well, a garbage truck, by its very nature, has its own percussive rhythms. My performance would match up with its syncopations."

"Why?" asked Pulaski, thoroughly bewildered, yet unable to hide his amusement – he found one-word questions tended to keep a teenager like Lee Lee talking.

"Because a little dawn music is really what I think everybody needs. Couldn't you use a little dawn music Mr. Pulaski? Hash?"

"I guess so," said Pulaski who I could tell just wanted to hug Lee Lee.

"Sure," I added, nodding to her encouragingly.

Lee Lee's participation might come in handy. Pulaski had indicated to me that no matter what he'd tried (appealing to a sense of decency, helping Frick's trouble youth, fostering civic responsibility . . .), the sanitation board was determined to set a hearing to decide the fate of Operation Pick-up Kids. Heine simply wielded too much power. Lee Lee's presence could give the program added weight and influence when the board deliberated.

Lee Lee looked past us to the dumpster in the parking lot. "I was thinking I could coordinate specific performances with pick-up days: you know Bach to start the week, Mozart for recycling, and Beethoven for heavy trash."

"I like the Beethoven particularly." I had visions of an entire orchestra hanging off handles of the truck, performing the 9th Symphony, the chorus popping up from the rooftops.

I was not certain, but that might have been the day I fell in love.

I was particularly struck by the notion that given Lee Lee's current pattern of behavior, she was just as likely to be tap dancing in a driver's ed class as she was to show up regularly on the trash runs. But as usual, I got it wrong.

* * *

Lee Lee should've been a thousand places other than on the garbage truck at 5:30 that early November morning. She hooked her left arm through the big orange handle, put her hand on the fingerboard and jammed her chin against the rest, while her right arm lifted the bow.

She played Bach's "Jesus Joy of Man's Desiring." I had once heard this lovely, hypnotic melody on the organ. Now with her violin, Lee Lee pierced through the heavy, cold morning air. As we collected our trash, Louie and I felt like we were in a movie, such is the effect of musical accompaniment. I held my back straighter and lifted the pails higher. The world was watching now.

Serendipitously, a karaoke machine was cast to the curb early in the run. I grabbed its microphone and started singing nonsense lyrics to her endlessly circular tune. We had stopped for a pick-up, and without the truck's rumble, I was able to join in as Lee Lee returned to the work's beginning. I sang directly to the pails as I raised them.

"Today we are singing/
The garbage, the garbage, the garbage, the garbage/
Its notes are compacted, compacted, compacted/
To nuggets of lost dreams, of lost dreams, of lost dreams/
On into the air they go floating and floating and floating/
We toss it and trash it and break it and bust it/
But still it remains and remains/
Cause garbage won't leave us, won't leave us, won't leave us/
Just like our singing of garbage, of garbage, of garbage/
The garbage of singing, of singing, of singing/
Our gaaaar—bage song.
Today we are singing/
The garbage, the garbage, the garbage, the garbage . . ."

On we drove, Lee Lee playing and my singing and Louie happily carrying more of the pail load today. It may well have been the best day of my life . . . until Lee Lee's mother ran out of her car and started following us on foot.

"Lee Lee," she yelled to her daughter and then calming herself said, "you are supposed to be at the student council meeting."

Lee Lee kept playing while I sang heartily, the notes slowly elongating as I carefully enunciated, "Its notes are compacted, compacted, compacted . . ."

When we scooted over to the next house, with those horrible truck breaks screeching, Lee Lee's mom ran breathlessly alongside, her flat black shoes kicking up the dry brown leaves, drawing in enough air to say, "Lee Lee, you're supposed to study for your B.C. Calc exam."

Lee Lee answered with her bow and I accompanied her, "To nuggets of lost dreams, of lost dreams, of lost dreams . . ."

We continued our halted lumbering down the road, pails in front of us, music swirling all about us, and Lee Lee's mother chasing, forever chasing until the next stop. Lee Lee's mother did not say anything else to her daughter. She just tried to keep up.

I was surprised that Lee Lee's bow work was neither strengthened nor weakened by her mother's disapproving presence. Instead she played with the composure of someone who had entered another realm. God, she had been well-trained. She nodded to me, counting out four to pick up our song, and I accommodated, "On into the air they go floating and floating and floating . . ."

Since the truck was never fast to begin with and now slowed even further by our sing-along, Lee Lee's mom kept pace. When we stopped, she stopped, blew the hair from her face, the autumn wind buffeting her vision. Lee Lee was now answering questions her mother didn't ask. Tucking her bow into her underarm, Lee Lee grabbed a powdered donut from her pocket and bit into it.

I had the feeling Lee Lee was not allowed to eat powered donuts.

Smiling as if she had tasted the food of the gods, Lee Lee nodded for us to bring the song to its big finish. The garbage truck took off far down the block, as it headed onto the second zone of its run, and left Lee Lee's mom far in the blustery distance. My laughter was soon stifled by the thought of Lee Lee's mother calling up Heine and the sanitation board. Clearly, they would be sympathetic to her complaints given Heine's latest Tweet: "If Frick residents smell any unpleasant odors wafting from the sanitation workers, let me know immediately." I don't care how much Wobbly Butler cologne we spritzed over our orange jumpsuits, we had no way of fighting that one.

That Tweet coincided with Mayor Heine's latest visit to the curb. "Hey Hash," said Heine, pointing to the pail. "I made a nice stew last night." I opened up the lid and staggered from the stench, wretching a bit. Through the tall kitchen bag, I saw fish heads, cow tongues, and cruel portions of cabbage.

"You ate that?"

"No, Hash. I made it for you."

I refused to throw up as I dumped the stroganoff of doom into the compactor. I turned away, gulping the fresh, cool air, not allowing the nasty bastard to suck any more joy from me than he already had.

I would make sure that Pulaski gave Lee Lee's mom a call later to tell her what a wonderful scholarship essay this experience would offer.

Before I'd left at 4:30 that morning, I had shoved the harmonica in my pocket that my mother gave me for my fifteenth birthday. I knew I'd never learn how to play it, and I surmised Lee Lee would master a Mozart horn concerto on it by the next run. She received the harmonica with the same quiet acceptance she had the donut. I can tell you that day was the last I saw of that harmonica. No matter, Lee Lee was meant to carry the instrument.

We rambled down the road like traveling vagabonds, like gypsies, singing our song to the world, singing our song to absolutely nobody:
"We toss it and trash it and break it and bust it/
But still it remains and remains/
Cause garbage won't leave us, won't leave us, won't leave us/
Just like our singing of garbage, of garbage, of garbage/
The garbage of singing, of singing, of singing/
Our gaaaar—bage song."

Instead of Lee Lee's mother following, the next day it was Max, who decided to take a break from investigating Mayor Heine to video us after all. For anybody else, I would have been stiff. But it was Max. Plus Lee Lee was playing the whole time we were there, sheltering her violin from the soft, pattering rain, and she provided the backtrack so that Max could further syncopate the thumps and rumbles of the trucks with the thrashing and thuds of our pails. Max had the video up two days later.

Maybe, just maybe, some good publicity might be enough to get the sanitation board to keep us in business. Lee Lee's mother might also turn around. Her daughter would be a celebrity, even if it's from playing on a garbage truck. She would be a trendsetter. All the girls with perfect transcripts would want to be Lee Lee.

A day after that was when I got the first phone calls from TV reporters. In between, the days passed like they always have. I lamely prowled for girls, pored over Levon Gallagher's disks, and deleted Emails, reading a few that caught my eye. What better way to fill up the hours until the cameras arrived?

From the November 25 Trash Folder

Are you sure you want to permanently delete all the items and subfolders in the Deleted Items Folder?

The Daily Bread from Reverend Alexander Burr

A few years ago, the first big digital mapping program came out called Lost.com, and that instrument of Satan instantly fell into bottomless perdition as well those who embraced it. Wherever a pilgrim desired to sojourn, Lost.com never took a wayfarer there. The instrument led a traveler terribly astray. Nowadays, a wayfarer may suffer the delusion that mapping programs work. Don't be fooled, my friend. They are just illusions and carry you to as bad a place as Lost.com. I warned Mayor Heine against investing in that venture. It's borne of the arrogance of believing you are able to find yourself through a device.

Turn on your map app and you will see yourself as a loathsome spider dangling above a fiery and precarious pit. Do you want to delude yourself that you are any more than an infinitesimal speck in God's grandiose kingdom? It is a false prophet promising discovery, an abhorrent emissary. The very moment you locate yourself on your phone, you dislocate yourself from the earth beneath your feet. A god-fearing man, Mayor Heine should not neglect this catechism. Every few years our mayor must learn that stern lesson and I prophesy he will soon learn that lesson again. So to find your way, remember Mayor Heine to lift your head from the grid and gaze up to the heavens.

The Epic Life of Selena Omaha

So are you ready for the inside scoop about what's popping in Frick Village?

Mr. Pulaski walks the streets every night at three in the morning. I took a pic. Mupload that ish! I was looking for glam and super awesome stuff left out for garbage pick-up, and I caught Mr. Pulaski in his bathrobe again. Pretty creepy, for sure. Is this a thing? I mean he definitely didn't look like he knew where he was going, but when he saw a little polka-dotted stroller left out at the Alfords, he opened it up and pushed it along. I think it helped keep him steady. It was an insanely hot stroller. I mean I wanted to put it in the corner of my room and stack my stuffed animals on it. Am I right ladies?

I followed Mr. Pulaski back to his house (he took three wrong turns before he found his way), and he just left the stroller on his curb and shuffled inside. He also left a box of clocks out there. Some were superbasic, you know, digital alarm clocks and stuff, but he had this bird clock that was killin' it. It was definitely the most swag money clock I've ever seen, really smart and sassy. Every hour a different bird chirped. I put the bird clock in the stroller and rolled away. Mr. Pulaski had all his lights on in the house, so I thought it was way better for me to bounce.

As I hit delete, I fell into bed. Tomorrow morning the birds would awaken me. I wondered whether they sang out from a branch or a clock.

9

FOOD FOR THOUGHT

I was clearly in love with Lee Lee. She became a regular on the garbage run and now the neighbors came out more to hear her play than to see what I would save from their collections. I could tell she was fond of me too, but you try figuring out how to meet up with the girl. She was as likely to show up for one of her dates as she was to appear at a student council meeting or a physics extra help session. I was starting to identify with Lee Lee's mom a little bit.

Although she only played the violin, she had truly become one of Operation Pick-up Kids. She even was summoned to Mayor Heine's office to take the oath and sign about fifty papers that said you were serving Frick Village, but don't expect to be insured or receive any real form of compensation. Louie and I had been in there a couple of months ago and endured three of the most painful hours of our lives pretending not to hate Heine and listening to him tell stupid stories of how he is one of a long line of leaders of Frick Village, some of them great, implying he was one of them. He even compared his achievements to Ben Wright's and quietly wondered if he too, like Ben, would have a school named after him. Heine sat at his desk under a huge portrait of President Reagan. Framing that portrait were bookcases full, not of legal tomes like other lawyers and politicians might, but of eggheaded suspense thrillers by Dan Brown and murder mysteries whose titles started with different letters of the alphabet. God, putting up with his nonsense showed how badly we wanted to haul trash, and that Lee Lee was hooked too.

Unfortunately, my only time with her was on the trash run, where between her music and my hauling, I felt that we were both performing rather than connecting. Everything about the rubbish runs provided wonderful distractions, including my occasional glances at Lee Lee.

Each run would offer its comfortable rhythms. Let's see what's on the menu today. We've got broken light sabers, which is rotten news for the Jedi; we've got boxes of squeezed lemons, their rinds brighten and freshen the rancid matter; we've got chewed and injured stuffed animals looking particularly forlorn in the rain; and we've got diapers, oh god, ugh, ugh, we've got diapers, from a baby who must've been fed a steady diet of peas and refried beans. Thank God for the frosty November air to numb the stench.

Oh, the smells, the smells, I prayed I'd never get used to them, since I knew that would be the day I had become at one with the trash. I was beginning to understand Louie's sensibility because if you're not trash's destroyer, you begin to take on its qualities. You see, I was suddenly very interested in making myself alluring, an aura I wasn't certain the residue from the daily work was providing. By the time I got back to Pulaski's office to fill out the log sheets, another lovely classmate, Eva, was waiting in there. I don't know if it represented a feminist badge of honor, but Operation Pick-up Kids was certainly serving as a chick magnet. I quickly got over Lee Lee's notification that she could not hang around, something about a white board schedule she had to follow, and eavesdropped on Eva's conversation with Pulaski. I loved to hear that girl talk.

I was starting to wonder what was happening to me. Sure I had the usual teenage boy hormonal interests, but Jesus, with Jen, Lee Lee, and now Eva, I was starting to believe these rubbish runs were doing something to my testosterone levels.

It didn't help matters that Eva was wonderfully excessive. She had just a bit too much of everything: hair, weight, curves, personality, vitality. What a gorgeous force of nature! She was an economy out of control. To someone who hadn't studied her the way I did, she might have seemed perfectly balanced with her lively laugh and her water bottle in hand. That's if you didn't know that she's had a few other waters to break up the four sodas and five coffees (two of them iced). That's if you hadn't caught her smoking outside the school. That's if you hadn't watched her answering questions correctly in calculus as she thumbed away at her online poker games under the desk or carried on an argument over Teddy Roosevelt's inferiority complex in AP U.S. History while she habitually tapped on her cell phone to play virtual reality roulette. Or you hadn't eaten lunch with her as she stacked up her little blue-lidded containers and ran through one course after another of what appeared to be gourmet food that she described to you in detail, down to mince sizes of the garlic, and offered you mouthfuls, even as she cursed her blackjack hand on her I-Pad, her red lips forever glistening with oil, forever smiling because she got to taste so many good things.

She had mentioned when she walked into the office that she "wanted on the garbage truck," but had since wandered off in a long discussion about where Pulaski would travel once he retired. Eva seemed to have either seen too much of the globe or had plans to get there. Pulaski was amused by the conversation, but after about ten minutes felt obligated to return to work.

"Why do you want to join Operation Pick-up Kids?" he asked.

"It sounds like a blast."

"Do you want to join to cope with some problem you're having?" Pulaski, like the rest of us, knew about her rehab stints.

"No, why would I?"

"Well, that's the reason most people find their way in here. It's sort of like therapy."

"I wasn't thinking about it that way, but I could always use more therapy."

"Well, we have your application, and if a spot comes up, we'll keep you in mind, but I think you might have to wait a while." They were precisely the words I didn't want to hear. "It's not that I don't think you'd be good in the program, but there are just so many who seem desperate. Am I right, you don't seem desperate?"

"Definitely not. I'm very happy. I just thought dumping trash would make me even happier, but I certainly don't want to take anybody's spot who really needs this."

"I knew you'd understand."

"Do you have anything else? I'm looking for something new and stimulating to do."

"Just a political internship with Mayor Heine's office. I'm not sure if that fits into the category of new and stimulating."

"I get you." Heine had been mayor for our entire lives, and most of us had no idea how he managed to get re-elected. I'm sure nothing would make Heine happier than having Eva hanging around. Hell, I would think about working for that rotten bastard if I got a chance to work with Eva. "Give me the number and I'll think about it."

I could hear Pulaski pulling the card from his rolodex, the last man in America with one. "Here you go. I'm pretty sure he's running for county executive again, so this might even be interesting."

"Let me know when you go to Krakow and to St. Petersburg. I'll recommend some fine restaurants."

As Eva was leaving Pulaski's office, two competing thoughts entered into my mind. The first was whether Pulaski considered me among the desperate. I was, after all, on the truck when so many others were waitlisted or turned down (a running joke in the school was, "You think you're in bad shape because you got rejected from a few colleges. I couldn't even get on a garbage truck"). That concern was completely drummed out by the urge to drop my log onto Pulaski's desk and chase Eva out the door.

"Hey, Eva!"

"Hey, Hash."

Think of something, Hash, there're coffee drinks and smokes and blackjack and calc class, but food, best off with food. "Did you make the pesto yet with the walnuts?"

"No, not with walnuts, with pine nuts. I was only going to use walnuts if I ran out of pine nuts."

"So you didn't run out? Was it any good?"

"It was absolutely delicious. I am a very good cook." Eva was one of those people who managed to get away with this kind of bragging without making me break into a rash.

"Bring a sample to lunch some time so I can try it."

"How about I make you dinner instead?" Eva stared into my surprised eyes and frowned. "Look, don't get me wrong. I have a feeling you don't get a lot of homecooked meals."

"Do you want to cook it at my house?" I asked awkwardly.

Most people knew I lived alone in the Joan's house, and they also knew I made a point of not inviting anybody over. "I'm only asking because I'd have to clean first."

Eva smiled. "That'll work. I think I like the idea of you cleaning up the place. Make sure you get rid of the dead bodies."

"I'll at least make sure they're out of the kitchen. You want to shoot for Saturday."

"Sounds good."

I could see in her eyes that Eva in no way was considering this a date. Although I was starting to fall in love with her and feeling the strange guilt of loving two girls who didn't love me, I was relieved that no more would be involved in her visit than food. I could talk to her better that way, and might spend a little less time gawking at her hips, her eyes, her chest, the waves of her black hair, or the angle of her calves in her high heels. "By the way, are you O.K.?"

"What do you mean?"

"I don't see a drink in your hand. Why are you not collapsing of thirst?"

"Now that you mention it . . ." she pulled two Starbucks frappuccino bottles from her impossibly large purse (a purse that I don't believe could fit in the carry-on bin of an airplane). She popped one cap and took a slug that almost finished off the 10 ounces. "I'd offer you'd one, but you know I might pass out of dehydration." She winked at me.

"So when you come over and make me this meal, are you going to let me eat any of it, or should I just watch you work your way through the courses in anticipation of scaring away a bout with hypoglycemia?"

She finished the first frappuccino and popped open the next. "I might save you a crumb."

"Just how many vats of liquid should I have stored in the house in preparation for your arrival?"

"Do you have a swimming pool?"

"No."

"Damn."

As I left Eva to her drinking and to her gambling and to her searching for someone else to absorb her verbal jousts, I headed back to Pulaski's office. He looked up from papers. "Bad news. They set a date for the hearing. I got them to push it back a month, but I'm pretty sure the sanitation board will kill us off then."

"When does the world come to an end?"

"January 11."

"That sucks."

"Yeah," said Pulaski, "Heine's been working very hard."

"Don't I know it," I said. I thought about telling Pulaski about the mayor's latest shenanigan, but I didn't want to give Heine the satisfaction of knowing he'd gotten to me. This morning, on top of his tall kitchen bag were five 8 X 10 photos of me picking up pails all over the neighborhood. None of them were in front of Heine's house. Did he take them? Did someone send them to him? Did he hire someone to take them? God, with all the phones out there, the pictures could've been snapped by any one at any time. Curiously, the pictures didn't catch me doing anything wrong. In fact, they were flattering. I almost liked myself in them, and it took a little bit of inner strength to throw them away.

Could I have used them as evidence that Heine was stalking me? How could I say I acquired the photos? The only way would be if I had stolen them from his trash. Strangely, I wasn't creeped out from the photos. I had seen the way he'd looked at the Joan at board meetings, and the way he'd looked at every attractive woman. Thank God he never looked that way at me. I felt sorry for Eva for even thinking of taking a job in his office. No, Heine was messing with me, but he hadn't made me as uncomfortable as he had hoped.

This hearing was the real concern. I asked Pulaski, "Anything we can do about it?"

"I don't know. The publicity may help. But we've got a bigger problem."

"What's that?"

"We've got to figure out which residents hate us –"

I interrupted him. "Well, that's easy enough."

Pulaski finished his sentence – "and change their minds."

I didn't have an answer to that one.

Thinking about the program's future made me miserable, so I left Pulaski's office and turned my thoughts back to Eva. I headed to the supermarket for coffee and water and soda and juice. I carried out supersized cans and jumbo-pack cases. I wish I had a 21-year-old cousin who could buy me smokes and wine. Even without those more adult provisions, I felt a little like a young Levon Gallagher, child of the nuclear age, stocking up the bomb shelter for the apocalypse.

Hell, letting someone into to my house felt a little like doomsday to me. At home, since the Joan died, I had lived a monk-like existence, with a diet of pork n' beans, Cheerios, and peanut butter and jelly on toast. Now, I was opening the front door and letting hedonism enter with six bags of groceries and enough hair to block out a skylight.

Maybe I *was* desperate. All I know is that I thought about Eva enough to have a helluva time hallucinating.

10

THE DIARY OF LEVON GALLAGHER: TAKING MEASURE

July 21, 1969

I measured my house to see just how small it was, writing down the dimensions on a pad. I traveled end-to-end of what I had dubbed the "Great Room" (my only room). Then I scrawled on the pad the dimensions (12' 10 3/8" X 9' 10 3/4").

Then I managed to lose the tape measure.

Some room, eh?

So I made an exhaustive search for a tape measure that shielded itself from my eyes. I tapped flat surfaces for a good twenty minutes, cursing. I gave up and went down the street to Artie's to borrow his. Just for the hell of it, I remeasured the Great Room to find its length now 13" X 10". I put Artie's on the window sill. There I discovered my own tape measure acting like it had been staring at me all along. I measured the room again, only to find it had shrunk back down to 12' 10 3/8" X 9' 10 3/4".

I returned to Artie and told him, "There's something wrong with your tape measure."

Artie seemed quite offended by this suggestion. "There's absolutely nothing wrong with my tape measure, Levon."

I brought him into my Great Room and slid the ruler across the boards. Artie was a tough nut. He could crack an egg in your hand and tell you he'd never heard of a chicken. "The problem is not my tape measure; it's yours."

"But my measurements are good," I said, trying to reason with him.

"No they're not. Yours are all jagged. Mine are elegant, all feet and no inches."

"That makes them suspicious. What's the point of having fractions if you don't use them? My Great Room can't be a simple dimension like 13' X 10'.

"Why not? Wouldn't a builder be more likely to use those dimensions than your weird ones?"

"No. The builder may have started with even dimensions, but that was before he put in sheet rock and everything. No, the dimensions would end up odd like mine."

"That's a dumb argument."

"Well, why don't we borrow Sarah's tape measure?"

We did and her defective device measured the room 13' X 10' too. And so did Frank Mavella's next door. Doesn't anyone have a decent tape measure in the entire neighborhood?

"You see," Artie said, like he invented the yardstick. "I do believe your tape measure is exactly one-eighth of an inch short for every foot."

"You mean to tell me that everything in my life is an eighth of an inch more than I thought it was?"

"That's if you're talking about a mere foot. If you're talking about more, like say eight feet, then it's a whole inch. And if it's a 96 feet, then it's a whole foot."

The situation was worse than I had imagined. Right now Ben is down in Delaware at DuPont working with Steffie Kwolek to help strengthen her Kevlar vests. Ben's stopping bullets and I can't even properly measure my dick.

I headed to the hardware store where I bought my tape measure five years ago.

"We only guarantee our tape measures for a year," said the clerk. One look at him told me he liked to see customers as much as an alley cat wanted to greet a German shepherd. I barked at him anyway.

"But its measurements are off. It's defective." I grabbed a couple of other tape measures from the shelf to show him what was wrong.

"That doesn't mean anything. You could have damaged the tape measure."

"And changed its length? It's a 25-foot tape measure. Are you telling me I managed to remove an eighth of an inch from every foot of the tape measure? That I managed to do it precisely?"

"What you do in your free time is none of my business, sir."

"It's bad enough this tape measure misrepresented the size and scope of everything I own. Now you're telling me that you're not interested in hearing my complaint. Are you going to replace the defective tape measure you sold to me or not?"

"Of course not."

"You've gotta be kiddin' me."

I was tempted to go after him, but I figured he had a baseball bat behind the counter. All this fighting was wearing me out. Anyway, I didn't need him to beat me up to hold a grudge. Instead, I took my tape measure and sized him up from head to toe. "Do you feel smaller?" I asked. I flipped the tape measure to him and turned away dramatically. For once, I thought I had the better of a confrontation. Yet as I turned to make one small step, my knee locked. It was as if my right leg was just too short to touch the ground again, so I fell. I made a point not to see the clerk smile as I got up and hobbled away.

I returned home. I must admit with that bum knee it did feel more like 13 feet instead of mere 12' 10 3/8" to get across the Great Room. I remembered that additional one and 5/8 of an inch as I walked over to meet an old friend with a delivery. I knew the next time I entered the hardware store the clerk wouldn't be working there anymore.

* * *

The date of Levon's particularly frustrating encounter with the tape measure coincided with man's first walk on the moon. It's nice to know Levon had noteworthy experiences on days other than assassinations of American icons. As with the other two entries, Levon seemed to willfully avoid mentioning the titanic events of the outer world, although you wonder whether he would have used the phrase "one small step" on another day. Meanwhile, I didn't exactly get much family history out of that entry. The only scrap I learned about my grandmother was that

she owned a tape measure. And that my grandfather could get all worked up even about tape measures. Big surprise. Except for his little nod to Ben Wright, I could hardly connect the incident to the old drunken story Levon told me long ago.

The last comment of the entry stuck with me the most. The lack of a name for the clerk was particularly troublesome, since I would have so much less to go on to find out what happened to that poor fellow. I started to pore through the editions of *The Herald* and *The Frickin'* for the months that followed the events of the moon landing and the grand tape measure fiasco. My eyes glazed over quickly, and I was pretty sure even if an incident was reported, I would've missed it. My own measurements of investigation were defective.

11

GENERATION CELEBRITY

When the first local cable news station showed up on the garbage run, I was a little self-conscious. In the light snow of early December, I actually thought of how I was lifting a trash can before I pivoted it into the compactor. Of course, Mayor Heine was there for the entire journey, getting as much camera time as possible and limiting the credit Pulaski and Hannah received for the program. "Operation Pick-up Kids is a Frick Village original and should serve as a model for the entire country." Even as he delivered his sound bite, Heine couldn't resist checking a text on his phone and signing a proclamation that his aide conveniently pulled from a briefcase. I wondered why he would make such statements when he planned to pull the plug on the program on January 11. From what Big Bill and Pulaski have told me, I shouldn't take the praise as a good sign. Clearly, the mayor had something up his sleeve.

Soon, the city stations followed, even wandering through Ben Wright High to get a "fuller picture of these extraordinary young people." Then the story made it onto the NBC Nightly News. They interviewed Peggy Murphy who spoke about how

"These kids are helping make their community a better place," while Anthony Gullota told the cameras, "They saved Frick Village."

I tried to sound humble. "It's just a job that needs to be done, just like any other job, and I'm happy to do it."

Louie was the genuine article. "Why are you making such a big deal? It's trash. People put it on the curb and we pick it up. Why are you bothering us about it?"

Getting little else from us, the interviewers stopped asking questions. Lee Lee, however, they followed her every spectacular note. Lee Lee's mom even surfaced to explain that her daughter was the first chair in the state youth orchestra. The interviewer would invariably follow-up with, "And she plays this exquisite music on a garbage truck?"

Lee Lee's mom would choose not to answer that question. Instead, she pointed out, "Lee Lee has played with several professional philharmonics and has won many honors in science research."

Chomping on a celery stalk and popping up the village website up on his phone, Mayor Heine said that he'd hand-selected only the best of the best to be members of Operation Pick-up Kids, a lie I was surprised he would perpetrate since it was so easy for us and Pulaski to expose.

The calls from reporters kept coming, and radio disc jockeys wanted us to talk trash on the air. Again, his fangs into his third celery stalk, his fingers tapping the Jumble puzzle on his phone, and his ear against a walkie-talkie, Mayor Heine took most of these media opportunities, which made us quite relieved. I was happy to see that upon my suggestion to every reporter who questioned me, Max was given some attention for his original video on us. I told them, "It could be a nice sidebar about how the spotlight on our story was first cast by a young homegrown teenage talent."

Unlike Louie and me, Max wanted the publicity. His video didn't exactly go viral, but he got over a hundred thousand hits, which is pretty damn good. Even as he was soaking up the moment, Max had his eye on the other big attention whore in the village, Mayor Heine. Only Max's desire to record every hypocritical word of the mayor sent him behind the camera instead of in front of it. He was still digging deeper into Mayor Heine's data mining. "Real trash doesn't compare to the virtual form," he said.

I asked Max what virtual trash smells like.

"Decaying fear."

* * *

That afternoon, the Spirit Committee met again, this time to consider fundraisers for the Winter Carnival. I suggested an ice carving station where I could sell sculptures for $20 a pop, since I was pretty good with picks and chisels. To drum up interest, I thought I could make an ice carving of Ben Wright, with all his innovations of phones and printers and games floating above his skull in a frozen cloud of brainstorms.

Megan Stevens smiled cruelly. "What a sweet idea. But you know what Hash?"

"What?"

"Ice melts."

"When it gets warmer, yes. But even then, you could keep the sculpture in the freezer."

"Who would want that cluttering up your freezer?"

"I don't know, maybe it would cheer someone up every time they opened the door to see a happy little walrus."

I was trying to figure out whether I was making perfectly

reasonable recommendations that Megan shut down because they came from me or whether my comments were actually getting stranger, supplying what Megan expected me to say.

"Ah a walrus." Megan had dropped her voice almost to a whisper. "Oh Hash, you are a cute old man, aren't you?"

"No," I said, with the conviction of someone willing to grab a lead pipe and beat to a bloody pulp any cuteness in my soul. "I'm not at all cute."

Megan talked at me with the dismissive pity she reserves for the delusional. "Anyway, we decided this morning to offer a much better fundraiser."

I asked what this great idea was, trying to guess how much I would hate the plan.

"We are going to offer web tributes for a hundred dollars apiece. Because it's the Winter Carnival, we'll call them Frozen in Time. The Frozen in Time Tributes will tell the entire wonderful story of a teenager's life right up until today."

"How will they do that?"

"We will use their Facebook pages, old Emails, texts. The usual stuff."

Until that moment, Max had not lifted his head from his computer. He was probably in search of one of Mayor Heine's darker secrets. Now Max's incredibly active eyebrows raised and furrowed. "Hey, that's data mining."

"I guess," said Megan.

"Aren't you breaking the law?" asked Max, who tended to break the law every time he cracked open a laptop.

"Not if the kid gives you all his passwords and full access."

Max just answered with sharpened eyebrows and a low whistle. I had to ask Megan the question. "Are you telling me you can get somebody to willingly give up all that information and invade their privacy?"

"Someone? We've already got a list of 23 kids." She showed me the names. I tried not to look, feeling as if I was catching them sitting on the toilet.

"Why would they do it?"

"Why wouldn't you? When we're done making our Frozen in Time Tribute, you will feel wonderful, like you've already lived the greatest life ever. It's like a total makeover."

I guess it might be attractive to have your entire personal life rewritten and repackaged. It would be like hiring a PR firm to redesign your photo albums. I couldn't get out of my head how much wasted time and misery those tribute recipients would suffer in the years to come, just from the good news pulled from the data – all those companies flooding them with Emails, text blasts, and phone calls, selling them what they already have too much of. And what about the bad and disturbing data uncovered? I shuddered, thinking of Megan and the rest of the Spirit Committee members possessing that information. Oh the sneers and giggles! Oh the future of embarrassment and rejected applications! I had visions of the Spirit Committee sitting at booths all over the school, offering the tributes like they were merely providing pencils with giant erasers to their mistake-prone classmates.

Megan then turned to me and asked, "How about you, Hash? I think you could use a tribute makeover."

I gave my answer to Max about an hour later. I wrote a letter warning of the dangers of receiving a Frozen in Time Tribute, describing how it would leave you with your privacy destroyed and vulnerable to attack by anyone who wanted power over you. Since my life as a trash man would soon end, I thought I should try to be more than a zombie at Ben Wright High.

Despite committing the very act of intrusive data mining on Mayor Heine, Max was willing to shoot out a mass Email of my letter to the entire student body. I thought about putting my name on it, but, given my reputation, I thought the message was much more powerful if sent by an anonymous hacker who in the mailing could show how easily systems can be penetrated.

A couple of days later I passed Megan in the halls and asked her how tribute sales were going. "Great," she smiled. "We're over a hundred."

So much for returning to my old life.

I walked away, wondering whether my letter had disturbingly increased interest. Oh, if only the rest of the world could be as reliable as garbage.

* * *

I can't tell you the next bunch of days on the rubbish run were normal. When I told Max about all the attention, he smiled at me. "Now I understand why you don't want a Frozen in Time Tribute. Why would you need one? I already made one for you."

Trying not to notice what was going on around us, Louie and I returned to our regular routines. I pulled a ragged dark stick wrapped in clear plastic from my pocket.

Louie looked at it in amazement. "Is that actually a piece of meat in your paw there?"

"Yeah, it's jerky."

"How appropriate. Could you be actually eating man food?"

"Well . . . the cows had a nutritious diet of quinoa and kale."

"Can't I have just one lousy conversation with you without you ruining it?" Yet Louie didn't seem disappointed that he was once again disappointed by me.

More residents than ever were either looking out their windows, walking their dogs, or getting their newspapers when we rumbled by. Even Mayor Heine got into the act. On top his trash can rested something called Paradise Ox Sun-Dried Kale. The environmentally friendly packaging claimed that *"This kale was nurtured in fields ploughed by oxen that retire to organic plains of amber grain."* I didn't know which disturbed me more: the knowledge that Heine gave me a present or that he knew enough about me to get me the right present. "What game is Heine playing?" I asked Louie.

"Not sure," he said, "but I think he's winning."

Some residents had their cameras out. "Don't you feel like we should do something to entertain these people?" I asked Louie.

"We could beat the crap out of each other," Louie suggested.

"That might be good."

"But then there'd be more oglers the next day."

"Forget it then." I pointed my right index finger at my head like I had a bright idea. "I know, let's try to make trash pick-up as boring as we can."

"That's gonna be hard," said Louie. "Trash pick-up being so thrilling and all."

In the frosty Christmas air, I motioned to Lee Lee who was playing a lively, jaunty waltz. "Hey, can you play out of key and hit some bad notes."

"No," was all Lee would give me.

"Then I guess it's just the two of us, Louie. If you do something interesting, like go after Nonna D'Antonio's lions again, I'll kill you."

* * *

When Louie finally got fully off probation, he was hardly chastened. If it had been anyone else, I would have said he became emboldened by his newfound stardom, but not Louie. If he saw a video camera set up on a tripod in a front lawn, he'd crush it in the compactor before you could hit the record button.

He peered out across the many curbs for something just beyond. As I spotted him eying a lamppost, I tried to rein him in. I pointed to the lamp, "Better watch out, those are the gateway drugs to mailboxes." I wasn't sure if they were hallucinations or nightmares, but I regularly saw Louie ripping up posts like some crazed videogame avatar while mailmen tossed letters onto the lonely grass.

Fortunately, Louie found something more enticing. It was the most beautifully arranged trash display ever installed on an American street. Each family member possessed an individual pail. But Louie took little note of Papa Joseph Gulotta's or Mamma Angela's or son Anthony's pails, even though he had to be a bit impressed how each of their pails was named, compartmentalized and sanitized (in the best nature of the word). Nicole, the daughter, now she had a bucket Louie couldn't keep his eyes off of. First of all it was pink, and she painted angels dancing about its rounded walls. But Nicole was not just flash without substance. As Louie had always told me, "It's what's inside the pail that matters." Once Louie caught a glimpse of her trash, he was truly smitten. Oh, she separated with the zeal of a true believer. Her trash was hopelessly tidy – little cotton balls, fig stems, olive pits, a pair of broken black leather pumps, and a very tiny white spandex top with a rip along the right collar bone. Plus the recyclables, my God, the recyclables were a feast for Louie's black Italian eyes. There were the crushed tomato cans and the Pellegrino bottles and the antipasto jars and what appeared to be a vial of an exotic balsamic reduction glaze. He sucked in deeply and clouds of cold smoke billowed from his mouth.

"Why don't I know this woman?"

I explained that Nicole Gulotta did not attend our school. "She goes to St. Mary's."

"Like a good Catholic girl should," he said, smiling at me. "Is she legal?"

"I'm not sure. What, to marry?"

Louie always impressed me as the type who wouldn't make it through a year on the truck before tying the knot.

"She's not in ninth grade, is she?" He asked this question with the kind of grim determination that he would wait for her, if necessary.

"She's our age."

"Good. Then I can ask her out."

"Louie, you haven't seen this girl or spoken to her."

He looked at me with the sincerity of the infatuated. "Hash, I've seen Nicole's garbage, so I've seen Nicole."

Lee Lee broke into Tchaikovsky's "Romeo and Juliet," and I sidled next to her, suddenly wanting to ask what was in her pail.

After he spent a careful couple of minutes disposing each little piece of lovely garbage luxuriating in her can, Louie tenderly returned it to its hallowed ground and left a note on it.

Dearest Nicole,

I love your refuse. It will haunt my dreams.

Your Admiring Trash Man,

Louie

I wondered whether Louie's note would destroy his beautiful relationship with his beloved Nicole before it started.

On the next run, Nicole once again put out her beautiful can. This time it contained only three delicately arranged dried lilies and a small note card that read, "*As you have haunted mine.*"

For the first and only time in all my garbage runs with

Louie, he did not dispose of the trash before him. Instead, he gently lifted Nicole's lilies and her note and slid them under his shirt. God, given the frigid temperature, he should've shivered and convulsed embracing those chilly mementoes. Yet, he merely smiled serenely. He did so a little bashfully, knowing I might have something to say about his ridiculous Mediterranean gesture.

Louie left a reply. *"May I escort you Friday night to Cardinale's?"*

Cardinale's was the type of place you wear a suit to, the type of place that would cost a trash man two week's pay, and that's if we actually got more than the minimum wage.

Oh, man, this was getting good. I smiled at Louie. "Boy, if I'd've known, I would've filled my bucket with dead roses long ago, so I could get a good meal of out of you."

"She gave me fresh lilies, not dead roses, you idiot," he said, a little testily. "That's why she gets dinner and you get gots."

"Get gots?" I didn't understand, so I spent the rest of the run torturing Louie, promising to sneak by his house Friday night and snap pictures of his sharp-dressed self to plaster onto the truck. Then I sang songs in a romantic voice completely out of sync with a scowling Lee Lee, songs about macaroni and cannoli and Nicoli.

When my rhymes became a little questionable, Louie wagged his middle finger and said, "Now, now, you are singing about the future Mrs. Sacco. If you continue, I am going to dispose of you where your body will never be found."

I put my hand to my chin to give the appearance of being in deep thought. "I wonder if that's the same place where all of the other lost Frick garbage has disappeared to?"

"You won't be around to know."

I kept singing and Louie kept threatening, and when the

date finally happened, I called him the next morning, a Saturday at 4:30 a.m. (we both woke up now at that time whether we needed to or not), and he told me every course they ate, and what foods they shared. Louie spoke of future dates; he was now committed to seeing either Nicole or her can every day from this day forward. I couldn't help but feel that Louie's romance was spurred on by an awareness that January 11 was coming and everything would change. He better get the girl now or he'd never get another chance.

I laughed at the insanity of it all.

And yet, and yet, I found myself in front of Eva's house, now making a much more careful inspection of her family refuse, trying to figure out what was once hers.

12

NO TRASH HOUSE

Louie and I didn't limit our investigation of sanitation in Frick to prospective girlfriends. We noticed that the Fredricksons never put a scrap of garbage to the curb, but the constantly burning fireplace offered at least some form of explanation. No, we couldn't quite work out what they did with the Styrofoam or the aluminum foil or batteries. What kind of toxins were emitting from that chimney?

But we were completely puzzled by the Mavellas' absence of garbage. They had no fireplace. Could it be possible they made no trash? Did they stack it in their backyard? We surely would have smelled it? Their basement? Their attic? Did they dissolve everything in hydrochloric acid? If so, where did they get a lake's worth of acid from?

Louie thought I asked too many questions.

"Let's just break into the goddamn house and find out where they put all the garbage."

"Why?" I asked. "What are we going to do even if we find the garbage?"

"Whatdaya think we're going to do? We're going to take the

crap out of the house and put it in the truck."

"What? Now you want to go into people's houses to get trash. Why don't you just follow the neighbors around with a garbage bag, so they don't even have to bend to drop it in the can?"

"The Mavella house is going to explode if we don't do something about it."

I chuckled, touched by Louie's concern. "That'd be something to see, wouldn't it? So what's your plan? Cleaning the whole house at once? We'd need an army of trucks to clear the place out."

Now it was Louie's turn to laugh. "No," he said slowly, and repeated, "no, man. Clear out the place? What, are you crazy? We just go in and take out a couple of pails, like a normal pick-up . . ." He thought for a minute and then threw in, "well maybe an extra pail, to start catching up on the backload."

"And with that game plan we'll have the Mavella household trash free by . . ."

". . . the time I'm on social security. Hell we have long-term plans, don't we?"

"Everybody's got to dream." We pretended to forget about January 11, but clearly we wouldn't even be talking about these mysterious houses if we didn't want to tie up loose ends before we were given the boot.

Lee Lee talked us into stopping the truck in front of the Fredrickson house so she could play a song. Usually, she tended to play a waltz, in the rhythm of the smoke billowing from the chimney. She insisted that the Fredricksons deserve to be celebrated since they were just like us, in the trash disposal business.

Hanging off the truck's orange handle, Louie yelled out. "They're trying to take our jobs!"

Deprived of new garbage, he compulsively toyed with the compactor lever. You wouldn't know that two minutes ago I had watched Louie, with three deft yanks of that lever, crush a huge sofa down into a loveseat, then to a beanbag chair, then to a mere arm rest, the compressed seating buried deep in the bowels of the truck. "What if everyone was like the Fredericksons," he grumbled. "I think we should cement over their chimney so they can't burn anything anymore."

"You can't do that to your brothers," Lee Lee told him as she swayed to Strauss.

"Yeah," I chimed in. "Don't turn your back on your brothers."

"They're not my brothers," Louie shook his head. "They're friggin' pyromaniacs."

Lee Lee played more passionately, and I belted out in time to the Strauss waltz, "They're really our friends, they are, they are," as I hugged the stinking Louie with a love that did not know noses.

When we arrived at the forever pailless Mavella house, Lee Lee stopped us once again to play a funeral dirge by Chopin. While Louie had objected to the Fredrickson concert, he was all for Lee Lee bowing for hours in front of the Mavella house as he scoped out the doors and windows to figure out the best way to break-in.

"How long can they hold up here?" Louie wondered. "How much crap can a family take in without ever letting anything out?"

I speculated that maybe the Mavellas are taking out a little bit of trash at a time in their cars. "They could be dropping it off in a dumpster, or even just one of those outside big bins at McDonalds or Taco Bell."

Louie kept staring at the house and said, "I don't think so, man."

"Why?"

"I can feel the weight of the house. It's filled to the gills, man."

I was a little envious of Louie's possession of such visionary gifts.

The next morning when we headed off on our route, Louie's head drooped as he hung off the truck handle like a drugged gorilla.

"What were you out with Nicole last night, buddy?"

"Nah, staking out the Mavella house."

"Crazy bastard. You should've invited Lee Lee. She could've played a whole requiem for you."

Louie rolled his eyes, regularly annoyed by my use of fancy terms. "Hey, I was right about the house. The cars left three times last night and they weren't carrying a scrap of trash." Louie's eyes rolled back, so tired he didn't notice how incredibly cold the truck handles were or admire the dusting of Christmas snow on the ground. The scene would've been lovely if I could feel my fingers. I scowled at Louie for being too oblivious to suffer.

"You're a sick bugger, you know that."

"I'm sick," Louie shook his head like I didn't understand, as usual, what was really going on. "Look at you with Heine's trash."

I couldn't argue with him. While Louie had his trash obsession, I had mine.

Picking up trash at Mayor Heine's big grey home always gave me the creeps and not for the reasons you might think, although the mayor is indeed one of the more disturbing people I've ever encountered. No, his trash did not consist of piles of cute, furry animals all dead. Instead, his trash looked terribly familiar. It was one half-filled pail like mine, featuring an empty frozen waffle box like mine; his recycling bin had cans of pork and beans, coke and jelly jars like mine; our trash shared toenail clippings, electric razor shavings, soiled sheets of paper towels that clearly served as plates, allegedly nutritious fruit-grain bars, ice cream cartons, and coffee grounds.

I was under the impression that Heine and I were the only bachelors in the village, the only men who lived entirely alone in this town. So Heine and I had a lot in common, walking into an empty house, eating in ways that required the least amount of cleanup possible, enjoying the peace of solitude.

Yes, we had a lot in common, except about 50 years of age and the fact that he was an ambitious jackass, and I hadn't become one yet. And oh yeah, he was trying to ruin my life. Yesterday, he even called me into his office for a disturbing conversation.

"Have you ever acted before?" Heine asked me.

"No," I said. "Why?"

"Oh, I was just wondering." Heine fiddled with his phone and slurped on a Frappuccino. "You sure look like an actor."

I flashed back to the photos of me he had left out in his trash. I was coming to understand that the mayor was not just messing with me. I would be part of a plan. "Why do you say that?"

"Cause some people are naturals." As I followed the brown coffee dripping down his chin and his fat fingers sliding from his phone to his belly, I struggled for a reply. "I see something special in you, Hash, something I haven't seen in this village since Ben Wright."

"Thank you, sir." I said. I hated myself for being polite to the man. Somehow I knew this conversation would both save my job and ruin it. But I had no idea how.

Whatever our connections and differences, I wouldn't let Louie dump Heine's pail. Louie pointed out how I loved the really light pails. I did too, of course, but I somehow also saw Heine's trash as my personal domain.

I would often go to Hannah and ask him about Mayor Heine. I knew he didn't like the mayor (the only person I knew Bill didn't like), but I also knew he would tell me about Frick's leader as fairly as he could manage. He'd tell me about a man who lived every breathing second of his days to be mayor of Frick Village, or if the fair people of the surrounding townships would deem it so, county executive. He did not have a wife and children, since as he said, "Village Hall is his wife and we are all his children."

"Does he really believe that?"

"He certainly does, my good lad. But problem is," here Bill Hannah dropped his voice a bit, almost to a whisper, "nobody else does, especially after all the missing garbage."

"They blame him."

"They used to." Hannah told of how after the scandal of the missing garbage in the mid-1990s, the authorities heavily investigated Heine. They tried to get a warrant to search his big grey house and he fought them like crazy, using every legal trick he could find to thwart them.

"You think he was stalling them to sneak stuff out of his house."

"Well, that's the funny thing," said Bill. "I tell you, my good man, ever since the scandal broke, they had twenty-four-hour surveillance on his house. If he took a Tic Tac off his couch, the authorities would've known."

"Did they ever get a warrant?"

"They did and they combed every last inch of his house. They didn't miss a hair in his shower drain."

"And?"

"Nothing, absolutely nothing. Heine even sued the feds for harassment and got a healthy out-of-court settlement. Oddly, he became a sympathetic figure, as if he had been falsely accused. He got re-elected mayor. It almost got him into the county executive chair."

"But he lost again."

"Well, Heine started yapping and of course, the suspicions were raised all over again. He had this way of talking that he knew secrets about people, the kind of secrets you might know if you had been rummaging through trash for 20 years."

"So people still think he's responsible for all those years of missing trash."

"I am afraid they do."

I thought about that missing trash a bit, but I thought more about my connections to Mayor Heine. Was I too delving into the souls of Frick residents by picking through their trash and taking scraps for myself? Was I living my life through their trash? Was that how I had been filling up the hole left by the Joan's death?

A memory of the Joan's father, Grandpa Artie, came hurtling back to me. I was in fifth grade and we were down in the basement on some mats. Artie had taken off his belt, folded the buckle and strap, and snapped his wrist, cracking the leather against my back. I howled. "I told you to pay attention," he scowled. "Stop staring out like you see dragons floating on the moon."

"Do you think my father's near?"

"Him," Artie snapped the belt against my shoulder blade to make sure he exacted proper payment for the information. "No, he's probably in New Mexico looking for Atari cartridges."

"What?"

"He used to talk about all these video games that were buried in landfills. He wanted to rescue them. Moron."

As I rubbed my shoulder, Artie eyed me with a stew of affection and pity. I knew he never felt sorry for hitting me ("Builds character in momma's boy") but for saying terrible things about my lost father. "Too many lies ruined my life and a few others. I won't ruin yours." Squaring off with me in a grappler's stance, he spent an hour teaching me arm bars, half nelsons, leg hooks, and granby rolls. He frowned a week later when I told him I decided not to join the wrestling team. Then he kissed me on the forehead and told me, "That's alright. I'll make sure to kick your ass whenever you need it."

Unfortunately, now Artie would never kick my ass again. I thought of Lee Lee. I heard music in my ears. But I needed words. I thought of Eva. I was very happy she was coming to dinner. That would certainly make me a little different from Mayor Heine, wouldn't it? Even a little different than my father?

But Eva was still a few hours away. My phone dinged with a text from Aunt Vicky. It was the usual, "How u doing?" As always, I answered, "K and u?" She'd text back, "K2." And so we were both free for another month. Aunt Vicky even sent me a Best Buy gift card for Christmas, which was unexpected. I sent her a Starbucks one in return. Since I was taking care of business, I made that dreaded, but unavoidable trip to the bathroom where I once again saw before my eyes the rolling video of the reality TV show *True Evacuations*. Forever searching for cameras on the mirror, the sink, the tile, the tank, I could tell myself once again that the scenes were not really recorded and that the reality show did not exist. I saw the images before me anyway.

I couldn't have that vision whirling around in my head for

too long, so I turned to my laptop and hacked away at the forest of old Emails. I only stopped deleting when I stumbled onto something that might actually be about me.

From the December 25 Trash Folder

Are you sure you want to permanently delete all the items and subfolders in the Deleted Items Folder?

The Daily Bread from Reverend Alexander Burr

The U.S. Department of Transportation released a survey finding that at any given daylight moment across America, 660,000 drivers are using cell phones or manipulating electronic devices while driving. My friends, I sayeth, if that result doesn't tell you how sad the state of affairs is, I don't know what will. What used to be worth dying for? Freedom and liberty? The protection of those loved ones around you? The precious life of a child? The Almighty Lord God? As John said in Revelations 22:15, "Outside are the dogs and sorcerers and the sexually immoral and murderers and idolaters, and everyone who loves and practices falsehood."

I have walked the streets of Frick Village and I have seen those who covet not only these devilish mechanisms, but everything they might procure. Some even hold onto their garbage like it has been consecrated and sanctified. The wicked have confounded possessions with abilities. Every moment we clutch our phones, our possessions, our trash, we deny our true selves. As Matthew said about talents in 25:29-30, the Lord will "cast the worthless servant into the outer darkness. In that place there will be weeping and gnashing of teeth."

A fine young man I know who lost his mother a few months back gathers the trash from our streets and disposes of it.

Deliver your wicked possessions unto him. May he possess the strength not to covet these vile instruments and instead pile the phones on high in his truck, letting them chatter and gibber to each other like they did in the Babel of yore.

The Epic Life of Selena Omaha

So are you ready for the inside scoop about what's popping in Frick Village?

Bill Hannah's on fleek. He's killin' it. That's all I have to say. He leaves out the hottest threads in big black bags for his boys to toss in the garbage truck. Big Bill must be totally wondering what happens to his bags. Last week, he left the most awesome mad blue suit with a checkered yellow pocket square. I threw it on and looked all classy and criss cross. And when I slipped on his green trousers with his red suspenders with a superbasic silver top, I felt like an insanely hot Christmas tree. Pretty crazy, right? I mean then I stood in front of the mirror and talked like Bill Hannah. I felt like I was royalty, like a prince or a princess. Oh gosh, I don't know which. It's like I'm a celeb, all iconic and stuff. Wow, nothing is better in this world than an epic black bag in front of Bill Hannah's yard. It's like Christmas comes every Tuesday!

As I hit delete, I considered my wicked possessions and wondered if Big Bill's suits would fit me.

13

DINNER WITH EVA

Trailing a cold gust of December wind, Eva came in carrying bags and boxes and sent me back to the car for the rest.

"What the hell did you bring here?"

"We live in a remarkable time, Hash," said Eva. "We can eat better than kings, and we will do that tonight."

I looked over the two tables filled with food. "Are we going to eat it all in one night?"

"Ohh," she groaned wistfully, "if only we could."

The Joan's familiar, uninteresting comment echoed through the corridors. I wanted to ask Eva if she heard that, but knew she didn't. Instead, I obeyed, taking out the garbage from the kitchen pail as Eva walked past the refrigerator, clicked on the oven, and threw pots and pans on all four burners. She had out three cutting boards with vegetables across each of them. Duck breasts were marinating in plastic bags and an octopus sat at the bottom of a stainless steel bowl of water, looking like its tentacles were still capable of lashing me across the cheek. She spoke of blanching and roux and ragout as she threatened me with big knives and chopped vegetables into impossibly small and uniform shapes. The pots and pans on the four burners alternately bubbled and simmered with waters and butters and oils. All the while she talked of the chemistry of cooking.

Eva must have spent a good twenty minutes on the egg alone. "Beware of the green ring that forms if you overheat the egg. You've released hydrogen and sulfur in the egg white and formed a gas. The hydrogen sulfide reacts with the iron and the egg yolk and then you get this alien-looking egg. That's why you should always throw your hard-boiled eggs right in a nice ice bath right when they're cooked." I had never had a hard-boiled egg in my life, but I was going to make one tomorrow, just to see what a green egg looked like.

Then there was custard: "You have to temper the egg. First, you add only a cup of the warm milk to the eggs. You can't put the eggs onto the heat or they'll curdle."

"Curdle?"

"You'll have scrambled eggs slopping around in your milk instead of a nice, creamy custard."

Then there were egg whites: "By whipping them, you are incorporating air into the watery protein mixture of the egg white, also causing the proteins to denature and unfold. The air bubbles attract the hydrophobic protein parts while the hydrophilic protein parts find their way to the water mixture. The whipping gets proteins to unfold and then form strong bonds with the air bubbles now incorporated into the mixture to make nice stiff egg whites."

"Huh," I said, showing I was paying attention. Unfortunately, my response had the opposite effect.

"I guess I better lay off the sexy egg talk, huh."

"Yeah, with all this chemistry being tossed about, I have a sudden urge to recite the periodic table in my underwear."

"Cool your ions there, boy."

I eyed the sink that was filled with the results of her caramelizing.

"My God," I said, trying my best to fake exasperation, "look at these dirty pots and pans and measuring cups. Are you serving me these for dinner?"

"Quit complaining."

"I'm not sure the entire kitchen in a diner has this size mess."

"Well, its food doesn't taste as good either."

She shut me up by feeding me a mango smoothie that like everything else she made tasted of many other things. As I sucked it down, she told me, "Slow down there, boy, you'll get a headache."

When the meal was finally ready, every inch of the table again was filled, this time with the colors and smells of a street full of restaurants. The octopus was broiled in paprika and the duck had some brown ginger sauce. The green beans had bacon and almonds while the biscuits had little warm puddles of cheddar. The butternut squash soup had nutmeg and the radiccio salad had cranberries and goat cheese. The meal was magnificent, but I struggled to describe her wonderful flavors. I had to resort to the language of cooking show judges, throwing around many "s" words like *succulent* and *savory* and *smoky* and . . . *succotash*.

As we ate, I told her of all the times I brought food to the Joan in the hospital. I confessed with some shame to Eva that I cooked none of it. "Every time I'd show up with a Chinese food container or a few slices of pizza in a box or a roast beef hero from the deli, she looked like the happiest woman in the world. She'd complain about the hospital food and take a couple of bites of whatever I brought, making joyful grunts. One time, I came back a few minutes later to drop off a magazine for her, and she was asleep. I couldn't help but notice that she had dumped all the Greek takeout I'd gotten for her, even the gyro sandwich, which she always loved, right in the garbage. The chemo had gutted her appetite. The Joan only pretended to like what I'd brought to make me happy."

Listening intently, Eva put more duck on my plate and waited for me to go on.

"Right to the end, I kept bringing her food because it strangely made each of us happier. The Joan would take her joyful nibbles, and I would never notice when the rest ended up in the garbage."

I was clearly eating too much and I could hear the food rumbling in my stomach. I was unprepared for such excess and knew tomorrow that my digestive track would behave like I'd swallowed a bag full of golf balls. Eva, however, had been training her entire life for such a moment. I admired how she could overindulge with such grace. I stood up, fearing that otherwise I might not rise again, and retired to the comfort of the dishes, where the sink could help steady my legs. I wondered why in God's name I had taken the mango smoothie with me and why was I still slurping away at it. Eva didn't help matters by constantly topping off my glass.

I had taken out the kitchen trash twice since Eva arrived, and the can was filling up quickly again. "You created more refuse in an evening than I generate in a month."

"I'm just trying to support your business, that's all. Hey, if everyone in the neighborhood was like you, you'd be out of a job." I didn't want to break the breezy mood by telling her that was the case anyway.

As I tossed the bag out into the garage, I asked, "Hey, speaking of jobs, did you take the internship in Heine's office?"

"Yes, we're making buttons and campaign pamphlets."

"What do they say?"

"Heine. A Leader for the Future. Pretty funny, eh. Maybe a leader for the nursing home."

"How does the mayor treat you?"

"He's very nice to me."

"I bet he is."

"He wants to teach me everything."

"I bet he does."

"He says I'm doing everything wrong, but he thinks I have potential."

"That makes sense. The only way he can get your attention is if he makes you think you're incompetent and he's really important."

"That may be true and he is a really annoying person."

"How so?"

Eva took an entire fifteen minutes to describe Heine's obsession with multitasking. He would constantly peruse the new Dan Brown thriller on his E-reader while he jabbed at his phone screen, scribbled in Jumble puzzles, and devoured his lunch. Being Eva, she focused on his terrible manners during eating: how he wouldn't stop talking as he ate a tunafish sandwich and how more than a little landed on her; how the mayo from the tuna would smear on his phone screen and how he left oil stains on long sheets of legal paper and how he would stain her spreadsheets and how he'd talk into the phone receiver even as he was giving you orders and taking big, gobbing bites from his sandwich; how she had learned to take long walks during Heine's feeding times, but she discovered he ate a lot. "He's a hard man to be near without being soiled." We both knew she was exaggerating, but we also knew it was one of her specialties. She thought for a moment in an attempt to be generous in spirit. "But he does know a lot about how to get voters to listen to him."

"Starting with you."

"Relax there, boy. It's not like I'm cooking him dinner or anything."

I was washing, as I had been much of the night, and she came next to me to dry. At first, it was kind of sweet, like we were an old married couple. Later, as I got into a rhythm of scrubbing and rinsing, she began to stand closer to me with her hair and curves a hand towel's distance from me. Eva had made a decision in that moment that she had not seemed to have thought about beforehand. I, however, had been thinking about such a wonderful possibility from the moment she invited herself over to cook dinner. I was not ready to experience what I had imagined more than once.

I had let someone for the first time truly into the house, and it wasn't just some wallflower. Her name wasn't Eva for nothing. She served up Eden on a half dozen platters. It wasn't her style to tempt me with an apple, but with an entire orchard. Tonight, she had taken over the kitchen. Although she had also taken over too many corridors of my mind, one physical room was enough for tonight.

Unfortunately, I couldn't run away, a drawback of inviting her into my house. Anyway, I didn't want Eva to leave. I wanted to keep talking. I didn't have to worry about that. As long as Eva had liquid, she had words and, with a water bottle in one hand and the remnants of a smoothie in the other, I was in business . . .

. . . At least until 3:30 in the morning, when her arms crossed onto the kitchen table and she dropped her head on them. All I could see of her was that mane of luxurious black hair. I woke her up with a cup of coffee and led her to her car. I gave her the Joan's favorite travel coffee mug. It featured a fat head with the words imprinted, "I make bald look good." I got her the mug after she'd started chemo and she'd drip in any liquid she could find to show it off to her friends and the ward nurses. I couldn't keep it in the kitchen cabinet anymore, yet I couldn't throw it away. Even in her weary stupor, Eva let out a low laugh when she read the mug. Eva could fill a wig shop with her mop of hair.

"Can I ask you a question?" she asked. I nodded. "Why do you call your mother the Joan?"

I looked at her and smiled. "Because that was her name." She waited for more.

"She always told me that because of our situation that I'd need to grow up fast. After the seventieth time she said that to me, I told her that I'd act like an adult as long as I got to call her by her first name. She said I could, but I still needed to show respect. That's where the 'the' in the Joan comes in." Eva hugged and kissed me like she was leaving on a trip.

I walked her out with an icy snow pelting us. I drew Eva close, sheltering her, pulling open her driver's side door. As I shut the door to her car, I said, "You're always on vacation, aren't you?"

Sliding down the window as she drove off, she yelled out, "Where else am I supposed to be?"

14

THE DIARY OF LEVON GALLAGHER: THE PRIMAL SCREAM

August 8, 1974

I tried to tell James Earl Jones about CB radios, but he wanted to keep yapping about his primal scream therapy. He told me how he'd been in the birth simulator at the Primal Institute.

"You give birth at the Institute?"

"No, no," James Earl Jones chuckled in a big booming baritone, like he owned shimmering nuggets of enlightenment while I held a bag of dirt. "You are born."

"Not again. Isn't once enough?"

"Everybody needs a clean slate."

"You come out of a womb?" I frowned.

"No, no," then more of the James Earl Jones chuckle. "You are in a simulator."

"A simulator?"

"It's a pressurized tube and you're covered in goop."

"What?"

James Earl Jones gazed at me with a knowing

smile that only a true believer possesses. I was feeling pretty uneasy. So I ventured –

"Can we talk about CB radios now?"

James Earl Jones stared down at me. "Primal Scream Therapy cured me of smoking and hemorrhoids." That voice was so deep I swear his underwear must've sagged to his knees just to carry the heavy audio equipment of his loins. "Has your blessed CB radio done that for you?"

I refused to notice he had six inches and sixty pounds on me. I would reason with him. "It is the most important device of our times. A CB radio is interactive. That makes it mighty powerful. It's almost like you have a phone that travels with you. It's remarkable. You can throw yourself out there and talk to anybody. You can contact someone miles away. With that kind of power, we'll be talking to everybody. We'll be talking while we're driving, while we're eating, while we're doing everything. We'll be doing so many things at once. One day we'll be able to communicate across the globe with one of these things."

"I'd hate to see the size of the car antenna for that one." There was more of that damn James Earl Jones chuckle. "Hey, with primal scream, you don't need stupid devices, you just need to release your anxieties. You're all pent up. I look at you, Levon, and I can tell you want to punch me really hard. That CB radio isn't going to calm you down. You know what's going to calm you down, this –"

That's when James Earl Jones started screaming, screaming in my ear. I did not think he could scream since he has such a deep bellow, but scream he did. It was a bottomless howl that lasted a good couple of minutes, the barbaric yawp of death itself. It reverberated through my ears across decades. I refused to move because I did not want James Earl Jones to believe he had any power over me.

When he finally stopped, my ears were ringing and I couldn't hear what he said to me. In fact, when I took up my assignment with truckers the next morning, I still couldn't hear well. Then James Earl Jones asked me a question I couldn't understand. I answered him anyway, "Wow, I think my hemorrhoids are cured."

He scowled and looked like he wanted to shove a CB radio right up into my recovery zone. Then the big man just walked away. I knew one day I would make James Earl Jones pay for considering me unworthy of assault. I no longer had to go out for supplies; the deliveries were coming right to my home.

But I didn't go home just yet. Since I'd be away with the truckers for a while, I wanted to stop in to see Sarah and Joan. Artie had been staying out longer and the rooms grew colder in the house. A couple of times I caught Artie and Sarah together there. Then I could hear beneath their clever jokes angry memories that thumped like a bass line in a sad song.

Artie spent most of his nights in Washington now, lobbying to create a fund to clean up toxic waste dumps. To open doors of Congressmen, he drew on the money he earned off investments with Ben Wright. It was one of those losing causes Artie specialized in. I'm sure he wondered whether his marriage fit in this category.

Joan jumped into my arms, yelled "Uncle Leev," and kissed on the cheek. That girl was already starting to become the beauty her mother once was. Every time I visited Sarah lately she looked like she'd been drained of a few pints of blood, a ghostly, pale goddess barely able to turn a can opener to give her daughter cream corn. Joan made me play Monopoly while she yakked away about how she was in love with Ponyboy from a book she read. She was seven going on seventeen.

"Boy, I wish I had her energy," Sarah said drearily. "All I want to do is sleep."

I handed Joan two hundred clams after she made it around the Monopoly board and asked Sarah, "Have you been to the doctor?"

"That's the thing about it," she said. "He can't find anything wrong with me." Sarah gave me a troubled glance while Joan moved her silver toy dog across the properties. We both knew what was wrong with her, but there was nothing to be done about it. "I cut back on my gallery hours. How many more hours can I sleep?"

I landed on Boardwalk and Joan punched my arm. That's when I started screaming like James Earl Jones. What I lacked in commitment to the scream, I made up in my talent for incorporating farm animal noises in every gasp of breath. As I built toward duck quacks and pig grunts, Joan laughed so loudly and infectiously that even Sarah smiled.

Goddamn James Earl Jones. I did feel better. I left Joan with a trucker hat and a CB radio, promising her we'd be big-rig buddies when I came home. I knew the only thing that seemed to make Sarah happy anymore was someone giving Joan attention. Sarah reminded me that Artie would meet me at Murphy's tonight for a whiskey. I knew we'd spend the evening talking around issues we couldn't speak of. I had no

idea at this point whether a chat on the CB or
a nice scream would be a more effective means
way of communication.

* * *

This log was on the day President Nixon resigned. The energy crisis was still roaring and the speed limits were dropping to fifty-five. When Levon went out on the road with the truckers the next day, he found many pissed off about the slower roads. Yet, according to Levon's accounts in *The Herald*, they spent most of the time joking on their CB radios (Levon's handle was "Thin-Skinned"). Levon didn't record any primal screams from them. Most of the time they had a big truck to make them feel better. Levon did not, which I guess is why he was getting deliveries.

After I was done studying old columns by Levon from August of 1974, I read every scrap of news about James Earl Jones from the Internet. It turns out he was a somewhat famous actor, not John Wayne, but he was known in his day. He was even the voice of Darth Vader. Who knew? I could find no evidence of Levon exacting revenge on the Sith Lord.

I had hoped these entries would shed light on the story Levon told me in the middle of the night when I was just an impressible teenager. He might just get around to telling that tale, but I guess not until he bitched and moaned about every pissy confrontation that annoyed him. I understood I would have to keep gathering bits and pieces of his story to make sense of it all. What was strange is how evasive he was in these entries. Aren't these supposed to be his secret thoughts? Clearly, the tale he told me had been a whirlpool spiraling Sarah downward, dragging her under, and from a distance, Artie too sounded like he was barely afloat. I envied the Joan of back then, vital and oblivious. As with her son, I knew that would not last long.

15

THE CARNIVAL ATTENDANT

The rubbish run had its demands. Mastering just how to lift the pails was the key. During the first couple of weeks, my arms and back throbbed with soreness. Only when my thighs joined in the lifting did the run seem like something I could withstand, that my body would not end up tossed in the compactor with the debris of a busted trash can. My shins and knees took the worst of it, since the damn plastic bags tended to have something sharp that would slice you, leaving cuts and scrapes and bruises across my legs.

I learned not to expect any pail to be like the previous one. This one lost a handle, this one was stuffed and jammed, so it required a brave and ruthless hand to set its contents free. This one weighed as much as Louie and reeked of rusted car parts, a rotting sourness that even a cologne of axel grease could not subdue. For those heavy ones, I'd crouch down low on it like it was a wild boar with a sharp set of tusks, tip it, slip a hand under its bottom, and prop its ass up until it tumbled over the truck lip. My triceps pulsed and throbbed with a power to discard anything that came my way.

Now the deep freeze of early January made even cotton balls seem like cannon balls with my stiff muscles and slow bones. In the desolate, leafless landscape, I scowled and lifted the pails quickly, best to keep blood flowing, huffs from my breath fogging up the neighborhood. The biggest item I confronted that day I left in front of the compactor, saving it for home. It was an outboard motor, with a propeller that looked like it had lost a fight with a coral reef, its blade tips mangled like broken teeth. I grunted as I bent my thighs down real low.

Big Bill yelled out from the truck, "There he goes, my good lad, mega mongo! Indeed, this is mongo worthy of the mongomaniac."

"Jesus," said Louie, "whatdaya hoisting an anchor, matey?"

"You got the wrong part of the boat, ya landlubber," I said. A couple of months ago, Big Bill and Louie would've busted on me for grabbing the motor, but now with the end coming tomorrow, they both shrugged as if to say, "What the hell . . . Why not?"

With her left glove snipped so she could finger the frets of her violin, Lee Lee abandoned the chamber music she was playing in favor of some sea shanties. I started singing, which made Lee Lee break off for what I thought was a dramatic pause. She didn't start playing again until I shut up. As she drew the bow across the strings jauntily, I yanked and pulled on pails like they were ropes on sails. My body rolled on and off the truck as a northerly wind bit our backs. The skeletal trees that loomed above scored the sky. The pails seemed to hardly need me anymore in order to find their way into the compactors. They were willing participants as I pivoted and swiveled with the easy movements of a discus thrower. Yeah, even in the tundra, this was a great way to live. As Lee Lee played a shanty about a drunken sailor, I danced with a joy so delirious I forgot that I should've been embarrassed.

When we were done with the run, we strolled back into the office, back into the rest of the world, into the stuffy internal air. We could smell ourselves, and know the smell was not something we could scrub off. All who encountered us could not miss our well-earned stench, even though the cold had tamped down Frick's memorable excess of odors. The trash had been massaged into our pores. Yes, the price we would pay for this Eden of sensual embrace and physical release was that anyone who led with his nose wouldn't get within a racetrack of us. We owned our smell, and would have branded it if we weren't certain that very act would have so neutralized the odor that we would have no smell at all. We felt welcome in Hannah's and Pulaski's offices because they knew the smell was the toll you paid to get to the other side. I wondered if I could stay there much longer.

Pulaski asked if he could drop by my house and take a look at what his buddy Hannah had called my Mongo Mashups. I took the outboard motor home and indeed turned it into an anchor for a sculpture. No, it was really the body of some futuristic person. Above the motor rose a rectangular head from a microwave discarded by Peggy Murphy (who I believe, like the Joan, was spooked by its cancerous waves). Like a good microwave would, it made a very empty, hollow head, a head that once upon a time could generate heat in everything that entered its consciousness. For hair, I pulled from the ribbons of weather stripping that Nicole Gulotta had placed neatly in her pail (I guess the world did not seem so cold to her now that Louie was cleaning up her debris). For a face, I used various pieces of Styrofoam that I had collected on a particularly dreary day of waste – what day couldn't I grab Styrofoam packing material? – but I took it knowing I'd need it someday. With the white, fluffy, puffy eyes, nose and mouth against a black, tinted microwave screen and the grey, spongy sticky hair, he looked like Frosty the Snowman's evil brother.

Inspecting the work carefully, Pulaski asked, "What's his name?"

"I will call him the Carnival Attendant."

As I said those words, I felt the blood rush to my face. Pulaski gave me the look of a man who could see shame in a turn of a shoulder, let alone in a reddened cheek.

"Who's that?" Pulaski pointed to me instead of my blockhead sculpture.

"My father."

"Oh," said Pulaski. "You trying to tell me your father was a carney?"

I know Pulaski, who might be the last human who believed everything Sigmund Freud said, was drawing all types of connections and conclusions right now. To get away from the topic, I spoke to Pulaski about the colleges I was considering as my mind wandered elsewhere. . . .

The Joan told me two things about my father, both of them when she was drunk. Once, with margaritas at Paco Loco, she slurred to me that "your father left on a motor boat." The only thing I'd heard about him before were whispers that he'd been a hacker. The Joan wiped some salsa from her lips and stared at me with an intensity that told me to listen now since the subject was not likely to surface again.

"Just before you were born, scientists were able to clone a sheep. I think they named her Dara. Anyway, hearing that, your father decided he could do a different kind of cloning." She stirred her finger in her slushy drink. "It's complicated." She downed the margarita and signaled the waiter for another. "Back then, they made a big deal about identity theft. Your father thought if he cloned people's cyber identities and made them all the same, then the corporations or crooks would have nothing to steal. Anyway, the program worked so well that the

FBI noticed and was ready to lock him up for twenty years."

"But wasn't he helping people?"

"You'll learn that it's never good to help people without asking permission, so he had to take off before the FBI gathered enough on him. He left most of the money with us though."

The sounds of everyone else in the restaurant were muffled. We could've been sitting around our kitchen table. "Where'd he go?"

"I think Costa Rica, but the Email was so confusing I'm not sure."

"Did you write him back?"

"Of course I did, but he never wrote me again."

"Why don't we go find him?"

"He doesn't want to be found." She didn't cry. I thought my next question would break the dams, so I shut my mouth.

The next morning I asked her about him, and she claimed she could not remember anything. I frowned. She swore she wasn't lying. For years, visions of a guy in a hunting hat next to a shaggy brown dog in an outboard puttered around my skull. He kept dropping in a fishing line, muttering Spanish to the mahi mahi and not catching a damn thing. Sometimes I had to wait for hours for that boat to head far enough down river not to see it anymore. Another time during two-for-one happy-hour merlots at Applebees, the Joan told me Dad used to work at the carnival. When I suggested that maybe he was a strong man who could ring the bell with one swing of the sledgehammer, the Joan started to laugh hysterically. She muttered something about his throwing out jackasses, and that they made a reality TV show about the carnival, but for some reason it never aired. Then I couldn't get another word out of her. Next morning, the Joan had nothing else to tell me except how much her head hurt. So he was on a reality TV show that never made it. How is that possible? What reality show doesn't make it onto TV, no matter how crappy? Add that piece of dirty laundry to the washing machine spinning in my head. Dad left the house before I had a clue. The Joan's story was that I was seven months old; Aunt Vicky claims I was almost two.

The Joan thought his name might be Ben, but she was really not sure. Deep in the recesses of my unspoken thoughts sat the hope that maybe Gallagher's entries would tell me more about my father. To make sure my visions would be foggy, the Joan claimed she didn't have a picture of him. "I couldn't stand to see him." I decided she was lying.

I rubbed her hungover head, "Didn't you think I'd be curious?"

"Yes." I thought someday I'd get a blender full of margaritas in her and learn which carnival can be arrived at by motor boat. Unfortunately, bars are not too common at hospitals. I still haven't found pictures of my father in the house. Since I don't know what he looks like, he could be in one of those random Polaroids I found in the basement. One day I'll have to interrogate Aunt Vicky under hot lights until she identifies him.

All the while as these memories were running through my head, I was going through my college options with Pulaski, shooting out the names of programs and fellowships that I thought I had long forgotten. Those college acceptances were there alright, buried right below the shame. While I could tell Pulaski was marking my every awkward movement, he was so happy that I finally spoke of a future beyond tomorrow's final garbage run that he would talk me through each one of them. There were moments he wandered in his words and made no sense at all, but he didn't look a damn bit embarrassed by it. He was in such a state that I knew I could dump yet another piece of my inheritance onto him. In the Joan's china cabinet rested these sweetly sickening Darling Cuddlies figurines. They were impossibly cute statues of apple-cheeked children hugging each other. Even the Joan hated them, but had been in no condition to shove them off on someone else. Yet they had value because they were once owned by Frick's greatest son. Receiving them as a gift from his mother, Ben Wright hated the figurines so he gave them to Levon, who also hated them, so he gave them to the Joan. I told Pulaski the story, who became more amused by every passing of the Darling Cuddlies. Then I reached into the china cabinet and handed him one called "Paddy Cake," a disgustingly sugary piece, a highlight of the entire miserable collection. He took it from me like I had handed him a tank of oxygen.

After Pulaski left, I asked Louie to stop by, an idea brewing. I took him right to the china cabinet and explained to him the story of the figurines. "Levon told the Joan that the pieces held many questions."

Louie shook his head. "I know one question he definitely had. Why the hell are you vandalizing your china cabinet with these trolls?"

"Hey, I gave Pulaski one and he loved it."

"That's because Pulaski's demented. You gave him a goldfish tank and he loved that too." I couldn't argue with Louie. Pulaski did love that damn goldfish tank.

From the back of the china cabinet, I pulled out a picture of Ben Wright standing next to the collection of Darling Cuddlies, his open right palm nudging toward the display like he was revealing something valuable; his sly, twisted grin said otherwise. "How about this idea?" I started, knowing Louie probably wouldn't like it. "I make copies of this picture, right. I put the picture, a Darling Cuddly, and a note on the doorstep of every resident we've really pissed off."

Louie counted the Darling Cuddlies. "You've got 23. That might just be enough." Surprisingly, he was warming to the idea. "What would the note say?"

"Something like we thank you for the opportunity to serve as your garbage men over these months, we apologize for our errors, and we are grateful for the opportunity to learn from your kindness and patience. And, as a token of our appreciation, we thought you might like a piece of history that Ben Wright left behind. Hell, with the name of Frick's great inventor associated with it, the value of these awful little Darling Cuddlies would at worst fetch 50 bucks on Ebay or more likely earn a cherished spot on the family mantle."

Louie shook his head. "Damn, they're ugly."

"But they might be enough to prevent the locals from trashing the trash boys."

Louie stared at one, his mouth twisting in disgust. "Oh, what the hell. I don't have any better ideas. This will either work or piss them off even more. I'm fine with both of those possibilities."

"Good," I said, taking a deep breath. "I'll get up real early and drop them off before our run." Then I paused. "The final run."

Not a sentimental type, Louie simply answered with "Yeah."

I looked back at the ridiculous carnival attendant I made. Like my old man, he too was not worthy of a reality TV show. Still, was my creation any worse than a Darling Cuddly? I chuckled. The next 24 hours would be crazy. Tonight, I'd see Eva, then I'd be out before dusk to drop off the figurines, then we go on the trash run and end the day at the hearing. I thought I knew how each event would turn out. As usual, I was wrong.

* * *

I was to meet Eva at Starbucks. I had asked her, "Where do you want to go from there?"

"Go from there? Why? Just bring your phone, O.K.?"

When I arrived and stood behind her in the line, Eva turned toward me and gave me a sniff, which always makes a guy who hauls garbage concerned.

"Is that rosemary scented deodorant?"

"Don't like it?"

"No. I love it. It's like you're carrying two roasted chickens under your arms."

Starbucks was so crowded that at nine o'clock we had to stand. We had seats at the counter by ten, and by ten thirty we finally got a small table.

We had what Eva called a phone date, not that we talked to each other on our phones. We just used our phones as the source of all our entertainment. It was a wonderful night. Eva taught me how to play a poker game where we were partners, battling against a computer. Then we'd look up strange videos on YouTube to share with each other. In between, we took turns ordering lattes and portioned servings of cheese and cake and fruit. Eva was forever sipping and nibbling. She didn't eat ravenously, but steadily, like something terrible would happen to her if she stopped. I tried to avoid having the worried studied look that she had avoided with me. She'd been through rehab for both drugs and alcohol so she got the same cocktail of student whispers and overbearing counselors that I received. On a night when we sent out to each other favorite songs and movie scenes as background noise, I tried to keep up with her pace of eating and drinking. Somehow, that felt reckless. I had spent two days in the bathroom after she cooked me dinner; clearly my body was not ready for Eva's nutritional program. I was going through cafés con leche like I was her caffeine soul mate, and we'd become awfully cozy as we leaned over each other's shoulder to catch lines of Twitter feeds or Max's latest video.

Max was now advertising in his promos, "From the director

who brought you Generation Dementia comes a new film about our troubled youth."

"Is Max one of the troubled youths?" asked Eva.

"You never get more credibility than if you're an insider."

As I got ready to hear what Max would say our problem was, Eva muttered "insider" and told me, "Can we see this later? I've got to show you something before I forget the name."

"O.K., but you'll have to last a few more minutes without knowing what's wrong with us."

"I could put that off for a couple of years." She starting tapping the keypad. "Let's see. It was something like No Garbage." She scrolled down the search results. "No, that's not it. How about Garbage Less?" She frowned and took a fortifying sip. "Let's try Garbage Free. I think that's it." She studied the results. "Yes," and pointed to the phone. "Now look."

On the screen were mountains of garbage rising up with trucks waiting off to the side and seagulls squawking and flapping around and above. Words were superimposed, "It doesn't have to be this way." Then flashed "GARBAGE FREE," followed by "The Way to the Next Millennium."

"What is this?" I asked.

"I don't know, but I know that Mayor Heine was meeting with these Garbage Free people."

"What did they tell him? What do they actually do?"

"I don't know. The mayor shut the door."

"You think this is part of the plan to dump us?"

"It seems that way, like they've already decided to get rid of Operation Pick-up Kids. I'm a little surprised given all the good publicity you've gotten lately. I wouldn't have shown it to you if I'm not a little worried."

I scrolled through the entire Garbage Free website. "They don't tell you anything else except that all the garbage in your community will go away."

"That would make your job a little less relevant, huh."

"Sure as hell sounds like it."

"I'll see what else I can find out. Do you want to watch Max's video now?"

"No." I ordered more coffee instead.

As Starbucks was closing and the barista tossed our cups and then us out (telling us three times to have a nice night before we got the hint), Eva said, "I want to see your trash art that everyone's been telling me about."

"Sure," I said, my head humming in a fog from the coffee, and a bit surprised by the request. "I didn't think you were interested the other night."

"Oh, I was interested, but you seemed to want to keep me in the kitchen, so I didn't want to be aggressive."

"And now you're O.K. being aggressive?"

"I've had four lattes. Do I have a choice?"

"Well, you could tremble and howl at the moon?"

"I'm a little tired of doing that."

"After you see my trash art, don't be surprised if you decide you're better off jumping up on a rock and barking."

Ignoring my mother's persistent question as I entered the house, I took Eva to the garage, the home of most of my efforts. She rejected my offers for coffee or anything else to eat or drink. Instead, she pulled up the garage door and lit a cigarette. She walked around the works and puffed, for once not saying a word as she passed the tower of stacked up TV sets, the abandoned yard tools wrapped in corn stalks, and the painted cans. She had gone through three cigarettes before she spoke again, which was not as long as you'd think: she was smoking like she had five lips.

I could tell she didn't like my work and was figuring out how to say that. I had been used to everyone who had even seen a glimpse of my pieces gushing about them. I knew most of that was either "Look how the boy's coping with his dead mother" or "Look what he's doing with my trash. Didn't I tell you my trash is worth something?"

As I watched her scrutinize each piece through a haze of smoke, sprinkling ashes around pedestals like she was trying to sanctify them, I came to the terrible realization of how little I had been doing to turn all these reclaimed materials into art. Clearly, I was much better at taking crap than figuring out how to transform it. Louie could've told me that. "Of course, you stupid bastard, you're a trash man. What'd you expect?"

As I watched her walk through the works a seventh time and saw her puffing and concentrating, refusing to be distracted by her phone, I suddenly knew my pieces were woefully inadequate. The work originally put into the objects I had taken from the curb was so much greater than the effort I had thrown into them.

Eva sat down and looked at me. "I like what you combined together in these works." She let that comment hang there. I knew criticism would follow. "I think for me though," she paused and puffed, "and this is just my taste," another puff, "I think you should reshape them so they become completely your own."

It wasn't hard to see her point. I looked at my glued and twisted chain of water bottles attached to an anchor. If I had carefully molded and sculpted those bottles so that they could pass for heavy nautical cables, then I might be presenting a useful commentary about gravity and water consumption. Typically, I had an idea, but the execution sucked.

I thought it was time to make it easier on Eva. "You mean instead of just slapping things together with nails and glue guns and splotches of paint?"

"I think you should make it a goal to transform what you have into something beautiful."

"I am more interested in it being disturbing."

"I believe it's more likely to be disturbing if you really try to make it beautiful."

"Yeah? That's the problem. I've got a lot of plastic here. I can't really reshape it."

She slid her hands across the outboard motor of the Carnival Attendant and the Styrofoam cups of The Calling. "I'd work more with the wood and metals and the foams that can be cut, carved, bent or sanded."

"I think I need to step back from some of this. I should throw away a bunch of it. You have any suggestions of what I should keep?"

She lit a new cigarette and strolled one more time through. Her statuesque figure made her look like a movie star walking among murder suspects. "This is what I'd do. Hire a cleaning lady and don't give her any instructions for the garage. See what she throws out and then consider the rest as potential works of art."

I tried not to show I was hurt, but I was pretty quiet after that. After a few minutes, Eva said she was tired and headed home. As I walked her across the cold sidewalk, she could tell that apologizing would make everything worse. I couldn't convince myself that to be so ruthless was necessary, yet I was really struggling to offer an alternate way for her to actually make me change what I had already considered completed works of art. I was struck by the waste of it all. Off the truck, I wouldn't be able to scrounge new raw materials. I seemed too late for everything.

That night, my hallucinations were limited to my trips to the bathroom. There, a voice rose from a remote speaker, "You didn't flush." I looked down at the clear water in the bowl. "Yes, I did." I curse myself for answering a rascally phantom. Out in the garage, I made my way through piece after piece, trying to imagine what in God's name I could do to make them beautiful. When I stumbled upon an honest possibility, I sketched the image. I huffed with the understanding that any transformation would take a couple hours work every night for a month, at least a month. Maybe I'd sculpt in the mornings to fill up those hours I had been spending on the truck.

I particularly thought about the Carnival Attendant. I would have to replace the Styrofoam face parts that stuck on the outside of the microwave door, looking like albino Mr. Potatohead reject pieces. Yes, the Styrofoam eyes, nose and lips made for a playful joke. But how much better would it be to actually sculpt a precise and realistic clay head that could be placed inside the microwave on the carousel, an intelligent, paternal head that could intensely peer out through the door. Oh, the skill and care I would have to summon. I would have to illuminate the inner rectangle of the microwave, but subtly . . . like the skull was radioactive.I tossed my right arm over my eyes and tried to imagine getting through even one of these reworkings. I took as some form of comfort that I would have more time since I wouldn't be distracted by Eva anymore. Pulling my arm away, I turned to the clock. It was time to start delivering the Darling Cuddlies.

16

THE RECYCLED BOTTLE

My final trash run was more memorable because it brought to a close my strange, yet satisfying experience with Cindy Stevens. Even though my thoughts should've been on the all-important sanitation board hearing later that day, I had invested too much into helping Cindy to not complete my mission.

It started more than a week ago, right at the beginning of the new year. At the top of the Stevens' recycling bucket rested an empty plastic water bottle with a piece of paper scrolled inside. Dumping the rest of the contents in the metals, plastics and glass bin, I unscrewed the bottle top and tapped out the scroll, unrolling it. It had a formal heading, Cindy Stevens, 11th Grade, English, January 2. Below it sat a single, neatly written line: "I am going to kill myself." I'd been in creative writing with Cindy. The only thing most students knew about her was that in ninth grade a topless picture of her popped up on Facebook. Even though Cindy deleted the photo within seconds, boys who wait around for such moments captured the image and it's haunted her ever since. Now, she eats her lunch in the bathroom. She was also the sister of super senior Megan, that mean teen of the Spirit Committee known to noisily suppress laughs about girls in the bathroom.

A part of me thought Cindy's message and the entire presentation was typical teenage girl stuff. Some juniors tend to threaten suicide once a week. Yet that's the thing about a cry for help; there's always the possibility she's not bluffing. Anyway, what's wrong with a cry for help? Aunt Vicky suggested in a text from Florida that my jumping onto the trash routes may have been one. When I wrote her back, considering the possibility, she didn't respond. Her next Email described the wonderful tropical sun and the refreshing afternoon rain showers.

There was something sweetly quaint and old fashioned about Cindy's plea. She didn't send it out in a YouTube video or post it on her Facebook page. It was all so charmingly private and secretive, which gave it an irresistible aura of authenticity. I carried the frosty recycling bucket off with me, so that later I could drop it on the Stevens' curb with her single bottle.

That very afternoon, I met again with Megan Stevens and Max after school for the Spirit Committee. The walls of the classroom were filled with recommendations to drink milk and warnings to not do drugs. Next to the posters sat a quote from Ben Wright that read, "Despite what people will tell you, something doesn't have to be well built to be powerful." For today's agenda, we were supposed to propose a new event for Competition Night.

"How about a video contest?" I suggested. Megan was already opening her mouth to shoot down my idea, so I had to get the rest out quickly. "But every entry can only be three seconds long. The video can keep looping."

"Three seconds?" Megan snickered. Maybe if she heard it again.

"A three-second video contest."

She groaned. "That's ridiculous. Who has the attention span to watch that?" Megan rolled her eyes at Max. I had a feeling Max might back me on this one, since he always stood on the side of video. Megan almost looked at me flirtatiously. "He's so cute, isn't he?" I loved being talked about like that. "What an old soul."

"What do *you* want? A one-second video contest?"

"No, don't be a silly head. That would never work. But a two-second video contest would be great!"

"What?"

Megan looked at me and turned to Max, as if to say, that old dog can't learn new tricks. But her eyes were a little friendlier and wetter. Man, those news stories about my time on the garbage truck had clearly done wonders for my reputation. Certainly, Megan's new fondness for me would disappear once I was dumped off the truck.

Max was pushing buttons on his phone for a few moments and then lifted the screen before our eyes. I saw a close-up of my face as I announced, "A three-second video contest." My pronouncement took exactly two seconds and repeated, again and again. The bottom of the screen read, "The Two-Second Video Contest."

"Should we use this to promote the contest?" asked Max.

"I look like I'm saying something wrong," I said.

"Old men often do," said Megan. "Let's use it."

I wondered whether my classmates who viewed the video would think of me as stupid or clever. I wasn't sure I cared. I don't know if my time on the garbage truck had damaged my eardrums, but I hardly could hear their voices anymore.

I stared intensely at Megan, "I will let you use my wonderful image on one condition."

"What?" She rolled her eyes.

"You are nice to your sister."

For those seconds you could shoot a competition night video, Megan looked upset, and then recovered with a "sure" so dripping with sarcasm that nobody in his right mind could believe her.

I believed her.

That cold, windy night I walked the Stevens' recycling bucket back to their house. I didn't care if Megan or anyone else knew. I figured Cindy needed me to hurl myself out to her.

Inside the bottle I left a small note with five basil leaves pulled from stalks Eva had left in a glass of water by my kitchen sink. "Why would you want to leave a world that can smell like this?"

The next pickup day she left that single bottle out in the blue bucket, even though it wasn't a recycling day. My basil leaves had been ground into a paste and caked up on the bottom. The edge of her note was saturated with a fragrant green. "A little pesto can't fix all the misery."

I thought of putting some pasta in the bottle to join with pesto and then accompany it with some stupid, barely uplifting note ("Misery feels better on a full stomach"), but instead I cleaned out the mess and started fresh. I feared maggots, which Big Bill called disco rice, would find their way into the bottle, not the gift suicidal types tend to embrace. I lined up dried kidney beans, black beans, green lentils, and yellow limas, carefully stacking each into pretty layers in the bottle. I took my time, spending half the night to make a bean rainbow. On the outside I taped a note, the size of a fortune plucked from a cookie: "May beans always brighten your day."

The next day she wrote back in the emptied bottle, still marked by her formal heading and her wonderfully clean, neat penmanship. "Beans tend to bend my days in other directions." I laughed, wondering if she smiled as she wrote that down.

More than once Louie scowled and howled at me for

holding onto that bottle. "What's next," he asked, "you going to start collecting the lint from freaky Cindy Stevens' belly button, so you can weave it into a friendship bracelet?"

I must admit that I was soon struggling to come up with inspirational junk to throw into the bottle: the opening was so small. It was amazing how quickly this dance of the water bottles moved from playful to stupid. If Cindy were truly suicidal, then I should stop messing around and talk to her. So I left my cell number in the bottle, asking her either to call me or to leave her number. That afternoon, she left her number. I called at 5:07. She was done talking at 7:34. Many people had treated her badly, especially Megan, who wrote regularly on the bathroom mirror, "Cindy fetches milk bones." I listened, occasionally saying "That sucks," to let her know I was paying attention.

Cindy spent most of her free time watching reality television, with special attention given to the real housewives shows that populated almost every city in the country. I've watched a terrible show called SuiciDolls too many times. All the teenagers on the show had been rescued from the ledge, so they could live in a house together. When they spoke in front of the camera, they were miserably, but intensely alive. In almost every episode, the director who calls himself Savior said, "What they need is attention." He clearly didn't mean attention as in counseling. "To be filmed gives them purpose," the Savior would say again and again. "SuiciDolls gives them a new lease on life."

I wondered what would happen if the cameras were shut off for good.

Meanwhile, I was struggling to pay attention to Cindy.

"Hey Cindy, I was miserable until I got on the garbage truck. Maybe if you found something to do, a hobby or something?"

She took a deep breath. I tried to figure out whether I steered the conversation in the wrong direction. "I've been thinking about that."

"Any idea what you'd like to do?"

"Yeah, but I don't feel like telling you now."

I thought of telling her about Frick's favorite son Ben Wright to serve as inspiration, but that story didn't end well, so I decided not to confuse matters. "Do me a favor Cindy?"

"Yeah?"

"Will you call me if you're having a tough time?" I winced when making the offer, but I could see no alternative.

"I will," she said. I thought Cindy was finally ready to get off her phone, but then she said she once had a hobby: taking pictures on her I-Phone. "That was so stressful."

"Why was that?"

"I took too many pictures. Thousands and thousands of pictures. I couldn't handle looking at all those images and deleting them."

"Oh." I could've suggested that maybe she shouldn't take so many pictures then, but I knew that nothing I said would make her want to take pictures again. The unlimited ability to snap pictures made Cindy sick, like taking a bath in chocolate syrup. "That sucks."

"Yeah, it does," she said and then she hung up.

On January 10, the day before the hearing, I left one more note for Cindy in the bottle, reminding her to call me at any time, and advising her, "Find a passion and make it a strange one."

And so today, January 11, I found in the Stevens' recycling bin a single bottle with a message, just like when I received the original suicide note. "Will this ever end?" I muttered to myself and pulled the message from the bottle. Scrawled on a note filled with hearts were the words, "I HAVE FOUND A PASSION. IT'S $(C_8H_8)_n$."

I wasn't sure what that meant, but I had a pretty good idea she would probably throw herself into the science research class. No, I don't think her passion was particularly strange, but there are worse places any of us could end up.

It was with suicidal Cindy on my mind that I made my way down to the sanitation board hearing. I saw many familiar faces: Stephanie Woods, Nonna D'Antonio, Keith Alford, Peggy Murphy, Derek Standish, and scores of other Frick residents. The news cameras were there and the locals dressed like they knew it.

Peggy Murphy stepped up to the podium first. "I can't tell you how happy I am to have these young people picking up my garbage. It's so good to see them out there in the fresh air, working with their bodies. It's wonderful. Keep it up!"

When I saw how heartily the residents clapped, I knew we had a chance. One after the other they came to the podium to praise Operation Pick-up Kids.

I whispered to Louie. "They must've really liked the Darling Cuddlies."

Louie frowned. "Don't kid yourself. The ceramic trolls had little to do with it. While they don't have much use for us, they like Pulaski, they really like Big Bill, and they absolutely love the cameras."

The sanitation board members particularly seemed to enjoy their glorious role in the festivities. For a moment, it looked like they would be heroes. But before they rendered their decision, Mayor Heine took to the podium. "What you have seen here today is a demonstration that the program I started is working. I ask you to approve the program for another two months when we can once again review the progress of these fine young representatives of Frick."

Following Heine's lead, the board approved the extension of Operation Pick-up Kids through March. Lee Lee almost smiled.

Louie actually did. And I had a big grin on my face . . . until I caught sight of Mayor Heine. His smirk told me he had something up his sleeve.

As I headed out, Mayor Heine came up to me and asked, "Do you know what methane gas is?"

"Isn't it what cows make when they fart?"

"Yes," Heine crinkled up his nose, "but it's also created from decomposing garbage. You know what's curious about that?"

"What?"

"The best way to take care of all that methane gas is to set it on fire." I was struck by the fact that Heine was not multitasking for once. How strange it was to have all his attention. "It makes a beautiful blue flame. You remind me of that methane flame."

"Quite a compliment sir," I said, trying for the just the right tone.

"What's funny about a methane fire is that when it burns too brightly, it extinguishes itself."

"Huh," I said.

"Funny the way things turn out, isn't it," he said and turned his attention to three devices and two legal-sized documents.

Yeah, Heine could drip sanitizer in your hand and give you an infection.

I had a funny feeling what he was planning would be even worse than killing off Operation Pick-up Kids. I had told myself again and again that my time on the truck was ending. All the build-up to that big hearing, for what? To gain a lousy two months before Heine would once again look to chop off our heads. Now I would continue, although not like before. By the way he was already looking past us, the mayor would make sure of that.

My thoughts returned to Cindy. That sanitation meeting was awfully short compared to the time I had spent turning Cindy around. I tried to figure why I was happy. Hell, my days consisted of picking up trash, sleepwalking through schools, and coming home to stare at the computer. Yet, I could sense something in Frick was happening, even from the Emails I read.

From the January 11 Trash Folder

Are you sure you want to permanently delete all the items and subfolders in the Deleted Items Folder?

The Daily Bread from Reverend Alexander Burr

Of late, much discussion in my home village of Frick has passed of garbage and the young people who collect it. I add my Amens to the chorus, yet shall warn that it is not the rubbish the youth take away that concerns me, but what remains. What dump truck can clean up cyberspace? Who can wrestle away those items plucked off the curb and brought back inside? Like those arrogant and foolish builders at Babel, we try to touch the heavens with our piles of data and the vessels that house them. And like those at Babel, our languages have been confused. Contrary to stackers of rubbish, cyberspace only expands the debris floating about in this age of misinformation, or as Genesis 11:8 so aptly presents, "they may not understand one another's speech." Yes, I too have been warmed by the rumble of the truck, the rattle of the pails and the ringing out of music across the plains, but these are voices, like Isiah's, crying out in a wilderness. They herald something grander coming, a pile of trash loftier than we had, heretofore, possibly imagined. It cannot be shuttered or buried for much longer. Hash, Louie, and Lee Lee are delivering a reckoning in a big orange truck. But who will eradicate the trash hurtling toward the heavens?

The Epic Life of Selena Omaha

So are you ready for the inside scoop about what's popping in Frick Village?

My best Facebook bae Mayor Heine caught scent of my rep of never leaving out my trash for anybody. He said it would be an honor if he could have some for the village archives. Mayor Heine muploaded this ish citation: "The refuse of Selena Omaha will serve as an emblem for all the trash of our time." And this is what he wrote on my Facebook wall as a personal thanks: "Selena, you only throw away the best, and the best of your waste is so much better than what most of us keep."

Mayor Heine knows better than anyone that I come from a fam that never gets rid of its stuff. Big Bill Hannah just drives the garbage truck by our house while dreamy Hash and loony Louie look for pails we don't put out. But because of this special request, I delivered my trash personally to the Mayor's office. In my trash bags were envelopes marked Top Secret, baggies stamped with the words Police Evidence, priceless coins and stamps, my confirmation dress, 17 single Banana Republic socks (I bet you there's an 18th hanging around the house somewhere), a military canteen from the 1940s, and a No Trespassing sign.

So don't be rachet, you thirsty scroungers. If you want a piece of me, go visit the village archives.

After I hit delete, I still couldn't sleep, so I fired up the Commodore 64 and gazed backward to see what Levon Gallagher had to say for himself.

17

THE DIARY OF LEVON GALLAGHER: PEDIGREE

July 25, 1978

I was at the Copacabana, an aptly named meat market, chatting up the red-headed Peggy Murphy who wore a tight blue dress. She must have been ten years older than me. She wore enough warpaint to trick me. Her gams ended with these six-inch platform shoes that gave her six inches on me, without taking in the height of her hair. A romance with Peggy would certainly require some climbing on my part. She told me she was a trade show rep. I asked her what's the most exciting product she's pitched? She smiled at me, half in love with me for my interest. "Well, there's this wonderful new thing called the Chia Pet."

"What kind of animal is that? Like a Chihuahua? I asked for a product, not a pet."

"That's what's amazing about the Chia Pet. It's a product that's also a pet."

"Like a Pet Rock."

"No, much better than a Pet Rock."

"Nothing is better than a Pet Rock."

"You have to understand, a Chia Pet is a figurine that has a plant growing out of it."
"So why's it called a Chia Pet?"

"Because the plant growing out of it is called a chia and you have to take care of it."

"Like a pet."

"Exactly."

"Who the hell would want that? That's the stupidest invention I've ever heard of."

"That's because you haven't seen it. Wait till you get a look at the Chia Guy and, even better, the Chia Ram."

This affection for the Chia Pet was dumb. Her pooh-poohing of the Pet Rock was dumber. I got in a few choice comments. "The thing about the Pet Rock is you don't have to act like you want to care for it. When you talk to it, you are truly talking to a rock, which I like. That rock was there before me and will be here after me. It is my lifelong buddy for a relative second in its long time on earth. It doesn't grow, it doesn't decay, it stays, and plays dead like a champ."

Peggy wouldn't hear of it. She said the Chia lasts longer in our minds - "where everything really counts, you know" — long after the pet rock is a forgotten fad. She tossed back her high and mighty hair and yapped about how "Chia hair isn't really hair, but it does the job. Wouldn't it be great if bald men could sprout follicles like Chia Guy?" On she raved, as if criminals would drop their heaters, pick up Chia Pets, and start kissing babies.

I couldn't listen to another word about her damned Chia Pet. I finally told her, "Look babe, you don't buy this Chia Pet because you want to take care of something. You do it because you get to take credit for raising something when all you're really doing is taking something out of a package. It's like all those people who talk to plants. They just want something to be there when they rattle on about their desperate, pathetic lives. They pretend a stalk of celery is being fed and nourished by their bullshit."

She responded in a fury. She stamped down with her right platform shoe on my left soft white leather sole. I had to snap down on my lower lip not to cry out in pain. I hope she didn't see my eyes getting wet. From her reaction, Peggy must've had long, herbal tea conversations with African violets and wandering Jews. It took all my inner courage to walk out of the Copa with only a limp. Spotting the weak and wounded member of the herd, a couple of Guidos with thick, black blown-dry heads and Italian horns glittering out from their hairy chests roughed me up a bit as I staggered to my car. They yelled what they considered clever taunts.

"Hey chump!"

"What are you Mork from Ork?"

I drove away before I got into another altercation I would lose.

The next morning I was supposed to meet Ben at Xerox where he was going to show me how he was tweaking this laser printer so the pages would look like they came straight out of a publishing house. But I was still in so much pain that I headed to the doctor for X-rays instead. I thought Peggy broke two of my metatarsals. The X-rays came back negative, but the doctor gave me painkillers anyway. I spent the next few days staggering around in a codeine haze, searching for Chia Pets in the stores. I didn't find any, although I did pick up a couple of more pet rocks, not to mention a couple of heaters for my Italian friends.

That very night I stumbled into Ben Wright's house. He was home for a change. Mostly, Ben acted like a fugitive on the run. Maybe the whispers about him and Sarah were true. I thought I'd catch him in front of a laser printer, tinkering. But instead he had a screwdriver twirling away in a big, boxy phone with no cord. Old restless Ben would drop by Marty Cooper's Illinois office at Motorola like he was stopping into the deli to grab a sandwich. I pointed to the phone.

"Who can you call with that thing?"

"Someone thirty years ahead of me. And guess what? I don't like him."

I shook my head. "So why don't you just smash that thing to bits."

Ben shook his head. "It won't matter. The call's already been made. You oughta know. Once the connection's been made, there's no cutting it."

He put his ear to that big, clunky phone and listened. I laughed. Ben looked like an idiot. "Hey man." I drew very close to him. "Are you O.K.?"

"Not really, but nothing can be done about it." Typical genius. Smart enough to split atoms, dumb enough to choose – of all the world's atoms to split – his own.

I took my favorite pet rock Edison from my pocket and gave it to Ben. He didn't seem to appreciate the gift. Maybe he would've preferred a chia pet.

* * *

I looked up the Chia Pet on Wikipedia and discovered that the first truly successful pet wasn't until 1982 when the ram was widely marketed. Old Peggy Murphy must have really been on the ground floor on this one (the pet was trademarked not a year earlier). July 25, 1978 was the day the first test tube baby, Louise Joy Brown, came into the world. The date's connection to Pet Rocks and Chia Pets was beyond my understanding, but I kept my distance from high heeled girls for quite some time after reading the account.

I took out the C Volume from the *Encyclopedia Britannica* Levon left for the Joan and me to look up Marty Cooper. However scattered was the nature of Ben's genius, Marty Cooper was the polar opposite as he focused on that damn cell phone for twenty years. Certainly right now I was receiving calls from the past, but the reception was all static, like I was picking up little pieces of Ben Wright, who had either invented my family's legacy or destroyed it.

18

THE FUTURE SANITATION WORKERS OF AMERICA

Simply, we saw our future in collecting trash. We did not want to go to college. We did not want to leave the gossip—who dyes his hair, who drinks two bottles of wine a night, who has a new inflatable man each month (and whose inflatable man is ultimately deflated and disposed of)? The information on the trash network is so much better than Facebook. We see strange couples sneak out in the early glacial morning. We know which owners don't pick up after their dogs. We've seen many a break-up from the collapsed boxes of memories. We know who got 3-D TVs and which phones, I-Pads, security systems, even what models and colors of toilet bowls (Glacial Bay gray) were installed in the Murphy house. We get to see people in their slippers and robes, shrouded in white hoods and black caps, occasionally if we're terribly unlucky, in their underwear. We watch them walk and jog and sprint and bike and skateboard and scooter by and behind us. We get to see what people eat (the Chinese food and the pizza) and what they don't (cabbage).

Lee Lee, Louie, and I spoke to Big Bill Hannah of our plans to continue on next year. He reminded us of the miserable pick-ups in the pouring rain. On those wet days, especially those frigid, bone-bending January ones, the pails weighed double, and, much worse, the cardboard boxes collapsed and the stinking, soupy debris drooped in uncollectable sodden blobs. Even though I scooped up this slop with thick latex gloves, the slime oozed into my palms like spider guts. Those rainy days were not the greatest, but they didn't happen *too* often.

Then Big Bill pointed to our cuts, scratches, scrapes and bruises. We shrugged. Big Bill then resorted to one of his stories, this one about a reporter, Murray Maslin, from *The Herald* who had been searching in the late nineties for the answer to the lost trash. One day, Maslin seemed to have finally discovered the secret. "All Murray said to me," Bill told us, "was 'tricky little devil.' A few days later, Murray was found dead in his house. The police ruled it a botched robbery, but I have strong suspicions it might have been something else. I can tell you from all my years in waste management, trash is a very rough business."

I twisted my mouth a little. "Are you trying to scare us, Bill?"

"Three times over the past dozen years state officials have shown up with a search warrant at my house," he said matter-of-factly. "I asked them why and they said, 'You know why.' I didn't know why, except that Mayor Heine liked it that way. They turned over my mattress like it had a treasure map for lost garbage pasted to its underside. They've lifted my rugs and rummaged through my files. As I said, it's a rough business."

I smiled. "I could see why they'd investigate you."

"Why is that my good man?"

"You're the perfect surprise villain." Bill looked puzzled.

"That would be a great story." I smiled at him again, this time enigmatically. "Who had a bigger motive to hide all that trash than you? After the scandal hit, you became head of sanitation, and you got the village residents to mistrust your sworn enemy, Mayor Heine, who come to think of it, seems to be your only enemy in the entire universe. It's a wonderful plan. It'd make a damn fine book too. It must be you or the story won't be half as good."

"I am sorry to break this to you," answered a very poised Bill, "but the story is never really that good."

I smiled again and this time Louie joined in. Even Lee Lee moved her lips a little as if she considered the possibility of looking amused. Louie nodded at me. "Look at him," nudging his head now to Big Bill, "cool as a cucumber, like he hadn't a care in the world."

"That's what makes it even better," I said. "Nobody suspects good ole Big Bill Hannah, servant of the people, a man of charm and impeccable manners, who is the very standard of what an upstanding citizen of Frick Village should be. That would turn the story right around, wouldn't it? Everyone suspects the oily, creepy mayor, but all the while, Big Bill's hoarding all our trash. You call me the Mongo Master, but you are the true Mongo King. It would make a great movie."

"Unfortunately," Bill said with some sadness, "the trash business, especially here in Frick, doesn't make for a good movie or story or anything else. The story, like the garbage it houses, just sits there piling up in our memories. And you, my good progenies of our fair village, carry the weight of that legacy. It's a much heavier burden than you realize. You're all excited because you've been given a two-month reprieve, a last minute stay of execution. Don't be."

"So you *are* trying to scare us."

"No, my lads and lass. I just don't want you to be too romantic about all this garbage. It wasn't long ago when you were just junior flips getting your shins mutilated. You're strong and your backs have not yet been gnarled and bent into question marks by carrying the heavy loads every day." When we started to answer, Bill reminded us that even Jesus, Pedro and Pablo walked around like old men after ten years at this job. Bill shook his head at all the attention we were receiving. "You guys have become rock stars. I can't figure it out."

We could all see that Bill was struggling to say what he wanted to. Louie clamped him on the shoulder and asked, "What's bothering you, Bill?"

"I don't want to scare you guys. I just want to let you know that there's more buried in Frick's trash than meets the eye, and I care about you enough to not want you to be dragged down in the mire."

Louie and I chuckled confidently, and Lee Lee played a jig that I'm sure would have made her mother faint in embarrassment. We stomped about raucously in what a generous soul might call a dance.

We were invincible.

* * *

Except for food and the occasional pair of jeans, I made my first major purchase since my mom died. It was a baker's dozen of Chia Pets, plus they threw in a Chia Guy for free. Ever since I read Gallagher's entry, I wanted a few of those for myself and thought I might someday present one to Peggy Murphy. She would have no idea how I knew, which would make the gift worth giving. I was sprinkling them with water when Lee Lee called.

"Can you come over?" she asked.

"Sure."

"Can you make sure your car's completely empty?"

I learned with Lee Lee, you don't ask why. Just say "Sure" and show up with your car empty.

Stepping through the front door, I walked into another country. Noticing the line of shoes on the yellow side mat, I added mine to the collection. The living room had Buddhas and the kitchen had noodles. I wanted to look around at the rich reds and golds and the vases with floral prints. I was hoping Lee Lee would give me a tour, but instead she handed me a big black plastic bag.

Why hadn't I considered that when Lee Lee called for me, it was for a rubbish run? This time instead of the streets of Frick Village, it was the halls of the Lee household.

I opened the bag so she could drop in her garbage. She didn't. Instead, she handed me her papers and looked into my eyes, hers were wet and sparkly. I wanted to believe they were eyes of romance, but I knew they were searching for something cleaner. She could not rid herself of all her work, but she *could* hand it to me so I could dispose of it.

I was reluctantly obedient. If she had called Louie, he would've already tossed a dozen black bags out to the curb and would've been eying the Ming vases next. In contrast, I gave every item she handed me a "once-over" before I tossed it in the black bag. One, a hundred-page science paper, was entitled "Concomitant Protease Inhibitor Salivary Cortisol Polyvinylamine Grafted Electrospun Polyacrylonitrile Membranes for Cr(VI) Adsorption in 3T3-L1 Adipocytes and OXPHOS Gene Expression and the Effects of Duration on Ion Currents."

I didn't throw that mouthful of brain pain right in. "Hey, isn't this your Intel Project?" I asked, rolling up the document and rapping it on her impossibly straight, shiny, black hair.

"Yes."

"And weren't you named a semi-finalist for the project?"

"Yes."

"And you want me to throw it away?"

"Well, Intel has it, and it's up in the Cloud. Don't worry, I'm only giving you hard copies. Everything I really value is up in the Cloud."

"And what if you can't access the Cloud? What if the Cloud bursts or floats away?" I imagined Louie staying up nights trying to figure out how he could stuff the Cloud into the compactor. "What if everything you've done, all your hard work, is irretrievable?"

"I have no other choice. I've done too much. It can't stay here. I feel too cluttered. I can't think clearly anymore. It's the Cloud or nowhere, and if I can't get it from the Cloud, that will just be too bad. I don't have any other choice."

After that, she sorted and handed stacks of paper to me. I dumped, all in silence. I was afraid to ask where the harmonica was that I dropped into her hands months ago. I hoped she didn't discard it so casually, and I hoped she didn't cling onto it either. I gave her the harmonica, still in its original box, so it'd no longer be my burden, a gift that reminded me how rarely I knew what to do with what I'd been given.

When I dragged the trash out of the house, I felt like I was carrying body bags. As I shuffled my shoes on and off, I didn't need Lee Lee to explain that her mother would be devastated to watch her eighteen years of parenting – parenting entranced by the intense discipline of love – tossed out on the curb. I'm glad she told me to empty the car. Lee Lee's labors stuffed the trunk, the entire back seat and floor, plus the front passenger seat. When every scrap of her past appeared to have been cleared out, Lee Lee took me to her room. On her long wall, where most teenage girls would have posters of kittens and boy bands, Lee Lee had a huge white board. I could see from the smudgy shadows it had been written on and erased countless times. Yet in deep, dark, permanent marker sat a final layer of ninety-six boxes, eight across and twelve long. Inside were a series of symbols and icons. I recognized some: music notes, fractals, vectors, Ying-Yang, Phi, Chi, and Z.

"Is this your schedule?" I ventured.

"Yes. Get it out of here."

After studying it for a couple of minutes, I confessed I couldn't understand it.

"Yeah, I can't either."

I was going to immediately call her a liar, but she looked too gravely serious for that. "You did understand it once though, didn't you?'

"Once."

I kept staring at the dense and confusing board, feeling a hallucination either coming on or already arriving. Breaking the trance, Lee Lee shoved in front of my snout a little white board, no bigger than a standard sheet of paper, and said, "This is what I understand now." What were once ninety-six boxes had been distilled to eight: they said A.P. Physics C, A.P. Calc BC, A.P. Lit, A.P. Span., A.P. Gov., Violin, Fencing, Garbage.

Before Lee Lee became confused, she was taking all kinds of additional upper-level courses at the local college. As Pulaski explained to me, "Ben Wright High ran out of knowledge here for Lee Lee." Now with her acceptance to Harvard, Princeton and a couple of other Ivys in her pocket, she struggled to scratch her way back to the superhuman existence of her previous 17 years. I wondered what this little white board would look like a month or a year from now. As I put my shoes on for the final time and slung the mighty white board onto my back, Lee Lee offered me something that appeared to be a smile of gratitude and promised to see me on the truck tomorrow. She even pointed to her new little streamlined whiteboard as confirmation. I knew someone of Lee Lee's caliber would only have so much time for trash in her life.

I hoisted the big white board over my shoulder like I was Atlas carrying the world.

Even though I put it in the backseat above the trash bags, I found I could not throw away Lee Lee's big board as I did everything else. I couldn't understand a quarter of it, but I could appreciate it as a testament to just how much one smart, endlessly curious teenager could squeeze into any given day, week, month or year. I gave the board an honored spot in my studio, but decided like everything I bought home, I couldn't just let it be. My Chia Pets were sprouting nicely. I took a hammer and screwdriver to them and cracked them open. Then I spread the chia fronds and tendrils all about the board.

I wanted the Chia jungle to slowly swallow up the board. I wanted Lee Lee's board to live on as a relic, like those Mayan calendars. Maybe someday the person smart enough to recognize what lay beneath the shaggy artifice would have the ability to decode her chart. I took out a knife to make one further addition to the piece, carving the name Lee Lee into the wooden frame.

Like everything else I had created, I knew most of the thought and effort had come from a place other than my hand.

In this case, I knew it would be particularly ungracious of me not to acknowledge the creator behind my façade. Each day that I watered the board, I would further shroud its memory from me, yet at least I didn't crush it in the compactor and send it off to be rendered in ashes.

19

THE DIARY OF LEVON GALLAGHER: ROCKY ENDING

January 28, 1986

Dennis Alford would not lay off the Rock Hudson jokes and the bar was laughing right along with him. I was not. Too bad, I had been in a wonderful mood. I was just on my sixth New Coke, the most delicious beverage in the world. The public, though, they hated it. All my buddies at the Frickin' Thirsty Saloon would only mix Coca Cola Classic into their rum or whiskey. They didn't see the future like I did. New Coke had the right jolt of caffeine, the taste was more humble, and it wasn't so damn familiar.

Dennis Alford was totally messing with my New World buzz. He slapped me on the shoulder with the same meathooks he once used to rip of quarterback heads. He thought he had funny things to say about Rock Hudson. He was one of those big, rough guys who demanded laughter from his audience. Would you like to laugh tonight or spit up blood tomorrow? Dennis had just finished his geographical gay jokes about the fallen actor ("I feel sorry for Rock Hudson, but all his good friends are behind him"). He moved onto what I can only call a transportation theme. He goaded me to the point that even a strategic sip of New Coke wasn't enough to stabilize my spleen.

"Hey Gallagher," here he goes again, "Why was Rock Hudson's car insurance so expensive?" I gripped the glass of New Coke tightly and slurped. "Because he got rammed in the rear too many times, huh-huh-huh." The whole Frickin' Thirsty Saloon roared. Few could resist Alford's cavernous chuckles. They were so impossibly bottomless that I was convinced his testicles hung to the floor. "Hey, Gallagher," he called. I didn't answer. "What do you call Rock Hudson in a wheelchair?" More queer locomotion jests. "Roll-Aids, huh-huh-huh."

They all laughed. I thought of attacking. I had punched many a big boy and have dearly paid for my decisions. Dennis Alford had four inches and 50 pounds on any of them. He could make a grizzly climb up a tree. I thought about how much New Coke I could buy very cheaply and store away in my bomb shelter. Alford would have his taste of Coca Cola Classic and be incinerated. My New Coke and I would live on. Alford until that time would torture me with rotten queer jokes. Did I mention that Rock Hudson was my favorite actor? Much better than John Wayne. That's for another time.

"Hey Gallagher," bellowed the loud mountainous bastard, "What's the difference between Rock Hudson and Ellis Island? Ellis Island is *ferry* terminal, huh-huh-huh." I felt it coming. I waited for the laughter to subside and tried to reason with Dennis.

"Alford. You know what was great about Rock Hudson?" Alford didn't respond, just stared at me. "He showed us all in the movies that we could be happily married."

"Of course he did," he yelled, pointing a finger at me. "Only a fag could pull that off." I went after him with both fists. He grabbed them in his big paws and my arms were stifled by his strength, so I tried to kick him. He pushed down my leg with his knee and the next thing I know he's stepping on both my feet with his big sneakers. He held me like that with my limbs locked up for a couple of minutes laughing with his friends while I struggled and cursed. I would've preferred that he broke my jaw.

I headed out to my car only to hear, "Hey Levon, wait up," behind me. It was Joan in tight jeans and a small top.

"What the hell are doing here?"

"Same as you, drinking."

"Drinking? How'd you get in? What are you eighteen?"

"Something like that. Girls tend to get in and drink free too."

Sure girls who looked like Joan did tend to get into the Frickin' Thirsty despite the 21-year-old drinking age. That didn't prevent me from scowling at her, like a good uncle should. "I hope you didn't see that nonsense."

"What? You with Alford. That was great."

"Yeah, if you like watching me being humiliated.'

"Nah, you were the only decent person in the saloon with any guts." Her tone approached pride.

I could've explained to her that what she

thought was bravery was just my inability to control myself. But I liked the way she was looking at me, and with the night I had, I could use a little idolization. Joan possessed an idealism long beaten out of me. She had her entire future mapped out. First law school, of all things. Then she'd clean up the world.

She had the family blood. Artie did some environmental advocacy work. Hell, the way he got to the Reps in the House to push through his Superfund bill was masterful. With Artie, it was personal. The only reason he started that Superfund fight twenty years ago was that the Mavella's poisoned backyard killed his mimosa tree. Since then, he's just gone back to making killings off of Ben Wright investments. Joan's different. With Joan, it's global. She would battle someone over a twig in Ethiopia, and unlike her father, she'd smile sweetly as she hoodwinked a military strongman to scatter seeds in the soil.

As I drove Joan home, I asked her about Sarah. Her answer of "the Same" told me her mother was still lost and spiraling downward. "And your Dad?"

"Always angry."

"Yeah," I told her. "Men of our age tend to get that way."

"Don't I know it," she said. "But why?"

"This is about the time when you sit down and add up the mistakes in your life, and then relive them all as you do a second counting, unable to believe how much you screwed up."

"But you're a lot younger than my Dad," she said with enough flirtation for me to understand Joan was growing up in that mess of a household a little too quickly.

"Yeah, but you see, you're not the only one

advanced for your age."

The following day I headed out to do my Off-To-Work column at a Buddhist Monastery and got many letters from an unenlightened public who questioned whether I was actually working. Instead of meditating, I spent the entire retreat thinking about Dennis Alford. Dennis Alford wasn't laughing for long.

* * *

I guess I find it quite characteristic that this, ahem, disagreement, didn't occur on a day that would make sense, like October 2, 1985, the day of Rock Hudson's death. Instead, it marked the Space Shuttle Challenger breaking up in the atmosphere, killing all seven of its crew members. I noodled around on Google looking for some sort of connection, ultimately finding the only commonality between Rock Hudson and the astronauts, teacher Christa McAuliffe in particular, was tasteless jokes about them. If Alford had served up any of those gems about the space shuttle disaster, Levon gave no such mention.

Then I googled Dennis Alford. I found about eight Dennis Alfords before I read this item in *The Herald* from April 12, 1986.

Former Jet Found Dead

Dennis "No End" Alford, who played for the Jets for seven years, was found dead last night in an abandoned Frick lot. Police discovered his body with two gunshot wounds to his chest. Alford, 37, had been retired the past nine years after a series of knee injuries slowed him considerably. Famous for his huge frame, Alford played defensive end and gained his

nickname for his ability to stuff the run. "He
was called No End," said his coach Sandy "Short
Order" Cook, "because nothing could get by his
end. When he was out there, he seemed to take
up half the field." Police are investigating
the circumstances of his death.

That was all. I searched another hour and a half for follow-ups and found nothing. You'd think "No End" would deserve more coverage than that. I was so frustrated that I researched New Coke for another hour just to read something. Who knows what I was looking for? Some hint that the beverage cultivated homicidal tendencies? No such luck. Yet, from what I could gather, Levon might have been the only person on the planet who preferred New Coke over the original. Did that make him a bad person?

Since this entry was the first that led to death, I couldn't help but connect it to the story Levon told me very late one night when I was just a teen. That was a helluva story, but not worth telling you about until I get to hear what else Levon had to say. In that story, Levon did something either terribly noble or just terrible. Even in his encounter with the Joan, I was not sure if he was completely noble. The rest of the disk would have to be combed over before I'd know. That will take some time since I had a good dose of reality to deal with first.

20

THE LOYALTY AGREEMENT

Let's see what's on the menu today. We've got a small box of Christmas angels. Each one probably had topped a tree for a year or two. Christmas can be a very ruthless business you know. We've got firewood, all beautifully split and ready to burn – obviously easier to toss than to give away. We've got six windows. I look at them and see only pane. We've got the rubble of a nasty divorce which I let Louie take care of, he being much better at disposing of emotional trash than I am. We've got a painting that's signed in intensely wild scrawl: Vincent. I risk that it's not a Van Gogh and let it sleep with the angels. We got Cindy Stevens rummaging through big cardboard boxes in search of God-knows-what. And we've got horrid remnants of a corn beef and cabbage meal, one with enough distance between cooking and disposal to let every noxious gas within its miserable Irish soul roil and release its belching song.

After we pulled into the resource recovery plant and Big Bill headed off on his rounds, we found Mayor Heine, smiling in his best suit, waiting for us in the trailer. He brought an aide with him, who immediately came up to shake our smelly, stinky hands as the mayor bellowed a hearty, but distant "Congratulations." I felt sorry for that aide, the poor bastard. He had to act like he hadn't been contaminated by touching us, like he didn't want desperately to power-wash his hands with bleach, though I'm pretty sure Mayor Heine's hands are a lot more soiled than mine.

Louie, who had encountered Heine less and therefore was less troubled by his presence, asked, "Congratulations for what?"

"Well, you're all going to be stars."

"How?" Louie was confused. "What?"

"I just signed with the Genuine TV network a deal for you guys to be featured in a new reality television show."

"Yeah," said Louie, "what's it called?"

"Generation Dementia." Lee Lee and I glanced at each other, immediately realizing that nothing good could come from this show. "See, it's named after you guys."

"What do we have to do?" asked Louie.

"That's the beauty of it." Heine had clearly been waiting for this question. I had never seen the man happier, even more gleeful than when he canned the Mexicans, and if I knew one thing about Heine, it was that he fired people with the kind of relish he otherwise reserved for eating knockwurst. "You just have to do what you've already been doing. You just pick up garbage and the cameras will do the rest."

We, Generation Dementia, had been collectively suckled and nourished by reality shows since the moment we left the womb. Louie, Lee Lee and I said nothing and just glanced back from the one to another, wondering how much else the show would demand from us. I remembered what Max told me months ago about Heine's connection to data mining, and wondered what the mayor already knew about each of us.

We politely thanked Mayor Heine, who looked terribly disappointed by our absence of enthusiasm. We knew it was unwise to say anything until we consulted Big Bill. We couldn't miss the fact that the mayor only appeared to us in our boss's absence and must've known that Big Bill spent Fridays testing air emissions from the plant.

As he drove away, Heine yelled from his car, "You're all going to be stars."

I muttered to Lee Lee and Louie, "Not if we can help it."

We waited in Big Bill's office until the late afternoon before he arrived. When we told him of the reality TV show, he didn't seem too concerned. As he grabbed a soda from his minifridge, Big Bill explained to us that "The Mayor can't put you on the reality television show unless you signed a loyalty agreement, which I'm certain you didn't do, my good young prodigies."

We all started fidgeting then. We each explained, somewhat haltingly, that upon our hiring the mayor had invited us individually to his office to personally thank us for our service to Frick Village and to have us sign some standard paperwork. Big Bill rolled his eyes, took a slug of soda, and said, "My good whipper snappers, no wonder our fine friend Pulaski calls you 'those dumb bastards of Generation Dementia'." I wanted to remind Big Bill that Lee Lee and I had been accepted to top universities, but I didn't think he would buy that argument any more than he did my claim last week that whiffle ball bats would someday be as treasured as Revolutionary War muskets. Big Bill paused a moment to see if we would speak as to confirm his suspicions about us. We demonstrated uncharacteristic restraint. "Well, that means you're going to have to either quit or be part of the show."

"We are not going to quit," said Louie. Lee Lee and I nodded in agreement.

"Then you'll have the opportunity that every other student in the school would want except you three."

"Does that make us stupid?"

"Unfortunately, it doesn't. It almost forces me to shower you with compliments, my good lads and lasses." Of course, Big Bill said not another word.

As I returned back home and opened the front door, I heard the echo of the Joan asking me if I had taken out the trash. She was no dumbbell. Why was it that the only time I could hear her voice was to tell me something so ordinary and domestic that it meant nothing to me at all? I knew the dreary rituals would continue at my next stop. To feel a little less violated, I had gotten into the habit of cleaning myself up before I slipped into the bathroom, dreading what I'd face in there. I would first go to the kitchen sink and pour water over my head from a container that previously held wanton soup. With my hair all slicked back, I entered the bathroom to confront the familiar video spooling before my eyes. I again told myself that my business becoming everybody's business was only a hallucination, which comforted me a little. I searched for cameras around the bowl and knew soon lenses would find their way into other crevices of my life.

That evening I took out a laptop that appeared yesterday on Eva's curb. I'd been waiting for one for months, and I wondered if Eva had left it as a peace offering. Part of me wanted to open it, especially since the aromas of coffee and tobacco indicated that the machine had indeed belonged to her and not her straitlaced parents. That shameful urge pushed me to a better idea. In the past month away from Eva, I had spent sleepless nights building a platform and surrounding it with carved Styrofoam that I had carefully covered with Nonna D'Antonio's abandoned, but perfectly clean, lace curtains. It took me five long nights to make a reasonable approximation of a cloud. Above it, I placed the open laptop. Against its back sat a metal rack, holding file folders renamed "Private," "Confidential," "Miscellaneous Missteps," "Secrets," "Personal," and other intimate headings. I had never been so careful with a mashup and the many hours of intense effort and concentration left me so lightheaded that I sprawled out on the garage floor next to that laptop cloud.

My eyes watered and I glazed over into a memory from 8th grade. Lifting up his boxing gloves, Grandpa Artie growled, "Come at me." I took a swing. I saw him duck, but barely spotted Artie's right to my jaw that dropped me. "Counterpunch," he said. "That's the key to boxing boy."

My braces gouged into my cheek and blood dripped from my mouth. I staggered back up before Artie could tell me. I understood that there was no better time to ask Artie about my father than when I was bloodied and dazed. "Is my dad a hacker?"

"What?" Artie looked confused enough by my question that I caught him in the ribs. Although he oomphed with something like surprised pain, Artie responded with a shot to my kidney that sent me down without thoughts of rising.

Lying on my back, I gained enough wind to ask again, "Is my dad a hacker?"

"No," he laughed at the absurdity of the question. "He liked playing video games. He didn't do anything bad with them." Artie seemed relieved that for a change he didn't have to spew black and foul descriptions about my father to me.

"Isn't the FBI after him?" I asked.

"Why?"

"For trying to protect people's identities."

Artie frowned and winced with pity. "Hash, you poor

bastard. Your father never did anything with his life. He wasn't a hacker. He didn't hurt people. He didn't help people."

Clearly, I was better off hallucinating than remembering my boxing matches with Artie.

The spell of the memory broken, I looked about my garage and spotted the eleven half-filled cans of polyurethane I'd gathered off the curbs. Then I carefully coated and recoated the piece next to me. I spent long hours of delicate application, making sure the lace clouds and the file folders remained in just the right place. I had never been more patient with a mashup than with what I now called "Secrets among the Clouds." If the work expressed that nothing private goes away forever anymore, I liked knowing at least Eva's laptop could no longer be physically violated.

* * *

Every day when I got done with the trash run and filtered into Pulaski's office to fill out the log, Eva found a way of passing by, looking nervous and awkward, words I wouldn't usually use to describe her. She wrote me on Facebook too, and said she would like to see me. I wrote her that "I'm busy right now hiring a cleaning lady."

Then she wrote again.

And again.

I tried to figure out whether I was still hurt or just acting like I was hurt (this whole reality TV stuff was messing a bit with my perspective). When I considered the risk Eva took and the gesture of trust she offered me in leaving out the laptop, I recognized a pettiness within me worthy of Levon Gallagher. I finally wrote back, "You can come by at eight tonight if you're available."

I heard her car pull up at 7:53. Standing inconspicuously in the hazy, brisk moonlight so that I had to crook my neck along the window sill to catch her silhouette, she smoked until 7:59 and knocked at my door at 8:00. We greeted each other. Her make-up couldn't hide how tired and haggard she looked. I wondered whether she was back on drugs. "You alright?"

"Yeah," she said, "I've been reading through Facebook, going through the couple of years of people's lives when I was in a fog." This was her form of saying hello. I think the constant writing and walking by me were her forms of apology. "I read the news and the Twitter feeds from those times, even watched some of the shows on Netflix, just as a way to get my balance about what I missed." I could tell she really wanted to smoke or something right now. She possessed the rare manners not to noodle around with her phone when she talked to me (I was scrolling on my screens while she spoke), but the absence of anything else to do but look at me and explain was clearly knocking the crap out of her. I was a little surprised about how miserable it made me to see her miserable.

"I was going to make some coffee," I said, "a very large pot. Why don't you come into the kitchen?"

"Great." I could see she was excited about the prospect of coffee. "I think the kitchen is the best room for me here anyway." I had filled the water tank and dropped three heaping tablespoons of my strongest coffee (Café Bustelo) into the filter. Eva sat on a stool and held her two hands cupped like she already cradled a mug in them. "As I was saying, I was reading through all my friend's Facebooks and I completely caught up on Jen Woods. I didn't know she was such a wreck. By the way, you should try scanning through five or six years of somebody's Facebook account. It's like reading a tell-all memoir. Anyway, I finally got up to the last couple of weeks in Jen's life and she had a lot to say about The Calling. Did you know she wrote about it?"

"No, I don't spend a lot of time on Facebook. What'd she say, that I was a dope and that she put it out in the trash?"

"No, no, she said you were a sweetheart and she had to give it back to you, so you could get in touch with someone else who really needed it."

"So, she really didn't need it."

"She did, but she saw it as something that should be passed around. So I thought I'd tell you that, just in case a cleaning lady does something stupid like throws it out. That would mean she has the same rotten taste as your personal chef."

"Nah, my chef can tell the difference between a hot dog and a filet mignon. It's just her carving knife is just a little sharper than I'm used to." Knowing that she was not one to wait for the whole pot to brew, I stuck a cup onto the heating coil, let it drip until it was three-quarters full, and handed her the cup. Eva looked like the happiest woman on the planet. "Come into the garage. I want to show you something." She followed, refusing to let go of the cup.

I led her to the sculpted clay head, which looked quite intensely human, certainly more alive than my father had been to me. "I still have to work a lot on the eyebrows. I seem to make them either too bushy or just strange bumpy ridges on the forehead."

"That's really something." I could tell Eva was genuinely relieved it wasn't horrible, so she wouldn't be left either lying to me or cutting my ego into crudités.

I explained how I was going to position it in the microwave for the Carnival Attendant and even showed her my first crack at illuminating the interior, using low wattage bulbs Ben Wright designed to ground the piece a local lore. "Right now, the shadows are in the wrong places. But I'll take my time and get it right." Then I showed her how from old planks I'd gathered I was designing a grandfather clock frame, featuring the phones of The Calling. "The rotary will serve as the clock face. I will connect its receiver above by the chord to the big old cell phone, which will serve as the pendulum."

"So you are playing with the interaction between time and communication. Pretty good stuff. Too bad no one leaves a grandfather clock on the curb."

"That's one thing I haven't seen."

"It's an awful lot of work for you."

"Sure as hell is." I think I almost sounded proud.

Then she spotted "Secrets among the Clouds." Eva's recognition of her laptop made me squirm.

I looked into her eyes. "As you know, I'd been looking for a laptop, so I'm glad you left it. I promise that I never turned it on." Eva's nod told me she trusted me. The three coats of polyurethane gave the piece a uniform sheen of protection. "And as you can see, it can never be turned on again."

"Your cloud is beautiful. It puffs and billows like you could float on it."

"Well, someone once told me a little beauty might not be a bad thing for a work of art."

"Can I have another cup of coffee?" Eva certainly wanted a cup of coffee, but I also could tell she wanted to get out of the garage before she said something that upset me (I knew Eva well enough to understand she couldn't control what she said). Back in the safety of the kitchen, she asked, "So tell me about the new reality series, Mr. Celebrity. The mayor is very excited about it. He took a lot of pictures with the Generation Dementia producers."

"Wonderful. Maybe they'll spend more time filming him

than us."

"I don't think so, but I think he's getting a mighty big paycheck in return."

"What, for his campaign?"

"No, he held a big press conference about how the added revenue would serve to build a Frick Village for the next millennium. That last part sound familiar?"

I thought for a moment. "That website, No Garbage."

"No, not No Garbage. That's what I thought it was first. It's Garbage Free."

"Oh, yeah, that stupid name. Our planet will be garbage free only after the apocalypse, and you know what, when that happens, the whole planet will be garbage. So what does Garbage Free have to do with the new reality show?"

"I'm not sure. It's hard to get near his office when he meets about it. I'm supposed to be limited to campaign work." Then she smiled at me. "Good thing the coffee urn is right outside his door."

"So you *do* know something."

"Well, I've overhead one of the reps talking about robotic arms and financing for trucks."

"They wouldn't have trucks if they weren't hauling trash, so that Garbage Free is bullshit, huh."

"Could be."

"Could you break into his office and get some better information?" Eva seemed like the type of person who wasn't too concerned about laws.

"When I get back *into* the office. This week and next I'm out visiting the town field operatives with Lanny, Heine's campaign advisor."

"That sounds painful."

"A little bit." She looked like she was, for once, understating her misery. She finished her coffee and I poured her more. "Let's talk about something else. This reality show could be a very exciting opportunity. Everyone in the village is talking about it."

"That's only because Lee Lee's playing in the background," I said.

She frowned with my mentioning of Lee Lee. "Oh always that Lee Lee playing in the background. I'd prefer Lee Lee to be playing at Carnegie Hall or even better the Sydney Opera House." She turned the cup over, smiling, signaling to the pot. "Yes, I think I'd like her best playing in Australia."

"Why?"

"She's the type of girl who could distract you."

"And you are?"

"The type of girl who leaves you with an empty can of coffee."

"Maybe I can use it for one of my pieces. I can title it Eva's Vices."

"You're going to need a whole other garage to complete that work." I poured her another coffee and poured myself a first cup. "Good idea," she pointed at the pot, "before it's all gone."

"Let me ask you something, Eva."

"Go ahead."

"Would you like to be a TV star?"

"Let's put it this way. They tried to put cameras in front of me for the reality show Unglued Teens when I was in rehab."

"What'd you do?"

"I ran up and threw a towel at the lens whenever I saw them filming near me. I carried a lot of towels. At first, they thought they could weave my attacks into the plot line. But once I got my hands on black spray paint and started ruining their lenses, I was moved to another ward."

"I could see why they would want you. You really would've been a star."

"I know I tend to overstate things, but I think if they would've put me on the show, I'd've killed myself by now."

"From embarrassment?"

"No, much worse. I was trying to figure things out. I don't know how you can ever be yourself with a camera around." She swiped her phone a few times and handed it to me. A gaunt-faced Eva with black rings below her eyes stared at me. "I call her Junkie Eva. I deleted her but someone on Facebook always brings her back. I can't get rid of her, even though I'm pretty sure I killed her off. You have to be ready, Hash." She turned her phone on its side, played with the camera function, and started framing me.

"Knock that off."

"Yeah. Don't tell me. Tell the paparazzi."

"I'm not letting them into my house."

"Not even your kitchen?"

"Not even my trash can."

"Then you'd better figure out what you're going to do about this reality show." She dropped the camera phone in her purse, gave me a kiss on the lips that could be interpreted by the optimistic as passionate and by the cynical as mocking, and headed out the door.

"Hey," I yelled, "do you always have to piss me off just before you walk out?" The air was scented with frozen cardboard boxes.

"Thanks for the coffee," she said as she lit a cigarette in the driver's seat.

"I hope it keeps you up all night."

"Are you kidding," she said as she drove away, "I'm already asleep."

Of course, I wasn't asleep. I stayed up all night reading Emails.

From the February 14 Trash Folder

Are you sure you want to permanently delete all the items and subfolders in the Deleted Items Folder?

The Daily Bread from Reverend Alexander Burr

The Mayor of Frick Village, Herman Heine, is offering to collect all cell phones from residents not only in his village but from everywhere around the world. "We don't want anyone to be chained to a phone who wants to be set free." He's even offering a case of Frick Village Water for each phone. I had a heartfelt conversation with Mayor Heine who confessed to me that he still indeed owns a cell phone. He claims he holds onto the phone in honor of one of its inventors, that overly praised Frick native Ben Wright. I hoped the Mayor would realize that Mr. Wright in one of the reasons Frick has been so cursed. And yet sometimes change demands a man who cannot renounce his own sins to lead others toward a cleansing. Yes, I would have preferred he had heeded Matthew who in 7:5 advised removing the log from your own eye so as to see clearly enough to take the speck from your brother's eye. The Mayor may be buried under the weight of too many possessions to free himself (I even hear, heaven forbid, that a Reality Show is coming to the village), but he has offered hope to others. I once heard Mayor Heine say, as he held his I-Phone, that he has "the whole world in his hands." I know a higher power who truly has the whole world in His hands. However, you cannot grasp His palm if you're clutching your phone.

The Epic Life of Selena Omaha

So are you ready for the inside scoop about what's popping in Frick Village?

That boy Hash O'Connell. Tell me you haven't seen him on

the truck with those big muscles and big words. He's definitely the hottest, most insanely talked about boy toy in Frick. The Hashtag is trending and what's really amazing is what our homegrown celeb trashman left out in the trash himself.

It's an authentically worn orange Frick Sanitation t-shirt.

I snatched it up at three in the morning and bounced before Mr. Pulaski shuffled by and blew his nose in it. What's amazing is how superbasic it is, and I don't mean superbasic as a dis. No, I mean like it was definitely used for all his hunky work. It even has a big rip by his right collarbone. So sorry thirsty girls, I'm not going to sell it on E-bay. It's mine. I'm putting it under glass and hanging it in my bedroom. Pretty crazy, right? Better luck next time ladies, but you better get up totally early because this sassy girl is ready to rumble.

Never had I been so happy to be so deeply disturbed.

21

REHEARSALS FOR REALITY

Louie was suspended again. He attacked Nonna D'Antonio's lions . . . again.

"What's with you and the lions, Louie?"

He raised his eyebrows mischievously, "It's an Italian thing. You wouldn't understand."

"Is it an Italian thing to always be dangling on the edge?" I picked up a bungee cord that was hooked to a trash lid. The trash lid jumped and danced as I wiggled the cord. Pointing to the lid, I told Louie, "That's you. Always in a state of suspended animation."

"Yeah, at times I like it that way."

"Who am I gonna be stuck with tomorrow then?"

Louie smiled. "Anthony."

Now I understood. "So which part is the Italian thing? Attacking the lions or getting your girlfriend's kid brother into the, ahem," I lifted my fingers to form quotation marks, "waste management, slash, sanitation industry."

"Yes," Louie answered.

While Big Bill in the driver's seat graciously welcomed his

junior flip, I knew from the second house that Anthony was not going to work out. Don't get me wrong. He's a great kid, but he wasn't raised on low class, stinky, rotting, rancid, putrid, oozing garbage. As I have mentioned before, the Gulotta trash is immaculate. Clean, neat, and sanitized, it smells better than most restaurants I've been in (Eva has noted I don't exactly frequent the finer dining establishments).

The warming of the mid-February air didn't help matters. Sure temperatures in the forties did alert the purple crocuses that dotted Frick's yawning lawns, but the odors were also awakened. So when Anthony got a whiff of Peggy Murphy's garbage with her cauliflower and broccoli stems decomposing in a sea of two-week-old tilapia, he reflexively barfed on her grass. He performed no better with Derek Standish's pails, which featured potatoes so decayed they liquefied, a long-forgotten lamb stew, and miserable English cheeses, whose odors apparently disintegrated their plastic wrappers. I'm sure if I pointed out the disco rice, he'd still be retching.

When we reached Alice Harvey with her buckets of dirty diapers and discarded drool rags, I tried to give Anthony a break. He wouldn't hear of it, even though now he sent out hard-earned blobs of bile that he fought nobly to keep down. "I'll do my job." Even Cindy Stevens, as she was dragging what looked like two huge bags of Styrofoam packaging material across the road, shot Anthony a concerned look. At Nonna D'Antonio's, he was dry-heaving over some lost chunks of bracciole. I wonder whether Nonna preferred a defiled lion or a soiled sidewalk.

Afterward, I sat with Anthony at the diner. Although he still looked quite green about the gills, he ordered pancakes and sausage. He pushed the plate to the middle of the table, so he could use his elbows to hold up his head. I got right to the point. "Look, you're finishing physics in 11th grade and are in the highest math you can take at Ben Wright High. You might want to consider engineering instead of waste management."

He looked at me like I'd just told him he had six weeks to live.

"When I was a little boy, my dad would take me to the resource recovery plant," he said, "and we'd watch the smoke come out of the stacks. 'Look,' he would say to me, 'they've elected another pope.' A pope was elected almost every Sunday. He would tell about how when he was young his father would take him to the dumps to, as he would say, 'Feed the seagulls.' It's the place where everything goes eventually."

"Sounds like a graveyard to me."

"Graveyards are also holy places."

I had a strong feeling I wasn't going to win any arguments with Anthony. "Look, you have to consider the realities of the situation. Frankly, you don't have the stomach to do this job."

"I'll prove it to you. I'll make the special run at the Covington house."

The Covingtons generated so much horrible trash that we always saved it as the last thing we did. I didn't know who in God's name they were feeding, but the trout heads, the rotting kale, the feta cheese crumbled across the pails like gaseous, dying snowflakes, so much sloppy, smelly crap, all unbagged (we left warnings of heavy fines; the Covingtons rightly figured we were bluffing).

By the time Anthony jumped down off the truck, he was heaving into this decaying stew. God, it was awful. Between the Covingtons' everyday stinks and Anthony's new vomitus contribution, even my stomach soured. It didn't help that I had to scoop up what looked like a dumpster's full of hospital waste all by myself.

As the truck rumbled away, Anthony barked out an apology.

"That's O.K.," I said sympathetically. I pulled from my pocket two magnets that I'd been given in ninth grade when I won one of those national science contests. Each was a striped red and black horseshoe about the size of my hand. They were stuck together and I'd forgotten how to separate them. I really didn't want to learn that trick again, and I thought there might be something illegal about tossing the magnets away. Anyway, I knew they'd just stick to the side of the truck if I tried to dispose of them on a run. "These are for you," I told Anthony with a generous warmth that indicated I may be giving him my finest precious metals. Anthony looked a bit glassy-eyed as he accepted them with an innocent, sweet gratitude. I was hoping he was thinking less about the trash run and more about separating the magnets. Hell, it's not every day you're there to witness someone's dreams being crushed. "How are you feeling?"

"That's the funny thing," said Anthony, "I feel wonderful. Like I've just cleansed my soul or something."

"Maybe I should give paid tours on the truck?"

Anthony grinned. "Yeah, you could call it Frick Village's Spiritual Spa Treatment."

"You could be the spokesman."

"I will be more than the spokesman. I'll be the president."

"At least you've found a new dream."

* * *

We met our director. He told me his name was "Psycho." I thought he should have been named "Trying too hard," but I didn't want to get off on the wrong foot. I carefully examined his tattoos. They looked like he hired an interior designer to decorate his body so he could impress the right clientele. Psycho said he loved our work, even though his wry smile told us only the public believed him. He said, "You have a true gift for picking up trash." I believe that was the first time the sentence had ever been uttered in English. Psycho told us he could make us even more special. He had this remarkable way of saying everything with so little sincerity that he seemed strangely believable. Anyone who made such an effort to demonstrate his untrustworthiness inspired faith. He suggested we need to play up the love triangle aspect of the trash runs. Louie explained that while Lee Lee was quite a catch, he gave his heart to Nicole Gulotta. I mentioned that the star-crossed love affair at the curb between Louie and Nicole would make for a wonderful storyline. I'm not sure Psycho properly heard what I was saying, since he suggested that Nicole could be used as a temptation to both Louie and me to stray from Lee Lee. That's when I had to restrain Louie from beating Psycho with a 32-gallon pail. "Now that attack would make some fine footage," I pointed out. Although he grinned in appreciation, Psycho did not seem interested in recording a scene where a charter member of Generation Dementia assaulted the director.

Then Psycho told Lee Lee how much he loved her performances. "I have never seen anyone play violin on a garbage truck so amazingly." Gee, neither have I, though I can't say I have any other classical industrial strength performances to compare it to. I'm sure Psycho was much more of an expert in such matters.

Lee Lee said "Thank you" with what I can only characterize as suspicious gratitude.

"But I think you should expand your horizons."

"Yeah?" Lee Lee seemed to be struggling with politeness.

"I was thinking classical hip-hop."

"What?"

"And your friend over here Hash could do some chillin' beat boxing."

"What?" This time I joined with Lee Lee and said, "How am I supposed to focus on picking up garbage?"

"Oh, you'll be fine. I can see you have a gift for such things."

I was trying to remember what the definition of "gift" was.

Psycho was too busy pitching to notice the building anger within both Lee Lee and me. He was used to saying ridiculous things, used to the anger of his "actors," used to pressing ahead to churn out a show. "Think about how cool it would be to have a hip-hop garbage truck with you guys occasionally bustin a rhyme."

As I glared at Psycho's tattooed neck (a beautiful print, by the way, reminiscent of an argyle sock), I wasn't sure what filled me with such brutal hatred. He was clearly intelligent and at least he didn't pretend he or any of us believed what he was saying. I think the way Psycho spoke didn't help matters. I had a strong suspicion his mission to create a reality TV series would destroy my happiness, a happiness I had not possessed until I stepped onto this truck. Louie scowled at Psycho. Psycho was an impressive physical specimen. He clearly spent many hours at the gym, but his muscles looked like they were much more designed to be beautiful rather than strong, which happened to be the exact opposite of Louie's physical makeup. You throw enough 50-pound pails into the truck, you'll understand. I also knew this muscular, tattooed street hustler of a director Psycho was the type who would immediately press charges. I made sure Louie wasn't going to do anything stupid.

Then Lee Lee twisted her face at Psycho, a reply she usually reserved only for idiots.

I smiled at Psycho and said, "Are you *sure* you don't want to record all this?"

The scriptwriter, who called himself "The Word," sat us down. He didn't wear socks and smiled like a thirtysomething man who eats organic tofu at business lunches and baloney in private moments. "We need to plan out what we are going to say and act out today."

"Act?" Lee Lee asked, touching her hair self-consciously.

"I mean what are you going to do?"

I shrugged my shoulders. "What we always do. Pick up pails, toss the garbage into the truck, hit the compactor, bale the truck, put back pails, and go to the next house."

"Yeah," said the Word. He gave off a no-nonsense vibe as he spoke to us. "But we need a little drama."

Louie looked at me with concern and told the Word, "The best thing about the job is that there is no drama."

"So the drama is hiding."

I chuckled, "So hidden that it doesn't exist."

The Word chuckled back, but much more condescendingly. "Yeah, yeah, when are you two going to fight over Lee Lee?"

"We've been through this with Psycho." Christ, Psycho and the Word (sound like morning radio hosts, don't they?) didn't hear what we were saying, and their names were pissing me off too. I'd hand The Word the last twenty I had in my pocket if he just let me call him Bob. Then, I decided what did I need to give him my twenty for? "Hey Bob, you're trying to manufacture something that's not there."

"My name's not Bob, by the way. It's the Word."

"Oh, sorry about that. You look more like a Bob to me."

"I can see you're hiding something."

"Whatever you say, Bob. But even if I was hiding something, why the hell would I want it to be recorded for an audience?"

"You don't understand. It's what you need to break free."

The Word paused for a moment as he was apparently summoning up a pep talk, one I'm sure he'd given to other non-performing actors in his shows. "Your privacy will pass away. You will give yourself to the greater world." He paused for a moment, like he was summoning up a speech. Then he gave one. "When the completeness of publicity comes, the partiality of privacy will disappear. When I was a child, I talked like a child, I thought like a child, I reasoned like a child. When I was a man, I put the ways of childhood behind me. For now we shall see only a reflection as in a mirror; soon we shall see face to face. Now I know in part; soon I shall know fully, even as I am fully known. You must mature from privacy to publicity." And with that last comment, The Word rested. He sat down. He looked so peaceful that I almost wanted to kiss his pen.

I was trying to figure out what was happening when I saw both Psycho and The Word take out their I-Pads, looking to set up a rehearsal schedule. I didn't understand.

"What the hell is there to rehearse?" asked Louie, who clearly wanted to shove bowling balls right up their asses.

Oh, why bother recounting the conversation. All I know was the next day Psycho had us in a warehouse tooling around in a golf cart through a replica Frick Village, with the streets taped off and mini trash cans at the curbs. Louie and I hoisted the little buckets with our thumbs and trounced around like giants while Lee Lee pretended to run a tiny bow across a hair clip. The Word shook his head disappointedly. "You have yet to leave your childhood behind. Stop hiding behind your private immaturities."

I chuckled. "Look at the size of everything in the place. Do you see anywhere to hide?"

The Word asked whether we were ready for the unexpected that we would encounter on our trash run. Louie explained,

"Sure the trash can get kind of strange, but it's all garbage, so it's all expected."

Psycho looked knowingly at The Word. "I don't think they understand what is happening here."

They were right, we didn't.

22

THE NEWLY PLANTED SHRUB

The next day, on the trash run, with the cameras out, we were administered a healthy dose of the unexpected. That foggy, damp morning, Eddie Jay, who told us he was an award-winning cinematographer, held a camera before us and explained, "Everything will be a close-up. If it ain't a closeup, it ain't real." Eddie told us he started out a lot like we did. Instead of garbage, he worked car accidents, shooting footage. "God, the things I saw would make you puke." With his heavy beard, his clunky boots, and his mighty camera, Eddie didn't exactly blend into the landscape. I had a feeling he could make a racket picking up a cotton ball.

And he was right on top of us. I hoped he might be less annoying than Psycho and the Word, since he had a dramatically less pretentious name, but unfortunately I had to rename him Probe to reflect his intrusive manner. "Don't pay any attention to the camera. Treat it like it's just a newly planted shrub." Easier said than done. Louie, Lee Lee, and I tried to do everything normally, but you can't be normal when Probe shoves into your personal space. Thankfully, we were so used to our daily rhythms that came with the squealing breaks, the banging of the cans across the compactor ledge, and Lee Lee's sweeping, thumping bow work, that we blocked out the camera for quite a while. For a good hour, the run almost seemed normal.

Then at the Mavella house, the Probe was no longer the lone cameraman. There were two more stationary cameras set up on the front lawn of a home that had never left a scrap of trash out on the curb in the entire time of our pickups.

Now an old steel can stood out defiantly. God, it seemed suspicious. Unfortunately, Louie was so excited by the prospect of fresh trash that he rushed over to the can before I could caution him. When Louie popped the lid, the cap shot up in the air and plumes of purple smoke rose from it. Louie jumped back reflexively, "Holy Mother." I should've been concerned for Louie, but I had a sneaky suspicion that I was merely witnessing Psycho and the Word's vision of drama. I stared at Probe, who let out a jeering laugh meant mostly for the audience. Louie frowned at this singed arm hairs.

Across the street from the Mavellas sat a stray and closed can. It was trash that seemed to belong to either nobody or everybody. My first inclination was to take it as the people's trash, although I could feel the stationary cameras boring down on my back and Probe's lens practically in my right nostril. I knew I should not open the pail. It was not my pail to open, but one manufactured for a reality TV show, one written by the Word and situated by a Psycho. Yet opening pails and dumping was my job and I knew if I left that pail untended, I would have it in my head all week. God, I'd have it in my mind for the rest of my life, the way I remember a single mitten I left ten years ago at a playground after falling off the monkey bars.

The planted pail had to be opened, even if I was behaving

like a trained chimp dancing for an organ grinder. I flinched as my fingers touched the tip of the lid. It didn't open on my first timid pass, so I had to yank on the handle with something like balls. As I popped up the lid, a furry critter scrambled out, yeowing. As it ran off, I could see it was a cat, not one I recognized from the neighborhood. Perhaps it was a stunt cat that got union wages and benefits. I couldn't miss the platform set in the can, so the critter's paws would be in proper position to leap right out and, with any luck, scare the bejesus out of me. I snickered instead. A more imaginative writer would have put in a rabid raccoon. Now that would've released some liquids. Maybe they are building up to such a possibility. For all I know, they'll have a Siberian tiger stuffed in there for the season finale.

As the week's shooting continued with similar "surprises" and shenanigans, we couldn't ever block out the camera and the accompanying self-consciousness of existing merely to feed the public's bored voyeurism. True to his nickname, Eddie Jay had a tendency to shove his lens right up your orifices. "Sorry buddies, but I'm committed to let the people see the real you."

I scratched my head and asked, "What if I don't have a real me."

He smiled knowingly, "Then it's my job to make one."

Three times a run, he would tell us, "Don't pay any attention to the camera. Treat it like it's just a newly planted shrub." By the end of the week, it seemed like every azalea, arborvitae and boxwood had eyes.

Psycho took pride in his fast turnaround from the filming to the airing of Generation Dementia, since it was on the Knowledge Channel a few days later. "It's the only way to keep it all real and raw, man."

Funny how overproduced raw can be. During what must have been late-night recording sessions, Psycho ended up voicing over a love-triangle plot and adding an entire orchestral soundtrack behind Lee Lee's violin. The three of us looked like whacky rock stars, drug addled, throwing garbage cans like we were trashing hotel rooms rather than cleaning up the neighborhood. Apparently, there was an entire rubbish subculture that we represented, living out this dream each morning, although no one bothered to tell us about it.

The lens had zoomed very close indeed, so close I couldn't recognize us. Now that I'd seen the show, I wasn't sure if I was picking pails the same way I had before reality so rudely intruded. In fact, I could now only remember my experience the way it had been portrayed on the "hottest show on basic cable."

For the first time in months, I thought about the Joan in the hospital. She drew me to the bed and made me hold her hand. "In a few days, Hash, I am going to die in the old fashioned way." She was not teary when she told me this.

"What do you mean, die in the old fashioned way?"

She took a deep breath. "What I mean is that my brain will be dead, but the machines will keep running a few days longer."

"You can still make it through," I said, my eyes getting wet and blurring a bit.

"No, Hash, you know I don't like to make a scene, but it's over." She peered into my spongy eyes. "I've heard too much from the doctors. I've seen the test results, and I actually feel it all shutting down, all my batteries are dying."

Although I tried not to show it, she could hear my sobbing and she started to cry along. She lifted up my head. "I am so sorry I'm leaving you all alone. God will I miss you."

"I'll be alright."

"Don't shut out your friends. Make sure you figure out how to spend time with Louie. He might not be as smart as you are, but it's really important to have someone like Louie around.

You can trust Louie. And you should hang out more with that boy with the video camera."

"Max?"

"Yeah, you know he wants to record my death."

"Moron."

"No, it's sweet."

"He's trying to make a viral video for Youtube."

"Not for this one. He said the only one who will see it is you."

Yeah, as if I'd want to relive this pain like it was some whacky cat video.

"You can count on Max too."

Maybe he'll record my loneliness. In her weakened voice, the Joan told me all those things that tear you up, about being proud of me and how much responsibility I've taken on so young and how her greatest regret was not being able to see me in the years to come. Of course, the two of us were bawling and dripping, my arms trying to hold some piece of her through all the tubes. Over those last few weeks, I had been learning what the end smells like, and I had inhaled it fully for the first time that day. By the time we ran out of ways to awkwardly caress and I sat back in that vinyl gray chair of insomniacs where I would sleep that night, I was weaker and dumber than she was.

Two days later, I was sitting next to her hospital bed with Aunt Vicky. The doctor came in. There were breaths from the machines, but she hadn't regained consciousness. So I asked him, "Doc, is she dead in the old fashioned way?"

He looked at me like I spoke a different language. Aunt Vicky stalked out the room, apparently angry about something.

The doctor spoke numbers and levels and no signs of neurological activity. The more technical he became, the more I knew, yes, that she was indeed dead in the old fashioned way. I put my hand on her face and kissed her on the cheeks and on the forehead and cried right up until the next nurse's shift.

I left after that, even though I felt rotten about doing so, smelling Aunt Vicky's disapproval across the 25 miles between hospital and house. Not staying would be that last thing I could do together with the Joan.

She was damn right. God I was alone, except for her persistent question that she greeted me with nightly as I came back home. Some days, as I obediently took out the kitchen trash, I would try to figure out if I'd rather she hovered above in a ghostly silence.

As I picked through and collected pieces of the past, many of them cheesy, plastic, tacky relics carrying within their cracked, brittle frames the most shallow of meanings, I wondered whether I was wallowing in self-pity or making my best stab at rejecting it. I carried sentimentality deep in my pockets even as I gave away those relics of my past. Was this my old fashioned way of coping with things? All I knew that with the cameras now upon me, I could not pick through my past without it seeming like a great invasion into my soul, a soul that I could not figure out whether it was filled with integrity or shame. For the sake of the reality show, I was going to play the part of integrity. You would have to acquire a better device than Probe possessed to discover otherwise.

23

THE DIARY OF LEVON GALLAGHER: DYE, YOU BASTARD

December 21, 1991

I fingered the picture of former President Ronald Reagan. It hung prominently in Mayor Heine's office. "You know," I said, scratching at Reagan's impossible head, "it's a dye job." I had been practicing mayor for the past week. I knew how my comment would go over. That's why I waited until my final day in office and until my story had been put to bed before I rattled the cage. Heine had only accepted my serving as mayor because Reagan let me serve as President for a week. Heine knew it wouldn't hurt to have more correlations between himself and his political god. Heine's big bushy eyebrows vibrated as I kept pushing. "I saw Reagan's hair up close, and the roots don't lie."

He walked up to me like he was going to make some important point about abortion or capital punishment or parking lots. "It isn't dyed. This is Ronald Reagan we're talking about." I was impressed he knew the topic of the moment. I expected to hear choirs singing. "The man oozes authenticity."

I wanted to suggest what Reagan really oozes or at least remind Heine of Reagan's acting career. But Heine just kept yapping. "You think it's dyed because his hair is so authentic that it's hard to believe it's real."

I studied Heine a bit. He wore a blue suit with a red tie. Both were almost high quality. He had what someone who liked him would call arresting gray eyes. They made me flinch a little bit. I wandered around with him for a week. Even with his best efforts, he couldn't hide the small-time combination of graft and corruption so common on the local level. He didn't let me come with him to visit the home of Nicky Mavella. Big Nicky had used his huge backyard as a toxic waste dump for a good twenty years. All the while, his neighbors held their noses and squawked. Heine suddenly knew how to shut his gub when it came to Mavella. Same thing with Kremer's huge donations to the Village Party.

I tried to get under his skin by casually bringing up Joan Cornwall pushing through landfill closures, particularly those in the surrounding area. My mention of Joan's environmental triumph should've caused Heine to spit snakes, but he acted like I'd just handed him a cookie. I returned to the president, a reliable chain-puller.

I ping-ponged my glance from the Reagan portrait to the mayor. Heine had styled his pompadour after his master. "You know that Reagan has a little head," I said. "That's a big reason he wore his hair like he did and why he always wore oversized collars." I moved closer to the portrait. "You don't have a ruler by any chance."

"No, I don't." Heine was clearly lying. "He has one of the great minds of the 20th century."

I kept my peepers glued to the portrait. "I think he might have had the smallest head of any of our presidents? Don't you think so?"

"Uh, I sincerely doubt it."

"Geez, between the dye and the small head, Reagan presents quite an intriguing figure."

"He's the finest president we've ever had."

When I worked with Reagan, I wasn't the only one fascinated by that shrunken dome of his. Don Regan, who was always hanging around, would even kid the President about his small head, that is when he wasn't telling Irish jokes.

I moved from the portrait to Heine's skull. "You don't have anything like Reagan's head. You have a big fat German head."

"Stop talking about my head and don't say anything else about Reagan's head." Heine delivered this command as he moved his big frame closer and peered down at me with his scary eyes.

"Wait a minute," I said, his head so close now that I could get a careful study. "Wow, you dye your hair just like Dutch Reagan."

He clearly was trying to control his anger. "No, I don't. I'm as authentic as Reagan is."

"I couldn't agree more."

That's when Heine ordered me out of his office.

I pulled out a device from my jacket. "You see this?" I waved the plastic rectangle before his eyes and pulled up the antenna. "Ben Wright called me on this phone from the future." Hell, Heine idolized Ben almost as much as he did old Ronnie. "You know what Ben told me. Whatever you do, don't give Heine my number." Then I stalked out of his office.

The next day I got a summons from Frick Village charging that I owed $5,723 back taxes, an outrageous, insupportable claim. He must've been really pissed to do something that stupid. My mayor-for-the-week columns ran not only pictures of me with Heine and Reagan's portrait, but with that tax summons next to my receipts for village payments. This act of vindictive pettiness did not reflect well on the village leader. I knew one thing for sure: Heine wasn't going to be county executive this election. And I was going to make sure Heine paid a little more after I went to see a friend.

* * *

Well, in my examination of *The Herald* for the 1992 county executive election, Herman Heine did indeed lose the race, and his fiscal attack on the beloved columnist Levon Gallagher seemed to have been a major factor in the election. As stated in the article entitled, "The Fall of a Rising Star," the one and only Bill Hannah (described as a longtime observer of local politics) is quoted as saying, "While many thought he had the charisma and skills to ultimately run for national office, that old bean Mayor Heine just seemed a little too unstable for the general electorate." Yet despite my careful examination of Heine news over the next few years, I saw no evidence that Gallagher got further revenge on the mayor. The altercation happened to occur on the very day the Soviet Union dissolved. Because the incident had been reported, it was one of the few entry dates Gallagher listed that I could verify.

211

I scanned through old copies of *The Herald* to confirm that the Joan's work on landfill closures had indeed been a big deal, even though she never talked to me about it. None other than Ben Wright was quoted as saying, "Getting all that garbage out of the ground will protect our groundwater for future generations." I couldn't help but feel Heine's relaxed reaction to the landfill closures signaled that he had another way of disposing Frick's trash.

I was starting to believe Levon Gallagher, and I wasn't too happy about it.

24

THE SYMPHONY

After seeing the first episode, an episode that was so twisted away from our sweat and asphalt world toward Psycho's MTV meth-consumed fantasy, we knew we had to fight back. But how?

If we acted out, we'd be putting on a show and only fuel his high-drama, self-promoting vision. No, our only actions would be trash pick-up. We would have to signal out the rest. We talked about behaving like we are being given clear acting directions and ask Psycho with the cameras running how he'd like us to perform for the show now. We would act like actors on a reality TV show, being awkwardly unnatural without ever being entertaining. Once the cameras rolled, Lee Lee stopped playing the violin, but lifted it up near her chin and vibrated the bow a good foot away from the strings to make impossibly clear that she was merely pretending to play, and doing a very poor job of it. I propped up an I-Pod with mighty speakers in a spot impossible for the cameras to miss and blasted violin solos with operatic vocals. I faked singing so out of sync with the performance that I made teen boy bands look downright organic. We wrote on our shirts in big black letters such phrases as "My words are fully scripted," and "My work is altered for your consumption." The only authentic entities on the curbs of Frick were the daffodils rising into the windy March air.

Neither Psycho nor Eddie Jay tried to change our approach or turn the camera away. When the next episode came out, we figured they would blur out the comments on our shirts and dramatically edit the "musical" aspects of the show. They did no such thing. Instead, they included every staged effort we made for Generation Dementia, even Louie's comment, "You should keep the camera rolling as I stare romantically at Lee Lee for you all out in TV land, though everyone who lives in this town knows I'm totally in love with Nicole Gullota. Got that?"

At key moments, Psycho would do voiceovers or be interviewed, so he could take the opportunity to point out how extraordinarily unhinged the three of us were. "What you are seeing are people who are so real, they have to pretend like their lives are scripted and that they have other lives that the camera can't see. Look how hard they try *not* to be real, like someone else is pulling the strings. They are on the show because they clearly don't want to be on the show. They are too real for reality TV. That's why they act so fake."

By the time the show cut to the last commercial, I was pretty certain that the American audience would believe Psycho and not any of us. Hey, when you watched the show and saw how well they packaged the narrative, I had trouble believing us over Psycho too.

Later on, Psycho summoned me to his trailer. After being turned away at two of his other trailers, I discovered that Psycho ate in a third. The one where he ultimately greeted me was simply a deluxe kitchen with a big stone island in the middle where Psycho cut vegetables next to a woman who came right out of cell phone ad. "Hash, this is Flora." I tried not to stare at her as I greeted, since she was ridiculously pretty and wore a braless blouse of minimal material.

Psycho had peeled onions in front of him and a glistening chef's knife. He held the knife like he knew what to do with it. "I'm sorry we got off to a rough start," he said, waving the knife handle. "I'm very protective of my people."

I looked around the room and understood cameras were everywhere. Even on the truck, we had heard whispers that Psycho would be producing yet another series entitled Dementia Raw where he'd star as the mighty fixer of all problems, especially in dealing with flakes like us. I mumbled something about his verbal abuse being no problem.

He smiled at me like we were best friends. I tried to look him straight in the eye, but Flora was incredibly active in her search for carrots, bending and stretching across the island. I had a feeling the cameras were not too concerned about me anyway. "I believe we should live every moment as if we're in front of a camera," said Psycho. I looked to see if there was a teleprompter next to the goose neck faucet. "That way we will be daring, alive, and interesting."

I smiled back, almost friendly. "Or at least appear to be."

"Look, I can tell what you're capable of. You could be a real star. I mean, not just on Generation Dementia, but on reality shows for years to come." As he flattered me, Psycho chopped onions with breathtaking speed and skill, all the time never taking his deep blue eyes off me. I almost stopped observing Flora's leanings over the sink long enough to see if each of his slices were of equal width.

"Wow," I said, holding off the sarcasm, not completely ready to abandon the idea that I might one day sit and have a photogenic meal in this trailer with the two of them.

Flora straightened up to address me. "I've already been working with Psycho for five years, and I have 'Following Flora' beginning next month."

"What's the show about," I asked, empty of anything else to say to her.

"Oh, the camera will watch my every move."

"That's great," I said, trying my best for sincerity. I attempted to figure out how many seasons would viewers be satisfied following Flora. I decided whatever number I would come up with would be doubled by reality itself. I turned to Psycho. "I want to thank you for inviting me in. I do appreciate what you're offering."

I fumbled about my deep pockets groping about for something worthy of giving to Psycho. Neither Mom's charm bracelet nor her apple corer seemed adequate. Then I fished out an old brass hand mirror wreathed with a raised profile of a goddess. My mother liked to press it up against her face right after a nasty chemo treatment and ask, "Who's the fairest of them all?" Her confident laugh would serve as her answer, thin wisps of her hair snowing as she convulsed happily. I didn't like harboring that little piece of disturbing courage, so I handed it to Psycho. "It was my mother's." Since I knew he knew my history, I was certain he would take it, if nothing else to use as a prop somewhere. Hell, if I could get rid of my most troubling possessions by rendering them onto Psycho, I would make that deal.

He gave my right hand a firm shake, intimating he had a grip that could hold me there for hours if he so desired. As I headed toward the door, he gestured with his chef's knife to the two tall kitchen bags, stuffed with vegetable carcasses and animal skins and neatly tied with red bows. They were almost beautiful. I shrugged and lifted them, understanding my role, removing the debris from Psycho's world. I wondered how far the cameras followed me as I carried the white sacks outside the trailer door.

I knew I would only see Flora again in the commercials of my dreams. After I deposited the garbage, I couldn't help notice that my hands smelled of Psycho's onions.

I couldn't say the TV show put me in a foul mood. Knowing a large national (maybe international) audience (could it be millions?) was watching me made me sit up in bed before the alarm rattled each morning. In the old days the neighbors smiled at me like I was a sweet paper boy, but now they stared at me like I was a celebrity. My aura shimmered in places where I had only been merely a shadow.

Even an insensitive dope like me could notice the difference when the Spirit Committee met to discuss the Spring Prom fundraiser. At first everything seemed normal. The walls of the classroom were covered in posters of mangled cars and bodies topped by big bold letters warning, "Don't Let Prom Night Be Your Last Night." The only change I initially spotted was the increasing inwardness of the once alert and camera-ready Max. During the meeting, Max worked on his laptop the entire time. His only contribution was to point out that Mayor Heine does most of his banking outside of U.S. borders. That left only me to decide the fate of the world with Megan.

This time Megan didn't wait for me to offer any suggestions. She eyed me in a way that could be interpreted as friendly and nervous, like she was meeting a Kardashian. "You know what we were saying at this morning's meeting that would be really cool – I mean if you were willing to do it, and you totally don't have to do it – if we could have Max film an exclusive segment of Generation Dementia just for us! We could sell it and make lots of money."

A simple "No" would have made sense, but I really did like the way Megan was almost groveling, just like I really liked the way some of my classmates yelled to me in the halls, "Hash! Dementia boy!" a term I took as affectionate. I actually started to notice what was happening around me during the school day. "What'd you have in mind?" I asked, sensing Megan would be flattered that I cared about her opinion.

"Well, we wanted to show the other side of Generation Dementia, you know, when you are not keeping the streets of Frick safe and clean." Oh my, how my job description had improved. "We'd like to follow you guys at night. We'd call it Generation Dementia After Dark."

I should have said, "You want to watch us sleep? When you're on the truck at five, you tend to go to sleep pretty freakin' early," but instead I answered, "Sure."

Megan's eyes brightened in a way that made me very happy. Don't get me wrong, I still hated the bitch, but I must say I really liked being admired and even a little worshipped.

"Great, I know how naughty you've been with my sister." I wondered what TV show she stole the word "naughty" from. "I can't wait to see what else you do at night." I didn't think inspiring Cindy Stevens to send me a chemical formula in a bottle made me a real bad ass.

Max was not so moved by our touching exchange. When Megan asked, "Max, so you'll follow around Louie, Lee Lee and Hash with your camera and create a segment," he answered without looking up from his laptop. "I can only do it for one night. I'm very busy right now."

Megan, of course, interpreted Max's frosty response as borne of jealousy. Why would Max heap more attention on Generation Dementia, while he, a wonderboy of cinema, remained underappreciated? I knew Max merely found Mayor Heine much more intriguing than three formerly marginalized classmates. Indeed, I knew Max was right, but I was happy Megan thought otherwise.

I headed back home like everybody was looking at me and nobody was laughing. After the Joan died, I spent a lot of time trying to not think about what other people thought of me, especially the kids at school. To be on the truck was to let go of my image of who I was. Now I was back wondering, since I had a feeling at least a couple of observers thought I was very cool. Unfortunately, the more I considered my elevated branch in the teen jungle, the more uneasy I became. As a starring cast member of Generation Dementia, my image had been so crafted and produced for mass consumption I could no longer claim it belonged to me. That evening I watched the episode one more time with an eye on either discovering myself in the frames or figuring out how to be the me that the viewers embraced. I felt a little bit like Ben Wright: the camera ripped skin off me the way Ben would tear at his own flesh.

After the episode ended a second time, my hallucinations returned. I had started to see music notes floating across my eyes followed by complicated sheet music, a riot of bars and clefts and crazy runs. I think I even spotted a couple of sixty-fourth notes float by. The music passed by in loops, with key signatures and tuplets, and exotic note relationships that I didn't even recognize. Meanwhile, not a single sound floated across my ears. While it never played, the sheet music didn't stop crossing my eyes. The Joan taught me how to play the piano when I was just a boy. I can't tell you where that piano is now. It left the house while I wasn't looking, although I don't know how that was possible. Clearly, I did not have the skill to play the music before me, even if that piano magically reappeared. I bet, though, that Lee Lee could play it. With a ruler in hand, I drew up sheet music, carefully measuring out the five lines for the bars. I made a good six pages, figuring that's what I would need to transcribe the music floating before me. It took nine pages instead.

I called Lee Lee and for once she answered when I wanted her to. Of course, I didn't have to tell her to bring her violin with her since she carried her instrument on her like the rest of us carry our cell phones. I greeted her at the door with the sheet music in hand, pretending I was the deaf and haggard Beethoven rising after scribbling the coda to the Ninth Symphony. Writing down what you see before your eyes is exhausting work. The whole time I wished I could've run my visions through a scanner. Yes, I had not composed a note of this score, but I had seen it float before my eyes like the promise of brilliance, and I presented it to Lee Lee like I had just completed the culmination of my life's work as an artist. God, this would be even better than my mongo mashups.

Lee Lee smelled of mangoes, the residue still sticky on her cheeks. Without greeting me, she studied the music in silence. I could see she was playing it in her head, like her brain was an intricate web of bow strings. After another minute, she pronounced: "This is not music. It makes no sense."

Crestfallen, I put the onus on Lee Lee. "Could it be because it is too difficult and original?"

"No." Typical Lee Lee, she would not elaborate.

I tried to see the musical notes before me, but all I could see was impassive, unimpressed Lee Lee. "Would you play it for me anyway?"

She did not answer. Merely took out her violin, looked down at the sheet music, sighed only once, and began to play.

The entire time that the notes floated before my eyes in my hallucination, a whispered hush roiled about my eardrums. I could not hear a thing, but now Lee Lee played on violin something that, for the first time since she was three, could not be called music. The cacophony that rose into the air made the grinding and banging of the garbage truck sound almost melodic by comparison.

"Make it stop!" I yelled.

Lee Lee pulled back her bow, handed me my composition, and left, since I could offer her nothing else to play.

I spent much of the rest of the evening artfully hot-gluing bars of my composition onto the screen of an old Zenith television that I had found outside Levon Gallagher's house two days after I had grabbed his five-and-a-quarter inch floppy disks. I was interrupted by Aunt Vicky's monthly text. "How u doing?" To which I answered my usual, "K and u?" She replied, "K2, but I'm moving," which meant she lost her job again, and which probably meant that old picture of her as a drunken firefighter resurfaced again. At a party back in college, Aunt Vicky wore the red hat and slicker, lifted an ax, and flashed a sloppy, rum-soaked smile. Whenever bosses saw that image, they felt compelled to fire her, since the picture told the world she was irresponsible and had insulted the sacred profession of firefighting the world over. I felt terrible for her and sincerely hoped she would find one employer who could forgive her drunken firefighter past.

Thanking Aunt Vicky for her new address and wishing her the best of luck, I plugged the Zenith in and was happy to see that 40-year-old relic still worked, even if all I saw and heard was static. I thought on a night like this one, that's what I needed to fall asleep. Instead, I spent another two hours in front of the laptop deleting Emails, opening up a few along way to get my fix of Generation Dementia chatter.

From the March 17 Trash Folder

Are you sure you want to permanently delete all the items and subfolders in the Deleted Items Folder?

The Daily Bread from Reverend Alexander Burr

I often wonder what would have happened if God told Adam and Eve to eat not from the tree of knowledge of good and evil in the Garden of Eden, but instead of tempting them with fruit, cell phones would dangle from the tree. Of course, they would have indulged in the cell phones just as they had the fruit. But I wonder would they have been too distracted and amused pushing buttons to notice that they were naked. Would they care if they were cast east of Eden, had to labor and die? They had cell phones now, so who thinks about anything else. Yes, Cain would still have slain Abel, but in this case because his brother got the newer I-Phone model with the deluxe package. I doubt if either of them would have placed their electronic devices on the altar for sacrifice. Would Noah have built the ark if he had a phone? Would Noah have taken pictures to post online?

With that Generation Dementia show invading our village, how could a spiritual man avoid such thoughts? Between the cell phones and the reality programs, the sins of pride, envy, greed, lust, sloth, and gluttony gallop in like six horses of the apocalypse. Would our great grandparents have been able to resist gazing downward at their phones or outward at these shows any more than Lot's wife was able to avoid looking back at Sodom and Gomorrah? To have a cell phone or to watch Generation Dementia is to turn thyself into a pillar of salt. Get thee behind me, cell phone. Oh, the trash in the village just piles up higher. Hash, my son, I warn thee, thou art perilously close to the perditious fall I have prophesied for our mayor. Tread lightly.

The Epic Life of Selena Omaha

So are you ready for the inside scoop about what's popping in Frick Village?

That adorable meatball on the garbage truck Louie Sacco. The Robin to Hash's Batman, Louie has his own amazing following, especially in the attention of a certain Catholic school bae who knows how to push buttons and one day may ring wedding bells. The buzz about Louie is he is a bad boy alright. Don't put any flower pots in the front yard, not even window boxes if any of you rachets want to keep them. Some Frick insiders have told me they don't feel their mailboxes are safe when Louie turns up the garbage truck. So, ladies, do you want the genuine skinny on what the man who throws away everything of everybody else's threw away himself?

His X-Box.

That's right. Seems like our boy won't be playing games anymore. You know what's crazy. I put his cartridges for Grand Theft Auto and Call of Duty into his system, and you can't believe how far along the dude was. He must've spent years breaking through all those levels. And he just threw it all away.

But that's Louie, right?

I was pretty sure Louie had a better approach to Emails than I did.

25

NOT NOTICING THE CAMERAS

The second episode was the last one we watched. We became determined to undermine Psycho's show at every turn. I visited Max with what I thought was a clever plan: he would record Psycho and the Word as they directed and scripted us. That would at least muddy reality a bit. It seemed like a project Max would jump at, instantly offering him more publicity.

I found Max in his room in front of his laptop, all eyebrows and no eyes. "When have you last left this dungeon?"

"Saturday."

"Smells like it. I've got a job for you." I explained to Max how he would chase around Psycho and the Word like he was producing his own show about the reality TV producers. At any other time in his life Max would've instantaneously shot out the door, shoving his lens up Psycho's tattooed nostril.

Not now though.

"I can't," muttered Max, his eyebrows still aimed at the screen.

"Why not? This is a great opportunity."

"Yeah, but I've got something bigger."

"What?'

"Mayor Heine. You can't believe the stuff he's done."

"Yeah, like what?" I admit that I was more than a little curious about our oily, power-hungry, anal-retentive mayor.

"Can't tell you yet." Eyebrows still on the screen.

"So when can you tell me?"

"When I tell the world."

Not in a particularly fine mood to begin with, I flew out the door before I was tempted to rip off Max's eyebrows.

With no Max to present an alternate version of events, we began to believe that subtle and clever were not going to work against Psycho. We decided to go after him on the front lines, where Eddie Jay, aka Probe, carried around what he called "the best and naturally most expensive equipment on TV." We met with the Gulottas, Peggy Murphy, and even Derek Standish, who certainly didn't like us, but hated the show and its shooting crew so much more. Initiating operation Steel Can, we convinced a number of key residents along our trash run to buy 32-gallon metal cans and to present us what amounted to neighborly requests. Peggy's was used as the template that others adapted: "Please kindly toss my can back off the curb. Feel free to fire the can far into my lawn, since it is sturdy, and I like to hear the clanging sound of it clattering across the front yard."

On the next run, we collected the trash like it was before Reality. Louie and I were all business, working like a couple of animals, albeit incredibly neat and considerate ones, while Lee Lee played Grieg's "Morning" from the Peer Gynt Suite – you could almost hear birds chirping from her strings. Here on the first day of spring, the buttery sun peeking through the green puffs of the budding oaks, tulips blanketing mailbox posts, I could sense the excitement in Eddie Jay's camera. Probe was drawn in by the way Louie lovingly returned to the curb Nicole Gulotta's pink pail covered with hand-painted cherubs, even caressing its handles. As he zoomed in for a close-up, Probe could not have expected that brother Anthony's steel can would come right at his HD lens. Louie's toss was impressive, since his back was turned away from the camera and he flung the can over his shoulder. Clearly, the practice at home the past week paid off. He ran immediately over to the fallen Eddie Jay, trying to act more interested in the bruise above his eyebrow than he was about the cracked top of the lens.

"Oh, I'm so sorry," said Louie. "I didn't expect you to be there. I was just fully into what I was doing, that's all."

Eddie got up. "That's alright. Maybe you were just showing off for your girlfriend."

By the time we got to Peggy Murphy's house, Eddie was back emboldened, shoving his back-up camera almost right into our armpits. He was more surprised than I was when I flung Peggy's two steel cans up high simultaneously – for garbage has made me strong, yah? – and watched them crack down on Eddie and his camera, crashing and thudding and pounding with sounds only such heavy duty trash cans seem capable of making. This time the damage to the camera was bad enough for Eddie to call it a day. By the way he held his balding skull, I suspected Eddie had a pretty bad headache too.

As he staggered away, I said to Probe, "I think I've got it now. I don't pay any attention to the camera anymore. You are just a shrub to me now. Thanks for your help."

The next day, the old Eddie was back, bandaged, with a new HD camera. We waited even further into the run this time. We tried not to smirk as we watched Eddie now taking all his shots from across the street, under the cover of billowing pink phlox, rather than right up our asses like usual. But as the run dragged on, Eddie grew bolder and drew himself right up to the curb. Now under the right conditions, he was in targeting range. I had to hold off until we arrived at Nonna D'Antonio's house, since she had written the best letter of all. She had four steel cans out that day; that old lady really knew how to make garbage out of almost anything (from old picture frames to her dead husband's hats to the many hair dryers of her long departed daughters). After dumping the debris in the compactor, Louie and I hoisted two each up by the metal handles and fired them across the street toward Derek Standish's curb, which was of course where Eddie was shooting. By the time he saw the steel cans coming, like incoming military ordinance, it was too late for the camera, as we hit it from every angle. It sounded like a tin shack collapsing in an earthquake. I saw Louie stare longingly at Nonna's stone lions and had to tug him back toward the newly injured Eddie.

We apologized with all the heartfelt sincerity that a reality show requires. Too bad the camera wasn't working to record such a touching moment.

Psycho was waiting for us in the office and was not too happy. I knew the last few days had become very expensive ones, days that get you hauled in front of your producers while they threaten to halt production or at the very least fire the director to get someone in charge with a better handle on the situation.

He yelled at us for a long time. I was so uninterested and detached that I can't even tell you what he said. When he was done, I took out a copy of the letter from Nonna D'Antonio, clearly written in her crimped, tortured, shaking hand.

Dear Nice Boys,

Could you please throw my pails into Mr. Standish's yard? He brings them into my garage. You boys do such nice job. Next week I will bake bread for you.

Thank you,
Mrs. D'Antonio

Psycho ripped up the note and tried to look tough. "You'll be hearing from our lawyers. If you do anything else, I'll make sure you'll be in jail."

I laughed, "For what, doing my job, a job that I'm barely paid for?" I tried to figure out if I could get fired. Only if Mayor Heine had the authority. No, with the extra time the sanitation board granted, Heine couldn't touch any of us this month. Only Pulaski had the authority to yank me out of Operation Pick-Up and only Big Bill Hannah had the jurisdiction to send me home. I didn't feel any danger in adding. "You told me not to notice the cameras, so I didn't. I would think such a strange, spontaneous accident would make the show exciting, just the way you like it."

26

THE SOILED NAPKIN

After our relatively bloodless rebellion, Psycho bought in a rival gang of rubbish haulers, a trio of actors who were billed as the true, hardcore Generation Dementia trashers. Their tattoos were even more elaborately designed than Psycho's. There were two guys and a girl of course. The girl, Scintilla, was not ethnically Chinese like Lee Lee, but she was what has been termed in the show business circles as vaguely Asian in a supermodelish way. The guys, Atom and Bomb, were better looking than Louie and me, although Louie objected to my assessment. I comforted him by explaining handsome does not make attractive. From his visitation to our office, I doubt that Psycho agreed.

"Dude," said Psycho. "I can't wait for the fireworks now."

I pretended to act excited, since I thought that might bother Psycho most. "Let's see what spontaneous conflict the scriptwriters can manufacture."

And in the beginning, the Word was busy. Atom, Bomb, and Scintilla did everything we wouldn't: drink product placement beverages, do celebratory dances, remove clothes, eat McDonalds during carefully filmed workbreaks, cry, yell

"Dude," punch each other, make highly suggestive gestures, pour liquids onto various body parts, tell "secrets" found in the neighbor's trash to the camera, cry, throw dog bones at Peggy Murphy's schnauzer, spray blue paint randomly, smell co-worker's socks, cry, steal garden gnomes, wave tequila bottles, smell specific items of rubbish, lick mailboxes, cry, cook a meal consisting of pail scraps, do somersaults off of the Gulotta's fig tree, vomit on command, make nasty comments about co-workers, cry, ignore Bill Hannah's directives, bang out a percussion solo from Derek Standish's trash cans, wear new and increasingly tighter jumpsuit uniforms for each episode, play with uniform zipper provocatively, cry, remove jumpsuit . . .

Psycho made the talk show rounds to explain how Louie, Lee Lee and I were the "actors" and that the rival gang were the real trash people.

Eddie "Probe" Jay no longer shot our route, instead following around those who caught reality the way it was meant to be – emotionally scarring contrived sexuality. For those beautiful people to haul, the producers even imported luscious, color-saturated garbage, garbage that looked like it was created by an unholy union of Disney and Playboy. Who wouldn't want to ride the garbage truck now? A nameless camera filmed us, respecting our privacy and distance. We really took to whatshisname. Louie, Lee Lee and I were becoming marginalized members of Generation Dementia. We pretended not to mind.

"I kinda liked the camera shoved up my ass," Louie admitted.

"Yeah," was all I was willing to confess.

Lee Lee hardly noticed how the audience for her violin solos diminished from millions to a couple of cultured, rabbit-eared neighbors.

Pulaski told us he wasn't sure whether we should be called Generation Dementia since we completely undermined his theories with our behavior. He bought us bacon-egg-and-cheese sandwiches. As we woofed them down, he asked, "Do they taste better than fame?"

We decided not to answer, but to continue eating. Despite the blossoming of spring, the morning light became a bit dimmer on the run, and Lee Lee played songs that sounded too familiar. All types of wet fronds fell from the trees and left the streets dirty. My muscles tired, and I wondered if they would be revived if I got a few tats on my biceps and forearms. A member called The Toss, added just today to the new crew, had ink right over his entire arm and it made his muscles look amazing.

I started to have this new recurring hallucination. For the first time it was during our rubbish runs. To the right of every pail I picked up, I saw a big soiled paper napkin; it looked like someone eating a hamburger – one with ketchup and pickles – had just wiped his mouth with it. Not until Louie spotted me reaching down for a napkin that wasn't there ("What are you doing? Some type of screwed up move like the jackasses from Psycho's crew?"), did I realize that the napkin was in my head. Yet, the napkin remained for me to pick up at every house. Sometimes, I was able to ignore it. Most of the time, I couldn't help myself from bending down and clutching a handful of nothing.

* * *

That afternoon, the Spirit Committee met. Max didn't show. I had visions of his arm hairs starting to wrap around his keyboard like vines as he clicked his way through a maze of financial statements Mayor Heine had rocketed into the black holes of cyberspace. Megan gave me a glance so drained of intensity that I could immediately sense my diminished value.

"I was hoping Max would be here," I said, "so we could finalize tonight's filming." I am ashamed to admit that Louie, Lee Lee, and I actually planned a good show, featuring a garbage-tossing Olympics emphasizing both distance and accuracy, a whacky obstacle course, and a spectacular musical performance by Lee Lee on electric violin with accompaniment by D.J. BeatOff.

"Uh," said Megan, giggling just a little, "didn't you hear?" I gave a look that told her I clearly hadn't heard. She only spoke words she learned from TV shows. "Oh, this is so embarrassing." I understood by the almost silent giggle, "embarrassing" for me, not her. "This morning, the committee decided to make the episode of Generation Dementia After Dark with the new cast members, you know Atom and Bomb, Scintilla, and we hope even The Toss."

She waited for me to respond. I didn't, so she kept talking.

"We thought we'd save you the trouble. Anyway, Psycho told us he was going to be producing the program no matter what, and we could sell the preview as a fundraiser. Then it'd be aired nationally. Isn't that great! We get to see it before anyone else!"

I considered saying something, but then I understood. Whatever I said would only make Megan happier, so I shut my mouth and walked quietly out of the last goddamn Spirit Committee meeting I'd ever attend for the rest of my increasingly anonymous life.

I tried to figure out if Megan gave me an extra dose of calm cruelty because of the embarrassment I caused by my influence on her sister Cindy, who had been wandering the streets in search of her passion. I wondered what the chemical formula

Cindy left in the bottle months ago $(C_8H_8)_n$ had to do with her gathering of this material. I admit that I wasn't really *that* curious. I knew eventually Megan would tell me if she knew it would wound me further or Cindy would tell me if she wanted me to pull a razor from her wrist again.

As I meandered back to the house, flowers bloomed everywhere, but all I kept seeing were those damn napkins on the ground, drawing on all my self-control to refrain from reaching down. The hallucination tumbled into memory. . . .

By the time I was in 9th grade, Grandpa Artie grew frail and had to use his cane as a weapon. "Try to block me," he said, lifting up the cane. Then with his left hand he threw sand in my eyes and spun the cane around in his right hand, lamming me on the skull. "Gotta be prepared for a dirty fighter," he warned me.

I held onto my head and asked, "How did the Joan and dad meet?" I expected another crack to the head, so I covered up, only to get a nasty rap to the shins.

Satisfied that I suffered the requisite agony, Artie told me, "Your father lived in that big grey house down the street. His mother had just died and he was by himself wasting away his days playing that damn Zelda game. Your mother knew I ruined my life trying to save someone, so she decided to be as stupid as I was. She dragged him out into the light. God he looked like an uncooked biscuit, but he browned and crisped right up after a few months with your mother. Hell, those months led to you." He frowned and jabbed me hard in the gut with the cane, and I collapsed, sucking my cheeks in to find air again. "Stop asking me about him. God, he's probably walking around the hills of San Francisco looking for abandoned joysticks."

Artie took no joy in making miserable prophecies about my

father, yet I suspected he was making up stories about him to get me off his back. He delivered his lies with a softness in his eyes that begged me not to ask any more questions.

So I asked him one more question, "Who owns the house now?"

"Mayor Heine," he growled, "who else would own that house?"

With that memory swirling, I called Big Bill and asked him who owned that house before Mayor Heine. "Lived in that house, my good man?" asked Bill. "Why no one. That house has been abandoned for as long as I can remember. Why do you ask, my good man?"

"Oh, it's nothing important."

* * *

At home that night, I found less ethereal and more substantive acts of disposal. First there was the trip to the bathroom, where I still saw the spooling video of *True Evacuations*. I had hoped that being on an actual reality TV show might preempt the appearance of the one that regularly aired in my toilet hallucinations. No such luck. The only difference was now the image wasn't me, but an actor playing me. I got out of there quickly and prepared for a more satisfying chance for disposal.

I used to delete a couple of hundred of Emails a day, but since the reality TV show aired, that number had doubled. I was nearly throwing away as much cybertrash as I was tossing the genuine articles. Even as I hit delete, the dread lingered that two of those Emails could've changed my life, but which two, eh? Tonight, no, this morning now, I just completed a massacre of my account only to see three new deliveries pop up bold and black. One had the subject heading: "Hash, I writhe too." Like it was a message in a bottle from some distant shore, I thought it was a good idea to open this Email from someone named Roger "Running Bullet" Ten. It read –

Never can look at your garbage the same again, can you? The camera can do that to a soul. I was once of the Apaca nation; now, I cannot see my home anymore. You are of Generation Dementia, but I am of the Girth Dimension.

And I will never find my way out.

Roger "Running Bullet" Ten was right about one thing: ever since the show started, I had this funny feeling I was lifting stage props instead of trash pails. I hesitated before sending the garbage into the compactor expecting Psycho to yell cut, so a stunt double could finish the job for me.

The Girth Dimension had already achieved the fame that Psycho coveted for Generation Dementia. The buzz about Girth Dimension on Twitter, gossip mags, and celebrity TV news was unavoidable, especially the bathing suit shots of Kim "Curving Path" Greenhorn. For so many years the Apaca tribe of Adabo had resisted persistent, smiling, threatening visitations from the casino owners of Resorts, Caesars, and Tropicana. The moguls would show up on the reservation with paper bags worth of money, cases of firewater, and promises of wealth for all. The pressure to build casinos on the Rez became so great from forces used to getting their way that tribal elders had to call in the FBI (an extraordinary move, given the fact that the village of Adabo traditionally steered clear of the government) to keep brutal interference to a minimum.

No, the village elders would not allow the huge American capitalistic forces to illuminate their clay terraces and pueblo huts with neon lights and flashing signs for breakfast buffets.

Then the producers of the *Girths* video game came into town and told the village elders that Adabo was the most beautiful village they had ever seen and had designed their entire video game series around its architecture. The game creators sat down in a circle with the village elders and offered free WiFi service for all of Adabo if they were able to film their new movie there. Oh yeah, the producers would have to paint the entire village red, to match the colors of the Girths who joyously blasted each other with rocket launchers from their cliff dwellings in the most popular app ever to hit a cell phone. One of the better features was the red goo dripping down the caves, oozing in lava-like rivulets through the crags and crevices. Oh yeah, in addition to the WiFi service, every child in the village would receive a cuddly, leaking Girth doll. And oh yeah, any village member willing to wear red body paint could appear in the movie, and anyone with natural talent like Kim "Curving Path" Greenhorn could receive a "prominent supporting" role.

I wrote back Roger "Running Bullet" Ten, thanking him for his sympathy. He responded immediately and we started Instant Messaging.

Me: "I bet you miss your old home."
Roger: "Can't remember what the village looked like before it was red."
Me: "That must be pretty rough."
Roger: "It's not so bad. I told my father that it's like we got a new red skin. He mumbled something about me being a self-hating racist."

When I didn't write back for a moment, Roger "Running Bullet" Ten went on.

Roger: "I think I have seen myself in the video game, not as a real character, but as one of the faces repeated in the background to make everything as familiar and natural as a good movie."
Me: "How does it make you feel?"
Roger: "I'm not sure . . . I have to go now. I have many Emails to wipe out."

So I sat in front of the screen deleting the two other Emails that had arrived with Roger "Running Bullet" Ten's, and the five others that had appeared since I had initiated contact with him. I waited for new ones to surface so I could delete them. They land on my cyber shores with a much greater certainty than offers to star in a reality TV show. Just like when I jumped onto the truck in the first place, I knew I would move on quickly from all this nonsense. I thought Max was heading in the right direction. Actually, it was two directions. I could either make something good or destroy something bad. I had to start somewhere. At least for now in front of this screen, all I had to do was wait a moment or two and I would have something to eradicate.

27

THE DIARY OF LEVON GALLAGHER: THE SEAL OF APPROVAL

April 19, 1995

My flesh started to hang down on my waist like cake batter. I did curls, bench presses, sit-ups, and squats in my war against 50 years, 35 of them under a fog of smoke and booze. I met each morning with Joan at the gym. Yes, she was like family. Yes, also, I must admit working out with a young beauty made me hit the weights harder. It took all my hatred of humanity not to fall for her.

Often I made a point of avoiding her.

As part of my training, I crawled out of bed at 4:50 and tracked the garbage route, outrunning the truck, my lungs and heart making more of a racket than the engine. I did not want to embarrass myself on my next column assignment. The last time I covered Frick Village I got a tax bill that screwed up my credit for years. But the place was reeling and rocking right now. The Mavellas, who had always carted the trash, were up on trial for turning many of their properties into toxic waste dumps. With the Mavellas out on their asses, the trustees tapped Big Bill Hannah, against Heine's wishes. Hannah, in turn, tapped Mexicans to ride the trucks, again against Heine's wishes.

I asked Hannah if I could ride on the truck with the Mexicans. "Of course, you can," he said, "my dear sir." I warned that my presence may upset the mayor. Hannah smiled and said, "I have no idea what you mean sir." I might be diving into dumpsters now, but that Hannah made you feel like a duke.

My six miles a day on the treadmill and my daily hour on the weight machines were completely inadequate preparation to lift pails with the Mexicans. For every one pail I grabbed, they handled three and they didn't wheeze, cough, or clutch their chests either. They took out the pails the way a Pro-Am bowler knocked down pins – fluidly, with enough crashing about to know good work had been done here. I was perfectly satisfied with writing a simple story of how the Mexicans were the best thing to happen to sanitation in Frick Village. Maybe toss in that their green card status should not be considered a threat to the local worker (there were no residential applicants), yeah, even end the story by making clear that despite Heine's insinuations, the Mexicans had no interest in scoping out the neighborhood houses for future robberies. Such a column would've been enough to twist Heine's mustache into a pretzel.

That was before I learned their names: Jesus, Pedro and Pablo. Hannah had nicknamed them the savior and the disciples. I wouldn't put it past old Bill to hire them specifically for their Biblical associations. Yet that wasn't the choicest nugget I picked up on the run.

There was the tattoo on Pedro's right wrist.

It was the Frick Village seal, and it also appeared on the wrists of Jesus and Pablo. I pointed at them to Bill. "Why'd they get them?"

"Heine made them." Big Bill smiled gleefully. I wondered whether he told his workers to flash their tattoos past my peepers. I couldn't miss spotting them any more than I could a cleavage at the Frickin' Thirsty.

"Why?"

"I have no idea, my good man." Oh, Big Bill Hannah definitely had an idea why Jesus, Pedro and Pablo carried around stamps on them like they were the permanent property of Frick Village. I think he preferred letting Heine explain the reason to me. Bill knew he would make it sound not nearly as horrific as the man who issued the edict.

Before I met with the mayor, Hannah made sure to take me to his basement, where Pablo dwelled. By staying down there, Pablo could send more money home. I asked him if he regretted leaving Michoacán and family for this lonely life in Frick Village. "No," he said. He had pictures of his wife, Elsa, and his two kids, Guillermo and Miguel, all over his walls. It was a life of singular discipline and purpose beyond my understanding. On the weekend, Pablo worked with a construction company owned by Hannah's brother. I tried to get Pablo to complain about his hard life. He smiled at me. I knew I would get nothing from him about the tattoo.

But who needed to talk to a saint when I had

a sinner so accessible?

"Hi Mayor," I said as politely as I could to the fathead who tried to deliver me to financial ruin a few years ago. "May I ask you just one question about the sanitation department?"

"Of course," he said, oily as ever, "anything for *The Herald's* star columnist." I made sure I caught none of his sarcasm. He didn't even look up from his Jumble puzzle.

"Mayor, why the tattoos on the Mexicans?"

"Now I wouldn't call them tattoos."

"Now what would you call them Mayor Heine?" The mayor had insisted over the years that I call him Herman.

"I would call them a seal of our approval."

"Were they required to wear them, Mayor Heine?"

"No, they didn't have to. They only wear the seal if they are employed by us."

I was confused, but tried not to show it. "Does anyone who is not a Mexican have to wear the seal?"

"It's not Mexicans. It's those who have green cards and who are not recognized U.S. citizens."

"Do any U.S. citizens have to wear the seal?"

"Of course not." He fingered his lips, now for the first time realizing I might be looking to make an issue out of this tattooing policy. "You don't understand. This seal is good for them."

I spoke to the good mayor for another half hour, but it was that initial line "The seal is good for them" that echoed first in my head and last in my column. I remembered what Ben told me a few years ago when he was working on digital cell phones. "If they're able to mark you, then they can always hunt you down." So I linked the Mexican tattoos with the serial numbers administered by Nazi SS officers and with the marks Stalin gave to dissidents in the Gulag and to the branding irons on cattle. I wrote about how Mayor Heine was treating his sanitation workers like property and that while the polite and gracious supervisor Bill Hannah might respectfully call his workers Master Jesus, Master Pedro and Master Pablo, Mayor Heine expected his slave Mexicans to bow down and call him Master. I went to the tattoo parlor and had the seal inked on my wrist. I took lots of pictures of Jesus, Pedro and Pablo revealing their stigmata. Of course, Heine was running for county executive again (when wasn't he?). Insiders thought he had an excellent chance of winning this time.

When the column came out, Heine didn't send me a tax summons. But I did get a truckload of trash dumped on my front lawn, courtesy of the Mavella boys. Of course, Joan, just to weaken me further, came by to help me clean up the mess. She moved with supple ferocity, stuffing the refuse back into the bags. She hated garbage and the messes it made. My anger was dwarfed by hers. Love searched for a discarded rose among the stench.

I didn't need to connect the dumping to Heine. The article on the brandings had done enough damage. And if they tried to track me down, I'd made sure they wouldn't know how to find me.

But the Mavellas would pay too. I'd make certain of it.

* * *

The Mavellas? Maybe that explains why they don't leave trash for pickups. I can't say the revelations about Heine surprised me. I was beginning to gain a little respect for Levon Gallagher. I'm pretty sure the Joan's attraction to Levon was grounded in his inability to hide his emotions, something the rest of her family struggled to provide. Perhaps his life added up to more than a series of pissing matches.

The date of Gallagher's battle over the Mexican conquest? That day Timothy McVeigh blew up the government office in Oklahoma City, killing 168 and injuring 800. Seems like Heine wasn't the only one who felt a little put upon at the time.

28

THE CASE OF THE MISSING GARBAGE

When I shared with Eva some of the entries from Levon Gallagher (she had been the first), Eva started reading through old stories about Heine, particularly after the Mavellas stopped carting garbage. "I don't get it," she frowned. "The garbage doesn't add up."

"Garbage doesn't tend to *add* up," I said authoritatively, "it piles up."

"Yeah, I get that, genius," she said, smiling and smoking like she just got a new carton of cigarettes. "It's that the Mavellas didn't dump enough garbage on their lands to account for even a small portion of the trash the residents of Frick Village generate."

"Well given that we haven't picked up any trash at the Mavellas since Louie started, maybe they have some secret way of breaking down garbage."

"Yeah, if they had a secret way, I'm pretty sure they'd either be rich or dead by now. And they're neither, so I have my doubts."

"Do the Mavellas have any other property?"

"None that I can find."

"How about Heine?"

"Already thought of that, boy. I haven't found anything yet, but I'll keep looking. All I know is that Hannah thought it was a mystery too. Once he hired his Mexican crew, he was taking enough trash from the village residents to fill up the Mavella property in less than a year and the Mavellas had been dumping for at least ten. That's what he told *The Frickin'* in the late 1990s."

I brought Eva to Bill, who naturally treated her like an honored maiden entering the court of Camelot. His chivalrous manner belied his monument of a forehead that was craggy and rough hewn, like something you'd see along the sides of a mountain pass. He could've easily been a brute of a man if it weren't for his nimble hands and his gentle smile. As always, a couple of minutes of small talk with Bill were required. Somehow he and Eva managed to get into a discussion about carving knives within moments of shaking hands.

When Eva finally explained what she was looking for, he answered, "Ah, my fair lass, that is a mystery I long have explored, only to be thwarted at every turn." He told her a long tale of searches through county and state records in search of a hidden property. "They clearly had to be dropping all that junk somewhere. But how could they possibly hide hundreds of thousands of cubic tons of trash?"

"Do you think Heine was involved?"

"Oh," Hannah smiled, "I know he was, my honorable lady. I can feel it in my shoulders, like the weight of a heavy pail."

"Then why can't we find a property?"

"I'm guessing there are many layers to the property title. Maybe Heine has another identity or put it under the name of a property or trust."

We tried out a whole bunch of possible alternate names for Heine and what in God's name he would call a corporation. All our suggestions descended into bad, profane jokes that made Bill Hannah bow his head while chuckling.

As the laughter died away, I pulled from my deep pockets a miniature dump truck. Levon Gallagher had given it to me when he was dating the Joan. He'd worked for a week in Germany for the Bruder Toy Company to write a column about the Euro and globalization. The dump truck was part of a set of twenty toy vehicles he'd brought me, each metal, carefully engineered little beasts weighing a couple of pounds. I had tossed the rest of them, but kept this one, believing the dump truck had a significance it really didn't possess. I thought about giving it to Louie, but I knew he would've tossed it away before I got out the door. Big Bill took it like I'd handed him a bottle of expensive scotch.

"Why thank you, my good man," he boomed. His reaction didn't mean he liked the dump truck. Hell, I could've handed Big Bill a gum wrapper. He polished the dump truck with his sleeve and put it up on his office mantle. That dump truck was safe at least for a few more minutes.

As we left Bill's office, I suggested that we visit Max next, since he'd been researching Heine or, should I say, hacking into his files for years. "If anyone would know, it'd be Max."

When I called Max, he wasn't exactly forthcoming. He paused a lot on the phone. "Uh, I really can't help you much, but I can show you this little video I've put together about the mayor called *Heine's Mines*. You're the only non-investor who will have seen it." I wanted to say to Max, "Wow, now I feel really special, you little prick," but I hoped maybe we'd pick up something. I asked him if I could bring Eva along. This time Max didn't pause. He clearly didn't mind Eva being in his house.

The cameras were everywhere in Max's room, a place where he created reality.

I pointed, "Can we shut some of those things off?"

"Never." I had a feeling he'd figure out a way to give Eva a starring role in some future video waiting to go viral. He nodded at me to indicate that the cameras were the price of admission to the premiere of *Heine's Mines*. Max was jumpier than usual.

"Don't tell anybody about this."

"Not even the cameras?" I pointed to the heavens of his room which sparkled with lenses instead of stars. Max frowned. "No problem." Eva was noticeably quiet, sipping her coffee, seemingly figuring out her role in this part of film, to look beautiful and try not to betray too many signs of intelligence.

Max zoomed toward me in a close-up. "I mean it. My lawyer said Heine could sue my family if I put it out right now."

"Why?" I asked, trying to block out of my head that Max, a high school senior, has a lawyer.

"Well, when you get evidence by hacking, it presents certain legal problems."

"What kind of problems?" I knew that Max had been peddling *Heine's Mines* as a promotional video to get financing for a full-length exposé on the mayor's data mining. Perversely, he was soliciting the very internet big wigs who had made their fortunes off of this type of information snooping and extraction.

Max did that fierce scrunching of his eyebrows to signal his impatience. "Did you come to see *Heine's Mines* or to annoy me with questions?"

Max clicked the screen. The images were a combination of live action and cartoon. The first scene framed the actual Mayor Heine in front of a computer terminal, a vision that quickly morphed into an animated version, his normally fat head even further enlarged, crowned by his impossibly big hair drenched with an appropriately cartoonish dye job. Before the animated screen bobbed the word "Private." Max's voice purred in the background, "There was once a mayor who liked to data mine, but he specialized in only one word: Private." The word grew larger than even Heine's head. "Indeed he prepared all his algorithms around that single word." The big word pulsed on the screen like a beating organ. "And accessing countless service providers, he made sure that no place would be private from his search of the word *private*." Now Heine's colossal head was gliding out from the computer circuitry into virtual worlds and landing in the laps of virtual users.

"What the mayor discovered in his search was not merely *private*, in the sense of the deeply personal and the alone, but there were private islands and private practices and private equities and private detectives and private sectors and private schools and private investments and even virtual private clouds." For every version of private popped up appropriate icons from sandy beaches to stethoscopes to fedoras to money bags. "Not to mention all the sexual ways private can be considered." In the background now played a particularly raunchy saxophone riff supporting many curvy shadows.

"The mayor had learned all things private. Did he keep his knowledge private? No, he earned tens of millions for what he mined from others." Now flashed printouts of off-shore bank accounts. "That data in the right retail targeting agencies would make sales simple. Indeed, how much would you pay to own someone's soul?" The shadows featured devil horns and the music hit notes Lee Lee would only play when her mother sent to her room without a physics textbook.

"The mayor has tried to cover up these acts." In come the

images of deleted files and shredded documents, which could well have been the slips of paper Max jammed in his pockets on the garbage truck all those months ago. "But don't be fooled. Every day the meanings of *private* and what it stands for expand." The mayor's head ballooned so grotesquely that I suddenly thought it could break through the screen and swallow me.

"So next time you're looking for some privacy, you should realize who owns it."

The screen went blank. Included in the credits was contract information for investment.

"Is this all true?" I asked Max.

"Every bit of it, except maybe the size of Heine's head."

"Yeah, you should've made it bigger. Do you have solid evidence?"

"Of course I do."

"Can I see it?"

"That's private."

"I'm not sure I know what that word means anymore."

"It means you can't see it."

"How'd you break in to his system?"

"Once I figured out Heine's obsessions, the rest was easy. Every one of his passwords is a simple variation." Max swallowed a little, seemingly disappointed that his desire to brag had trumped his increasing guardedness.

Eva, who had been waiting patiently, finally couldn't wait anymore. "Hey, in your research, by any chance, did you come across anything about a secret mound of trash."

"Not a peep."

Eva and I looked at each other. He responded spontaneously enough to sound like he wasn't lying. For Max to have gone through Heine's computer and find nothing about a dump site was not a good sign for our investigations.

As we left the darkness of Max's den, I asked Eva whether she learned anything useful from the video.

"Not much. It was intriguing and all, but it doesn't get us any closer to finding the garbage that's outside of Heine's hard drive." Eva lit a cigarette and starting blowing smoke in rings, looking suddenly refreshed and peaceful. "I think I'm going about this all wrong."

"How so?"

"I think I should start with the land and work backward." She noted my puzzled expression. "Look, there are not many big parcels of land around here, except for the nature preserve and I can tell you the hidden landfill's not there, since I stepped on every leaf in that place during rehab . . . They said it was therapeutic."

"Well, it's comforting to know the nature preserve is not a dump."

"Besides the preserve, there are probably only about five parcels where the dump could be. I think I'll find out who owns those properties."

"So," I said, "you're more than a caffeine crazed, nicotine driven, overly indulgent political aide."

"Whatever you say I am, I am more than that."

"You're really great with a compliment."

"I'm even better with an insult."

"So how are you going to find out this information?"

"I'm going to the county clerk's office."

"Won't Heine wonder what you're doing there?"

"Oh, I'll tell him I'm at the board of elections next door. He doesn't think I'm very bright."

"I wonder where he got that notion."

"Couldn't tell you," she smiled.

Most afternoons after classes, I found myself almost unconsciously heading over to Frick Village Hall to catch a glimpse of Eva. Usually, I ran into Mayor Heine shaking someone's hand for a grin-and-grip photo, even as the hand not appearing in the picture was tickling his cell phone. I drew close enough to Heine to hear scraps of his voice which managed to carry twice as far as anyone else's on the village green. "Tax rebates will be mailed . . . pot holes will be filled . . . dog doo will be scooped . . . toilets will be scoured." Heine knew what the people wanted.

When I asked Eva why the mayor was so ridiculously responsive to the public, she told me, "His goal is to make a personal connection with everyone in the county."

"Impossible," I said.

"Yeah?" She smiled at me, a little surprised by my naiveté. "He's got almost 40 Facebook accounts, each filled up with five thousand friends."

I whistled. "How does he keep up with them?"

"He's got staffers responding, clicking 'likes' all day long and spewing compliments."

"Is that one of your jobs?"

"He asked," hostility welling in Eva's eyes. "I told him to go take a hike."

I wanted to respect Eva's integrity, but I did notice her image was all over the Frick Village web site. When I pointed out her constant presence, Eva frowned and asked me to open the web site right now. Eva must've been in ten of the twelve pictures cycling through the village home page. I could see why she was featured. She could even make zoning board regulations stimulating.

"You notice anything about my pictures?"

Even though I could tell Eva was presenting me with a test

of my worthiness, I didn't notice a goddamn thing. So I answered, "Yes, you look especially beautiful," then I added for good measure, "as always."

Another frown. "You don't notice anything else about me." Since I didn't notice a goddamn thing, I thought it was better to not answer; perhaps her disappointment would be less. She paused a few extra moments to let my cluelessness sink down to my shoes. "I'm wearing the same clothes, you idiot."

I wanted to say so what, until I considered that I've never seen Eva repeat an outfit. I don't believe she had that many clothes, but she rotated blouses, bottoms, and pumps the way she shuffled cards. "Oh," I said, relieved that I might have finally understood. "They were all taken the same day?"

Eva put her right index finger to her nose, smiling. "I told him if he uses any more pictures of me on the website, I'm quitting."

"That's pretty noble of you."

She frowned again. Discussions of Mayor Heine tended to bring out the scowl in her. "He wanted me to take pictures with donors."

Now it was my turn to twist my face. "Did you break out in hives just hearing the suggestion?"

"A bit." Despite the disgust, I could sense that she had a measure of respect for him. She would casually mention to me that he never stopped working, talking to voters on the phone, sending texts to the heads of civic associations all over the county.

I rummaged through my pockets for something I wanted to give the mayor. When I cleaned up the house after the Joan died, I came across a set of old keys. They must've had twenty or so business tags from supermarkets, drug stores, and companies long dead like Blockbuster and Borders. But what kept me from tossing the ring were the seven keys themselves. Don't get me wrong. I didn't think there was some magical key that would open a door to paradise or Starbucks. I could tell they were all basic house keys letting me into places I had no interest in going. I tried all seven out anyway. They worked on none of the locks in my house, and all of them were too big and clunky to be safe deposit keys. I carried these keys around in my deep pockets for weeks, sometimes even mistakenly pawing them in an ill-founded effort to start the car, before I realized that Mayor Heine was just the man to have them. I could see him walking around the village, sticking them into every door. Eva gave me a curious look when I asked her to give them to the mayor. I explained to her that he could use another distraction. Give him a new set of keys and all that data he had mined, there was no telling what obsessions might take over that troubled, invasive brain of his. Later Eva told me that when she passed the keys onto the mayor, he smiled at her with something that approached desire. "Never ask me to give him something again," she warned me.

Heine's influence was clearly expanding, and I could see next fall he would be elected the most powerful man in the land. His looming presence gave us an urgency to hunt down the missing trash. Plus, this bit of detective work felt so diametrically opposed to all the reality television nonsense that its lure only intensified. Hell, I'd been hearing folklore about the mysterious missing garbage of Frick Village all quarter long from Pulaski. I wasn't sure if he told Louie and me these tales to make us feel more or less significant. Knowing Pulaski, he was looking to diminish our elevated opinions of ourselves. How valuable could we be if twenty years of trash could vanish without our lifting and tossing and compacting? With every pail I hoisted, the absence of all that trash weighed and heaped on me like I'd forgotten to pick it up myself.

Indeed, since Eva started working for Heine, my hallucinations along the rubbish run increased. Instead of the Murphy or Standish or Gullota curb, I'd see the mound of a great landfill, well curved and shaped like a Native American ritual hill. Then, near the top of the grassy mound, I'd see a clear open break that had been scraped back, exposing hundreds and hundreds of light bulbs. Though they were all extinguished, none were broken. I knew that these light bulbs could have withstood neither time nor burial. This nonsensical hallucination became as regular as the run itself; it was my daily visitation to the lost garbage.

As Eva explained her next steps, I said to her. "Hey, Sherlock, we're not looking for the lost city of Atlantis here."

"No, we're not. The lost city of Atlantis was never ours. This garbage was. It's our birthright."

I cannot underestimate how much Eva's enthusiasm for the quest drew me in. I knew one thing for sure, she was making more sense to me all the time.

29

DONALD HAGEN

While my first instincts were to search for that lost garbage, Louie saw the Mavella house as the key to everything. "Hey, they once hauled all the garbage. Now not a scrap leaves their home. I think the answers are in their basement."

Today, Louie texted me during school hours after our morning trash run. He clearly decided staking out the Mavella house again was more important than attending classes. "The daughter's carrying out big black plastic bags into a minivan. Looks like she's driving. I'm gonna follow."

"Be careful," I texted, feeling like I was suddenly in a straight-to-DVD movie. I tried to figure out just what Louie should be careful about. I had visions of chopped up limbs and torsos in those bags, and realized how once you started to think you're in a bad film, the awful possibilities follow. I decided to take the rest of the day off and wrote Louie that I'd like to join him. He called me a few minutes later. "I think she's going to the county dump. I'll swing by and pick you up." He was at the front circle of the school two minutes later.

When she was in school, Maria Mavella said very little, but

she would always smile at me like we were sharing some inside joke. For a few months, she wrote a blog about school gossip that left the halls buzzing, since most of what she revealed was miraculously true. When two senior girls spread on Facebook that Maria got her information by sleeping around, she abruptly shut the blog down. After that, many boys chased her, looking to get past her baggy clothes. Maria would roll her eyes at me, empathetically, as if to say, "Look, you're not the only one who must endure such stupidity." Now we were trailing her to the dump, catching up to her car, thanks to the many stop signs designed to slow down the garbage trucks through the neighborhood. It'd been a while since I felt such shame, but I had to follow her trash.

We kept our distance as she stopped at the depot and dragged out eight black bags, each pretty much the size of her. She moved her load with a grace and efficiency of someone who had done this before, almost like she'd spent some time hanging off the garbage truck. I could see from the way Louie leaned over the steering wheel that he might well have been tempted to invite the girl to Cardinale's if that special seat in the corner table had not already been occupied by Nicole Gullota.

"Should we talk to her?" I asked Louie, both of us uncomfortable with skulking around, waiting for her to finish her drop-off. In the end, I followed Louie's counsel. "Let's first look in the bags. Then we'll know if we need to talk to her."

We were fortunate that Maria's black bags were left unattended, the drop-off depot serving as a weigh station for the big trucks to deliver refuse to the resource recovery plant. In this place the sweet blossoms of spring were crushed by the suffocating embrace of ripening decay. We waited a good five minutes for Maria to drive down the road before rifling through the bags. We found plastic wrap, tissues, carrot peelings, and a broken dinner plate; we found Q-Tips yellowed from use and clumps of hair blackened by dye; we found one new sock and two old shoes. We found an extraordinary variety of debris in those huge black bags.

None of it to our untrained eyes felt like a clue.

I couldn't even find anything worth reclaiming for my garage. Louie didn't seem too disappointed. "At least we know what they've been doing with their garbage."

I could tell that mystery had really bothered Louie, and now that the issue was settled, the earth could continue to turn.

Still, I had questions: "But why not just leave the bags on the curb if they just had run-of-the-mill trash? Why all the secrecy? Why is Maria hauling instead of one of her lunkhead brothers?"

Louie drummed his fingers on his steering wheel. "I don't have any answers to that. I do believe some people like to have complete control of their own garbage."
"That's a bit crazy," I said.

"Not really," Louie was actually tapping out Beethoven's "Moonlight Sonata" on the steering wheel. Lee Lee had played it enough on the truck to find its way into our skulls whenever even the idea of garbage came up. "Trash is pretty private. Who wants a stranger pawing around what's private?"

We threw out enough raunchy answers to that question to chuckle over all the way back to my house.

About a half hour later, Eva walked through my door with a couple of pages ripped from a yellow legal pad and started naming owners of big land parcels. I had no idea who these people were, so after making coffee and filling up a huge to-go cup for her, we returned to Bill Hannah, who seemed to know everyone who ever stepped foot within a twenty-mile radius of Frick Village.

Before we entered into his office, I paused for a moment,

reconsidering the lingering possibility that maybe it was Hannah, not Heine, who had hidden the garbage. If he were the culprit, then how stupid were we to go to him for guidance and information? He could be leading us off the trail, or worse, right into harm's way. As I told him to his face months before, Hannah would be the perfect villain, so unexpected, so respected, so damn polite. Such a revelation felt like something in a cheesy murder mystery, or worse, a reality T.V. show. No, I trusted Big Bill Hannah because I had seen his hands on the pails, and I had spent too much time with him. I wasn't going to let my hallucinatory suspicions (the kind Max might conjure for a video) interfere with my instincts.

I walked into Bill's office, like I had a hundred times before, but now I let Eva do the talking.

"I am glad to be your humble servant again, my fine lass," said Bill in his patented courtly manner. "I hope I do not disappoint you and can properly address your outstanding concerns."

She started naming the owners, and Hannah ticked off a brief biography for each. "Howard Nudlebaum is a hedge fund manager whose estate encompasses an old apple orchard." Eva asked if the orchard was still there. "He has a big fall festival where the Mexicans press cider and make pies for him." She moved onto the next name. "Michael Flynn is a big real estate developer. He's actually thought about selling the entire Hawk Ridge property, and subdividing it into premium home sites. He's planning on expanding his villa in South Beach." Eva gave me a glance. No high-end developer would try to subdivide on an old landfill. She moved onto the next name. "Toby Merwin has the oldest estate in the county. His forefathers were big landowners since the Mayflower. You know, the landed gentry with fox hunts and everything. He has stables with more than

80 show horses on the property. He spends more time in the equine breeding business nowadays than anything else." Again, I could tell by Eva's expression she was crossing off Merwin too. Those types of horses were fragile babies; they would collapse of heart attacks if their delicate hoofs got soiled by an old hot dog wrapper, let alone Peggy Murphy 12-year-old Friday fish stew. She tossed out more names. "Manav and Sukanya Shah. Oh, the Shahs, they're both top flight cardiac specialists. They've also written a couple of heart-healthy advice books. I bet you've seen them on TV. They have, what is it, eleven children?" Not thinking eleven children could be tromping about a landfill site, Eva forged ahead. She got through another nine names, all of whom Hannah described in such a way that they seemed unlikely trash mongers. She got to Landor Nagera.

"Landor Nagera?" Hannah paused, that huge granite forehead of his percolating with all kinds of activity. "My good lass, I don't believe I know Landor Nagera."

"That's alright. You've already saved me many hours of work with what you've told me."

"Landor Nagera sounds like someone in Star Wars," I pointed out, helpful as ever. "Maybe he's from another galaxy."

Eva gave me a half smile and turned back to Hannah. "Can I give you the next name? I only have three more on the list."

"It would be my great honor, my lady."

Eva threw out Charles Wu and Alton Smith and Tommy Sisneros McCarthy, and Hannah spoke respectively of a tech industry mogul, a fashion guru, and a restaurateur who combined a tapas bar with an Irish pub to build a national chain. We didn't smell a whiff of decomposing trash in their portfolios.

Eva and I thanked Hannah, Eva more graciously. "I must say I've learned more about the noble people of our fair Frick village in a half hour with you than I learned in my eighteen years of rummaging through its convenience stores and markets," she said. Eva had the tendency to pick up the language and inflections of whomever she spoke to.

As we headed back out into the light, Eva and I debriefed. "I find it particularly intriguing that Heine isn't on that list," I said. "Max and the neighbors talk like he's the richest man in the state."

"It's very possible that Max and the neighbors don't know what the hell they're talking about." Eva was clearly frustrated. You could see that she'd been at it for days, obsessing over the lost garbage like it was a favorite food, beverage, cigarette, or online blackjack game.

"Come to my house and cook me dinner."

"Thank you," she said with sincerity. "Let's first run by the county clerk's office before it closes. I've gotten friendly with the deputy clerk."

"Of course you have."

Eva frowned and continued. "I want to give him the lot number for the parcel owned by that Landor Nagera guy, see what else we can find out about him and the property."

When we arrived at the county clerk's office, she asked me to wait in the car. She didn't have to explain to me that the assistant clerk might be a little less likely to try to impress her with his real estate expertise if a guy who thought he was her boyfriend was hovering over them. It was about three minutes to five when we arrived and the county workers were moving to their cars with a speed and efficiency worthy of an emergency drill. By five minutes after five, my car and the deputy clerk's seemed to be the only two left in the parking lot. A couple of minutes later, when I saw Eva and the assistant clerk (not a bad looking guy, but no movie star either) coming out, I scooted into the back seat.

They were laughing all the way to the car.

"So I'll see you then," he said.

"Well, I still have some more research to do on CV-2249 for my thesis project, so you definitely will."

She shut the door and headed into the driver's seat.

"I'm back here," I whispered.

"Thank God," she said a little bit panicked.

"What were you scared of."

"Well, I come back to the car and you aren't here. Plus this missing garbage investigation is freaking me out a bit."

"I thought Romeo might not look so forward to helping you tomorrow if he saw an incredibly handsome dude in the car."

"That was good thinking. I was afraid you were sulking."

"I wasn't sulking," I said pretty convincingly. "So you're working on your thesis now?"

"I don't think he'd be so helpful if he thought I was in high school."

"Oh, I think he'd be as helpful, but I think he might spend a lot of time worrying that he could end up in jail at the end of all this."

"Yeah, and who needs that kind of worrying." As she made her way out of the county offices back toward the market near my home, I crawled up into the front seat. She gave me a glance. "You upset with me?"

"No. I'm crazy jealous right now, but that's my problem." I decided I needed to change the subject. "Were you able to find out something?"

"Not much. I've got a better idea of the parcel. It looks undeveloped from what Brendan could tell me." I wondered if I'd have hallucinations later about Brendan, preferably hallucinations involving kicking him in the head.

"Well that's good news. A truly developed parcel is unlikely to be a garbage dump."

"At one time, it might have had an access road but that information's very sketchy, just a dotted line. Brendan says it could've been a plan for a road instead of an actual road."

"Again, that sounds promising. I think if the dump is anywhere, it's going be on something that has hazy details."

"The only other thing I found out was that the property was sold in 1998 to Landor Nagera from the previous owner Donald Hagen."

"Donald Hagen? I'll have to call Hannah later and see what he knows about him. How long did this Hagen guy own the property?"

"I don't know. I'll try to find out tomorrow. I got the impression Brendan really needed to go. It was very kind of him to stay late to help me."

"Yeah, I hear if you stay any later than five at the county offices, your head turns into a pumpkin like Heine's."

Eva giggled a little bit. We turned our attention to the parcel and decided it might be worth a visit since we didn't seem to have any better leads. Eva even suggested a private stroll through private property in search of a dump might be quite romantic.

We bought the groceries like we were a married couple. When we entered the house, like always, I heard the Joan's question. I wondered if Eva hung around long enough, that she might be able to hear it too. She got dinner started and I headed out to the garage to continue to work on The Calling. With some careful sanding and staining, the grandfather clock section was shaping up nicely. I had split and spread out the rotary so it would mimic the numbers on a clock face, and I was now drilling a bolt through the phone receiver to convert it to a pendulum. My mind was clearing now and I ran through all the names again, trying to find some kernel from our discussion with Bill that we had not seized upon initially. Each landowner seemed to be a highly implausible harborer of lost trash. Even if they bought the properties after the dumping, these parcels were too prominent to once serve as a landfill. I called Bill and asked him if he had heard of Donald Hagen. No, Bill hadn't heard of Donald Hagen, my good man.

Well, I guess that was something. Bill Hannah, who might as well have been the town historian, had heard of neither owner of plot CV-2249. I tried to think about the name Landor Nagera, but all I could envision was a guy in a white helmet flying a space ship. I'm not quite sure that I'm cut out for detective work.

Well, there was still the unknown Donald Hagen to investigate. As I tried out the pendulum, I repeated his name to the rhythm of the arc, "Don-ald Ha-gen, Don-ald Ha-gen, Don-ald Ha-gen, Don-ald Ha-gen, Don-ald Ha-gen, Don-ald Ha-gen, Don-ald Ha-gen."

I was ready to say something that just might be as stupid as my suggestions about Landor Nagera, yet the thought was swinging about my skull like that pendulum, and I knew I had better get it out or it'd be wreaking havoc in my visions all night. I headed out of the garage and watched Eva lovingly attend to the risotto. I whispered to her, just over the hum of the bubbling pots. "Donald Hagen could be Ronald Reagan."

"Ronald Reagan?"

"I know he's dead. But I also know someone who worships Ronald Reagan."

Not a slow processer, Eva said, "You mean someone with a big picture of him on his office wall." She thought for a minute. "That's not the dumbest thing you've ever said."

"Why thank you." I even remember Gallagher writing about a guy on Reagan's staff named Donald Regan. It's a name pretty similar to Reagan's. It'd make sense for Heine to pick such a first name as Donald as a substitute.

I called Max. "Whatdaya want now?" said Max as a form of greeting.

"Those passwords you used for Heine. By any chance, did they have to do with Ronald Reagan?"

"Yeah."

There was silence. I pressed ahead. "You want to elaborate on that?"

"No." Max hung up. I think he suspected we were producing our own documentary. Max was definitely either the exact same or a completely different kid than the one who saw bloody murder in every garbage pail.

Listening in on the conversation, I could see Eva was really thinking now. I expected wisps of smoke to rise from her luxurious black mane. "So you think the mayor sold the land to this Landor Nagera guy."

"He must be a very trustworthy friend."

Eva frowned. "Does Heine look like the kind of guy who has those types of friends?" She was now serving her 16-ingredient salad (featuring three types of nuts and two berries), and I quietly sighed catching the sight of the stack of bowls in the sink. "Maybe Landor Nagera is a phony name."

"Well, it sounds like a phony name, unless you hail from the planet Zotan."

Eva slapped a healthy spoon of 16-ingredient salad a little too aggressively onto my plate, leaving my green waffle shirt splattered with 8-ingredient dressing. She smiled at me and muttered, "jerk." I was trying to figure out whether she liked my jokes. I think she was trying to decide the same thing.

Suddenly, Eva stopped serving and merely held the spoon like she was posing for a bakeoff. I considered tossing out another one of my witticisms, but she was in one of those intense states of concentration that I had only witnessed when she was seriously gambling. Hell, for Eva to halt the ceremonies of feasting, she must have been pierced through with a thunderbolt forged by the gods. "Of course," she said. "Landor Nagera is Ronald Reagan."

Confused, I couldn't resist asking, "Ronald Reagan is from the planet Zotan? Well that explains a lot."

"It's an anagram," she said, but with an expression that added "moron" to her comment. I didn't reply, not sure if I'd ever learned what an anagram was, or I had learned it once and forgotten it. Eva was doing her best to be patient with me. "It's when you take one word and mix around the letters to make another word. Ronald turns into Landor and Reagan becomes Nagera."

"Oh, I get it now, like the Jumble puzzles." Like all puzzles, Eva loved the Jumble and like all puzzles, she was a whiz at it. More to the point, Jumble was one of the 42 distractions Heine fiddled with when he pretended to listen to you. "So you think this is Heine's land and has always been Heine's land."

"I'm coming around to that way of thinking."

"And he transferred the property from himself to himself from Donald Hagen to Landor Nagera."

"It sounds stupid, I know, but it sounds like Heine. I can't figure out why he changed the name."

I had an inkling. "When was the transfer again?"

"Brendan says 1998."

I decided I hated the name Brendan. "Hannah once told me the story about a reporter, Murray Maslin, who thought he knew where the trash was and then wound up dead. If I remember correctly, it was about that time."

"So Heine could've gotten spooked. We weren't the first people to realize that Donald Hagen was a really stupid phony name for Heine to come up with."

"Yet you could see Heine doing it."

"Of course I could, just like I could see him coming up with that anagram for Ronald Reagan. It's like he planned out his entire life as if it were a cheesy mystery movie."

"So that means . . ."

"That means Max and your stupid neighbors might be right about Heine having some financial resources."

"I think you should get on the truck tomorrow and stop at each one of their houses and offer your sincerest apology."

"First of all, I'm not known for my sincere apologies. Second, let's wait to see if anything comes of further investigations before you get all smug and smart with me. Third, hand me my phone."

She slapped in the address on her keypad and looked at the map. "Your risotto's going to burn," I warned her.

"To hell with the risotto. Take a look at this map." She dragged her finger along roadways and enlarged the image. "It's a ways out of town."

"You want to go there tonight?"

"And look at it in the dark? No, tonight we're going to eat this slightly overcooked, but still quite heavenly risotto. Tomorrow morning, you're doing your trash run, I'm gonna do some research." I muttered the words "goddamn Brendan" barely low enough for her to miss. "Then we're both going to skip school, and you're going to drive us out there. How's that sound?"

"What do you mean how's that sound? I'm the one who made the plan."

Eva was ready to argue with me, but realized I was joking, so she punched me instead. "Funny, Donald Hagen doesn't sound like someone who'd be big in the solid waste management industry."

"Well, maybe not Donald Hagen, but Landor Nagera sounds like he could run the trash business for the whole galaxy."

She raised a glass of 12-ingredient fruit juice. "Here's hoping we find out some answers tomorrow." We clicked glasses. The juice was very good, although I could only recognize seven of the ingredients.

That night my mind kept racing through all the possibilities Eva and I had discussed. When I tried to settle into bed, I got up to go to the bathroom twice. Each time I didn't see one damn camera. Unbelievable. Now, when I could've used the attention. . . . Then I got out of bed and read Emails.

They didn't help me sleep.

From the March 28 Trash Folder

Are you sure you want to permanently delete all the items and subfolders in the Deleted Items Folder?
The Daily Bread from Reverend Alexander Burr

A survey says that 19 percent of the population uses a cell phone in church. That survey was conducted a year ago, so I guess the percentage is now up to 26 percent. I wonder when they check their phones. During a hymn? During prayer? During my sermon? Why do they come to church? They have the rest of their lives to pile the trash of distraction between themselves and the Lord. They have turned my sanctuary into a reality television show that could be entitled Real Parishioners of Frick. In this new age, entering the hallowed altar situated between themselves and the vault of heaven, they stream live chats, Twitter feeds, YouTube videos, and alerts on dog food sales.

Still, I see goodness remains in this world. I thank the Lord that the lambs of our village have been removed from Generation Dementia. Those who now preen for the cameras are damned anyway. Hash may yet be saved from a wicked existence, for he may bring order to this cluttered world. It used to be that the trash only filled our houses and streets. Now it fills our air. When it enters our sanctuaries, we know there is nowhere to hide from its probing eyes.

Still that which hath been hidden may yet be revealed, and Hash may yet deliver.

The Epic Life of Selena Omaha

So are you ready for the inside scoop about what's popping in Frick Village?

Mr. Pulaski isn't the only one besides me walking the streets at three in the morning to look and see what people have left out on the curb. Our little diva of the trash truck Lee Lee is out turning up a few hours before she climbs up next to Hash and Louie. I can't tell you I've gotten anything useful of hers that she's left out. That girl doesn't throw out anything but shade.

But one early morning I was following Lee Lee (I was just curious, that's all), and I saw her open up Nonna D'Antonio's pail and drop in a small cardboard box. I waited until she turned up the next street before I looked in the pail. And do you know what it was?

The packaging for a harmonica. No harmonica, though.

Could you see Lee Lee playing the harmonica? Could you see Lee Lee's mother? I'm wondering if Lee Lee was so thirsty that she was trying to grab more attention for Generation Dementia, especially with her and her friends being replaced by those real garbagemen. The next thing I know she'd be showing up at my curb trying to take something of mine.

But I won't get chirped. Selena Omaha doesn't leave out anything for anybody.

I wished I had a harmonica right now since I knew a good tune to play.

30

GARBAGE FREE

After the garbage run and before I could meet up with Eva, Big Bill, Lee Lee, Louie and I were summoned to Frick Village Hall for an important announcement. Mayor Heine was already behind the podium and there were many members of the press murmuring.

I turned to Bill, "You know what this is about?"

"No idea, my good man."

Heine had many pieces of oak tag before him and a projector screen blinking behind him. After much hand shaking and many insincere laughs, he made his introductory remarks, including far too many needless thankyous.

"Well, I brought you here today to announce that not only is Frick Village out of bankruptcy, but with the new revenue streams gained from our partnership with the Generation Dementia show producers, we can embark on a state-of-the-art resource recovery program. Starting in two months, we will switch over to a completely automated garbage pick-up. There will be no more human error, there will be no excessive clanging of pails, there will be no leftover mess on the streets. There will

only be precision trash removal."

The screen behind Heine showed a truck with two thin, long mechanical arms hooking onto pail handles, lifting up the pails high, and dropping them into the compactor. Floating softly in the background like harmless clouds were the words, "Garbage Free." The pails were then gently replaced at the curb, and the arms started reaching out invitingly toward the pails of the next customer. Heine walked so close to the screen that he appeared to be on the street with the truck. "Isn't that a thing of beauty?"

"What's this all mean?" asked Louie to Big Bill.

"That the pooch has been screwed," he answered.

"You mean we're losing our jobs—"

"To machines."

"That's creepy, man."

I looked at the three of them, a little stunned. "I thought we were safe with the trash. I mean who would want the job? If machines were going take over, why didn't they do it twenty, thirty, forty years ago, like they did with all the other industrial jobs? I thought the automatons had passed us by."

"Apparently not," said Lee Lee.

"Especially if you have a mayor running for county executive," Big Bill said.

"Not again," Louie said. "How many times can one man lose?"

"I don't know," said Big Bill. "I hate the man, but I've never seen him so popular, and I've been keeping an eye on his movements for a lot of years."

We watched the animated, state-of-the-art truck on the screen like we were peering into summer: visions on such screens tend to leave an indelible impression, especially if they project a higher definition than everyday life, than a reality that has merely been experienced instead of professionally produced. After the automated Garbage Free truck headed through the neighborhood and seemed to have cleaned up the entire village in minutes, the thin metal arms had one final pick-up. There were two trash men in orange jump suits standing as stiff as two trash cans. One of them was short and squat and could've been Louie and the other was a tall one who could have been . . . me. The metal arms lifted and deposited them into the compactor with the word "Dump!" repeated, as in "Dump! Dump!" The image was on a loop. The press corps laughed. I found the illustration less amusing.

I tried to hallucinate, but all I could see was the stupid disposal of our avatars with the word "Dump" repeated right out into infinity.

Louie put the situation in proper context. "It's like those new Garbage Free trucks are unmanned drones and they're firing their heat-seeking missiles at us."

I shook my head. "Look, when they took us off the trash run on Generation Dementia, we had a pretty good idea of what would be coming next. If you are not on reality TV, your chances of functioning in everyday life are mighty slim."

"But to be replaced by machines . . ."

"Is that worse than being replaced by actors? My God, they're not even actors, they're reality show actors."

"That's quite a fine menu of options we've been presented with."

Meanwhile, Mayor Heine linked his freaky robot garbage trucks to Frick's favorite son. "I see the spirit of our great inventor Benjamin Roosevelt Wright floating above our Garbage

Free village. Wright always propelled us into the future, and with these trucks, we will forge our way into a new age."

"He wants to be so much like Wright," said Louie. "Maybe he'll start ripping his skin to shreds like that crazy bastard did." Somehow I didn't think we'd be so lucky.

Heine ended his presentation with the bottom line. "Ultimately, with this new state-of-art sanitation delivery system we will save the taxpayers of Frick Village millions in the years to come."

I turned to Louie. "Were you getting paid over minimum? Because I wasn't." Louie pulled out the inside of his pockets to reveal his fine lint collection.

Mayor Heine stood at the podium ready to answer questions. A reporter from the local cable station asked what color the new truck would be. "Orange." Jesus Christ, I was hoping he'd asked Heine next what he liked to eat for breakfast. Another reporter asked for a ride on the Garbage Free truck. Maybe Heine might let her trot around on a pony at the petting zoo while he was at it.

Thankfully, *The Herald* reporter, Tanvi Jain, asked a real question and it happened to be about us. "Are you at all bothered that you will be getting rid of the members of Operation Pick-up Kids, especially since it was their success that got Frick Village the attention to make the Generation Dementia reality show possible and to provide the revenue to fund this new program?"

Mayor Heine smiled. "Certainly, I'd like to thank the fine young students in Operation Pick-up for their service to our community at a particularly difficult moment in Frick Village history. However, the current members are all graduating seniors, so it is time for them to move on with their lives."

Rising up on her flat heels, Tanvi did not seem to want to let it go at that. "Aren't you getting rid of a successful program in both the village and in the school system by abandoning Operation Pick-up Kids?"

Mayor Heine cleared his throat, "Well, we're not exactly getting rid of the program. We will see Operation Pick-up Kids continuing to serve the community, perhaps with kids cleaning up the sidewalks or something like that."

Tanvi was not done. "Am I accurate to assume that you don't have a clear plan in place of how to continue what has been a program that gives the youth of Frick Village a greater stake in the community?"

"My dear," Mayor Heine paused for effect. "There is always a plan." With that comment, the mayor zipped out of the room, even as Tanvi was asking for concrete details of that plan.

Clearly, in inviting his current trash haulers to the press conference, Heine was serving notice that he had finally buried the three of us. Over the past couple of months, the nonsense with the reality show had completely soured us from wanting to continue on our rubbish runs. But now, now that Heine was ripping it away from us, I wanted to stay on. I could see in Lee Lee's eyes that she wanted to stay on too, even it that meant her delaying college and bearing the wrath of her mother. And Louie . . . Louie was ready to burst out the door, hitch a tent to the back of the truck, and live out his days hauling trash in and out of Frick Village.

I went up to Tanvi Jain. "What the mayor said about us isn't totally accurate."

"How?"

"We want to stay on the truck, and we're ready to stay for another year. He'd have to pay us a lot less than the cost of that entire system."

I don't know if I meant anything I just told Tanvi, but I knew one thing: Screw Heine. That quote was as good as a way to start as any. I was hoping my meeting with Eva would move things a step further.

* * *

With shovels slung over our shoulders, we walked on Landor Nagera's property a good hour before we were absolutely, totally, hopelessly lost. I really can't explain how it happened. The car ride had been so promising. You could see how trash trucks could function here unnoticed, since after you got off the turnpike, you headed down Jerusalem Road, a road of scrub pines and no houses. Then you turned left onto another houseless street, Nazareth Path, for a mile or so, until you finally landed on Calvary Lane, where we rolled up to lot CV-2247 about 500 yards on the right. We had traveled roads to nowhere, and the final dotted line that might've hidden an entrance then could not be spotted now. If a dirt road had existed, Heine and nature had done a fine job of shrouding its past. After we walked by the No Trespassing signs, I thought we would have no problem finding the landfill, that once on the property it would appear majestically before our eyes like the Statue of Liberty – twenty years of Frick trash rousing and rising like a slumbering dragon. I thought the GPS on my phone would guide me through the land, but the GPS didn't work. We were in a dead zone. Initially I had imagined this expedition would be a terribly romantic quest with Eva. If I had been better prepared and thinking clearly, I would've made all the proper precautions for going into the wild, marking trees with a pocket knife, snapping twigs to blaze the trail, carrying some water, granola, maybe a signal flare . . . you get the idea.

Instead I was just thrashing about.

Thankfully, although the paths were sketchy, there wasn't much in the way of underbrush among the birch and maple and oaks. The leafy ground was damp as if a few rivulets of fresh water trickled through the land that gently sloped toward all points. The property gave you the strange impression that you were going nowhere in every direction.

There was nothing else to do but keep walking. I could offer to Eva little else than an assortment of survival tricks, useless today of course, but nonetheless making for pretty diverting conversation. "You know if a mountain lion attacks," I said, Eva being courteous enough not to remind me that mountain lions are not found within a thousand miles of Frick Village, "you should lift a small child in front of you to make yourself look larger."

"Plus," Eva added, "the mountain lion knows that the baby's tastier, with all that subcutaneous fat."

I told her about the necessity of carrying a long stick on every journey (of course, I didn't have one in my possession), so that when you hit quicksand, you could slip the stick behind your back to keep you from sinking under. Eva countered that you couldn't expect to escape killer bees by jumping into water. "When you surface, they'll be waiting for you."

We spoke of climbing up from a well, surviving snake bites (do not, do NOT, do NOT! suck the venom), fighting sharks, fishing with a branch, and combating scorpion attacks.

None of this expert knowledge got us any less lost, but we *felt* less lost and more at home as we talked our way across nowhere, trudging forever ahead, unsure if that was in a particular direction or merely in circles. I didn't care. I could be lost with Eva for hours. I was so happy I almost forgot that Heine was in the process of destroying my career and that we might be on the precipice of discovering the waste of a generation.

At our backs, the warming April sun was dropping into the horizon. Through all this trail talk, we finally got to deciding which way was west. "We've been heading east," I said confidently, like I had always been aware of our direction.

"That's great. See we've been heading in the right direction the whole time."

"Aren't we the lucky bastards?" We walked and talked, cutting methodically from one end of Landor Nagera's property to another. Eva got around to telling me what else she found out from the incredibly annoying Brendan. It seemed that Landor Nagera bought the land from Donald Hagen for straight cash, so the transfer probably only took a week.

"Somebody must've been in a hurry. This Landor must be a very wealthy man." I paused. "Landor? I never realized his name started with Land."

"Duh?"

"But it's also an anagram for Ronald. That's pretty cool. Landor. It's like land or . . . what?

"Like land or Nagera? Are you sure you want to stick with the pretty cool statement?"

"Well, it's like Heine himself. It starts pretty intriguing, then it all turns to crap."

The shovels were making some major indents on our shoulders before we turned onto a wider path, and we were on that for a couple of minutes before we realized that it was an old broken road. We looked far behind toward what we hoped was Calvary Road and could see only some huge fallen trees blocking the entry a few hundred yards back. Pointing to them, Eva said, "You think Heine put them there, so no one would come up here?"

"I hope the hell so."

We could see the land rise before us and our pace quickened. As the hill came into our vision, I was heartened by its height and width (now *that* could house the refuse of Frick's past), but the metal pipe in front of the mound offered clearer evidence. "Eva, I think that's a methane pipe."

"A what?"

"Methane pipe. It prevents explosions when the garbage decomposes in a landfill."

"Would a pipe like that be installed in the middle of woods for any other reason?" As I started to answer, Eva cut me off. "That was a rhetorical question."

Eva took pictures of the pipe and the mound, walking around its vast perimeter to get the overgrown contours of the landfill from many angles. I climbed up the hill and dropped the shovel into the dirt. I expected to get a spade full of garbage. I got weeds and topsoil. I stuck the shovel in again, dragging out more weeds and topsoil. This shoveling continued until I unearthed a wheelbarrow or two of dirt, calling over Eva to stop taking pictures and get digging.

After I had done most of the digging (a point which I reminded her of whenever we later told the tale to friends), Eva hit the first man-made object. Of course, it was hard plastic, something that would have still remained if the first shovels had been scooped into the mound centuries later. A big black boom box emerged, the speakers broken, but the cassette deck still intact. Eva also found plastic bottles and plastic bags. Naturally, I found diapers, which managed to hold their stink all these years. I found lots of cardboard and old folders with lots of files. Eva kept taking pictures. I found some cans, they could've been soup or beans, their labels long fallen away. All this treasure was nice, but it wasn't incriminating. Eva and I both knew what we were looking for. Neither of us brought it up after that, afraid we would jinx our efforts. The light was dying in the west. Soon we wouldn't be able to take pictures.

Fortunately, after a few more minutes of digging, Eva hit the stash. The pile of newspapers was still bundled in twine. I chopped through the rope with the spade and Eva started separating the papers. While the first of the pile was pretty deteriorated, the next bunch were in fine shape, their front pages readable. The April 23, 1994 edition of *The Herald* announced the death of Richard Nixon. Three other April editions had less timeless news. One featured a housing scandal, another pointed out tax breaks for the rich, and the third marked a detailed investigation into gun violence in America. I did not read on, since I recognized the next paper in the stack was smaller and thinner.

The April 22, 1994 edition of *The Frickin'* dedicated the entire front page to a major new initiative by Mayor Heine called the Frick Survey project. Instead of continuing to rummage through the twenty years of village garbage before me, I stopped right here and read the story, as if I was sitting at a kitchen table, a cup of coffee in my hand, just perusing the local rag like any other day.

The second paragraph quoted Heine, "With this comprehensive survey, we will generate the greatest, most detailed profile of a community the world has ever known. With such a treasure trove of demographic information, the commercial sector will get the kind of data it craves to be able to properly address our community needs. This survey will transform the village."

While most of the story seemed quite positive, it did feature a few grumbles from residents, the most telling coming from Peggy Murphy: "This is just another attempt by the village to infringe onto our private lives."

I lifted the newspaper up gently like it belonged in a museum archive as Eva snapped pictures. "That's some pretty fine evidence right there, eh?"

I tucked *The Frickin'* back inside *The Herald* copies to protect it. I was hoping it wouldn't rain tonight. I thought about shoveling dirt back on top of it, but my instincts told me to leave everything where it was right now.

We took our shovels and decided to get the hell out of here for the night.

"So, how do we get this story out?" asked Eva.

"Well, we've got to be a little cautious about this," I said. "We made the discovery by trespassing."

"The good news is, I don't think Heine can cover this up. You can only figure out how to hide twenty years of garbage so many times in your life."

I suggested that we feed the story to the press and let it go from there.

"You know anybody you can trust?" Eva asked.

"I think so, even though I just met her."

Eva groaned a bit, an indication she had noticed a pattern in how easily I put faith in women. We followed the abandoned road back toward Calvary Lane, stepping over many a felled tree. Eventually, we left the dead zone and I had a bar or two on my cell phone. I called Tanvi Jain and told her what we discovered. Eva sent her pictures and her research on Lot CV-2249. I could hear the excitement in Tanvi's voice. She promised she'd be investigating and was sure her editor would get a few more staff members on the story.

"I'll see you at the village hall tonight, right?" Tanvi asked.

"Why?"

"I'm surprised you don't know."

I reminded Tanvi I had been out in a dead zone unearthing

the greatest story in the history of Frick Village.

"Oh," she answered. Then she told me that the village council members had gotten word of a flash mob tonight at village hall (sounds like Louie had been busy too), and that residents were planning on dumping trash on the Frick Village Green in protest of the new automated rubbish removal system. Even Heine agreed a hearing, however raucous, would be preferable to such a scene. "It seems like I'm going to be spending some time in your village."

"Well," I said, "I think you might be spending a few moments on the outskirts of the village too."

Tanvi said she had a few close contacts at the state Department of Environmental Conservation who might be traveling with her.

"Good," I said. "Can't you skip the meeting?"

"My editor would kill me. Robotic arms lifting garbage? People love that kind of stuff." I think she could see my frown through the phone. "Don't worry, I won't be sleeping for at least the next couple of days. I know how big the story is, and I know you didn't have to call me, and I'm glad you did. By the way, the picture of *The Frickin* cover from '94 is freaking amazing."

"I'll make sure to let the photographer know," I smiled over at Eva. "When we both have the time, remind me to tell you the story about a beautiful young intern in Mayor Heine's office who cracked the ancient mysterious case of Frick's missing garbage. I tell you it's the stuff you could base a reality TV show on." I did a hop-step as Eva swung a shovel at my ankle. "Yeah, I think your headline writer might be able to come up with something good. Will you put something in tomorrow's paper?"

"No, but I'll throw it on the website as soon as I can get a DEC official down there."

We made our way to the car. As I drove back home, I asked

Eva if she wanted to go to the village hall meeting tonight.

"Are you asking me out on another date?"

"Sure, if you're willing to continue to maintain your very low standard of what a date is?"

"Are you kidding? I have a feeling we'll be seeing some very good theatre."

31

THE DIARY OF LEVON GALLAGHER: THE CLIFF

September 11, 2001

I had wanted to meet Chuck Jones my entire life. His Bugs Bunny cartoons filled hours of my childhood. They had started right along with the war and by the time I was born more people went to the movies to see Bugs than the feature film. Now it was my last shot to see the rabbit. As I grew older, the newspaper column became more about what I wanted than what the public demanded. Shelley first scheduled me to visit these guys who made a cartoon called *South Park*. I ignored him. He pressed for *The Simpsons*. I booked a plane to Los Angeles to see Chuck instead.

I headed out of the newsroom. Shelley said to me sadly, "Levon, nobody even knows who Chuck Jones is anymore."

"That's the case for just about everybody

I've ever heard of."

I hadn't been out to California since I had visited Ben. He had been tweaking Java script for Jimmy Gosling. Then the authorities found the note. Ben had dumped the file in his trash folder months earlier, but when the SEC confiscated his hard drive over patent-infringement charges, the note was resurrected from the trash and leaked to the press. You wouldn't think anyone would get worked up over his calling Americans cruel, selfish bastards, but the outrage from commentators was spectacular. Ben was branded as the worst kind of traitor (is there a best kind?). I almost got lynched writing a column defending him. Ben's "apology" that he certainly belonged to that "klan of flag-waving, narcissistic bastards" didn't help matters. He became public enemy number one.

A few months later Ben was dead. After that, Sarah returned to the institution for good, embracing what she already knew, that no prescription of Prozac or OxyContin would release her. Artie spent most of his time looking for walls to smash his hands through, or when that wouldn't do, he taught his young grandson to become something he could never be. Joan was the only one left in the family who wasn't brought down with the fever. If anything happened to her, I tell you . . .

I hoped Chuck would make me forget my bad memories about the left coast. I brought him a gift of gel pens. I knew he probably had never seen them before. "They smudge more," I told Chuck, "but you get a much bolder line with them."

Chuck growled at me, "Great, all I need in my life is more smudges." Chuck's breath smelled of burgers ground from mad cows. He agreed to let me animate with him, but he refused to use my gel pens. I was sad. When you draw with a gel pen, it's like the paper is shot through with light. For the past few weeks I left notes with my gel pen on sticky pads for everyone in the newsroom. Some didn't appreciate my gesture. Instead of smiling at my sparkling note, "Off to the Post Office," festooned with letters that shimmered and splashed like sunshine through a fountain, Evelyn slapped the note right on my forehead. Then she said, "Levon, who the hell cares."

Chuck Jones wouldn't use my gel pens, and he didn't want to draw Bugs Bunny with me either. All he cared about was Wile E. Coyote. "I like him much better because he doesn't really say anything except his name with the moniker, 'Super Genius,' like that is his profession. Gravity joined forces with the Road Runner. You've got to love a character like Wile E. Coyote who defies gravity, even when it hurtles him off a cliff everyday. Bugs Bunny talks too much." Oh, Christ, that's what I loved about Bugs!

We didn't agree on anything. The worst was when I asked Chuck what was the best subatomic particle name? Who would have a better sense of such a riddle than a zany cartoonist? He answered that I had just asked him a very stupid question. Then he said, "Neutrino, of course." I tried to hide my deep disappointment.

"What about Quark?"

"That's a stinky name," he said dismissively. He waved his hand to shoo away the bad odor it emitted.

"Howso?"

"Sounds like a name when you can't think of a name, like if you called your dog Gurgish."

"You like Neutrino better? Doesn't that sound like a fitness powder marketed for muscular Italians?"

"No, it does not. Anyway, it's much better than Quark. Hell, Gauge Boson is even a better name than Quark." Now I think Chuck was trying to get under my skin the way old Bugs did with Daffy Duck. "Gauge Boson, god, I wish I had named my son that."

"I think you underestimate Quark," I said, trying to reason with him. "First of all, the word starts with a 'Q.' And it's a short word. We are talking about the tiniest particles here. The 'ark' part rhymes with lively words like spark or joyous words like lark or bucolic words like park . . ." I was running out of rhymes, "or branding words like mark."

He frowned and drew those big ears on Wile E. Coyote. "I really don't think you get absurdity," he said gravely. I can't recall anyone saying something so painful to me. From five years old, from Bugs Bunny on, I thought I had gotten absurdity and that was the one thing that made life bearable. Its ridiculousness was an antiseptic against an infectious, toxic world. No wonder this whole business has been such a struggle! I'd rather he'd have stabbed

me several times in my ear drum with his
fountain pen. That night I conjured up images
of all the ways a cartoonist could be erased.
What's better, if anybody found out, I knew how
to erase myself without a smudge on my oh-so-
private soul.

I threw away the most miserable files on my
disks. Ben has warned me, that even with such
precautions, my foul words could reappear miles
and months away. Those dark thoughts I tossed
out could bounce right back in cyberspace, like
Wile E. Coyote, waiting for another fall.

* * *

How strange it was that Levon Gallagher, the lifelong Easterner,
was on the other coast on September 11, 2001. Yes, he seemed to
relish completely ignoring earth-shattering events around him
as he waged his tiny personal battles. Those nasty little spats
collected in my consciousness like so many of those nuggets I
rescued from the trash heap. Sure Chuck Jones was a very old
man by then, but I couldn't help noticing that an awful lot of
people who argue with Levon didn't live much longer. Jones
died in February of the next year. And I got a suspicion
something bigger may have been behind Ben Wright's death. I
clearly wanted Levon's life to read like a murder mystery, to
add up to something, and, in turn, for my family legacy to add
to something more than a fragmented boy reading about broken
ancestors. How much time was I wasting on Levon Gallagher's
trivial memories? . . . And the accompanying deaths? I forced
pieces together. September 11 made clear that the Cold War had
ended and a new era was upon us. Levon's entire existence was
wedded to that nuclear age, an age where every day meant

being pushed off a cliff. You'd fall, seemingly die, and end up back on the cliff, only to drop back down. He would get up off the ground and search for a cliff that wasn't there anymore, like it had been outsourced or something. Where the hell do you go when you can't find a cliff?

I was terribly afraid of Levon, this dead man, and I couldn't figure out why.

32

GENERATION DEMENTIA

Pulaski was still in his office when I returned at 6:30 p.m. He scratched his graying beard and stretched like a bear at the zoo, replete with growling noises and a twisted maw. We had become friendly enough that I could ask him, "Do you have a life?"

"Isn't it obvious?"

"What are you going to do next year when you retire?"

"Stare into oblivion." He peered out beyond me, past the walls, as if rehearsing for his future role.

"Can I ask you a question?"

"As opposed to what you have been doing?"

I smiled. He stared out into the darkness. "Why do you call us Generation Dementia?" he raised his eyebrow as if to answer – Again, isn't it obvious. I clarified. "I mean it isn't a particularly politically correct thing to say. Aren't you counselors all about sensitivity training?"

"At my age, all my sensitive parts are numb." It was my turn to stare into the great nothingness. "Anyway two years ago my doctor thought I suffered from early dementia. I first started seeing his point when I'd go for my daily walk through the neighborhood only to discover that after a few minutes I had no idea where the hell I was. After a lot of soul searching, I realized that not only do I have signs of oncoming dementia, so do many of you."

"You're serious."

He learned forward now, eyes right on me, in full counselor mode. "Explain the hallucinations."

I looked down on the floor. "I can't."

He knew that he would be doing the talking for quite a while because I wasn't going to say a word. "It's not you. It's the world that you grew up in." Pulaski said. He made a point to say that today was no worse than any other time in history, just stranger to him, with all the reality shows and the virtual reality games. "The lines between being an audience and an actual participant in everyday life have been so blurred that you don't know how to behave," he said. "It leads to awkward outbursts and crazed attention-starved antics. You have more information thrown at you in a week than I had to absorb in my first 50 years and you wonder why you can't sort out your thoughts and struggle making clear plans and organizing what you think you might understand." Pulaski was getting worked up. "You sit together in groups, not talking to each other, but sending choppy little texts out to a disinterested universe and scroll down on your tiny phones forever searching for an image or a sound that may distract you. What else could you be? The hallucinations might be the sanest thing happening to you."

Pulaski tried to suppress a belch. He was unsuccessful.

"Are you telling me that we'll have to be dealing with this for the rest of our lives?"

"Yes." He said so with a finality that indicated there was nothing left to discuss. I waited for him to realize that he was not done talking. It was all part of the dementia. "That's why I sent you all out onto the garbage trucks. You need to stay active. Sending you out on the runs was my directive of unconditional love."

"But when the garbageman robots take over –"

"You'll have to find something else." He smiled devilishly. "There's always cesspool cleaning. There will never be a shortage of crap, that's for sure."

"Yeah," I answered with mock sadness, "until the robot turd men come." Pulaski gave one of his cynical chuckles, a reminder that his main source of amusement derived from the ridiculousness of misery. "But, jeez, don't you think Generation Dementia is pretty harsh. How the hell have you gotten away with saying it all this time?"

"I have been quite charmed in my life in that I never seem to get in trouble for what I say. Most people would have been fired six times over, and yet, look at me, they're going to give me a nice watch and beg me to stay on – although we know they want me out of the school faster than a kid with head lice."

Pulaski had the big goldfish bowl I gave him filled with water on his desk. But no goldfish. I had visions of him carrying the bowl with his briefcase off to retirement neglecting to dump the water before he left.

I told Pulaski I heard the Joan's voice in the house (though I wouldn't tell him what she said). He asked me if she appeared in my hallucinations. "Never, but the visions have gotten stranger, if that's possible."

As I described a few of the more troubling hallucinations, he grunted and said, "It's part of the grieving process . . . your mother's voice, all these crazy visions."

I asked him whether I can do anything to get rid of them.

"No."

I liked Pulaski because he wasn't interested in lying to me.

I asked him if he thought the hallucinations had some hidden subconscious meaning. "Highly unlikely."

"Didn't you tell me that you're also a trained psychologist?"

"Yes."

I left Pulaski and tumbled into a memory – unsurprisingly, a family memory.

The last time I saw Grandpa Artie was when I turned seventeen last spring. He was in a wheelchair then and a week later he would be found dead in it. We were at a firing range. "It's time, my boy, that you learn how to shoot a gun." Artie had out his old Colt '45. I shuddered with 4th grade memories of Artie's rifle lessons – every pull of the trigger sent me flying onto my back.

"You're a man now, and I don't imagine me or your mother will be around to wipe your ass, so you better figure out how to fire this thing." He gave me a rap on the neck with the butt of the Colt for old time's sake. He was so frail that it hit me with a soft thud. In the old days, he would've sent me into lala land with such a stroke, but now the smack felt therapeutic. After a few awkward squeezes, I fired the gun better than I expected, hitting the outside of the target.

"Now if someone comes at you, you might be able to wing him."

When we left the shooting range, he handed me the old Colt, a hundred bullets ("if you have a hundred, maybe you'll get lucky with one"), and a surprising warning: "Watch out for using this gun. It ruined my life, your grandma's life, and the life of someone you should've met."

"What happened with this gun?" I asked. "Did my dad use it?"

"No, of course your father didn't use it. When are you going to get it? Your father never did anything, I mean anything except maybe impregnate your mother, and I'm not even sure about that. No, this gun is part of a story of love and honor, and your father has nothing to do with it whatsoever."

"Then tell me what happened with the Colt?"

"Someday, someone will tell you the story. God, enough people in Frick know it. Go listen to 'The Long, Black Veil' if you want to figure a few things out about it."

"Will it tell me the story?"

"No, but it's time you learn the family anthem."

I thought it wise not to tell Artie that I knew the song and that I also knew the story to go with it. I carried the song and story around in my skull like prized possessions the way Artie bequeathed that damn Colt 45 unto me. For now, everything seemed tied up with Levon Gallagher, so I waited to see if there was more to learn, always waiting for another nugget of trash to show up on the curb.

33

KITTENS AND DEVIL DOGS

Outside the doors of Frick Village Hall were stuffed animals stacked against the wall ten feet wide and five feet deep, lined up like they were in a firing squad. A sign in front of them read: *When they have to go, do you want them taken away by mechanical arms?*

I didn't think that was the most compelling argument, but there was something effectively sad about all those furry little critters. I was wishing for rain so they would look truly pathetic.

The hall was jammed to the rafters and the place smelled of whiskey, mud, and anger. Mayor Heine was showing the same PowerPoint that he presented to the press a few hours ago, but now all he heard were yells, boos, and hollers. Somebody, I think it was Nonna D'Antonio, was even hissing.

"You want everything to fit into your boxy containers, don'tcha Heine," said the irate Mr. Alford over the PowerPoint narrator. "The world doesn't work that way. No matter what you and your robot trucks expect, some trash can't be confined or contained."

After Heine made a long speech, during which the fair

people of Frick Village displayed a stunning lack of courtesy, the line formed for public comment. Derek Standish pulled (seemingly out of his rear end) a long steel tube, some branches, a big arm chair, and a bag of marbles. "Tell me how your trucks are going to handle this stuff."

"They're not," said Mayor Heine. "You're going to have to break everything down."

"I never had to do that. The garbage men would do that."

"This is progress," Heine answered. "Let go of the Stone Age. You have to keep up with the times. I will not have Frick Village be a backwater."

"It's like you're making us do more, so you have to do less, and then pretending we're getting this great improvement on our lives," said Standish. "It sounds like a scam to me."

Nonna D'Antonio yelled at Heine in broken Italian for five minutes, incorporating much foot stomping and finger pointing (man, does that old lady have some crooked digits). Nobody understood her, but the entire audience gave her a standing ovation.

Mayor Heine wryly thanked her for her "enlightening, gracious, and distinguished remarks."

Naturally, most disturbed by the news of the automated pick-up was the Gullota clan. Joseph, the patriarch, spoke eloquently about how garbage was a private, deeply personal matter and that it needed to be handled by caring, highly trained professionals, not an army of thoughtless machines.

"Morning will become cold and robotic. The village will lose its poetry. We now wake up to the sounds of workers whose vitality washes the sleep from our eyes? Tomorrow, we will arise from sweet dreams into a metallic reality."

Mayor Heine explained, "That's all well and good, but machines don't need health care or need to be insured, machines don't miss days, machines don't send pails rolling into the street."

As a response, the good son Anthony attached metal pipes to his arms. Nicole kept putting material in front of him that he tried to pick up. Some, like the log, rolled off as he lifted it; others, like a forty-pound sack of rice, bent and dropped down, with little white grains scattering across the village hall floor. Anthony then lifted a net that left him trapped and tangled. "You look like a baccala," said Nicole. Louie laughed loudest.

The parade of speeches continued, but I spotted Tanvi Jain and knew I'd better touch base with her. She told me she had contacted the DEC officials and they'd be meeting her in front of the property tomorrow morning. I gave her clear directions to the abandoned road, so she wouldn't have to spend hours wandering in the wilderness like Eva and I did.

I stopped talking when Pulaski strode up the podium. "I started Operation Pick-up Kids because in all my years at the high school almost every senior I've ever met suffered an existential crisis." Existential crisis? The conversation at village hall suddenly elevated a bit. "After all those years of preparing to get into college, they get in. Then they wonder what it all means. Was all the effort worth it? Can they handle losing the comforts of home and the familiarity of their lives being carved into 40-minute bites? Have they actually been ready for college for years, and if so, what the hell are they still doing in high school in the second semester of their senior year? They are clearly too young and too old. In today's wireless world, they are more alienated and detached than ever. Don't get me wrong. I am not criticizing progress. I don't want our forward-thinking mayor to accuse me of being a Neanderthal."

Pulaski's voice oozed of such contempt, a listener might easily believe he had been actually calling the mayor a Cro-

Magnon man who grunted the phrase forward-thinking like it dropped out of his bottom. As Pulaski spoke, Cindy Stevens – yes, little suicidal Cindy Stevens – was milling about handing out baggies to the crowd. "The wireless world has allowed the youth of our generation to possess broad knowledge and agile minds, but they have lost the physicality and the ease of sincere communication that gives solace to these teens, a group prone to depression. Operation Pick-up Kids was designed to throw these teens out into the community where they would learn to have a stake in making Frick function. Sadly, it worked so well that the mayor decided to allow a reality television series to come in here to tear apart the fabric that we were trying to weave. What do you think this cyborg trash scheme is going to do to those teens and to the rest of us in Frick Village?"

In answer, Cindy Stevens yelled "Now," and the crowd in something like unison tossed up handfuls of white Styrofoam packing peanuts. They floated up high toward the rafters and then flitted down, less like snow, more like ash from a nuclear winter.

Mayor Heine was trying to explain that Operation Pick-up Kids would continue to play a vital role in the village, but the crowd was preoccupied with the packing peanuts, making sure each one left their bodies and made its way to the floor.

"Let your robots clean up this mess, Heine," said Cindy Stevens as she stormed out. Even as Heine continued to explain, the rest of the crowd filed out, leaving the hailstorm of Styrofoam in their wake. The only one left in the room beside the mayor was Max, propped up on a wobbly folding table, filming the exodus from the room and the isolated mayor. I'm sure Max was looking to capture a private moment.

Now I understood what the formula $(C_8H_8)_n$ stood for. So Cindy had taken my advice all those months ago: to devote her life to Styrofoam was indeed a strange passion. Yet, what could be more plentiful? I could see Cindy's angry sister Megan trying to push her way into Cindy's room past this protective, spongy cocoon. Awfully hard to hurt a sister so immersed in packing peanuts.

As we departed, April showers didn't arrive to render the stuffed animals sodden and desolate. But someone decided to peg them with junk food, so Peter the Penguin was desecrated by a six-pack of yodels and Benny the Bear was nailed with a dozen Twinkies and Katrina the Kitten was attacked by her arch enemies, a pack of devil dogs. The tasty cakes were all broken on the fur, their white cream somehow looking more like pus than shaving cream. Oh the horror, the inhumanity!

One look at this abomination would be enough to send a courageous man screaming from the dreaded automated garbage trucks.

Of course, after such a night, I could not sleep, so I headed into the bathroom, flushing what should always be buried and my hallucinations with them.

Then I rifled through my Emails. You'd think I'd learn to stop looking at them before I hit delete.

From the April 1 Trash Folder

Are you sure you want to permanently delete all the items and subfolders in the Deleted Items Folder?

The Daily Bread from Reverend Alexander Burr

I'm deeply saddened by the decision of Mayor Herman Heine of Frick Village to move to an automated trash system. I must say that our greatest folly is to separate ourselves further from the waste we produce as if we did not create it, as if we do not have to take responsibility for its disposal. I do believe that understanding will save sons like Hash and Louie and daughters like Lee Lee for they now know what it is to carry that load.

We must never forget that our waste is Adam's curse. That devil Freud might call it our subconscious, but whatever the case, it is the stain that makes us embarrassingly fallible. When a machine lifts these burdens off our narrow shoulders, it reminds us of our tendency to deny our responsibility like Peter's denial three times before the crowing of the cock. Is Mayor Heine Peter or Judas? I cannot see that far ahead. Yet I prophesize he will believe he bears the cross only to discover that he has instead buried it like many talents into a soil where even the willing cannot unearth it.

The Epic Life of Selena Omaha

So are you ready for the inside scoop about what's popping in Frick Village?

I don't mean this to be a dis, but that poor hunk Hash has really fallen into the grind. I mean yesterday he bounced a shoebox of painkillers. What kind of thirsty sicko gets rid of them? And that's not all. You should've seen the mad swerve headscarves and the two baseball caps. Then there were the way smart sandals and pumps, all size 9, my size. I don't know if I'll use the pocketbooks, all are in pretty good condition, but a little too Beyonce for my taste. Though I definitely wanted the stack of self-help books he left. Most of them looked brand new and on fleek. I took three epic bags of toys too. They will be great for target practice (especially the Legos) once I get more BBs for Levon Gallagher's gun. I'm always running out of BBs. I wonder if Hash will be the one actually throwing into the garbage truck all the stuff from his home (he's definitely turned up some serious housecleaning, and I only took about a quarter of it), or will it be those glam studs from the real cast of Generation Dementia?

Oh, it's getting very sassy in Frick.

The Email inspired me to continue my housecleaning, starting with—

34

OUR UNDERWEAR DRAWERS

The DEC officials had officers and a search warrant in hand the next morning. Besides the evidence Eva and I provided, they were able to use the major land rise off of Google maps as further indication of a landfill. It didn't hurt that the authorizing judge had a long and ugly history with Heine, just distant enough that he decided not to recuse himself as an interested party. Of course, Tanvi Jain was there, but we couldn't be, since we would essentially be admitting to breaking the law. Now Jain and the authorities could make some vague claim that anonymous squatters had sent them the information.

Clearly, Tanvi had a better cell phone than I did, since she sent me a series of text messages as a running commentary of what was being unearthed. From the very beginning, the officials didn't doubt they were standing on the landfill. Their only question was how wide and how deep. One DEC official, who had surveying equipment, walked the hill's perimeter rolling a wheel about the edge. Another had a long skinny drill that burrowed down about six feet. "They started at the hole you already dug and saw no end in sight."

I could tell from her texts that Tanvi was conducting many interviews. "Miller tells me this is a major find."

A half an hour later, Tanvi wrote me again. "Everything's great. They're heavy into the work right now. They haven't noticed I'm off digging on my own."

After another fifteen minutes, Tanvi rained on me a shower of brief texts.

"OMG, new jeans with old rips!"

"LOL, a huge toaster oven!"

"Could it be? A cubic zirconium ring. I think it's from QVC."

I asked her, "Did you find any missing statues from the Renaissance?"

"LOL, a Baywatch lunch box!"

"No, not a silk vest for a poodle. This is great!

"A video for Police Academy 6!"

"A green supersoaker!"

"Fruit Roll-ups and Slim Jims. They still look edible, barely, although that was always the case."

She continued on, using up so much text space that I had to delete almost everything right after I received it. On she would go, recording Frick's miserable record of consumer shallowness.

"OMG, a walkman."

"LOL, platform shoes. I think they're from the disco era."

"Spackling buckets, busted sheet rock."

"Resin chairs with Hello Kitty stickers."

I could see Tanvi hiding this secret stash away, so she could one day open the Frick Historical Museum.

"I could blog about Frick's trash for months!"

I recoiled a little at the word blog, still stung by the embarrassment of Mom's incessant, obsessive commentaries. I couldn't quite shake from my skull that blogging sounds more like gossiping than analyzing.

The more Tanvi talked, the more I wanted to throw the phone against the wall. What if the garbage Tanvi was picking through and mocking was my mother's? Did she have the right to rifle through what the Joan had intended to discard, what she had every reason to believe no other human eyes would ever see? The invasion of privacy on an entire village was colossal, and Eva and I had led that charge. What had been long buried and sealed in every other community in America was now being opened to the public and its pictures exposed like it was lurid porn. I wasn't sure we were only bringing down Heine with this revelation. I argued with myself. Big deal, so reporters and state officials will be picking through your trash, and maybe as a form of land remediation, they may even carry it out, parade it through the streets, until it reaches its final destination at a resource recovery plant. Doesn't everyone tend to be ashamed of what he abandoned? What he purchased and then rejected? What he turned to waste?

I was torn between damning what I'd done and seeing if I could get another peek at the ancient waste. Hell there might be artistic gold in them there hills. What the hell am I? A peeping Tom raking through the underwear drawers of Frick Village?

I expressed to Eva my misgivings. Eva sighed. "During the rehab program, I figured out how to give up shame," she said. She thought only those locals with a distorted image of themselves would have a problem. She said that the landfill gave us a chance to better understand how we lived, and that the newly discovered trash invigorated Frick. "I believe this will be giving Frick a chance to be a very interesting place for a long time and that's not a bad thing. Maybe I'll open up a restaurant and call it the Hidden Trash Café."

"Yeah, I wish I was as optimistic. The media will lose interest in about a week, and all people will remember about us is the silly garbage we made."

"I don't know about you, but I'm going to stick my spoon in that garbage and stir it around a bit like it's a new stew recipe."

Later that afternoon, Tanvi Jain posted her story, and within hours the Village of Frick was in an uproar. I half expected to see torches and pitchforks. The next day prosecutors were closing in on the notion that Landor Nagera was an alias for Mayor Heine, a conclusion that had already been arrived at by the village residents. Someday, Eva might get credit for seeing the entire picture before anyone else imagined it, like she had counted the cards and knew each player's hand as it was being dealt. For now, the only praise she would be hearing was my hearty approval of her lamb ragout, ratatouille, and cheddar biscuits to mop it all up.

That night I could only offer Eva my trust in her: I fired up the Commodore 64 and called up what looked like the final file of Levon Gallagher. After all this nonsense, I needed a little distraction from the trash that has passed, is passing or is to come.

35

THE DIARY OF LEVON GALLAGHER: MAPPED OUT

July 11, 2008

"Let's find out where you are, Levon."

Joan put the Garmin GPS in my car. Minutes later I became a dot on a screen. I was on the map. I spent my life trying to stay off the map. I grew up with maps where Greenland was huge, five times as large as it had any right to be, where the top of world was as wide as its middle. I grew up with Hagstroms, my finger always following the roads. I grew up where I was never on the map, in a time when the world was so very large and I was so very small that you could not find me.

I liked it that way.

I had no credit cards, did no banking online, carried no cell phones. I did not want government or anybody else to know my whereabouts. Now this machine beeps in my car. I can be targeted like I'm a munitions dump.

"So Garmin knows where I am?"

"Sure," said Joan matter-of-factly, clearly not understanding the ramifications of what was happening here.

"And if Garmin knows, I can presume the government knows too."

"That's a good assumption."

I grabbed her wrist. "Why the hell did you put that thing in my car?"

"So you can find out where to go."

"I don't need to know where to go. I don't need to go anywhere if it means they can find me." It figures she'd use a mapping program that works. If she just had lost.com like our Mayor Heine, then I wouldn't have to worry about a damn thing. In fact, I'd be harder to find than ever.

"I don't understand. You don't think the government has always known where you are. My God, you're Levon Gallagher, a Pulitzer Prize-winning reporter."

"Sure they can find me at the newsroom, but not here."

She snickered at me – and I had considered marrying the woman. "You really don't think the government knows where you are."

"I get all my mail delivered to the newsroom. My address is not published."

"Oh Levon, just because something is unpublished doesn't mean it's not documented."

"My private life isn't documented either."

"Oh Levon, just because it's not documented, doesn't mean it's not recorded."

"How is that possible?"

"Data mining. Between the government and the corporations, there're many interests that want to know how you spend your money."

"I spend only cash."

"That's one of the things they want to

know."

"They wouldn't know anything if they didn't find me just now on that GPS."

"Are you kidding me?" She pointed to the sky. "Do you know how many satellites are looking down on you? My God, they know when you pee."

I tried to calm myself, remembering that Joan, while quite a looker for her age, had just been diagnosed with brain cancer and may even have early dementia, and should not be considered a trustworthy source about such sensitive information. I have known Joan since she was born and have watched her exhaust her entire life looking for an intimacy that her family was in no condition to provide. Now she turned again to me. As before, it didn't matter how good of a person Joan was and how happy she'd make me, I would not be trapped by the geography of this situation.

I thought of my crawl space and my jaw started to tighten. How deep did the cameras probe? I did not want to appear suspicious in front of her. The damage was already done with the Garmin. I might as well talk to her about it. "Does it set routes?"

"It guides you to wherever you want to go."

"What if I want to go right here."

"Then it confirms where you're located."

"Big deal."

"Don't underestimate that. It grounds you. I put on the GPS every time I want to make sure I'm still here." Her eyes became a little moist and she swallowed a couple of times. "After I had Hash, his father wanted me to run off with him." I knew this story very well, but she clearly thought I needed to hear it again. "He told me, 'I can't be a father and do what I have to do.' And I asked him 'What do expect me to do?' He held my hand, saying, 'Come with me. Let's get lost together and see the world. Let Artie take care of the child. He's done for anyway. Getting lost is the only way.' I looked into his eyes, making sure I wasn't crying, and said 'For you it is. I've gotta make sure Hash has the chance to get lost too when he grows old enough. I can't just leave him.' We didn't say much as he packed."

I studied Joan carefully and said, "That was another time."

She smiled the way someone does when reading a postcard sent by a friend miles and years gone. "As he carried his duffle bag out the door – his worldly possessions could fit in an airplane carry-on bin – he looked back once. 'You sure?' he said, 'because once I go there'll be no way to find me.' I thought about Hash in the other room and told him, 'I won't be lookin'.'"

She smiled at me sweetly. "Turns out, he really didn't go away. Oh, he disappeared for a time, after he dug up that picture of me with Ben Wright on MySpace." She shook her head. "Still can't figure out how he found that photo. I thought I'd wiped it out long ago." Joan gazed into my eyes with an intensity that could be interpreted as love. "There's a price that you pay to be part of this world, Levon. I've definitely paid it. Hash will pay it too. Sure, they can find you, and sadly, every miserable thing you've ever done, but it's easier to find yourself here than anywhere else."

I looked at Joan, reabsorbing her lines like they were part of a movie I had watched too many times. I wanted to kiss her and hold her, but I was old enough to know that some things are not worth having. The price is too great. I had spent my life under the radar. She would sacrifice it all, just because she was terminally lost.

I walked up to her and told her gently. "Look Joan, I don't think this is going to work between us. I need my privacy."

"We can be private together," she said coyly.

"God, I wish that was the case, but we're going to have to be private alone."

"Maybe *you* have to be."

I imagined her private with someone else, maybe with Shelley Kornfeld, and I wanted to strangle the two of them. I would clearly be making a delivery to my crawl space.

"I do." I handed her the Garmin GPS. "Please take this with you." As she drove away, I knew she was comforted by knowing where she was, while I was equally comforted by having no idea whatsoever.

* * *

I would have been disappointed if the Joan hadn't appeared in Levon's last journal. I was no less disappointed after reading this entry. She must've told me the story of my dad being a hacker who got tangled up with the law for trying to help people just to make me feel less rotten about who my father was. She didn't count on me rummaging so carefully through the trash.

I looked up the entry date only to discover it was the unveiling of I-Phone 3G – really the first phone where the internet and all the apps landed in your hand. Typical Levon. I checked the disk repeatedly. That was indeed the last file. He must've decided that even this type of communication needed to be off limits.

I dug deep into my pockets for my own dormant electronic device. Near the end, the Joan brought me a new cell phone, which she told me not to activate until after she died. "You don't need my number and my messages rattling around your screen." But I kept my old phone and opened her old texts regularly.

Now I gave Eva that phone. "What would you like me to do with it?" Eva asked gently.

"Throw it away for me, but just don't throw away today, O.K.?" In the days that followed, I wondered whether Eva tossed it. I wanted to ask, but didn't, since I knew I'd be unhappy with whatever answer she gave me. I shook my head, hoping to shuttle away the last lumps of hideous sentimentality that had weighed down my pockets these many months. Levon's final entry got to me though, like I had opened a lost box in the attic.

What now? Sure, I could research the Joan, and even my Dad. All the research in the world only leads to a series of questions and dead ends. No, it was time to break into Levon's house. Clearly, his nephews and nieces had combed over the place, but I had a feeling they might not have made their way down to the crawl space.

36

TOILET PAPER

Eva and I broke into the Gallagher's home at 3 a.m., flashlights in hand, and stepped down to the crawl space.

"Why do most of the dates you take me on involve trespassing?" she asked.

"Because I'm a much bigger believer in my own privacy than I am anybody else's."

It took about ten minutes before we stumbled across the guns. Naturally, they were shoved in the corner, stacked up like they were pieces of wood set to start a roaring fire. I lifted a rifle, tentatively, pointing it toward the wall, afraid it was loaded. I was struck by its weight, like I needed to be stronger to use it well. Eva was even less familiar with guns than I was, and we studied them like we had encountered a strange new species in a cave. We did not run from them, yet we did not take them.

"I have a signal," Eva said, pointing from her phone to the weapons. "Let's figure these things out." We spent the rest of that morning examining each gun. As I read off names and model numbers, Eva scrolled around on her phone, piecing together what each one was. Some took a couple of seconds. Others took ten or twenty minutes, but I was somewhat surprised we could indeed identify all of them.

I would alternate the sizes and shapes of the weaponry, just to keep myself engaged, since the load was so heavy. Eva would input the inventory. After a couple of hours, she ticked off what we had figured out so far: "a Smith and Wesson .38 revolver, an AR-15 assault rifle, a .40-caliber Glock, a Ruger 9 mm semiautomatic, a .223 Bushmaster semiautomatic assault rifle, a Smith and Wesson .357 revolver, a 9 mm Beretta, a .45-caliber Springfield semiautomatic handgun, an AK-47 Norinco Arms variant, an AK-47 Romarm Cugir variant automatic rifle, a .38-caliber Colt revolver, a Winchester 1300 pump-action shotgun, a .9mm Browning P35 Hi-Power semiautomatic handgun, a 9 mm Israeli Military Industries Uzi Model A carbine semiautomatic rifle, a 12-gauge Winchester 1200 pump-action shotgun, a .380 ACP Browning, a 9 mm Smith & Wesson semiautomatic handgun; a Ruger M-77 .22-250 bolt-action rifle with scope; a Mossberg 12-gauge pump-action, a 12-gauge Benelli semiautomatic shotgun; a .357 Magnum Smith & Wesson, a .22 Sentinel WMR revolver, a .380 ACP Browning, a .45-caliber Heckler & Koch, a 9 mm Springfield semiautomatic handgun, and a .44 Magnum Smith & Wesson revolver.

Then there were the magazines, boxes and belts of ammo, which added up into the thousands.

"Do you think he ever fired these things?"

"I hope not," I said. "They all seem pretty new. Maybe a few of them at a firing range, but I don't think much else." Perhaps he had purchased one weapon after another following every slight, spite and fight he endured. If so, he had more episodes than revealed on the five-and-a-quarter-inch floppies.

After we had completed the inventory of the arsenal, enough

to finish off every soul in Frick, I sat back against the crawl space wall, sprawled my legs outward and exhaled deeply. I closed my eyes and heard Eva scramble her way out of the crawl space. Maybe it was the reality TV series or the automated trash trucks or the twenty years of garbage that sunk me so low that I felt the bones had been yanked from my body. I was developing a suspicion my desolate state had everything to do with Levon Gallagher, this strange, argumentative, alienated man whom I liked tremendously, a ghost who had something ghastly lurking in his basement. I know I would be skittish to enter my own basement now, fearful of what I might find. I don't know how long I sat in the dank darkness, sniffing the damp cement before Eva returned.

She pegged me in the head with something big and soft. I thought it might be a nerf ball, but as I flashed my light upon it, I saw a roll of toilet paper now sprinkled with the grey cement dust that slept on the crawl space floor.

"It's not as bad as you think," said Eva.

"Yeah? Does that mean it's worse?" I picked up the roll, stuck my finger in the cardboard tube, and mindlessly spun the toilet paper around.

"No," she said with an energy designed to rouse me, "you hold in your hand compelling evidence to the contrary." I muttered "compelling evidence to the contrary." If Eva didn't become a friggin' lawyer, that'd be quite a waste. "He's got ten times as many rolls of toilet paper as he has guns."

I did a little calculation. That was an awful load of toilet paper, but I didn't catch Eva's reason for optimism. "Great. Toilet paper, guns . . . if you find a fat deck of credit cards, then Levon Gallagher would have indeed possessed the holy American trinity."

Eva sighed, realizing that being my girlfriend was going to

be more work than she had originally anticipated. She lit a cigarette. I raised my eyebrows. "What?" she said. "Dead men don't get cancer." She exhaled a plume of smoke that shot through the crawl space and consigned to its short-ceilinged atmosphere to low, puffy clouds of cement dust. "Look, a guy with that many rolls of toilet paper had plans to live a long time. He didn't have cans of chipped beef and beans, like he'd be stashed up for a siege, fighting it out with the police after he wreaked mayhem. No, a very big part of him had no intentions of using the guns."

"How do you know that?"

"Because he lived all those years and never fired them. Sure he stored up all his anger and yeah, this is very rough to see. But he left it here, like he left those floppy disks."

"I would have never known if I hadn't been nosing around. I wouldn't have found out a thing, and nobody else would've either. His family sure didn't find out."

"So what are you going to do?" Eva asked.

"I have an idea," I said, "but it's going to be a lot of work."

"You know how I hate work," said Eva.

"Yeah, that's why I want to you to help me."

"I get it." Eva blew smoke in my face. "But I'm not happy about it."

37

THE CLEAN UP

My plans to address Levon Gallagher's legacy would have to wait a day because of a call the next morning from Lee Lee and her request for a favor.

The story of Frick's lost garbage had moved at the breathtaking speed that only events in our cyberworld can propel, and no one had the intellect and the capacity to see opportunity in its dense, layered mounds more than Lee Lee. She got her massively relieved mother to use her Harvard's acceptance to leverage the microbiology chair at MIT to press the renowned professor Richard Chu to answer her Emails about a research study which she'd like him to oversee. Then she convinced me to take her to the lost garbage site where she pulled out something that looked like a rectal thermometer attached to a GPS device.

"It's a methane measuring gas analyzer," she told me as she marched across the landfill taking readings.

"Of course it is," I said, my flashlight beaming at Lee Lee who seemed to me like a scientist on the moon. "I'm sure those are available at any drug store." She whipped out swabs and dropped them into Petri dishes, sprinkled with agar and nutrients.

While I had found what I was looking for just by digging a few feet down, I had a feeling Lee Lee's quest was a little more sophisticated. "Are you trying to discover radioactive material?" I asked.

"No, I'm looking for microbes. Some researchers think there's a microbe responsible for all the other methane producers. It's an anaerobic bacterium called Methansarcina Barkeri. This is a great place to make a study since the landfill has been completely untouched for years. It's like a fresh breast of the new world." Only Lee Lee could make a garbage dump sound like Eden.

"I wouldn't get my hopes up about the authorities letting you study it."

"I think Dr. Chu carries a lot of weight. If he pushes for me to conduct this study, I think I'll be practically living at this landfill this summer."

"I guess you won't be playing much violin out here."

Lee Lee didn't respond. She was too busy taking notes and making calculations. In fact, we hardly spoke for the next few hours as she continued to run tests.

I told Eva the next morning about my adventure with Lee Lee. Eva smoked more cigarettes than usual, which seemed hardly possible, but there it was. I was so used to doing whatever I wanted that I had not thought taking Lee Lee to the landfill would hurt Eva. By the way she spent much more time looking at the poker screen on her phone than at me, I eventually figured out the landfill had become *our* romantic getaway. It took a good hour of my explaining that Lee Lee was simply using me to get the data necessary for Dr. Chu to push her MIT research project with the local authorities. "I was part of the old garbage she was interested in. Now she's into this new garbage. Believe me, she has no interest in me."

"But do you have interest in her?"

I paused and decided to be honest. "I was attracted to her when she was broken. Now I'm not."

"Are you attracted to me because I'm broken?"

"Very much so."

"And when I'm pieced back together?"

"Oh that's not going to happen, at least as long as you're with me."

Neither of us was sure if I gave the right answer, but at that moment we were both willing to accept it.

I was no less enraptured by the landfill than Lee Lee was. When we crossed paths there during the spring, I was happy she was off doing all those tests so I could spend more time by myself. In the few hours I slept, I dreamt of walking its perimeter. The hallucinations of that pile of perfectly unshattered lightbulbs glowing majestically under the weight of that rubble returned. I found myself driving to the lost landfill instead of to 7-Eleven. Eva and I talked about bringing chairs and thermoses of coffee there and staring at the wild forsythias that found Frick's old refuse as hospitable as we did.

When I told her how impressed I was with her solving the mystery of the missing garbage, Eva was uncharacteristically modest. "Hey, it's not like I found something useful like a rare coffee bean."

"Still," I told her, "finding this mountain is a good day's work."

"Yeah, it was."

That's more like my Eva.

The only one who didn't seem to be attracted to the landfill was Louie, the true trash man among us. I had imagined Louie secretly dragging hunks of garbage away from there to the resource recovery plant where it could be properly disposed of. Louie could've made that mess a lifelong mission.

You can understand something about my mental state by the fact that I dared Louie to take on this quest. He had no such obsession. "That trash has already been tossed. There's too much being made here and now to worry about that garbage."

Louie didn't take a job as a trash man in another village either. Instead, Pulaski, bless his heart, got him in with the school custodian's union. The old chief custodian, Clarence Cioffi, was retiring. He and Pulaski were best friends. Clarence's son, Nicky, would be taking over. Pulaski had made sure Louie had taken every civil service exam, which he aced. As Pulaski told me, "the boy's got brains, but he'd rather have his wisdom teeth yanked out without Novocain than enroll in college." Pulaski even pushed Louie to take sensitivity training courses, submit to drug tests, and avail himself to background checks. Simply put, Louie was very easy to hire as the youngest custodian ever to sweep the halls of Ben Wright High.

"Are you sure you want to do this, Louie?" I asked, like a concerned parent. "You have trash running through your blood, man."

"Not really," he said matter-of-factly. "It was a good job and this is another good job." He saw how disturbed I was that he left behind the garbage truck so nonchalantly, so he punched me on the arm hard enough that it might knock some sense in me. "Look, you're overthinking this."

"It's what I do."

"I know. Now, let me try to simplify this all for you. People live, they make messes, and I clean them up."

"Sounds like a crappy job to me."

"It's better than making the messes."

"You should talk to Eva one day when she's cooking."

"No, my friend, I'd say that's your territory."

When Nicole arrived, I figured out I was happy for Louie. I could tell by the way they grabbed each other, Nicole was either pregnant or would be by next Tuesday. As Louie said to me, "A custodian is a good position. I have a steady salary and good benefits."

I drew from my deep pocket a book Levon Gallagher gave me many years ago, *How to Become a Millionaire in a Year*, and handed it to Louie. Louie looked at me kindly and said, "One day I was walking on the street when a blind man with his seeing eye dog called out to me. 'Hey,' he said, 'can you tell me where's a garbage can around here?' The blind guy's holding in his hand a plastic bag of his dog's crap. The nearest garbage can was a few turns and a couple of hundred feet away. I asked him to give me the bag and I'd take care of it. 'You sure?' he asked. I told him I'm sure. Thanks for the book."

Maybe I should've given it to Mayor Heine.

I don't know whether I've seen too many movies or what, but I had to confront Mayor Heine about the hidden garbage, even though Bill Hannah had already told me that Heine knew Eva and I were responsible for the discovery. In Frick Village, secrets tend to keep shorter than milk. Trying to create a little drama worthy of, I don't know, a reality television show, I put together with Eva a new village flag, consisting of a big hill with a flat top, riddled with old tires, fish bones, broken chairs, and refrigerator doors. Plastic bags and bottles were sprinkled throughout while seagulls hovered forever searching the landfill below. We made all the images on the computer and ironed them onto the flag, giving the product a cheesy, crude quality.

Though I wasn't even sure Mayor Heine would be willing to take our appointment, he met with us immediately. When we arrived, he greeted us with the warmth of an old friend. We presented him with the flag, clearly feeling more uncomfortable than he did. Mayor Heine unfurled it, laughed, and called us over to him, so his photographer could take a picture of the three of us surrounding the flag. Heine instructed the photographer, "Make sure you post this on the village website and on all my Facebook pages."

As we left, he said, "Don't be strangers. I like to hear about how my enterprising young residents are advancing."

When I got in Eva's car, I was shaking. "What the hell was that?"

Eva lit a cigarette. "We have a new best bud."

"He didn't yell at us. He didn't threaten us. He acts like we didn't destroy his career." Eva arched her eyebrows at me, and I soon understood what she had already realized. If the mayor didn't act like the landfill discovery was a problem, then it may not be one. Eva just smoked as she watched me punch my right fist into my opened left palm a few times. I thought about how Levon Gallagher had gotten under Heine's skin. All I wanted from Heine was some threat, like "you better watch out boy because one day I'll be coming after you." Next my failures in my battles with Psycho popped into my head. I laughed. "You know something. I really suck at this humiliation thing."

Eva squashed the cigarette butt. "You do, but that's O.K." Then she lit another one and looked off far beyond me. "Sure, some people are still easily humiliated. So many more now are impossible to humiliate."

"Like Mayor Heine."

Eva smiled.

As usual, when I needed to feel better, I ended up in Pulaski office. It had taken most of the school year for me to decide that Pulaski wasn't as burnt out as he appeared. That he knew what the hell he was doing. Today, I sat down in his office, no longer to fill out logs, but just to be in a place where I felt comfortable. Our conversation would invariably return to the lost landfill and the motivations of Mayor Heine. "I think he felt power in the possession of all that debris," said Pulaski. "It's like he owns Frick's entire history, its soul."

"That's kind of skeevy."

"Don't you sense it?" asked Pulaski. "I've never walked around this village before and felt this skittish. It's like everybody and everything, down to the worms in the flower beds, are so creeped out."

"I'm surprised the landfill wasn't discovered earlier?"

Pulaski rubbed his long nose. "Remember, most of the people here didn't want to know about a secret landfill. They liked their low taxes and sanitation fees. Plus, Heine did drop that trash in the middle of nowhere. You'd have to get lost just to wander within miles of it. And you know garbagemen, especially the Mavellas. They're a tight group. In a place where everybody knows everybody's business, nobody knows their business." As Pulaski spoke, hope flickered within me that Heine would somehow pay for his crimes.

Rallying, I chipped in. "I hear a lot from residents talking about the old landfill and the new, automated trash program like they're the same thing."

"I get that," said Pulaski. "It's like some twisted form of control. I think Freud might have had something to say about the curious behavior of Mayor Heine."

The voting public would also have something to say. Pulaski told me that based on polling data, the electoral sentiment reflected that Mayor Heine was *too* perverse to be a viable candidate. Pulaski said he'd been walking the streets a lot lately talking to people. "You know what Derek Standish told me," he said. "He says to me, 'What kind of sick bastard hoards an entire village's garbage?' Now that's the kind of reaction that makes me think Heine is in some serious trouble."

Heine may as well have raided the panty drawers of every female in Frick Village and hung them on the Daughters of the American Revolution flagpole. More than 20,000 dropped him as a Facebook friend off his various accounts. No, Heine wouldn't be county executive. Max's full-length exposé on the data mining exploits of the mayor was now fully financed. The working title was *The Man Who Owns Your Privacy*. Further clouding his future, DEC officials are trying to link Heine and the Mavellas to a gas monitoring system at the landfill site, a system that required regular visitations. To give an idea of how low Heine's star had sunk, a grassroots group called the Take Back the Trash Party selected Bill Hannah to run against him for mayor.

I had a feeling Levon Gallagher would approve.

38

A HOLE OF MY OWN

Digging a large hole in my backyard, I made it straight and narrow, like a grave. I had worried mightily in the hours of dragging Levon Gallagher's guns and ammo from his crawl space to my basement. I was tired of worrying. If I got caught, I really couldn't offer a reasonable explanation, although I had a sneaking suspicion Eva would think of something

Hey, at this point, to hell with it. I had been digging for hours now, and I had to lift the shovel high above my head to dump the dirt out.

Eva peered down at me, backlit, creating a lovely silhouette. "Is it deep enough?"

"It's going to have to be, since my arms feel like two strangled snakes."

When Eva yanked me out of the hole, I saw that damn pile of light bulbs before my eyes again. It took me a minute or two to rediscover Eva. She had on her cooking apron and had lined up big measuring cups of water to pour into the cement mix that she had already dropped into the trough. As I headed toward the back door, I told her, "You can start mixing now. I'm going to get the weapons."

When I staggered my way up from my basement with a third of the arsenal cradled in my shaky limbs, I heard Eva scraping the hoe back and forth in the trough. I drew myself close to the cement. "That's good," I told her. "Just let it slake for a few minutes."

Eva was sweating. "We should've ordered a cement truck."

"That wouldn't have been too conspicuous."

When the cement became a little fluffy, I dropped it in the hole and opened up the next sack. Eva lined up the water jugs and drizzled them in. I did the rough folding in, but soon Eva was scraping the hoe back and forth through the second trough. "This is like combining the ingredients to make bread."

"Yeah, if you're serving an army."

"Or my family."

"Do me a favor. Just don't start kneading it, O.K.?"

"Yeah, I might end up looking like one of those statues of fat Venuses outside the Gulotta house."

I dropped some weapons down the hole and we started the cement mixing all over again. We used every one of those twenty bags of cement to make sure we choked the firepower out of the arsenal. For some reason I kept the 9 millimeter Beretta stuffed in my jeans during the entire burial process. It was a small, elegant gun and I had trouble getting rid of it. Who knew when you might need such a thing?

Eva pointed to my waist and said, "You've got one more, tough guy."

I thought of trying to explain my misgivings of relinquishing the final gun of Levon Gallagher's deadly stash, but I was tired of presenting justifications for my contradictions and hypocrisies. I was not in any condition to have Eva think less of me, so I dropped the Beretta down with the rest. I didn't mention to her that I still held Artie's old Colt 45 in my basement. I simply was not ready to get rid of it yet.

"They're fossils now," Eva said. "If an archaeologist finds them a thousand years from now, I bet she'd theorize that the fine people of Frick were engaged in strange spiritual rituals."

"That would be the least disturbing thing an archaeologist would discover about us." I moved to the pile of dirt to start shoveling it down the hole.

"Don't you want to wait for the cement to dry?"

"Nah. I want to cover this all up as soon as possible. The cement will have eternity to dry."

Above the dirt I placed one of those concrete slabs that were stamped to look like a herring-bone brick pattern. Once I had it nice and level I installed The Calling on top of it. The phone pendulum was ticking, perpetually, at least for now. It would mark out time like the inscription dates on a tombstone.

"Good thing Louie's not on the rubbish run anymore," Eva said, pointing to my newly installed sculpture. "But it is in the backyard, so maybe it'd be safe."

"Are you kidding? Louie would sniff out that thing. It'd be in the truck before I scavenged my first mongo of the day."

We both took long, hot showers. As a trash man, I knew that after all the soaping and scrubbing and washing that I would feel almost clean. The soreness and the cement dust that I blew out of my nose left me sitting at the kitchen table afterward weak and ragged. Eva moved toward the stove and lit the gas, but she could barely lift her arms.

I looked about the yard to see how many rose bushes were blooming despite my neglect, the warm May days propelling horizons beyond graveyards old and new.

"I feel like Chinese tonight," I said.

"Yeah?" said Eva, "I could stir fry something."

"You've stirred enough today. Let's just get takeout."

Eva winced at the word "takeout," but was too tired to argue. As we waited for the delivery, Eva told me about her orientation for the state university at Buckminster. "They're going to have jugglers and comedians."

"Sounds enlightening."

I had not told Eva that I had seriously considered joining her there. I'm glad I didn't, since I ultimately decided that would be a bad idea. For all Eva knew, I would be staying home and taking classes at the local community college. But I was no longer sure staying in Frick was a good idea. I had been accepted to the state university at Noyes, which was only an hour away from Buckminster. From what Pulaski told me, I'd have no problem claiming hardship (they considered no parents a hardship), so I could have my car up there.

Writing out the enrollment check and sending in the forms, I told Eva my plans over the beef and broccoli. "I thought we might be able to have dinner every once and while."

Eva raised her eyebrows, smiling, "Not if you make me fill in a hole before every meal."

I put the commitment letter in the mailbox. I can't say I was jumping for joy. College seemed so abstract and irrelevant to me right now. I wasn't sure I could simply sit there anymore to listen and learn. No, I couldn't be a dinosaur like Louie, who embraced a life that somebody's great grandparents would admire. I couldn't be like most of my schoolmates either, who managed to pass time in the classes by scrolling around on their phones. I got the impression that for seniors, college was the only possible place to go to continue that wild dance between information and distraction. Yes, I liked to think I was different, but I had this deflating notion that the distinction was more in my mind.

As it was for now, I had to figure out how I would not visit that damn landfill all summer long, and what I would do with my arms now that I wasn't picking up trash pails. Yes, I'd imagine Eva and I would be sharing a few meals together. The way these evenings tend to go, I could be three hundred pounds by August.

I asked the inevitable, "You want to take a ride to the landfill?"

"Well," said Eva hesitating, "I thought maybe we'd do something else."

"Like what?"

"Let's talk about privacy," she said. So we did. We agreed to many things, and then we stopped talking for a long time . . . .

When we spoke again, Eva told me, "I have a present for you." She headed out to the car. Naturally, with such a mysterious offer, all I could think about was grabbing a hold of her.

She returned with an actual wrapped gift.

It was small and looked like a book. Ripping off the paper, I read the cover jacket, "*The Many Lives of Levon Gallagher* by (who else?) Levon Gallagher. Thank you."

"I thought it might be nice for you to get something you didn't pick out of the garbage," said Eva. "He actually wrote this one for public consumption. I thought we'd read it together, you know, take turns."

Dropping down on the couch next to her, I opened up the first chapter entitled "The Assembly Line" and started reading aloud.

That was the night I started my college education.

We each read a chapter apiece, and then I said to Eva, "Did I ever tell you the strange and disturbing tale Levon told me when me when I was young?"

Of course I knew I hadn't told her, but now was the time for her to hear . . . and for you too.

39

THE STORY

I was 14 years old when Levon Gallagher told me the story that made me want to become a writer. Levon and the Joan had been drinking margaritas and by midnight the Joan had passed out. A half hour later with no one to talk to but a salty glass, Levon unfolded such a convincing tale that I couldn't help but believe it to be true.

"The story opens with a shaken Ben Wright cradling a still warm Colt 45 in his bloody left hand walking into his best friend's house to say goodbye." Levon explained how Ben had killed Nathan Strout down on the banks of the Pequa River. Wracked by nervous desolation, Ben told Artie Cornwall and his wife Sarah that he had gone to the Universal Processing Factory simply to reason with Nathan, but when he saw the huge pipes dumping PCBs into the Pequa, he understood what he must do. "I knew that the dumping would only stop over Nathan's dead body," Ben told Artie. "With Strout dead, the factory would go under and the authorities would move in and the Pequa wouldn't end up destroyed like the Hudson." To escape the factory, Ben threw himself over the security fence, slicing his hand on the barbed wire. Levon explained to me the future that had been previously laid out for Ben Wright. "He could've been the greatest mind of his generation. The inventions that could have shot from that skull were mind-boggling. Now Ben would spend his days behind bars. Ben might've been able to simply use Artie and Sarah as an alibi – that he spent the night over at their house – but the cuts on his hand from the barbed wire looked mighty suspicious. Artie Cornwall saw the terrible waste in it all. He refused to allow such a tragedy to transpire." That sure sounded like Artie, whether it was a belt strap to my back or a cane to my gut, when Artie got a notion in his shorts . . .

Levon raised his finger dramatically. "That's when Artie concocted the most ridiculous scheme." Levon explained that the idea stemmed from the old song "The Long Black Veil," a dirge which centered on a man who was wrongly convicted of murder. The man was executed because he refused to reveal the fact that at the time of the crime he was sleeping with his best friend's wife. Artie said, "What if we turn the song around? What if we *say* at the time Nathan Strout was killed that Ben was sleeping with you, Sarah." Both Ben and Sarah looked horrified. "And I came in and caught you both doing the deed." Ben protested heavily, but Artie could only talk about the power of the alibi. "What could be more credible? Hell, if I'm willing to make an official statement that publicly humiliates me and Sarah is willing to too, then Ben, you will be free to do the work you were meant to do."

Levon spoke into the late night of the heroic convictions and speeches Artie delivered to sway Sarah. "Sarah asked, 'but what about our daughter?' To which Artie answered, 'Joan will understand. We will be teaching her how to sacrifice.' Of course, Ben acted reluctant, but the specter of life imprisonment swayed him." They proceeded to arrange the details of their statements with a precision worthy of three bright interrogators. Artie knew he had walked in on the two at exactly 10:43 because he lifted the digital clock at that moment and fired it at the lovers, who were completely naked, except for Ben's black shin-high dress socks and Sarah's sapphire necklace (Levon's story was becoming increasingly intriguing to me). They even reenacted the scene with Artie storming in, tossing the clock, yelling "You rotten bastards," and punching Ben in the cheek as Sarah fell off the bed and bruised her hip. Artie continued to yell at them, knowing he would have to stretch out the scene to give the incident enough scope and scale to protect Ben. He smashed the lamp down on a sprawling Ben, who held his left arm out to protect himself, spewing shattered glass into the already damaged hand, a clear effort to strengthen the alibi.

Artie eventually broke down in the corner by the TV set, sobbing, while Sarah tried to console him, and Ben shamefully rested his lacerated hand on his swollen cheek. Artie gathered himself and pored back over the details, making certain all three would tell the same story. Ben was the wild card, since he still wanted to confess, but he relented when Artie told him, "I need you to do this for me." Sarah nodded to Ben assuredly, her gentle gray eyes framed by the soft brown hair and the classical cheekbones.

After Artie buried the Colt 45 deep in his basement in a spot inaccessible to all but him, the three waited for the cops to come calling. The detectives inevitably arrived once they couldn't find Ben at his apartment. All three were dragged downtown, where they told their lurid tales, with Ben's swollen cheek, Sarah's bruised hip, Artie's gnarled hand, and a broken clock to corroborate the accounts. With Ben's alibi, the investigation soon moved onto the corporate competitors of Nathan Strout, a man who had too many enemies for anyone to reconsider a brilliant, rogue environmentalist with a spectacular, but airtight, alibi.

It wasn't until the dim light of dawn awakened when Levon unfolded the next chapter of the tale, one of damaged, conflicted feelings on all sides. Sure, the cover-up wasn't a complete disaster. Ben did indeed achieve something, working with Marty Cooper on the cell phone at Motorola. He was also there to collaborate on everything from liquid crystal displays with Jim Ferguson to the Pong video game with Nolan Bushnell. "He seemed to never be able to use his genius to create anything on his own," Levon told me. "He was always collaborating and playing the secondary role. It's like he was operating with part of that brilliant brain in sleep mode."

Levon mumbled a great deal about the messy scenes that followed every success. "Ben would dig into his own skin like he was a wild beast. I saw him tear at his calf once. It bled so much and the gash was so deep, I tried to take him to the hospital to get stitches. He wouldn't let me . . . said he'd kill himself if I tried." Levon expressed some confusion about whether Ben and Sarah had indeed subsequently slept together before Ben committed suicide. Levon suggested that Ben may have ended his days with the very gun Artie thought unreachable to all but him. Nine months later, Sarah was institutionalized and would be in and out of psych wards for the rest of her life. The broken Artie wandered from job to job looking to find meaning in a world where he had ultimately destroyed the two people he most wanted to save. He kept an eye on his daughter, whom he thought he cursed, and dreaded that his misbegotten legacy might even tumble down upon his clever, misguided grandson.

As Levon ended his story and we both headed to get some sleep, he said to me, "That's the book I want to write someday. You think it will sell?"

I had combed through his five-and-a-quarter-inch floppy disks hoping to find this story, or at least some clues about it. I had wondered if Artie or the Joan had told Levon the story. From what Levon described, the Joan had Sarah's eyes, hair and cheeks, even her necklace. Sarah could've been one of those women last viewed in an Italian renaissance painting, which was the type of compliment Levon had often rendered onto the Joan. How Levon told the story and the overarching sadness of his reminiscences had convinced me that he was actually revealing the ruptured spine of his own life, one of great sacrifice for everyone and everything Levon cared about. Even Ben and Artie's wandering from job to job was another way of describing Levon's columns.

After all that time, Levon had never committed the story to either paper or screen, only in a drunken whisper to me. Whether it was merely a story, something made up in Levon's troubled mind, or something more, he had decided to never allow it to see the light of day. No, instead, he carried the memories that rested on these five-and-a-quarter inch floppies, tiny, petty, seemingly inconsequential memories that stayed with him up to his grave. He bequeathed the story unto me as a birthright.

The song "Long Black Veil" speaks of the woman who had been the dead man's lover now perpetually walking the streets, haunted by her illicit, tragic secret. I was no less haunted, but I couldn't figure out whether it was from that old story Levon told me or the diary entries I'd been reading for the last few months. Those big, old clunky Motorola phones piled up in my hallucinations, like so much E-waste, and I could not figure out how to dispose of them.

Eva looked as beaten up as I felt. "Is that the whole story?" she asked, her dark skin lightening. As I nodded, Eva blew out air and relaxed. "Thank God. I thought your story would reveal that Levon was your father."

I frowned, thinking. "No, I can't say that. I thought it was a possibility, maybe still think so. I've been gathering all this garbage from the past, yet I can't say anything for certain."

"Only someone really on the inside of your family would know that story. And the little you've told me about your father . . . well … he sounds a lot like Levon. You know, don't get offended by this," uh-oh, here comes the pain, "but Levon really couldn't tolerate people."

She could've said worse. "I'm starting to think the Joan had a type, that's all."

"No wonder she got brain cancer."

I laughed. "Yeah, I'd drive away as fast as you can if I were you. I carry around those genes."

"Don't think I haven't considered it. But that's really all you want to tell me. No horrifying stories about what you've got stored in your crawl space or anything?"

"No, I haven't started my collection yet." She looked at me, waiting for words closer to forthrightness. "I just wanted to tell you something that has stuck with me for a long time, that's all." She kept staring at me as I rubbed my forehead. "Anyway, I'm not sure it was a good idea to try to dig my father's story up from the trash."

Eva sipped coffee, puffed her cigarette, and asked, "Do you think Ben Wright is your father?"

I smiled. Eva didn't tend to let things go. "That would mean he had a fling with both my grandma and the Joan. Don't you think I have enough problems without lifting that load?"

We both laughed, neither of us sure why.

Eva worked the coffee and the cigarette. "Maybe your dad's Landor Negera? Donald Hagen?"

I pulled the cigarette from her mouth. I might as well have ripped out her kidney. Eva looked so stunned I returned the cigarette to her lips before she had a seizure. Eva held up her hands to indicate a truce and softened her line of questioning.

"So you're not going to keep trying to figure out if Levon, Ben or someone else is your father?"

"Not this year," I told her. "I've got better things to do." I knew it was time to stop constructing my father out of the rubble.

Eva dropped her cigarette in her coffee.

That night I read about the PCBs General Electric had dumped into the Hudson River for thirty years from 1947-1977, which were close to the first thirty years of Levon Gallagher's existence. Yeah, the trash courses through the rivers, hell it's installed in my house and buried in my yard.

If I don't get it out of my system, I could crush under the weight of it. So I tell Eva one more story about Levon Gallagher, read through my Emails, open a word document, and start typing.

From the May 10 Trash Folder

Are you sure you want to permanently delete all the items and subfolders in the Deleted Items Folder?

The Daily Bread from Reverend Alexander Burr

Mayor Heine staggered into my church seeking sanctuary, which I gladly administered. He relinquished his cell phone unto me. He has spent many days looking down into his hands for something that isn't there. His gesture appears strangely similar to praying, but I know I will exert much time and energy to teach him the difference. He brought to me some of his possessions. It was a bizarre collection, including an old military canteen, a baggie that had Police Evidence stamped on it, and even a young lady's white dress. I was comforted that among his abandoned items was a No Trespassing sign. I believe he was telling me that he was letting God into his life. Such a man requires patience. As Proverbs 25:15 tells us, "With patience a ruler may be persuaded, and a soft tongue will break a bone." Unfortunately, last night I caught him rummaging through my garbage. I wasn't certain, but he might have slipped some item, I believe it was the sermon I had given last week, into his pocket, an act of thievery reminiscent of Achan and Micah. Indeed, the road to redemption is a long one.

The Epic Life of Selena Omaha

So are you ready for the inside scoop about what's popping in Frick Village?

I, Selena Omaha, have a mad awesome confession to make: while in my lifetime I have thrown away nothing of importance, I *have* abandoned my name. I didn't think it was a good idea to continue to remain a Mavella. You might listen to me for the wrong reasons, like you were trying to track down something you threw away long ago that I might still have. Now you can hold onto everything as easy as I can. What my fam used to collect and what Mayor Heine held onto is now in the clouds. We dump today way better than in the past. Playas, we have nothing to be ashamed of there. We definitely make so much more garbage now, the stuff all the hot dweebs call data, and we shove it into that misty, hazy vault. There it hangs and hovers, burying into the insanely epic sky more than my fam or even Mayor Heine could ever hold. So don't lose touch with me, ladies. The next time we talk, my head will be up chilling in the clouds.

40

GOODBYE

I put the Commodore 64 and Levon Gallagher's five-and-one-quarter-inch floppy disks to my curb. I wasn't sure whether the actors playing trash man or the automated machines would be picking them up. I can't say I hated one more than the other. Either way I was certain neither would rescue the machine or Gallagher's private diary. That knowledge made me quite happy.

My phone dinged with a text from Aunt Vicky. "How u doing?" I answered, "K and u?" She replied, "K2," and then added, "might b returning soon." I knew she wouldn't and she knew that better than I did. But I think she needed to say it anyway. I might've needed to hear it. Texts can be helpful that way. I returned through the front door and heard the Joan's question echo through the corridor. Then as I headed into the kitchen, Eva asked me that very question: "Did you take out the garbage?"

They were not words that would change your world, were they? Indeed, my mother's post-mortem question was embarrassingly unexciting, but stayed in house. Now that Eva asked, for the first time in a year, the question had a face. You would think after all the times I had answered "Yes" to the question that I wouldn't have to hear it anymore. But no, it was there in the house, and I wouldn't be surprised if it was up in my dorm room next year.

I knew I wouldn't tell my story to the world on a blog like my mother, even though I did have offers – seems you can even be a failure on a reality TV show and still get a fair share of attention. In fact, I'm pretty sure that notoriety derived from the magnitude of my failures. No, I would follow Levon Gallagher's lead, and put my story on a USB drive, label it Generation Dementia, and shove it in a drawer. If someone decades later still has a machine that can open the file, that strange anachronism of a soul mate will be welcome to read it.

All I have to say is, I'm happy it was you.

Purchase other Black Rose Writing titles at www.blackrosewriting.com/books

and use promo code PRINT to receive a 20% discount.

www.ingramcontent.com/pod-product-compliance
Lightning Source LLC
Chambersburg PA
CBHW060937120726
47910CB00002B/375